The Grandissimes

The
Grandissimes

BY GEORGE W. CABLE

**Foreword by
W. Kenneth Holditch**

PELICAN PUBLISHING COMPANY
Gretna 2001

*The word "Pelican" and the depiction of a pelican are trademarks
of Pelican Publishing Company, Inc., and are registered in the
U.S. Patent and Trademark Office.*

Library of Congress Cataloging-in-Publication Data

Cable, George Washington, 1844-1925.
    The Grandissimes / by George W. Cable ; foreword by
    W. Kenneth Holditch.
        p. cm.
    ISBN 1-56554-901-5 (pbk. : alk. paper)
    1. New Orleans (La.)—Fiction. 2. Culture conflict—
Fiction. 3. Vendetta—Fiction. 4. Creoles—Fiction. I. Title.

PS1244 .G6 2001
813'.4—dc21

                                                    2001021962

Illustrations by Albert Herter

Printed in Canada

Published by Pelican Publishing Company, Inc.
1000 Burmaster Street, Gretna, Louisiana 70053

CONTENTS

Contents.

Contents

PHOTOGRAVURES

** *In addition to the foregoing, the stories are illustrated
with eight smaller photogravures from drawings by Mr.
Herter.*

FOREWORD

George Washington Cable was arguably one of the best fiction writers in the South in the second half of the nineteenth century and certainly one of the most popular. Born in New Orleans in 1844, he employed the atmosphere, people, customs, and language of that city and other areas of South Louisiana to create memorable novels and short stories in the Local Color tradition. With the exception of Tennessee Williams, George Washington Cable is more than anyone responsible for the image of New Orleans lodged in the collective imagination of readers. Until the 1947 Broadway production of Williams' drama *A Streetcar Named Desire,* the New Orleans that Cable portrayed in his two major works, *Old Creole Days* and *The Grandissimes,* was the picture that came to the mind of readers anywhere the city was mentioned. So popular was his work that he went on lecture tours throughout the United States with his friend Mark Twain, reading from his work to large and appreciative audiences. Despite the ravages of time, progress, and the work of politicians and investors that have in recent decades altered New Orleans, erasing many vestiges of the old

French town, the reader walking through the area today can still catch occasional glimpses not only of the French Quarter that Cable knew but of the Vieux Carré of 1804, the time of the action of *The Grandissimes.*

Cable was born in a most propitious era for a writer; by the time he put pen to paper to create his first works of fiction, the Local Color movement was beginning to flower. Several factors contributed to the development of that school of literature in America after the Civil War. In an age of growing literacy, there was a proliferation of newspapers and periodicals. These provided a large new market for short fiction, so that editors actually traveled the country in search of new authors. During the Civil War (1861-65) soldiers had been exposed to unfamiliar parts of the United States—New Orleans, for example, was occupied by federal troops beginning in 1862—and the general population as well learned about areas other than their own. As a result, there developed a hunger for knowledge of how other people lived. Local Color writers, although associated with the school of Realism, often tended toward the romantic, concentrating their attention on those elements that distinguished their region from the rest of the nation, including customs, dialects, idioms, food, architecture, and others.

After service in the Fourth Mississippi Cavalry from 1863 to 1865, Cable, like many another Confederate veteran, returned home to New Orleans to build a new life for himself and his family. In the years that followed, he worked as an accountant for cotton brokers and as a columnist for the *Picayune*, a major New Orleans newspaper. In 1873, when Edward King, an editor of *Scribner's Magazine*, visited New Orleans, Cable had been writing fiction for some time. When the two men met, Cable showed King some of his work, and within a few months, "'Sieur George" became his first published short story when it appeared in *Scribner's*. It introduced readers all over the country to the unfamiliar atmosphere of the old French Quarter as revealed by a new and unique literary voice. His work continued to appear in the magazine for the next few years, and in 1879, *Old Creole Days*, a collection of seven short stories, was published by Scribner's.

By that time, Cable, at the urging of his editor, had been working on his first novel for two years, and by the end of 1879, *Scribner's Magazine* began to serialize it. For the next twelve months, chapters of *The Grandissimes* appeared in each issue of the periodical and attracted widespread attention. In 1880, the novel was published in book form and promptly established Cable as a popular novelist nationwide. Readers unfamiliar with the unique and exotic history and atmosphere revealed in his narratives, so different from the rest of the United States as to be almost another country, were charmed and amazed by their introduction to the city. Fiction about the old South had achieved a wide popularity soon after the Civil War, but to date, no one of note had dealt in a novel with the rich vein of material in New Orleans. Cable would continue to mine that ore for the rest of his life.

Cable, unique in that he was both a romantic and a realist, challenged the accepted literary tradition of the old South and its aristocracy while at the same time portraying the dramatic, glamorous, and appealing elements of the region. His work was a marked contrast to the sort of sentimental "magnolias and crinoline" fiction being produced in the South in the years after the Civil War, and Northern critics were almost universal in their praise of what he had accomplished in *The Grandissimes*.

What negative reviews of the novel there were came mostly from Southern critics, especially those in New Orleans. The reviewer in *The Bee*, a French-language newspaper associated with the Creoles, was very harsh in his evaluation. An anonymous author, probably Adrien Rouquette, a Creole who was both a Roman Catholic priest and an author, wrote a scurrilous attack on the novel, suggesting that Cable was aligned with practitioners of voodoo and even sexually intimate with one of them. This kind of unjust assault was a foretaste of the intense dislike of Cable that would develop in the city within a few years, not only as a result of his fiction but also because of his liberal stance on the question of race.

Even in his native city, however, some powerful voices came to the defense of *The Grandissimes*. Lafcadio Hearn, a friend of the novelist and himself a writer of Local Color material, had been inspired to come live in New Orleans after reading some of Cable's stories. Hearn became a staunch supporter of the novelist and his fiction, countering local adverse criticism by attesting to the credibility of Cable's characters, language, and incidents and proclaiming the novel superior in almost every way.

Cable wisely had chosen to set *The Grandissimes,* his best novel, in 1804 and the following years, perhaps the most crucial time in New Orleans history, that period following Napoleon's 1803 sale of Louisiana to the United States. This act the Creoles looked upon as a betrayal—the French emperor is scornfully referred to by one of them in *The Grandissimes* as "the dread Corsican"—even though there continued to be strong support for him when he fell from power shortly thereafter and was sent into exile. Subsequent to the sale, referred to in the novel as "the cession," there occurred a large influx of *"les américains,"* whose very presence was a serious affront to the descendants of the French and Spanish settlers.

In a city in which French had been the predominant language since its founding in 1718, suddenly there was a large portion of the population speaking English and even insisting that official documents be written in both languages. In addition, those "invaders" from the North introduced new and decidedly unwelcome customs and attitudes into the established Creole culture. They were looked upon as crude, illiterate, and beyond redemption because most of them were Protestants. The conflict between the two ethnic groups and their lifestyles is effectively dramatized in Cable's portrayal of Joseph Frowenfeld, his protagonist in *The Grandissimes*, who comes with his German-American parents from the North to New Orleans, where he and his father expect to open an apothecary shop (or drugstore).

The "immigrants" are disappointed by the absence of hills in the Louisiana Delta as they enter "a land of reptiles, silence, shadow, decay," and by the abundance of mosquitoes, which soon prove fatal to Joseph's parents, who die of yellow fever. That plague often raged in the eighteenth and nineteenth centuries in South Louisiana with fatal results before it was discovered that the pesky insects were responsible for its spread. After recovering from the same disease, Joseph, who like Cable is a Protestant and a reformer, settles into the community and soon begins to comment on the injustices he observes in the social and ethnic stratification in the city. He immediately runs afoul of the hot-blooded young Creoles unwilling to tolerate any suggestion that their culture is in any way inferior. Their destruction of his first apothecary shop ironically foreshadows the subsequent rejection of Cable and his work by the Creoles that would ultimately lead to his leaving his native city to live in the North.

In addition, the American settlement in the city added a new complication to an already complex social structure, in which blacks (most of them slaves at that time) occupied the lowest level. The free people of color (known locally as Creoles of color and identified officially by the initials f.p.c. or, for men, f.m.c. after their names) were several steps above the slaves, and the white Creoles occupied the upper and unscalable heights. It was an inflexible stratification with no opportunity for upward mobility. Through his portrayal of the Grandissime family, in which there are two half-brothers, one white, the other of mixed blood, Cable dramatizes effectively the irony and injustice of the society.

A caste system founded on money was certainly not unique to Louisiana, but what distinguished that of New Orleans from the rest of the United States was the very existence of the Creoles of color, descendants of white Creole men and their mistresses of mixed blood, quadroons or octoroons. In a society in which even the Catholic church did not openly condemn such arrangements, so much a part of the social fabric had they become, it was not only customary but even expected for Creole men to choose a young mistress from among the large population of "free people of color" and set up a second household.

The inevitable outcome of the practice, which seems to have had its origin in the West Indies and was so well established that it even had a name, *plaçage*, was a steady increase in the number of people with mixed blood in the city. Members of this "shadow class" occupied an ironic and unique place in the hierarchy of New Orleans society: they could own property—indeed, many of them became quite wealthy and some of them even owned slaves—but they could not vote. They could attend the opera, but a special gallery was reserved for them, segregating them from the white audience to some of whom they were certainly closely related. The quadroon and octoroon mistresses and their children lived in districts around the French Quarter in which planters and their other families had their townhouses. Needless to say, the Americans who settled in the city before and after the cession of Louisiana to the United States found this Byzantine system not only strange but, for most of them, immoral.

The result of such a complex cultural hierarchy among the Creoles, both white and black, pitted against the newer, rougher lifestyle of *les américains* provides the novel with its tension and suspense. Much of the action emanates from the clash that, not surprisingly, develops between the established citizenry and the brash newcomers with their decidedly un-Creole ways. This tension, combined with the unique elements that set New Orleans apart from the rest of the country, then even moreso than now, provided Cable with a seemingly inexhaustible supply of exotic material for his fiction.

The canvas on which George Washington Cable painted his grandest picture, *The Grandissimes,* was a large one, and he filled it with an abundance of Local Color details, using the unique patois of each of the social classes, their songs and dances, their dress, the way in which they spent their days and nights, all cast against the backdrop of the enervating climate of swampy South Louisiana, which Cable and other authors have seen as contributing to a characteristic torpor among the natives. It was his practice in fiction to use exact identifiable locations, and in this novel he writes of the *Place d'Armes* (originally a parade ground for French soldiers, now the park at Jackson Square), Maspero's slave exchange, St. Louis Cathedral, the Calabazo (jail), and Congo Square. At the last site, which is now Louis Armstrong Park, slaves were afforded their only recreation when on Sunday afternoons their owners allowed them to congregate there to sing and dance. America's only indigenous music, jazz, developed partially as a result of this custom, and one of the climactic scenes of *The Grandissimes,* the set piece involving Bras-Coupé, occurs in this location.

All of Cable's descriptions of local sites, characters, and customs reveal his marked ambivalence toward New Orleans and the state of Louisiana. On a few occasions, he directly voices his devotion, as in the description of a March afternoon that is so glorious as to "make one wonder how the rest of the world avoids emigrating to Louisiana in a body." Yet Cable saw as well the faults of the city, and for him, as for such later writers as Tennessee Williams, the Vieux Carré was the very embodiment of decadence. For Cable, it exemplified the weaknesses and sins of the Creoles, a people to whom he was unavoidably drawn even as he condemned what he saw as immoral in their lifestyle. A devout Protestant, he was nevertheless intrigued by their Catholicism, a blend, peculiar to New Orleans, of Roman orthodoxy and such elements as voodoo (or *voudou,* as Cable spells it) that had been introduced into the city by slaves and by planters and their families fleeing slave insurrections in the West Indies in the late eighteenth century.

In chapter 18, Cable dramatizes Frowenfeld's walk through the Vieux Carré "to begin at once the perusal of this newly found book, the Community of New Orleans." This device of the walk by a careful observer, later to be used by such authors as Thomas Wolfe in *Look Homeward, Angel,* gave Cable a means to introduce numerous sites and details that made clear to readers how different New Orleans was from the rest of the country. The fact that Frowenfeld is an outsider makes him keenly aware of those elements that distinguish the area from any other place in the country. Walking along the grandest street of the old Quarter, the rue Royale, Frowenfeld encounters a wide range of ethnic types and languages.

Among the white Creoles and blacks, Frowenfeld sees Indians, Mexicans, and *les américains,* many of them come downriver on rafts. In the nineteenth century and even the early 1900s, vendors hawked their wares in the streets, and along the way he encounters a *marchande des calas,* a seller of calas, rice cakes that were a staple of the diet in the city until recent decades. Her song, in the black Creole patois referred to in New Orleans as "Gumbo," is a typical element of Local Color fiction. Other uses of patois in conversation in *The Grandissimes* may deter some modern readers, but at the time of the novel's publication, the public seemed to have an insatiable hunger for such writing, as attested to by the works of Joel Chandler Harris, Thomas Nelson Page, and Cable, among others.

The Grandissimes, Cable's most effective portrayal of New Orleans, is also embellished with tensely dramatic situations and a very large cast of Romantic characters, larger than life yet recognizable to those who know the history of the city. Cable considered Aurore Nancanou the most fully realized of all the characters in his fiction, a judgment in which several scholars and other novelists concurred. His characters represent a broad spectrum of New Orleans before the Civil War: *les américains;* Creoles, both wealthy and impoverished, old and young; slaves; and even descendants of the Choctaw Indians who once dwelt across Lake Pontchartrain north of the city. There are also actual historical figures: W. C. C. Claiborne, the first American governor of the newly acquired Louisiana province, Edward Livingstone, Daniel Clark, James Wilkinson, and the privateer Jean Lafitte. In some scenes, cast against such local landmarks as the *Place d'Armes*, Cable moved these real-life figures among his fictional creatures in a kind of historical pageant to add a sense of credibility to the novel.

One essential element of all good literature, according to Cleanth Brooks, is tension, and most of Cable's best writing results from the conflict between the Creole attitudes and the author's own Presbyterian outlook. Cable was at once fascinated by the customs and beliefs of the Creoles and appalled at their vices. Often in *The Grandissimes,* as well as in his nonfiction history *The Creoles*, Cable, in the novel through his alter ego Joseph Frowenfeld, condemns the character flaws of the Creoles en masse. The deficiencies of the Creoles, in his view, included their lack of initiative, lethargy, inflammability, stubbornness, impracticality—especially in economic matters—vanity, and a "poetic and pathetic pride" that resulted in a "perennial rebellion against common sense." That "overweening pride," which Aristotle identified as a trait of the tragic hero, is present, according to one of Cable's characters, Doctor Keene, in all the Creoles, "this same preposterous, apathetic, fantastic, suicidal pride."

In his nonfiction work entitled *The Creoles*, Cable contends that the lifestyle of the New Orleans natives is characterized by "Latin ductility," "untrained sensuality," "fierce exclusiveness," "love of pleasure," and "ostentatious living." They were, as he portrayed them, "unreflecting," "illiterate," "coarse, boastful, vain," and "licentious." Some of these faults he attributed to a combination of their Gallic heritage and the "luxurious and enervating climate." Doctor Keene characterizes that climate as "lethargic and ferocious as an alligator" and suggests that it is the reason for the Creole's always being, or thinking he is, "on the defensive." It may contribute as well to the frequent outbreaks of violence in the novel, a violence that is often evidenced in the best of Southern fiction. Much of the action of the novel is connected with a duel that occurred in the past between a member of the De Grapion family and a Grandissime, as a result of which the families have remained sworn enemies. The ending, a variation on the Romeo and Juliet story, brings the two families together belatedly and presumably terminates the long, fruitless, and destructive quarrel.

In contrast to the Yankees, who in their conversation tend to go "straight to the root of things," the Creoles, Joseph Frowenfeld observes, sneak around subjects, never addressing them directly and even using dissimulation when it serves their purpose. They are ambitious, but at the same time, they "murder time" and are scornful of labor, too indolent to bring their dreams to reality. Their hedonism, exhibited in their love of talk, of parties, of dancing, leads Frowenfeld to believe that their problems stem from the fact that they concern themselves with "Expediency" rather than with "Divine Justice," which he, as a Calvinist, believes they must face in the future. All these traits, at odds with the Protestant work ethic of the author and his protagonist, are presented in this novel as not just shameful but also immoral.

Although always a good storyteller, portraying credible characters in dramatic situations in both *Old Creole Days* and *The Grandissimes*, Cable was also a polemicist. He wrote not only in his essays but also in his fiction protests against injustices in government and elsewhere. He was an outspoken opponent of racial injustice, the Louisiana lottery, and the convict lease system, in which prisoners were rented as laborers to the private sector. He even addresses women's rights in *The Grandissimes*, when Aurore Nancanou complains that although she is poor, she is first forced to be a lady, then must live in a world that does not permit her to earn her livelihood. In speeches and essays Cable criticized the caste system in the South, particularly in the uniquely stratified society in New Orleans; the failure of local governments to grant civil rights to freed slaves; and the segregation of schools.

The dramatic event that seems to have triggered his social consciousness was the forcible segregation of a girls' school in the Haunted House on Royal Street in the French Quarter, which he would write about in *Strange True Stories of Louisiana*. A group of men entered the school and separated the white students from those presumed to be of mixed blood, forcing the latter to leave. In response, Cable began to write his social-protest essays to dramatize what he considered the inequities and cruelties of the caste system, and he portrays the same in *The Grandissimes*. He not only published his protests but delivered numerous public speeches on the topic around the country. Fiction offered him yet another outlet for his views on social and political problems.

What most troubled Cable about the Creoles was another ingrained practice, the stratification of castes resulting in injustices against those who were because of race or social standing excluded from the establishment. By contrasting the positions of the two Honoré Grandissimes, one white, one a free man of color, he dramatized what most appalled him in the history of the Creoles, the effects of which continued to be in evidence in the late 1800s when Cable was writing, although slavery had been abolished more than a quarter-century before. In Cable's view, however, abolition had not substantially improved the lot of black people. He believed that the caste system produced "a double bondage," for the owners are just as enslaved to the system as are their human chattel. It was a bondage that tainted and bound the entire society, black and white, enslaved and free, and always over it, Frowenfeld remarks, looms the "shadow of the Ethiopian." Much to the horror of the Calvinistic Frowenfeld, the white Creoles look down on the blacks. When one of them shouts, "Shoot the black devils without mercy!" the narrator, obviously expressing both Frowenfeld and Cable's view, observes that this remark embodies "the whole Creole treatment of race troubles."

Cable used a standard device of Local Color authors when he introduced an outsider into this bizarre and for the most part secret and closed society. Frowenfeld can "make no conscious compromise with any sort of evil," and in this reflects the attitudes of the novelist who created him. With his "frankness and ardent zeal for truth," Frowenfeld is compared to the biblical Joshua, who brought down the walls of the enemy city Jericho. A staunch advocate of the Puritan work ethic, Frowenfeld insists to his Creole friends that "nothing on earth can take the place of hard and patient labor." One of the major conflicts of the novel involves Frowenfeld's dilemma; he must decide whether or not he will "compromise" with the standards of the community of which he has become a part ("When in Rome, do as the Romans do"), and it is his triumph that his morality will not let him do so. Some reviewers at the time deemed Frowenfeld to be too good, faultless almost, but Cable nevertheless manages to make him credible and even appealing.

Although the author was adamant in his condemnation of what he saw as the Creoles' sins in the past, he was, as noted above, clearly ambivalent toward the culture, drawn to it at the same time he was repelled by what he saw as its faults. Despite the fact that *The Grandissimes* may be regarded as a condemnation of the Creole lifestyle, especially as related to its view of race, it is the Creole characters who are the most interesting, the most alive. Near the end of the book, Cable to some degree exonerates the Creoles when he observes that in his own age, the late 1800s, because time has "diluted and sweetened" the Creole's character, "almost all the savagery that can justly be charged against Louisiana must—strange to say—be laid at the door of the *Américain*."

Like his protagonist in *The Grandissimes,* Cable, an uptown Presbyterian and a descendant of one of the "American" families, was himself, ironically, very much an outsider in his native New Orleans. He surely must have felt a stranger in relationship to the remnants of the Creole society in the French Quarter and the Creole faubourgs (suburbs), even though he numbered a few of them among his friends.

Ultimately, his controversial views on civil rights and the caste system, expressed in his fiction and essays, would lead to his being made so uncomfortable in the city of his birth that he moved to New England, where he continued to write in exile about his beloved New Orleans. One of his last works was a novel with the intriguingly ambiguous title *Lovers of Louisiana.*

The Grandissimes is permeated with a sharp irony as Cable portrays the events and traditions that are unique to the culture of the old Creole city, and to some extent the rest of the South before the Civil War. For example, the most noble and virtuous characters are often the most scorned by those in a position of political and social power. Honoré Grandissime, f.m.c., has achieved wealth with the inheritance left to him by his white father, but he must be subservient in the presence of his white relatives and others of the dominant race, never being allowed to forget that he is a second-rate citizen—and even, in fact, not quite a citizen at all. Yet it is through his generous intervention that the family is saved from financial disaster.

Bras-Coupé, the African prince whose tragic tale Cable had first told in an unpublished piece of fiction, "Bibi," was based on a real character who had become something of a legend in the history and folklore of the city. Bras-Coupé is brutalized when he violates the code of slave behavior, and the story is related by Cable in graphic and even painful detail but without any of the overt moralizing that characterized much of the fiction about slavery. The sad tale is referred to a number of times in the novel and is indeed inter-woven into the narrative of the Grandissimes. Often the author speaks directly to the reader to make an ironic comment, as when he observes that many white people call blacks "the happiest people under the sun" and adds, "We ought to stop saying that."

In addition to irony, another element of Cable's narrative method is the use of humor, which on several occasions prevents passages of the novel from becoming merely sermonizing. Humor is pervasive in the novel, as when the narrator observes, after an exaggerated boast by Raoul Innerarity, "We have the afflatus in Louisiana, if nothing else." Agricole Fusilier is described as an "anti-voudou" because whereas the voodoo practitioners poured rum on the ground in their ceremonies, he preferred to drink his. In one passage, Cable refers to the Louisiana courts as "those famous cupping-leeching-and-bleeding establishments." These humorous touches alleviate some of the gloom of the tragic story that the novel relates.

Despite shifting literary tastes through the past one hundred years and more, the works of Cable continue to appeal. His style, especially relating to the use of various local dialects, may seem to many readers now as quaint and even incomprehensible, but the reader who is willing to make the effort to read *The Grandissimes* finds beneath that sometimes forbidding surface a rich treasure: a tremendous cast of characters involved in a tense and exciting drama. Through the decades, Cable has exerted considerable influence over other authors, notably William Faulkner, whose *Absalom, Absalom!,* one of his major novels, exhibits a distinct debt to some of Cable's short stories and *The Grandissimes.* In addition, Cable deserves attention as the first fiction writer in the South to attack head on the injustices of the caste system and to campaign directly through his essays and indirectly through his stories and novels for reform. Thus *The Grandissimes* continues to entertain readers at the same time that it reveals the mind of a humane and caring author determined to improve his world.

W. KENNETH HOLDITCH

CHAPTER I

MASKED BATTERIES

T was in the Théatre St. Philippe (they
had laid a temporary floor over the
parquette seats) in the city we now call
New Orleans, in the month of September, and in the year 1803. Under the twinkle of
numberless candles, and in a perfumed air thrilled
with the wailing ecstasy of violins, the little Creole
capital's proudest and best were offering up the first
cool night of the languidly departing summer to the
divine Terpsichore. For summer there, bear in
mind, is a loitering gossip, that only begins to talk
of leaving when September rises to go. It was like
hustling her out, it is true, to give a select *bal
masqué* at such a very early — such an amusingly

early date; but it was fitting that something should be done for the sick and the destitute; and why not this? Everybody knows the Lord loveth a cheerful giver.

And so, to repeat, it was in the Théatre St. Philippe (the oldest, the first one), and, as may have been noticed, in the year in which the First Consul of France gave away Louisiana. Some might call it "sold." Old Agricola Fusilier in the rumbling pomp of his natural voice — for he had an hour ago forgotten that he was in mask and domino — called it "gave away." Not that he believed it had been done; for, look you, how could it be? The pretended treaty contained, for instance, no provision relative to the great family of Brahmin Mandarin Fusilier de Grandissime. It was evidently spurious.

Being bumped against, he moved a step or two aside, and was going on to denounce further the detestable rumor, when a masker — one of four who had just finished the contra-dance and were moving away in the column of promenaders — brought him smartly around with the salutation:

" *Comment to yé, Citoyen Agricola!* "

" H-you young kitten! " said the old man in a growling voice, and with the teased, half laugh of aged vanity as he bent a baffled scrutiny at the back-turned face of an ideal Indian Queen. It was not merely the *tutoiement* that struck him as saucy, but the further familiarity of using the slave dialect. His French was unprovincial.

" H-the cool rascal ! " he added laughingly, and, only half to himself; " get into the garb of your true sex, sir, h-and I will guess who you are ! "

But the Queen, in the same feigned voice as before, retorted :

" *Ah! mo piti fils, to pas connais to zancestres?* Don't you know your ancestors, my little son ! "

" H-the g-hods preserve us ! " said Agricola, with a pompous laugh muffled under his mask, " the queen of the Tchoupitoulas I proudly acknowledge, and my great-grandfather, Epaminondas Fusilier, lieutenant of dragoons under Bienville ; but," — he laid his hand upon his heart, and bowed to the other two figures, whose smaller stature betrayed the gentler sex — " pardon me, ladies, neither Monks nor *Filles à la Cassette* grow on our family tree."

The four maskers at once turned their glance upon the old man in the domino ; but if any retort was intended it gave way as the violins burst into an agony of laughter. The floor was immediately filled with waltzers and the four figures disappeared.

" I wonder," murmured Agricola to himself, " if that Dragoon can possibly be Honoré Grandissime."

Wherever those four maskers went there were cries of delight: " Ho, ho, ho ! see there ! here ! there ! a group of first colonists ! One of Iberville's Dragoons ! don't you remember great-great grandfather Fusilier's portrait — the gilded casque and heron plumes ? And that one behind in the fawn-skin leggings and shirt of birds' skins is an Indian Queen. As sure as sure can be, they are intended for Epaminondas and his wife, Lufki-Humma!" All, of course, in Louisiana French.

"But why, then, does he not walk with her?"

"Why, because, Simplicity, both of them are men, while the little Monk on his arm is a lady, as you can see, and so is the masque that has the arm of the Indian Queen; look at their little hands."

In another part of the room the four were greeted with, "Ha, ha, ha! well, that is magnificent! But see that Huguenotte Girl on the Indian Queen's arm! Isn't that fine! Ha, ha! she carries a little trunk. She is a *Fille à la Cassette!*"

Two partners in a cotillion were speaking in an undertone, behind a fan.

"And you think you know who it is?" asked one.

"Know?" replied the other. "Do I know I have a head on my shoulders? If that Dragoon is not our cousin Honoré Grandissime — well ——"

"Honoré in mask? he is too sober-sided to do such a thing."

"I tell you it is he! Listen. Yesterday I heard Doctor Charlie Keene begging him to go, and telling him there were two ladies, strangers, newly arrived in the city, who would be there, and whom he wished him to meet. Depend upon it the Dragoon is Honoré, Lufki-Humma is Charlie Keene, and the Monk and the Huguenotte are those two ladies."

But all this is an outside view; let us draw nearer and see what chance may discover to us behind those four masks.

An hour has passed by. The dance goes on; hearts are beating, wit is flashing, eyes encounter eyes with the leveled lances of their beams, merriment and joy and sudden bright surprises thrill the breast, voices are throwing off disguise, and beauty's coy ear is bending with a venturesome docility; here love is baffled, there deceived, yonder takes prisoners and here surrenders. The very air seems to breathe, to sigh, to laugh, while the musicians, with disheveled locks, streaming brows and furious bows, strike, draw, drive, scatter from the anguished violins a never-ending rout of screaming harmonies. But the Monk and the Huguenotte are not on the floor. They are sitting where they have been left by their two companions, in one of the boxes of the theater, looking out upon the unwearied whirl and flash of gauze and light and color.

"Oh, *chérie, chérie!*" murmured the little lady in the Monk's disguise to her quieter companion, and speaking in the soft dialect of old Louisiana, "now you get a good idea of heaven!"

The *Fille à la Cassette* replied with a sudden turn of her masked face and a murmur of surprise and protest against this impiety. A low, merry laugh came out of the Monk's cowl, and the Huguenotte let her form sink a little in her chair with a gentle sigh.

"Ah, for shame, tired!" softly laughed the other;

then suddenly, with her eyes fixed across the room, she seized her companion's hand and pressed it tightly. " Do you not see it ? " she whispered eagerly, " just by the door — the casque with the heron feathers. Ah, Clotilde, I *cannot* believe he is one of those Grandissimes ! "

" Well," replied the Huguenotte, " Doctor Keene says he is not."

Doctor Charlie Keene, speaking from under the disguise of the Indian Queen, had indeed so said; but the Recording Angel, whom we understand to be particular about those things, had immediately made a memorandum of it to the debit of Doctor Keene's account.

" If I had believed that it was he," continued the whisperer, " I would have turned about and left him in the midst of the contra-dance ! "

Behind them sat unmasked a well-aged pair, " *bredouillé*," as they used to say of the wall-flowers, with that look of blissful repose which marks the married and established Creole. The lady in monk's attire turned about in her chair and leaned back to laugh with these. The passing maskers looked that way, with a certain instinct that there was beauty under those two costumes. As they did so, they saw the *Fille à la Cassette* join in this over-shoulder conversation. A moment later, they saw the old gentleman protector and the *Fille à la Cassette* rising to the dance. And when presently the distant passers took a final backward glance, that same Lieutenant of Dragoons had returned and he and the little Monk were once more upon the floor, waiting for the music.

"But your late companion?" said the voice in the cowl.

"My Indian Queen?" asked the Creole Epaminondas.

"Say, rather, your Medicine-Man," archly replied the Monk.

"In these times," responded the Cavalier, "a medicine-man cannot dance long without professional interruption, even when he dances for a charitable object. He has been called to two relapsed patients." The music struck up; the speaker addressed himself to the dance; but the lady did not respond.

"Do dragoons ever moralize?" she asked.

"They do more," replied her partner; "sometimes, when beauty's enjoyment of the ball is drawing toward its twilight, they catch its pleasant melancholy, and confess; will the good father sit in the confessional?"

The pair turned slowly about and moved toward the box from which they had come, the lady remaining silent; but just as they were entering she half withdrew her arm from his, and, confronting him with a rich sparkle of the eyes within the immobile mask of the monk, said:

"Why should the conscience of one poor little monk carry all the frivolity of this ball? I have a right to dance, if I wish. I give you my word, Monsieur Dragoon, I dance only for the benefit of the sick and the destitute. It is you men — you dragoons and others — who will not help them without a compensation in this sort of nonsense. Why should we shrive you when you ought to burn?"

"Then lead us to the altar," said the Dragoon.

"Pardon, sir," she retorted, her words entangled with a musical, open-hearted laugh, "I am not going in that direction." She cast her glance around the ball-room. "As you say, it is the twilight of the ball; I am looking for the evening star, — that is, my little Huguenotte."

"Then you are well mated."

"How?"

"For you are Aurora."

The lady gave a displeased start.

"Sir!"

"Pardon," said the Cavalier, "if by accident I have hit upon your real name —— "

She laughed again — a laugh which was as exultantly joyous as it was high-bred.

"Ah, my name? Oh no, indeed!" (More work for the Recording Angel.)

She turned to her protectress.

"Madame, I know you think we should be going home."

The senior lady replied in amiable speech, but with sleepy eyes, and the Monk began to lift and unfold a wrapping. As the Cavalier drew it into his own possession, and, agreeably to his gesture, the Monk and he sat down side by side, he said, in a low tone:

"One more laugh before we part."

"A monk cannot laugh for nothing."

"I will pay for it."

"But with nothing to laugh at?" The thought of laughing at nothing made her laugh a little on the spot.

"We will make something to laugh at," said the Cavalier; "we will unmask to each other, and when we find each other first cousins, the laugh will come of itself."

"Ah! we will unmask?—no! I have no cousins. I am certain we are strangers."

"Then we will laugh to think that I paid for the disappointment."

Much more of this childlike badinage followed, and by and by they came around again to the same last statement. Another little laugh escaped from the cowl.

"You will pay? Let us see; how much will you give to the sick and destitute?"

"To see who it is I am laughing with, I will give whatever you ask."

"Two hundred and fifty dollars, cash, into the hands of the managers!"

"A bargain!"

The Monk laughed, and her chaperon opened her eyes and smiled apologetically. The Cavalier laughed, too, and said:

"Good! That was the laugh; now the unmasking."

"And you positively will give the money to the managers not later than to-morrow evening?"

" Not later.   It shall be done without fail."

" Well, wait till I put on my wrappings; I must be ready to run."

This delightful nonsense was interrupted by the return of the *Fille à la Cassette* and her aged, but sprightly, escort, from a circuit of the floor.   Madame again opened her eyes, and the four prepared to depart.   The Dragoon helped the Monk to fortify herself against the outer air.   She was ready before the others.   There was a pause, a low laugh, a whispered " Now ! "   She looked upon an unmasked, noble countenance, lifted her own mask a little, and then a little more ; and then shut it quickly down again upon a face whose beauty was more than even those fascinating graces had promised which Honoré Grandissime had fitly named the Morning ; but it was a face he had never seen before.

" Hush ! " she said, " the enemies of religion are watching us ; the Huguenotte saw me.   Adieu " — and they were gone.

M. Honoré Grandissime turned on his heel and very soon left the ball.

" Now, sir," thought he to himself, " we 'll return to our senses."

" Now I 'll put my feathers on again," says the plucked bird.

CHAPTER II

THE FATE OF THE IMMIGRANT

IT was just a fortnight after the ball, that one Joseph Frowenfeld opened his eyes upon Louisiana. He was an American by birth, rearing and sentiment, yet German enough through his parents, and the only son in a family consisting of father, mother, self, and two sisters, new-blown flowers of womanhood. It was an October dawn, when, long wearied of the ocean, and with bright anticipations of verdure, and fragrance, and tropical gorgeousness, this simple-hearted family awoke to find the bark that had borne them from their far northern home already entering upon the ascent of the Mississippi.

We may easily imagine the grave group, as they came up one by one from below, that morning of first disappointment, and stood (with a whirligig of jubilant mosquitoes spinning about each head) looking out across the waste, seeing the sky and the marsh meet in the east, the north, and the west, and receiving with patient silence the father's suggestion that the hills would, no doubt, rise into view after a while.

" My children, we may turn this disappointment into a lesson ; if the good people of this country could speak to us now, they might well ask us not to judge them or their land upon one or two hasty glances, or by the experiences of a few short days or weeks."

But no hills rose. However, by and by they found solace in the appearance of distant forest, and in the afternoon they entered a land — but such a land ! A land hung in mourning, darkened by gigantic cypresses, submerged ; a land of reptiles, silence, shadow, decay.

" The captain told father, when we went to engage passage, that New Orleans was on high land," said the younger daughter, with a tremor in the voice, and ignoring the remonstrative touch of her sister.

" On high land ? " said the captain, turning from the pilot ; "well, so it is — higher than the swamp, but not higher than the river," and he checked a broadening smile.

But the Frowenfelds were not a family to complain. It was characteristic of them to recognize the bright as well as the solemn virtues, and to keep each other reminded of the duty of cheerfulness. A smile, starting from the quiet elder sister, went around the group, directed against the abstracted and somewhat rueful countenance of Joseph, whereat he turned with a better face and said that what the Creator had pronounced very good they could hardly feel free to condemn. The old father was still more stout of heart.

" These mosquitoes, children, are thought by some to keep the air pure," he said.

" Better keep out of it after sunset," put in the captain.

After that day and night, the prospect grew less

repellent. A gradually matured conviction that New Orleans would not be found standing on stilts in the quagmire enabled the eye to become educated to a better appreciation of the solemn landscape. Nor was the landscape always solemn. There were long openings, now and then, to right and left, of emerald-green savannah, with the dazzling blue of the Gulf far beyond, waving a thousand white-handed good-byes as the funereal swamps slowly shut out again the horizon. How sweet the soft breezes off the moist prairies! How weird, how very near, the crimson and green and black and yellow sunsets! How dream-like the land and the great, whispering river! The profound stillness and breath reminded the old German, so he said, of that early time when the evenings and mornings were the first days of the half-built world. The barking of a dog in Fort Plaquemines seemed to come before its turn in the panorama of creation — before the earth was ready for the dog's master.

But he was assured that to live in those swamps was not entirely impossible to man — "if one may call a negro a man." Runaway slaves were not so rare in them as one — a lost hunter, for example — might wish. His informant was a new passenger, taken aboard at the fort. He spoke English.

"Yes, sir! Did n' I had to run from Bras-Coupé in de haidge of de swamp be'ine de 'abitation of my cousin Honoré, one time? You can hask 'oo you like!" (A Creole always provides against incredulity.)   At this point he digressed a moment: "You know my cousin, Honoré Grandissime, w'at give two hund' fifty dolla' to de 'ospill laz mont'?   An' juz because my cousin Honoré give it, somebody helse give de semm.   Fo' w'y don't he give his nemm?"

The reason (which this person did not know) was that the second donor was the first one over again, resolved that the little unknown Monk should not know whom she had baffled.

"Who was Bras-Coupé?" the good German asked in French.

The stranger sat upon the capstan, and, in the shadow of the cypress forest, where the vessel lay moored for a change of wind, told in a *patois* difficult, but not impossible, to understand, the story of a man who chose rather to be hunted like a wild beast among those awful labyrinths, than to be yoked and beaten like a tame one.   Joseph, drawing near as the story was coming to a close, overheard the following English:

"Friend, if you dislike heated discussion, do not tell that to my son."

The nights were strangely beautiful.   The immigrants almost consumed them on deck, the mother and daughters attending in silent delight while the father and son, facing south, rejoiced in learned recognition of stars and constellations hitherto known to them only on globes and charts.

"Yes, my dear son," said the father, in a moment of ecstatic admiration, "wherever man may go,

around this globe — however uninviting his lateral
surroundings may be, the heavens are ever over his
head, and I am glad to find the stars your favorite
objects of study."

So passed the time as the vessel, hour by hour,
now slowly pushed by the wind against the turbid
current, now warping along the fragrant precincts
of orange or magnolia groves or fields of sugar-
cane, or moored by night in the deep shade of
mighty willow-jungles, patiently crept toward the
end of their pilgrimage ; and in the length of time
which would at present be consumed in making the
whole journey from their Northern home to their
Southern goal, accomplished the distance of ninety-
eight miles, and found themselves before the little,
hybrid city of "Nouvelle Orléans." There was
the cathedral, and standing beside it, like Sancho
beside Don Quixote, the squat hall of the Cabildo
with the calabozo in the rear. There were the
forts, the military bakery, the hospitals, the plaza,
the Almonaster stores, and the busy rue Toulouse ;
and, for the rest of the town, a pleasant confusion
of green tree-tops, red and gray roofs, and glimpses
of white or yellow wall, spreading back a few hundred yards behind the cathedral, and tapering into
a single rank of gardened and belvedered villas, that
studded either horn of the river's crescent with a
style of home than which there is probably nothing
in the world more maternally homelike.

"And now," said the "captain," bidding the
immigrants good-by, "keep out of the sun and

stay in after dark; you're not 'acclimated,' as they call it, you know, and the city is full of the fever."

Such were the Frowenfelds. Out of such a mold and into such a place came the young Américain, whom even Agricola Fusilier, as we shall see, by and by thought worthy to be made an exception of, and honored with his recognition.

The family rented a two-story brick house in the rue Bienville, No. 17, it seems. The third day after, at daybreak, Joseph called his father to his bedside to say that he had had a chill, and was suffering such pains in his head and back that he would like to lie quiet until they passed off. The gentle father replied that it was undoubtedly best to do so, and preserved an outward calm. He looked at his son's eyes; their pupils were contracted to tiny beads. He felt his pulse and his brow; there was no room for doubt; it was the dreaded scourge — the fever. We say, sometimes, of hearts that they sink like lead; it does not express the agony.

On the second day, while the unsated fever was running through every vein and artery, like soldiery through the streets of a burning city, and far down in the caverns of the body the poison was ransacking every palpitating corner, the poor immigrant fell into a moment's sleep. But what of that? The enemy that moment had mounted to the brain. And then there happened to Joseph an experience rare to the sufferer by this disease, but not entirely unknown, — a delirium of mingled pleasures and distresses. He seemed to awake somewhere between heaven and earth, reclining in a gorgeous barge, which was draped in curtains of interwoven silver and silk, cushioned with rich stuffs of every beautiful dye, and perfumed *ad nauseam* with orange-leaf tea. The crew was a single old negress, whose head was wound about with a blue Madras handkerchief, and who stood at the prow, and by a singular rotary motion, rowed the barge with a teaspoon. He could not get his head out of the hot sun ; and the barge went continually round and round with a heavy, throbbing motion, in the regular beat of which certain spirits of the air — one of whom appeared to be a beautiful girl and another a small, red-haired man, — confronted each other with the continual call and response :

" Keep the bedclothes on him and the room shut tight, keep the bedclothes on him and the room shut tight," — " An' don' give 'im some watta, an' don' give 'im some watta."

During what lapse of time — whether moments or days — this lasted, Joseph could not then know ; but at last these things faded away, and there came to him a positive knowledge that he was on a sick-bed, where unless something could be done for him he should be dead in an hour. Then a spoon touched his lips, and a taste of brandy and water went all through him ; and when he fell into sweet slumber and awoke, and found the teaspoon ready at his lips again, he had to lift a little the two hands lying before him on the coverlet to know that they were his — they were so wasted and yellow. He turned his eyes, and through the white gauze of the mosquito-bar saw, for an instant, a strange and beautiful young face; but the lids fell over his eyes, and when he raised them again the blue-turbaned black nurse was tucking the covering about his feet.

" Sister ! "

No answer.

" Where is my mother ? "

The negress shook her head.

He was too weak to speak again, but asked with his eyes so persistently, and so pleadingly, that by and by she gave him an audible answer. He tried hard to understand it, but could not, it being in these words :

"Li pa' oulé vini 'ci — li pas capabe."

Thrice a day, for three days more, came a little man with a large head surrounded by short, red curls and with small freckles in a fine skin, and sat down by the bed with a word of good cheer and the air of a commander. At length they had something like an extended conversation.

" So you concluded not to die, eh ? Yes, I 'm the doctor — Doctor Keene. A young lady ? What young lady ? No, sir, there has been no young lady here. You 're mistaken. Vagary of your fever. There has been no one here but this black girl and me. No, my dear fellow, your father and mother can't see you yet; you don't want them to catch the fever, do you ? Good-bye. Do as your

nurse tells you, and next week you may raise your
head and shoulders a little; but if you don't mind
her you 'll have a backset, and the devil himself
would n't engage to cure you."

The patient had been sitting up a little at a time
for several days, when at length the doctor came to
pay a final call, " as a matter of form ; " but, after
a few pleasantries, he drew his chair up gravely,
and, in a tender tone —— need we say it ? He had
come to tell Joseph that his father, mother, sisters,
all, were gone on a second — a longer — voyage, to
shores where there could be no disappointments and
no fevers, forever.

" And, Frowenfeld," he said, at the end of their
long and painful talk, " if there is any blame attached
to not letting you go with them, I think I can take
part of it ; but if you ever want a friend, — one
who is courteous to strangers and ill-mannered only
to those he likes, — you can call for Charlie Keene.
I 'll drop in to see you, anyhow, from time to time,
till you get stronger. I have taken a heap of trouble
to keep you alive, and if you should relapse now
and give us the slip, it would be a deal of good
physic wasted ; so keep in the house."

The polite neighbors who lifted their cocked hats
to Joseph, as he spent a slow convalescence just
within his open door, were not bound to know how
or when he might have suffered. There were no
" Howards " or " Y. M. C. A.'s " in those days ; no
" Peabody Reliefs." Even had the neighbors
chosen to take cognizance of those bereavements,

they were not so unusual as to fix upon him any extraordinary interest as an object of sight; and he was beginning most distressfully to realize that "great solitude" which the philosopher attributes to towns, when matters took a decided turn.

CHAPTER III

" AND WHO IS MY NEIGHBOR ? "

WE say matters took a turn; or, better, that Frowenfeld's interest in affairs received a new life. This had its beginning in Doctor Keene's making himself specially entertaining in an old-family-history way, with a view to keeping his patient within doors for a safe period. He had conceived a great liking for Frowenfeld, and often, of an afternoon, would drift in to challenge him to a game of chess — a game, by the way, for which neither of them cared a farthing. The immigrant had learned its moves to gratify his father, and the doctor — the truth is, the doctor had never quite learned them ; but he was one of those men who cannot easily consent to acknowledge a mere affection for one, least of all one of their own sex. It may safely be supposed, then, that the board often displayed an arrangement of pieces that would have bewildered Morphy himself.

" By the by, Frowenfeld," he said one evening, after the one preliminary move with which he in-

variably opened his game, "you have n't made
the acquaintance of your pretty neighbors next
door."

Frowenfeld knew of no specially pretty neighbors next door on either side — had noticed no
ladies.

"Well, I will take you in to see them some
time." The doctor laughed a little, rubbing his
face and his thin, red curls with one hand, as he
laughed.

The convalescent wondered what there could be
to laugh at.

"Who are they?" he inquired.

"Their name is De Grapion — oh, De Grapion,
says I! their name is Nancanou. They are, without
exception, the finest women — the brightest, the
best, and the bravest — that I know in New Orleans." The doctor resumed a cigar which lay
against the edge of the chess-board, found it extin-
guished, and proceeded to relight it. "Best blood
of the province; good as the Grandissimes. Blood
is a great thing here, in certain odd ways," he went
on. "Very curious sometimes." He stooped to
the floor where his coat had fallen, and took his
handkerchief from a breast-pocket. "At a grand
mask ball about two months ago, where I had a
bewilderingly fine time with those ladies, the proudest old turkey in the theater was an old fellow whose
Indian blood shows in his very behavior, and yet —
ha, ha! I saw that same old man, at a quadroon ball
a few years ago, walk up to the handsomest, best

dressed man in the house, a man with a skin whiter than his own, — a perfect gentleman as to looks and manners, — and without a word slap him in the face."

" You laugh ? " asked Frowenfeld.

" Laugh ? Why should n't I ? The fellow had no business there. Those balls are not given to quadroon *males*, my friend. He was lucky to get out alive, and that was about all he did.

" They are right ! " the doctor persisted, in response to Frowenfeld's puzzled look. " The people here have got to be particular. However, that is not what we were talking about. Quadroon balls are not to be mentioned in connection. Those ladies —— " He addressed himself to the resuscitation of his cigar. " Singular people in this country," he resumed ; but his cigar would not revive. He was a poor story-teller. To Frowenfeld — as it would have been to any one, except a Creole or the most thoroughly Creolized Américain — his narrative, when it was done, was little more than a thick mist of strange names, places and events ; yet there shone a light of romance upon it that filled it with color and populated it with phantoms. Frowenfeld's interest rose — was allured into this mist — and there was left befogged. As a physician, Doctor Keene thus accomplished his end, — the mental diversion of his late patient, — for in the midst of the mist Frowenfeld encountered and grappled a problem of human life in Creole type, the possible correlations of whose quantities we shall presently find him revolving in a studious and sympathetic mind, as the poet of to-day ponders the

"Flower in the crannied wall."

The quantities in that problem were the ancestral — the maternal — roots of those two rival and hostile families whose descendants — some brave, others fair — we find unwittingly thrown together at the ball, and with whom we are shortly to have the honor of an unmasked acquaintance.

CHAPTER IV

FAMILY TREES

In the year 1673, and in the royal hovel of a Tchoupitoulas village not far removed from that "Buffalo's Grazing-ground," now better known as New Orleans, was born Lufki-Humma, otherwise Red Clay. The mother of Red Clay was a princess by birth as well as by marriage. For the father, with that devotion to his people's interests presumably common to rulers, had ten moons before ventured northward into the territory of the proud and exclusive Natchez nation, and had so prevailed with — so outsmoked — their "Great Sun," as to find himself, as he finally knocked the ashes from his successful calumet, possessor of a wife whose pedigree included a long line of royal mothers — fathers being of little account in Natchez heraldry — extending back beyond the Mexican origin of her nation, and disappearing only in the effulgence of her great original, the orb of day himself. As to Red Clay's paternal ancestry, we must content ourselves with the fact that the father was not only the diplomate we have already found him, but a chief of considerable eminence; that is to say, of seven feet stature.

It scarce need be said that when Lufki-Humma was born, the mother arose at once from her couch of skins, herself bore the infant to the neighboring bayou and bathed it — not for singularity, nor for independence, nor for vainglory, but only as one of the heart-curdling conventionalities which made up the experience of that most pitiful of holy things, an Indian mother.

Outside the lodge door sat and continued to sit, as she passed out, her master or husband. His interest in the trivialities of the moment may be summed up in this, that he was as fully prepared as some men are in more civilized times and places to hold his queen to strict account for the sex of her offspring. Girls for the Natchez, if they preferred them, but the chief of the Tchoupitoulas wanted a son. She returned from the water, came near, sank upon her knees, laid the infant at his feet, and lo! a daughter.

Then she fell forward heavily upon her face. It may have been muscular exhaustion, it may have been the mere wind of her hasty-tempered matrimonial master's stone hatchet as it whiffed by her

skull; an inquest now would be too great an irony;
but something blew out her "vile candle."

Among the squaws who came to offer the accustomed funeral howlings, and seize mementoes from
the deceased lady's scant leavings, was one who had
in her own palmetto hut an empty cradle scarcely
cold, and therefore a necessity at her breast, if not
a place in her heart, for the unfortunate Lufki-
Humma; and thus it was that this little waif came
to be tossed, a droll hypothesis of flesh, blood,
nerve and brain, into the hands of wild nature with
carte blanche as to the disposal of it. And now,
since this was Agricola's most boasted ancestor —
since it appears the darkness of her cheek had no
effect to make him less white, or qualify his right to
smite the fairest and most distant descendant of an
African on the face, and since this proud station and
right could not have sprung from the squalid surroundings of her birth, let us for a moment contemplate these crude materials.

As for the flesh, it was indeed only some of that
"one flesh" of which we all are made; but the
blood — to go into finer distinctions — the blood,
as distinguished from the milk of her Alibamon
foster-mother, was the blood of the royal caste of
the great Toltec mother-race, which, before it yielded
its Mexican splendors to the conquering Aztec,
throned the jeweled and gold-laden Inca in the
South, and sent the sacred fire of its temples into the
North by the hand of the Natchez. For it is a
short way of expressing the truth concerning Red

Clay's tissues to say she had the blood of her mother
and the nerve of her father, the nerve of the true
North American Indian, and had it in its finest
strength.

As to her infantine bones, they were such as
needed not to fail of straightness in the limbs, com-
pactness in the body, smallness in hands and feet,
and exceeding symmetry and comeliness throughout.　　Possibly between the two sides of the occipital
profile there may have been an Incæan tendency to
inequality ; but if by any good fortune her impressible little cranium should escape the cradle-straps,
the shapeliness that nature loves would soon appear.
And this very fortune befell her.　Her father's detestation of an infant that had not consulted his
wishes as to sex prompted a verbal decree which,
among other prohibitions, forbade her skull the
distortions that ambitious and fashionable Indian
mothers delighted to produce upon their offspring.

And as to her brain : what can we say?　The
casket in which Nature sealed that brain, and in
which Nature's great step-sister, Death, finally laid
it away, has never fallen into the delighted fingers —
and the remarkable fineness of its texture will never
kindle admiration in the triumphant eyes — of those
whose scientific hunger drives them to dig for *crania
Americana ;* nor yet will all their learned excavatings
ever draw forth one of those pale souvenirs of mor-
tality with walls of shapelier contour or more delicate
fineness, or an interior of more admirable spaciousness, than the fair council-chamber under whose

dome the mind of Lufki-Humma used, about two centuries ago, to sit in frequent conclave with high thoughts.

"I have these facts," it was Agricola Fusilier's habit to say, "by family tradition; but you know, sir, h-tradition is much more authentic than history!"

Listening Crane, the tribal medicine-man, one day stepped softly into the lodge of the giant chief, sat down opposite him on a mat of plaited rushes, accepted a lighted calumet, and, after the silence of a decent hour, broken at length by the warrior's intimation that "the ear of Raging Buffalo listened for the voice of his brother," said, in effect, that if that ear would turn toward the village play-ground, it would catch a murmur like the pleasing sound of bees among the blossoms of the catalpa, albeit the catalpa was now dropping her leaves, for it was the moon of turkeys. No, it was the repressed laughter of squaws, wallowing with their young ones about the village pole, wondering at the Natchez-Tchoupi-toulas child, whose eye was the eye of the panther, and whose words were the words of an aged chief in council.

There was more added; we record only enough to indicate the direction of Listening Crane's aim. The eye of Raging Buffalo was opened to see a vision: the daughter of the Natchez sitting in majesty, clothed in many-colored robes of shining feathers crossed and recrossed with girdles of serpent-skins and of wampum, her feet in quilled and painted moccasins, her head under a glory of plumes, the carpet of buffalo-robes about her throne covered with the trophies of conquest, and the atmosphere of her lodge blue with the smoke of embassadors' calumets; and this extravagant dream the capricious chief at once resolved should eventually become reality. " Let her be taken to the village temple," he said to his prime-minister, "and be fed by warriors on the flesh of wolves."

The Listening Crane was a patient man ; he was the " man that waits " of the old French proverb ; all things came to him. He had waited for an opportunity to change his brother's mind, and it had come. Again, he waited for him to die ; and, like Methuselah and others, he died. He had heard of a race more powerful than the Natchez — a white race ; he waited for them ; and when the year 1682 saw a humble " black gown " dragging and splashing his way, with La Salle and Tonti, through the swamps of Louisiana, holding forth the crucifix and backed by French carbines and Mohican tomahawks, among the marvels of that wilderness was found this : a child of nine sitting, and — with some unostentatious aid from her med-icine-man — ruling ; queen of her tribe and high-priestess of their temple. Fortified by the acumen and self-collected ambition of Listening Crane, con-firmed in her regal title by the white man's Manitou through the medium of the " black gown," and in-heriting her father's fear-compelling frown, she ruled with majesty and wisdom, sometimes a decreer of

bloody justice, sometimes an Amazonian counselor
of warriors, and at all times — year after year, until
she had reached the perfect womanhood of twenty-
six — a virgin queen.

On the 11th of March, 1699, two overbold
young Frenchmen of M. D'Iberville's little explor-
ing party tossed guns on shoulder, and ventured
away from their canoes on the bank of the Mississippi into the wilderness. Two men they were whom
an explorer would have been justified in hoarding
up, rather than in letting out at such risks; a pair
to lean on, noble and strong. They hunted, killed
nothing, were overtaken by rain, then by night,
hunger, alarm, despair.

And when they had lain down to die, and had
only succeeded in falling asleep, the Diana of the
Tchoupitoulas, ranging the magnolia groves with
bow and quiver, came upon them in all the poetry
of their hope-forsaken strength and beauty, and fell
sick of love. We say not whether with Zephyr
Grandissime or Epaminondas Fusilier; that, for the
time being, was her secret.

The two captives were made guests. Listening
Crane rejoiced in them as representatives of the
great gift-making race, and indulged himself in a
dream of pipe-smoking, orations, treaties, presents
and alliances, finding its climax in the marriage of
his virgin queen to the king of France, and unvary-
ingly tending to the swiftly increasing aggrandize-
ment of Listening Crane. They sat down to bear's
meat, sagamite and beans. The queen sat down

with them, clothed in her entire wardrobe : vest of
swan's skin, with facings of purple and green from
the neck of the mallard ; petticoat of plaited hair,
with embroideries of quills ; leggings of fawn-skin ;
garters of wampum ; black and green serpent-skin
moccasins, that rested on pelts of tiger-cat and buffalo ; armlets of gars' scales, necklaces of bears'
claws and alligators' teeth, plaited tresses, plumes of
raven and flamingo, wing of the pink curlew, and
odors of bay and sassafras. Young men danced before them, blowing upon reeds, hooting, yelling,
rattling beans in gourds and touching hands and
feet. One day was like another, and the nights
were made brilliant with flambeau dances and
processions.

Some days later M. D'Iberville's canoe fleet, returning down the river, found and took from the
shore the two men, whom they had given up for
dead, and with them, by her own request, the abdi-
cating queen, who left behind her a crowd of weeping and howling squaws and warriors. Three
canoes that put off in their wake, at a word from
her, turned back ; but one old man leaped into the
water, swam after them a little way, and then unexpectedly sank. It was that cautious wader but inexperienced swimmer, the Listening Crane.

When the expedition reached Biloxi, there were
two suitors for the hand of Agricola's great ancestress. Neither of them was Zephyr Grandissime.
(Ah ! the strong heads of those Grandissimes.)

They threw dice for her. Demosthenes De

Grapion — he who, tradition says, first hoisted the
flag of France over the little fort — seemed to think
he ought to have a chance, and being accorded it,
cast an astonishingly high number ; but Epaminondas cast a number higher by one (which Demosthenes never could quite understand), and got a wife
who had loved him from first sight.

Thus, while the pilgrim fathers of the Mississippi
Delta with Gallic recklessness were taking wives and
moot-wives from the ill specimens of three races,
arose, with the church's benediction, the royal house
of the Fusiliers in Louisiana. But the true, main
Grandissime stock, on which the Fusiliers did early,
ever, and yet do, love to marry, has kept itself lily-
white ever since France has loved lilies — as to
marriage, that is ; as to less responsible entanglements, why, of course ——

After a little, the disappointed Demosthenes, with
due ecclesiastical sanction, also took a most excellent
wife, from the first cargo of House of Correction
girls. Her biography, too, is as short as Methuselah's, or shorter ; she died. Zephyr Grandissime
married, still later, a lady of rank, a widow without
children, sent from France to Biloxi under a *lettre
de cachet*. Demosthenes De Grapion, himself an
only son, left but one son, who also left but one.
Yet they were prone to early marriages.

So also were the Grandissimes, or, as the name is
signed in all the old notarial papers, the Brahmin
Mandarin de Grandissimes. That was one thing
that kept their many-stranded family line so free

from knots and kinks. Once the leisurely Zephyr gave them a start, generation followed generation with a rapidity that kept the competing De Grapions incessantly exasperated, and new-made Grandissime fathers continually throwing themselves into the fond arms and upon the proud necks of congratulatory grandsires. Verily it seemed as though their family tree was a fig-tree; you could not look for blossoms on it, but there, instead, was the fruit full of seed. And with all their speed they were for the most part fine of stature, strong of limb and fair of face. The old nobility of their stock, including particularly the unnamed blood of her of the *lettre de cachet*, showed forth in a gracefulness of carriage, that almost identified a De Grandissime wherever you saw him, and in a transparency of flesh and classic beauty of feature, that made their daughters extra-marriageable in a land and day which was bearing a wide reproach for a male celibacy not of the pious sort.

In a flock of Grandissimes might always be seen a Fusilier or two; fierce-eyed, strong-beaked, dark, heavy-taloned birds, who, if they could not sing, were of rich plumage, and could talk, and bite, and strike, and keep up a ruffled crest and a self-exalting bad humor. They early learned one favorite cry, with which they greeted all strangers, crying the louder the more the endeavor was made to appease them: "Invaders! Invaders!"

There was a real pathos in the contrast offered to this family line by that other which sprang up, as

slenderly as a stalk of wild oats, from the loins of
Demosthenes De Grapion. A lone son following
a lone son, and he another — it was sad to contemplate, in that colonial beginning of days, three gen-
erations of good, Gallic blood tripping jocundly
along in attenuated Indian file. It made it no less
pathetic to see that they were brilliant, gallant,
much-loved, early epauletted fellows, who did not
let twenty-one catch them without wives sealed with
the authentic wedding kiss, nor allow twenty-two to
find them without an heir. But they had a sad aptness for dying young. It was altogether supposable
that they would have spread out broadly in the land;
but they were such inveterate duelists, such brave
Indian-fighters, such adventurous swamp-rangers,
and such lively free-livers, that, however numer-
ously their half-kin may have been scattered about
in an unacknowledged way, the avowed name of
De Grapion had become less and less frequent in
lists where leading citizens subscribed their signa-
tures, and was not to be seen in the list of managers
of the late ball.

It is not at all certain that so hot a blood would
not have boiled away entirely before the night of
the *bal masqué*, but for an event which led to the
union of that blood with a stream equally clear and
ruddy, but of a milder vintage. This event fell out
some fifty-two years after that cast of the dice which
made the princess Lufki-Humma the mother of all
the Fusiliers and of none of the De Grapions.
Clotilde, the Casket-Girl, the little maid who would

not marry, was one of an heroic sort, worth — the
De Grapions maintained — whole swampfuls of
Indian queens. And yet the portrait of this great
ancestress, which served as a pattern to one who, at
the ball, personated the long-deceased heroine *en
masque*, is hopelessly lost in some garret. Those
Creoles have such a shocking way of filing their
family relics and records in rat-holes.

One fact alone remains to be stated : that the
De Grapions, try to spurn it as they would, never
could quite suppress a hard feeling in the face of
the record, that from the two young men, who,
when lost in the horrors of Louisiana's swamps, had
been esteemed as good as dead, and particularly
from him who married at his leisure, — from Zephyr
de Grandissime, — sprang there so many as the
sands of the Mississippi innumerable.

CHAPTER V

A MAIDEN WHO WILL NOT MARRY

MIDWAY between the times of Lufki-Humma
and those of her proud descendant, Agricola Fusilier,
fifty-two years lying on either side, were the days of
Pierre Rigaut, the magnificent, the " Grand Marquis," the Governor, De Vaudreuil. He was the
Solomon of Louisiana. For splendor, however,
not for wisdom. Those were the gala days of
license, extravagance and pomp. He made paper

money to be as the leaves of the forest for multitude; it was nothing accounted of in the days of the Grand Marquis. For Louis Quinze was king.

Clotilde, orphan of a murdered Huguenot, was one of sixty, the last royal allotment to Louisiana, of imported wives. The king's agents had inveigled her away from France with fair stories : " They will give you a quiet home with some lady of the colony. Have to marry ? — not unless it pleases you. The king himself pays your passage and gives you a casket of clothes. Think of that these times, fillette; and passage free, withal, to — the garden of Eden, as you may call it — what more, say you, can a poor girl want ? Without doubt, too, like a model colonist, you will accept a good husband and have a great many beautiful children, who will say with pride, ' Me, I am no House-of-Correction-girl stock; my mother ' — or ' grandmother,' as the case may be — ' was a *fille à la cassette !* ' "

The sixty were landed in New Orleans and given into the care of the Ursuline nuns; and, before many days had elapsed, fifty-nine soldiers of the king were well wived and ready to settle upon their riparian land-grants. The residuum in the nuns' hands was one stiff-necked little heretic, named, in part, Clotilde. They bore with her for sixty days, and then complained to the Grand Marquis. But the Grand Marquis, with all his pomp, was gracious and kind-hearted, and loved his ease almost as much as his marchioness loved money. He bade them try her another month. They did so, and then returned with her; she would neither marry nor pray to Mary.

Here is the way they talked in New Orleans in those days. If you care to understand why Louisiana has grown up so out of joint, note the tone of those who governed her in the middle of the last century:

"What, my child," the Grand Marquis said, "you a *fille à la cassette?* France, for shame! Come here by my side. Will you take a little advice from an old soldier? It is in one word — submit. Whatever is inevitable, submit to it. If you want to live easy and sleep easy, do as other people do — submit. Consider submission in the present case; how easy, how comfortable, and how little it amounts to! A little hearing of mass, a little telling of beads, a little crossing of one's self — what is that? One need not believe in them. Don't shake your head. Take my example; look at me; all these things go in at this ear and out at this. Do king or clergy trouble me? Not at all. For how does the king in these matters of religion? I shall not even tell you, he is such a bad boy. Do you not know that all the *noblesse*, and all the *savants*, and especially all the archbishops and cardinals, — all, in a word, but such silly little chicks as yourself, — have found out that this religious business is a joke? Actually a joke, every whit; except, to be sure, this heresy phase; that is a joke they cannot take. Now, I wish you well, pretty child; so if you — eh? — truly, my pet, I fear we shall have to

call you unreasonable. Stop; they can spare me
here a moment; I will take you to the Marquise:
she is in the next room. * * * Behold," said he, as
he entered the presence of his marchioness, "the
little maid who will not marry!"

The Marquise was as cold and hard-hearted as
the Marquis was loose and kind; but we need not
recount the slow tortures of the *fille à la cassette's*
second verbal temptation. The colony had to have
soldiers, she was given to understand, and the
soldiers must have wives. "Why, I am a soldier's
wife, myself!" said the gorgeously attired lady,
laying her hand upon the governor-general's epau-
let. She explained, further, that he was rather soft-
hearted, while she was a business woman; also that
the royal commissary's rolls did not comprehend
such a thing as a spinster, and — incidentally — that
living by principle was rather out of fashion in the
province just then.

After she had offered much torment of this sort,
a definite notion seemed to take her; she turned
her lord by a touch of the elbow, and exchanged
two or three business-like whispers with him at a
window overlooking the Levee.

"Fillette," she said, returning, "you are going
to live on the sea-coast. I am sending an aged
lady there to gather the wax of the wild myrtle.
This good soldier of mine buys it for our king at
twelve livres the pound. Do you not know that
women can make money? The place is not safe;
but there are no safe places in Louisiana. There are

no nuns to trouble you there; only a few Indians and soldiers. You and Madame will live together, quite to yourselves, and can pray as you like."

"And not marry a soldier," said the Grand Marquis.

"No," said the lady, "not if you can gather enough myrtle-berries to afford me a profit and you a living."

It was some thirty leagues or more eastward to the country of the Biloxis, a beautiful land of low, evergreen hills looking out across the pine-covered sand-keys of Mississippi Sound to the Gulf of Mexico. The northern shore of Biloxi Bay was rich in candleberry-myrtle. In Clotilde's day, though Biloxi was no longer the capital of the Mississippi Valley, the fort which D'Iberville had built in 1699, and the first timber of which is said to have been lifted by Zephyr Grandissime at one end and Epaminondas Fusilier at the other, was still there, making brave against the possible advent of corsairs, with a few old culverines and one wooden mortar.

And did the orphan, in despite of Indians and soldiers and wilderness, settle down here and make a moderate fortune? Alas, she never gathered a berry! When she — with the aged lady, her appointed companion in exile, the young commandant of the fort, in whose pinnace they had come, and two or three French sailors and Canadians — stepped out upon the white sand of Biloxi beach, she was bound with invisible fetters hand and foot, by that Olympian rogue of a boy, who likes no better prey than a little maiden who thinks she will never marry.

The officer's name was De Grapion — Georges De Grapion. The Marquis gave him a choice grant of land on that part of the Mississippi river "coast" known as the Cannes Brulées.

"Of course you know where Cannes Brulées is, don't you?" asked Doctor Keene of Joseph Frowenfeld.

"Yes," said Joseph, with a twinge of reminiscence that recalled the study of Louisiana on paper with his father and sisters.

There Georges De Grapion settled, with the laudable determination to make a fresh start against the mortifyingly numerous Grandissimes.

"My father's policy was every way bad," he said to his spouse; "it is useless, and probably wrong, this trying to thin them out by duels; we will try another plan. Thank you," he added, as she handed his coat back to him, with the shoulderstraps cut off. In pursuance of the new plan, Madame De Grapion, — the precious little heroine! — before the myrtles offered another crop of berries, bore him a boy not much smaller (saith tradition) than herself.

Only one thing qualified the father's elation. On that very day Numa Grandissime (Brahmin-Mandarin de Grandissime), a mere child, received from Governor de Vaudreuil a cadetship.

"Never mind, Messieurs Grandissime, go on with your tricks; we shall see! Ha! we shall see!"

"We shall see what?" asked a remote relative of that family. "Will Monsieur be so good as to explain himself?"

.   .   .   .

Bang! bang!

Alas, Madame De Grapion!

It may be recorded that no affair of honor in Louisiana ever left a braver little widow. When Joseph and his doctor pretended to play chess together, but little more than a half-century had elapsed since the *fille à la cassette* stood before the Grand Marquis and refused to wed. Yet she had been long gone into the skies, leaving a worthy example behind her in twenty years of beautiful widowhood. Her son, the heir and resident of the plantation at Cannes Brulées, at the age of — they do say — eighteen, had married a blithe and pretty lady of Franco-Spanish extraction, and, after a fair length of life divided between campaigning under the brilliant young Galvez and raising unremunerative indigo crops, had lately lain down to sleep, leaving only two descendants — females — how shall we describe them? — a Monk and a *Fille à la Cassette*. It was very hard to have to go leaving his family name snuffed out and certain Grandissime-ward grievances burning.

"There are so many Grandissimes," said the weary-eyed Frowenfeld, "I cannot distinguish between — I can scarcely count them."

" Well, now," said the doctor, "let me tell you, don't try. They can't do it themselves. Take them in the mass — as you would shrimps."

CHAPTER VI

LOST OPPORTUNITIES

THE little doctor tipped his chair back against the wall, drew up his knees, and laughed whimperingly in his freckled hands.

" I had to do some prodigious lying at that ball. I did n't dare let the De Grapion ladies know they were in company with a Grandissime."

" I thought you said their name was Nancanou."

" Well, certainly — De Grapion-Nancanou. You see, that is one of their charms : one is a widow, the other is her daughter, and both as young and beautiful as Hebe. Ask Honoré Grandissime ; he has seen the little widow ; but then he don't know who she is. He will not ask me, and I will not tell him. Oh, yes ; it is about eighteen years now since old De Grapion — elegant, high-stepping old fellow — married her, then only sixteen years of age, to young Nancanou, an indigo-planter on the Fausse Rivière — the old bend, you know, behind Pointe Coupée. The young couple went there to live. I have been told they had one of the prettiest places in Louisiana. He was a man of cultivated tastes, educated in Paris, spoke English, was handsome (convivial, of course), and of perfectly pure blood. But there was one thing old De Grapion overlooked : he and his son-in-law were the last of their names. In Louisiana a man needs kinsfolk. He ought to have married his daughter into a strong house. They say that Numa Grandissime (Honoré's father) and he had patched up a peace between the two families that included even old Agricola, and that he could have married her to a Grandissime. However, he is supposed to have known what he was about.

" A matter of business called young Nancanou to New Orleans. He had no friends here ; he was a Creole, but what part of his life had not been spent on his plantation he had passed in Europe. He could not leave his young girl of a wife alone in that exiled sort of plantation life, so he brought her and the child (a girl) down with him as far as to her father's place, left them there, and came on to the city alone.

" Now, what does the old man do but give him a letter of introduction to old Agricole Fusilier ! (His name is Agricola, but we shorten it to Agricole.) It seems that old De Grapion and Agricole had had the indiscretion to scrape up a mutually complimentary correspondence. And to Agricole the young man went.

" They became intimate at once, drank together, danced with the quadroons together, and got into as much mischief in three days as I ever did in a fortnight. So affairs went on until by and by they were gambling together. One night they were at the Piety Club, playing hard, and the planter lost his last quarti. He became desperate, and did a thing I have known more than one planter to do : wrote his pledge for every arpent of his land and every slave on it, and staked that. Agricole refused to play. 'You shall play,' said Nancanou, and when the game was ended he said : 'Monsieur Agricola Fusilier, you cheated.' You see? Just as I have frequently been tempted to remark to my friend, Mr. Frowenfeld.

"But, Frowenfeld, you must know, withal the Creoles are such gamblers, they never cheat ; they play absolutely fair. So Agricole had to challenge the planter. He could not be blamed for that ; there was no choice — oh, now, Frowenfeld, keep quiet ! I tell you there was no choice. And the fellow was no coward. He sent Agricole a clear title to the real estate and slaves, — lacking only the wife's signature, — accepted the challenge and fell dead at the first fire.

"Stop, now, and let me finish. Agricole sat down and wrote to the widow that he did not wish to deprive her of her home, and that if she would state in writing her belief that the stakes had been won fairly, he would give back the whole estate, slaves and all ; but that if she would not, he should feel compelled to retain it in vindication of his honor. Now was n't that drawing a fine point ? " The doctor laughed according to his habit, with his face down in his hands. "You see, he wanted to stand before all creation — the Creator did not make so much difference — in the most exquisitely proper light; so he puts the laws of humanity under his feet, and anoints himself from head to foot with Creole punctilio."

" Did she sign the paper ? " asked Joseph.

" She ? Wait till you know her ! No, indeed ; she had the true scorn. She and her father sent down another and a better title. Creole-like, they managed to bestir themselves to that extent and there they stopped.

" And the airs with which they did it ! They kept all their rage to themselves, and sent the polite word, that they were not acquainted with the merits of the case, that they were not disposed to make the long and arduous trip to the city and back, and that if M. Fusilier de Grandissime thought he could find any pleasure or profit in owning the place, he was welcome ; that the widow of *his late friend* was not disposed to live on it, but would remain with her father at the paternal home at Cannes Brulées.

" Did you ever hear of a more perfect specimen of Creole pride? That is the way with all of them. Show me any Creole, or any number of Creoles, in any sort of contest, and right down at the foundation of it all, I will find you this same preposterous, apathetic, fantastic, suicidal pride. It is as lethargic and ferocious as an alligator. That is why the Creole almost always is (or thinks he is) on the defensive. See these De Grapions' haughty

good manners to old Agricole; yet there was n't
a Grandissime in Louisiana who could have set
foot on the De Grapion lands but at the risk of
his life.

"But I will finish the story: and here is the
really sad part. Not many months ago old De
Grapion — 'old,' said I; they don't grow old; I
call him old — a few months ago he died. He must
have left everything smothered in debt; for, like his
race, he had stuck to indigo because his father
planted it, and it is a crop that has lost money
steadily for years and years. His daughter and
granddaughter were left like babes in the wood;
and, to crown their disasters, have now made the
grave mistake of coming to the city, where they
find they have n't a friend — not one, sir! They
called me in to prescribe for a trivial indisposition,
shortly after their arrival; and I tell you, Frowenfeld, it made me shiver to see two such beautiful
women in such a town as this without a male protector, and even " — the doctor lowered his voice
— "without adequate support. The mother says
they are perfectly comfortable; tells the old couple
so who took them to the ball, and whose little girl
is their embroidery scholar; but you cannot believe
a Creole on that subject, and I don't believe her.
Would you like to make their acquaintance?"

Frowenfeld hesitated, disliking to say no to his
friend, and then shook his head.

"After a while — at least not now, sir, if you
please."

The doctor made a gesture of disappointment.

"Um-hum," he said grumly — "the only man in New Orleans I would honor with an invitation! — but all right; I'll go alone."

He laughed a little at himself, and left Frowenfeld, if ever he should desire it, to make the acquaintance of his pretty neighbors as best he could.

CHAPTER VII

WAS IT HONORÉ GRANDISSIME?

A CREOLE gentleman, on horseback one morning with some practical object in view, — drainage, possibly, — had got what he sought, — the evidence of his own eyes on certain points, — and now moved quietly across some old fields toward the town, where more absorbing interests awaited him in the Rue Toulouse; for this Creole gentleman was a merchant, and because he would presently find himself among the appointments and restraints of the counting-room, he heartily gave himself up, for the moment, to the surrounding influences of nature.

It was late in November; but the air was mild and the grass and foliage green and dewy. Wild flowers bloomed plentifully and in all directions; the bushes were hung, and often covered, with vines of sprightly green, sprinkled thickly with smart-looking little worthless berries, whose sparkling complacency the combined contempt of man, beast

and bird could not dim.   The call of the field-lark
came continually out of the grass, where now and
then could be seen his yellow breast; the orchard
oriole was executing his fantasias in every tree; a
covey of partridges ran across the path close under
the horse's feet, and stopped to look back almost
within reach of the riding-whip; clouds of starlings,
in their odd, irresolute way, rose from the high bul-
rushes and settled again, without discernible cause;
little wandering companies of sparrows undulated
from hedge to hedge; a great rabbit-hawk sat alone
in the top of a lofty pecan-tree; that petted rowdy,
the mocking-bird, dropped down into the path to
offer fight to the horse, and, failing in that, flew up
again and drove a crow into ignominious retirement
beyond the plain; from a place of flags and reeds a
white crane shot upward, turned, and then, with the
slow and stately beat peculiar to her wing, sped
away until, against the tallest cypress of the distant
forest, she became a tiny white speck on its black,
and suddenly disappeared, like one flake of snow.

The scene was altogether such as to fill any hearty
soul with impulses of genial friendliness and gentle
candor; such a scene as will sometimes prepare a
man of the world, upon the least direct incentive, to
throw open the windows of his private thought with
a freedom which the atmosphere of no counting-
room or drawing-room tends to induce.

The young merchant — he was young — felt this.
Moreover, the matter of business which had brought
him out had responded to his inquiring eye with a

somewhat golden radiance; and your true man of business — he who has reached that elevated pitch of serene, good-natured reserve which is of the high art of his calling — is never so generous with his pennyworths of thought as when newly in possession of some little secret worth many pounds.

By and by the behavior of the horse indicated the near presence of a stranger; and the next moment the rider drew rein under an immense live-oak where there was a bit of paling about some graves, and raised his hat.

"Good-morning, sir." But for the silent r's, his pronunciation was exact, yet evidently an acquired one. While he spoke his salutation in English, he was thinking in French: "Without doubt, this rather oversized, bareheaded, interrupted-looking convalescent who stands before me, wondering how I should know in what language to address him, is Joseph Frowenfeld, of whom Doctor Keene has had so much to say to me. A good face — unsophisticated, but intelligent, mettlesome and honest. He will make his mark; it will probably be a white one; I will subscribe to the adventure.

"You will excuse me, sir?" he asked after a pause, dismounting, and noticing, as he did so, that Frowenfeld's knees showed recent contact with the turf; "I have, myself, some interest in two of these graves, sir, as I suppose — you will pardon my freedom — you have in the other four."

He approached the old but newly whitened paling, which encircled the tree's trunk as well as the six graves about it.   There was in his face and manner a sort of impersonal human kindness, well calculated to engage a diffident and sensitive stranger, standing in dread of gratuitous benevolence or pity.

"Yes, sir," said the convalescent, and ceased; but the other leaned against the palings in an attitude of attention, and he felt induced to add: "I have buried here my father, mother, and two sisters," — he had expected to continue in an unemotional tone; but a deep respiration usurped the place of speech.   He stooped quickly to pick up his hat, and, as he rose again and looked into his listener's face, the respectful, unobtrusive sympathy there expressed went directly to his heart.

"Victims of the fever," said the Creole with great gravity.   "How did that happen?"

As Frowenfeld, after a moment's hesitation, began to speak, the stranger let go the bridle of his horse and sat down upon the turf.   Joseph appreciated the courtesy and sat down, too; and thus the ice was broken.

The immigrant told his story; he was young — often younger than his years — and his listener several years his senior; but the Creole, true to his blood, was able at any time to make himself as young as need be, and possessed the rare magic of drawing one's confidence without seeming to do more than merely pay attention.   It followed that the story was told in full detail, including grateful acknowledgment of the goodness of an unknown friend, who had granted this burial-place on condi-

4

tion that he should not be sought out for the purpose of thanking him.

So a considerable time passed by, in which
acquaintance grew with delightful rapidity.

"What will you do now?" asked the stranger,
when a short silence had followed the conclusion
of the story.

"I hardly know. I am taken somewhat by surprise. I have not chosen a definite course in life —
as yet. I have been a general student, but have
not prepared myself for any profession; I am not
sure what I shall be."

A certain energy in the immigrant's face half
redeemed this childlike speech. Yet the Creole's
lips, as he opened them to reply, betrayed amusement; so he hastened to say:

"I appreciate your position, Mr. Frowenfeld, —
excuse me, I believe you said that was your father's
name. And yet," — the shadow of an amused
smile lurked another instant about a corner of his
mouth, — "if you would understand me kindly I
would say, take care ―― "

What little blood the convalescent had rushed
violently to his face, and the Creole added:

"I do not insinuate you would willingly be idle.
I think I know what you want. You want to
make up your mind *now* what you will *do*, and at
your leisure what you will *be*; eh? To be, it
seems to me," he said in summing up, — "that to
be is not so necessary as to do, eh? or am I wrong?"

"No, sir," replied Joseph, still red, "I was feeling that just now. I will do the first thing that offers ; I can dig."

The Creole shrugged and pouted.

" And be called a *dos brûlé* — a ' burnt-back.' "

" But " —— began the immigrant, with over-much warmth.

The other interrupted him, shaking his head slowly and smiling as he spoke.

" Mr. Frowenfeld, it is of no use to talk ; you may hold in contempt the Creole scorn of toil — just as I do, myself, but in theory, my-de'-seh, not too much in practice. You cannot afford to be *entirely* different from the community in which you live ; is that not so ? "

" A friend of mine," said Frowenfeld, " has told me I must ' compromise.' "

" You must get acclimated," responded the Creole ; " not in body only, that you have done ; but in mind — in taste — in conversation — and in convictions too, yes, ha, ha ! They all do it — all who come. They hold out a little while — a very little ; then they open their stores on Sunday, they import cargoes of Africans, they bribe the officials, they smuggle goods, they have colored house-keepers. My-de'-seh, the water must expect to take the shape of the bucket ; eh ? "

" One need not be water ! " said the immigrant.

" Ah ! " said the Creole, with another amiable shrug, and a wave of his hand ; " certainly you do not suppose that is my advice — that those things have my approval."

Must we repeat already that Frowenfeld was abnormally young? "Why have they not your condemnation?" cried he with an earnestness that made the Creole's horse drop the grass from his teeth and wheel half around.

The answer came slowly and gently.

"Mr. Frowenfeld, my habit is to buy cheap and sell at a profit. My condemnation? My-de'-seh, there is no sa-a-ale for it! it spoils the sale of other goods, my-de'-seh. It is not to condemn that you want; you want to suc-*ceed*. Ha, ha, ha! you see I am a merchant, eh? My-de'-seh, can *you* afford not to succeed?"

The speaker had grown very much in earnest in the course of these few words, and as he asked the closing question, arose, arranged his horse's bridle and, with his elbow in the saddle, leaned his handsome head on his equally beautiful hand. His whole appearance was a dazzling contradiction of the notion that a Creole is a person of mixed blood.

"I think I can!" replied the convalescent, with much spirit, rising with more haste than was good, and staggering a moment.

The horseman laughed outright.

"Your principle is the best, I cannot dispute that; but whether you can act it out — reformers do not make money, you know." He examined his saddle-girth and began to tighten it. "One can condemn — too cautiously — by a kind of — elevated cowardice (I have that fault); but one can also condemn too rashly; I remember when I did

so. One of the occupants of those two graves
you see yonder side by side — I think might have
lived longer if I had not spoken so rashly for his
rights. Did you ever hear of Bras-Coupé, Mr.
Frowenfeld?"

"I have heard only the name."

"Ah! Mr. Frowenfeld, *there* was a bold man's
chance to denounce wrong and oppression! Why,
that negro's death changed the whole channel of
my convictions."

The speaker had turned and thrown up his arm
with frowning earnestness; he dropped it and
smiled at himself.

"Do not mistake me for one of your new-
fashioned Philadelphia '*negrophiles*'; I am a merchant, my-de'-seh, a good subject of His Catholic
Majesty, a Creole of the Creoles, and so forth, and
so forth. Come!"

He slapped the saddle.

To have seen and heard them a little later as they
moved toward the city, the Creole walking before
the horse, and Frowenfeld sitting in the saddle,
you might have supposed them old acquaintances.
Yet the immigrant was wondering who his companion might be. He had not introduced himself
— seemed to think that even an immigrant might
know his name without asking. Was it Honoré
Grandissime? Joseph was tempted to guess so;
but the initials inscribed on the silver-mounted
pommel of the fine old Spanish saddle did not bear
out that conjecture.

The stranger talked freely. The sun's rays seemed to set all the sweetness in him a-working, and his pleasant worldly wisdom foamed up and out like fermenting honey.

By and by the way led through a broad, grassy lane where the path turned alternately to right and left among some wild acacias. The Creole waved his hand toward one of them and said:

"Now, Mr. Frowenfeld, you see? one man walks where he sees another's track; that is what makes a path; but you want a man, instead of passing around this prickly bush, to lay hold of it with his naked hands and pull it up by the roots."

"But a man armed with the truth is far from being barehanded," replied the convalescent, and they went on, more and more interested at every step, — one in this very raw imported material for an excellent man, the other in so striking an exponent of a unique land and people.

They came at length to the crossing of two streets, and the Creole, pausing in his speech, laid his hand upon the bridle.

Frowenfeld dismounted.

"Do we part here?" asked the Creole. "Well, Mr. Frowenfeld, I hope to meet you soon again."

"Indeed, I thank you, sir," said Joseph, "and I hope we shall, although — "

The Creole paused with a foot in the stirrup and interrupted him with a playful gesture; then as the horse stirred, he mounted and drew in the rein.

"I know; you want to say you cannot accept my

philosophy and I cannot appreciate yours ; but I appreciate it more than you think, my-de'-seh."

The convalescent's smile showed much fatigue.

The Creole extended his hand ; the immigrant seized it, wished to ask his name, but did not ; and the next moment he was gone.

The convalescent walked meditatively toward his quarters, with a faint feeling of having been found asleep on duty and awakened by a passing stranger. It was an unpleasant feeling, and he caught himself more than once shaking his head. He stopped, at length, and looked back ; but the Creole was long since out of sight. The mortified self-accuser little knew how very similar a feeling that vanished person was carrying away with him. He turned and resumed his walk, wondering who Monsieur might be, and a little impatient with himself that he had not asked.

" It is Honoré Grandissime ; it must be he !" he said.

Yet see how soon he felt obliged to change his mind.

CHAPTER VIII

SIGNED — HONORÉ GRANDISSIME

On the afternoon of the same day, having decided what he would " do," he started out in search of new quarters. He found nothing then, but next morning came upon a small, single-story building in the rue Royale, — corner of Conti, — which he thought would suit his plans. There were a door and show-window in the rue Royale, two doors in the intersecting street, and a small apartment in the rear which would answer for sleeping, eating, and studying purposes, and which connected with the front apartment by a door in the left-hand corner. This connection he would partially conceal by a prescription-desk. A counter would run lengthwise toward the rue Royale, along the wall opposite the side-doors. Such was the spot that soon became known as "Frowenfeld's Corner."

The notice "À Louer" directed him to inquire at numero — rue Condé. Here he was ushered through the wicket of a *porte cochère* into a broad, paved corridor, and up a stair into a large, cool room, and into the presence of a man who seemed, in some respects, the most remarkable figure he had yet seen in this little city of strange people. A strong, clear, olive complexion; features that were faultless (unless a woman-like delicacy, that was yet not effeminate, was a fault); hair *en queue*, the handsomer for its premature streakings of gray; a tall, well knit form, attired in cloth, linen and leather of the utmost fineness; manners Castilian, with a gravity almost oriental, — made him one of those rare masculine figures which, on the public promenade, men look back at and ladies inquire about.

Now, who might *this* be? The rent poster had given no name. Even the incurious Frowenfeld would fain guess a little. For a man to be just of this sort, it seemed plain that he must live in an isolated ease upon the unceasing droppings of coupons, rents, and like receivables. Such was the immigrant's first conjecture; and, as with slow, scant questions and answers they made their bargain, every new glance strengthened it; he was evidently a *rentier*. What, then, was his astonishment when Monsieur bent down and made himself Frowenfeld's landlord, by writing what the universal mind esteemed the synonym of enterprise and activity — the name of Honoré Grandissime. The landlord did not see, or ignored, his tenant's glance of surprise, and the tenant asked no questions.

We may add here an incident which seemed, when it took place, as unimportant as a single fact well could be.

The little sum that Frowenfeld had inherited from his father had been sadly depleted by the expenses of four funerals; yet he was still able to pay a month's rent in advance, to supply his shop with a scant stock of drugs, to purchase a celestial globe and some scientific apparatus, and to buy a dinner or two of sausages and crackers; but after this there was no necessity of hiding his purse.

His landlord early contracted a fondness for dropping in upon him, and conversing with him, as best the few and labored English phrases at his command would allow. Frowenfeld soon noticed that he never entered the shop unless its proprietor was alone, never sat down, and always, with the same

perfection of dignity that characterized all his movements, departed immediately upon the arrival of any
third person. One day, when the landlord was
making one of these standing calls, — he always
stood beside a high glass case, on the side of the
shop opposite the counter, — he noticed in Joseph's
hand a sprig of basil, and spoke of it.

"You ligue?"

The tenant did not understand. "You — find —
dad — nize?"

Frowenfeld replied that it had been left by the
oversight of a customer, and expressed a liking for
its odor.

"I sand you," said the landlord, — a speech
whose meaning Frowenfeld was not sure of until
the next morning, when a small, nearly naked
black boy, who could not speak a word of English,
brought to the apothecary a luxuriant bunch of this
basil, growing in a rough box.

CHAPTER IX

ILLUSTRATING THE TRACTIVE POWER OF BASIL

On the twenty-fourth day of December, 1803, at
two o'clock, P. M., the thermometer standing at
79, hygrometer 17, barometer 29.880, sky partly
clouded, wind west, light, the apothecary of the rue
Royale, now something more than a month established in his calling, might have been seen standing

behind his counter and beginning to show embarrassment in the presence of a lady, who, since she had
got her prescription filled and had paid for it, ought
in the conventional course of things to have hurried
out, followed by the pathetically ugly black woman
who tarried at the door as her attendant; for to be
in an apothecary's shop at all was unconventional.
She was heavily veiled; but the sparkle of her eyes,
which no multiplication of veils could quite extin-
guish, her symmetrical and well-fitted figure, just
escaping smallness, her grace of movement, and a
soft, joyous voice, had several days before led
Frowenfeld to the confident conclusion that she
was young and beautiful.

For this was now the third time she had come
to buy; and, though the purchases were unaccount-
ably trivial, the purchaser seemed not so. On the
two previous occasions she had been accompanied
by a slender girl, somewhat taller than she, veiled
also, of graver movement, a bearing that seemed
to Joseph almost too regal, and a discernible unwillingness to enter or tarry. There seemed a certain family resemblance between her voice and that
of the other, which proclaimed them — he incau-
tiously assumed — sisters. This time, as we see,
the smaller, and probably elder, came alone.

She still held in her hand the small silver which
Frowenfeld had given her in change, and sighed
after the laugh they had just enjoyed together over
a slip in her English. A very grateful sip of sweet
the laugh was to the all but friendless apothecary,

and the embarrassment that rushed in after it may
have arisen in part from a conscious casting about
in his mind for something — anything — that might
prolong her stay an instant. He opened his lips
to speak; but she was quicker than he, and said,
in a stealthy way that seemed oddly unnecessary:

" You 'ave some basilic ? "

She accompanied her words with a little peeping
movement, directing his attention, through the open
door, to his box of basil, on the floor in the rear
room.

Frowenfeld stepped back to it, cut half the bunch
and returned, with the bold intention of making
her a present of it; but as he hastened back to the
spot he had left, he was astonished to see the lady
disappearing from his farthest front door, followed
by her negress.

" Did she change her mind, or did she misunderstand me?" he asked himself; and, in the hope
that she might return for the basil, he put it in
water in his back room.

The day being, as the figures have already shown,
an unusually mild one, even for a Louisiana
December, and the finger of the clock drawing by
and by toward the last hour of sunlight, some half
dozen of Frowenfeld's townsmen had gathered,
inside and out, some standing, some sitting, about
his front door, and all discussing the popular topics
of the day. For it might have been anticipated
that, in a city where so very little English was
spoken and no newspaper published except that

beneficiary of eighty subscribers, the "Moniteur de la Louisiane," the apothecary's shop in the rue Royale would be the rendezvous for a select company of English-speaking gentlemen, with a smart majority of physicians.

The Cession had become an accomplished fact. With due drum-beatings and act-reading, flag-raising, cannonading and galloping of aides-de-camp, Nouvelle Orléans had become New Orleans, and Louisiane was Louisiana. This afternoon, the first week of American jurisdiction was only something over half gone, and the main topic of public debate was still the Cession. Was it genuine? and, if so, would it stand?

"Mark my words," said one, "the British flag will be floating over this town within ninety days!" and he went on whittling the back of his chair.

From this main question, the conversation branched out to the subject of land titles. Would that great majority of Spanish titles, derived from the concessions of post-commandants and others of minor authority, hold good?

"I suppose you know what —— thinks about it?"

"No."

"Well, he has quietly purchased the grant made by Carondelet to the Marquis of —— , thirty thousand acres, and now says the grant is two hundred *and* thirty thousand. That is one style of men Governor Claiborne is going to have on his hands. The town will presently be as full of them as my

pocket is of tobacco crumbs, — every one of them
with a Spanish grant as long as Clark's ropewalk
and made up since the rumor of the Cession."

" I hear that some of Honoré Grandissime's titles
are likely to turn out bad, — some of the old Brahmin properties and some of the Mandarin lands."

" Fudge ! " said Dr. Keene.

There was also the subject of rotation in office.
Would this provisional governor-general himself be
able to stand fast ? Had not a man better tempo-
rize a while, and see what Ex-Governor-general Casa
Calvo and Trudeau were going to do ? Would not
men who sacrificed old prejudices, braved the popular contumely, and came forward and gave in their
allegiance to the President's appointee, have to take
the chances of losing their official positions at last ?
Men like Camille Brahmin, for instance, or Charlie
Mandarin : suppose Spain or France should get the
province back, then where would they be ?

" One of the things I pity most in this vain
world," drawled Doctor Keene, " is a hive of patriots
who don't know where to swarm."

The apothecary was drawn into the discussion —
at least he thought he was. Inexperience is apt to
think that Truth will be knocked down and murdered unless she comes to the rescue. Somehow,
Frowenfeld's really excellent arguments seemed to
give out more heat than light. They were merci-
less ; their principles were not only lofty to dizzi-
ness, but precipitous, and their heights unoccupied,
and — to the common sight — unattainable. In

consequence, they provoked hostility and even resentment. With the kindest, the most honest, and even the most modest, intentions, he found himself—to his bewilderment and surprise—sniffed at by the ungenerous, frowned upon by the impatient, and smiled down by the good-natured in a manner that brought sudden blushes of exasperation to his face, and often made him ashamed to find himself going over these sham battles again in much savageness of spirit, when alone with his books ; or, in moments of weakness, casting about for such unworthy weapons as irony and satire. In the present debate, he had just provoked a sneer that made his blood leap and his friends laugh, when Doctor Keene, suddenly rising and beckoning across the street, exclaimed:

"Oh! Agricole! Agricole! *venez ici;* we want you."

A murmur of vexed protest arose from two or three.

"He's coming," said the whittler, who had also beckoned.

"Good evening, Citizen Fusilier," said Doctor Keene. "Citizen Fusilier, allow me to present my friend, Professor Frowenfeld — yes, you are a professor — yes, you are. He is one of your sort, Citizen Fusilier, a man of thorough scientific education. I believe on my soul, sir, he knows nearly as much as you do!"

The person who confronted the apothecary was a large, heavily built, but well-molded and vigorous

man, of whom one might say that he was adorned
with old age. His brow was dark, and furrowed
partly by time and partly by a persistent, ostentatious
frown. His eyes were large, black and bold, and
the gray locks above them curled short and harsh
like the front of a bull. His nose was fine and
strong, and if there was any deficiency in mouth or
chin, it was hidden by a beard that swept down
over his broad breast like the beard of a prophet.
In his dress, which was noticeably soiled, the fash-
ions of three decades were hinted at; he seemed
to have donned whatever he thought his friends
would most have liked him to leave off.

"Professor," said the old man, extending something like the paw of a lion, and giving Frowenfeld
plenty of time to become thoroughly awed, "this is
a pleasure as magnificent as unexpected! A scientific man? — in Louisiana?" He looked around
upon the doctors as upon a graduating class.
"Professor, I am rejoiced!" He paused again,
shaking the apothecary's hand with great ceremony.
"I do assure you, sir, I dislike to relinquish your
grasp. Do me the honor to allow me to become
your friend! I congratulate my down-trodden
country on the acquisition of such a citizen! I
hope, sir, — at least I might have hoped, had not
Louisiana just passed into the hands of the most
clap-trap government in the universe, notwithstanding it pretends to be a republic, — I might have
hoped that you had come among us to fasten the
lie direct upon a late author, who writes of us

that 'the air of this region is deadly to the Muses.'"

"He didn't say that?" asked one of the debaters, with pretended indignation.

"He did, sir, after eating our bread!"

"And sucking our sugar-cane, too, no doubt!" said the wag; but the old man took no notice.

Frowenfeld, naturally, was not anxious to reply, and was greatly relieved to be touched on the elbow by a child with a picayune in one hand and a tumbler in the other. He escaped behind the counter and gladly remained there.

"Citizen Fusilier," asked one of the gossips, "what has the new government to do with the health of the Muses?"

"It introduces the English tongue," said the old man, scowling.

"Oh, well," replied the questioner, "the Creoles will soon learn the language."

"English is not a language, sir; it is a jargon! And when this young simpleton, Claiborne, attempts to cram it down the public windpipe in the courts, as I understand he intends, he will fail! Hah! sir, I know men in this city who would rather eat a dog than speak English! *I* speak it, but I also speak Choctaw."

"The new land titles will be in English."

"They will spurn his rotten titles. And if he attempts to invalidate their old ones, why, let him do it! Napoleon Buonaparte" (Italian pronunciation) "will make good every arpent within the

next two years. *Think so?* I know it! *How?*
H-I perceive it! H-I hope the yellow fever may
spare you to witness it."

A sullen grunt from the circle showed the "citizen" that he had presumed too much upon the license
commonly accorded his advanced age, and by way
of a diversion he looked around for Frowenfeld to
pour new flatteries upon. But Joseph, behind his
counter, unaware of either the offense or the resentment, was blushing with pleasure before a visitor
who had entered by the side door farthest from the
company.

"Gentlemen," said Agricola, "h-my dear friends,
you must not expect an old Creole to like anything
in comparison with *la belle langue*."

"Which language do you call *la belle?*" asked
Doctor Keene, with pretended simplicity.

The old man bent upon him a look of unspeakable contempt, which nobody noticed. The gossips
were one by one stealing a glance toward that which
ever was, is and must be an irresistible lodestone to
the eyes of all the sons of Adam, to wit, a chaste
and graceful complement of—skirts. Then in a
lower tone they resumed their desultory conversation.

It was the seeker after basil who stood before the
counter, holding in her hand, with her purse, the
heavy veil whose folds had before concealed her
features.

CHAPTER X

" OO DAD IS, 'SIEUR FROWENFEL ' ? "

WHETHER the removal of the veil was because of the milder light of the evening, or the result of accident, or of haste, or both, or whether, by reason of some exciting or absorbing course of thought, the wearer had withdrawn it unconsciously, was a matter that occupied the apothecary as little as did Agricola's continued harangue. As he looked upon the fair face through the light gauze which still overhung but not obscured it, he readily perceived, despite the sprightly smile, something like distress, and as she spoke this became still more evident in her hurried undertone.

" 'Sieur Frowenfel', I want you to sell me doze *basilic*."

As she slipped the rings of her purse apart her fingers trembled.

" It is waiting for you," said Frowenfeld; but the lady did not hear him; she was giving her attention to the loud voice of Agricola saying in the course of discussion :

" The Louisiana Creole is the noblest variety of enlightened man ! "

" Oo dad is, 'Sieur Frowenfel' ? " she asked, softly, but with an excited eye.

" That is Mr. Agricola Fusilier," answered Joseph in the same tone, his heart leaping inexplicably as he met her glance. With an angry flush she looked quickly around, scrutinized the old man in an instantaneous, thorough way, and then glanced back at the apothecary again, as if asking him to fulfil her request the quicker.

He hesitated, in doubt as to her meaning.

"Wrap it yonder," she almost whispered.

He went, and in a moment returned, with the basil only partially hid in a paper covering.

But the lady, muffled again in her manifold veil, had once more lost her eagerness for it; at least, instead of taking it, she moved aside, offering room for a masculine figure just entering. She did not look to see who it might be — plenty of time to do that by accident, by and by. There she made a mistake; for the new-comer, with a silent bow of thanks, declined the place made for him, moved across the shop, and occupied his eyes with the contents of the glass case, his back being turned to the lady and Frowenfeld. The apothecary recognized the Creole whom he had met under the live-oak.

The lady put forth her hand suddenly to receive the package. As she took it and turned to depart, another small hand was laid upon it and it was returned to the counter. Something was said in a low-pitched undertone, and the two sisters — if Frowenfeld's guess was right — confronted each other. For a single instant only they stood so; an earnest and hurried murmur of French words passed between them, and they turned together, bowed with great suavity, and were gone.

"The Cession is a mere temporary political manœuvre!" growled M. Fusilier.

Frowenfeld's merchant friend came from his place of waiting, and spoke twice before he attracted the attention of the bewildered apothecary.

"Good-day, Mr. Frowenfeld; I have been told that ——"

Joseph gazed after the two ladies crossing the street, and felt uncomfortable that the group of gossips did the same. So did the black attendant who glanced furtively back.

"Good-day, Mr. Frowenfeld; I ——"

"Oh! how do you do, sir?" exclaimed the apothecary, with great pleasantness of face. It seemed the most natural thing that they should resume their late conversation just where they had left off, and that would certainly be pleasant. But the man of more experience showed an unresponsive expression, that was as if he remembered no conversation of any note.

"I have been told that you might be able to replace the glass in this thing out of your private stock."

He presented a small, leather-covered case, evidently containing some optical instrument. "It will give me a pretext for going," he had said to himself, as he put it into his pocket in his counting-room. He was not going to let the apothecary know he had taken such a fancy to him.

"I do not know," replied Frowenfeld, as he touched the spring of the case; "I will see what I have."

He passed into the back room, more than willing to get out of sight till he might better collect himself.

" I do not keep these things for sale," said he as he went.

" Sir ? " asked the Creole, as if he had not understood, and followed through the open door.

" Is this what that lady was getting ? " he asked, touching the remnant of the basil in the box.

" Yes, sir," said the apothecary, with his face in the drawer of a table.

" They had no carriage with them." The Creole spoke with his back turned, at the same time running his eyes along a shelf of books. Frowenfeld made only the sound of rejecting bits of crystal and taking up others. " I do not know who they are," ventured the merchant.

Joseph still gave no answer, but a moment after approached, with the instrument in his extended hand.

" You had it ? I am glad," said the owner, receiving it, but keeping one hand still on the books.

Frowenfeld put up his materials.

" Mr. Frowenfeld, are these your books ? I mean do you use these books ? "

" Yes, sir."

The Creole stepped back to the door.

" Agricola ! "

" *Quoi !* "

" *Vien ici.* "

Citizen Fusilier entered, followed by a small

volley of retorts from those with whom he had been disputing, and who rose as he did. The stranger said something very sprightly in French, running the back of one finger down the rank of books, and a lively dialogue followed.

"You must be a great scholar," said the unknown by and by, addressing the apothecary.

"He is a professor of chimistry," said the old man.

"I am nothing, as yet, but a student," said Joseph, as the three returned into the shop; "certainly not a scholar, and still less a professor." He spoke with a new quietness of manner that made the younger Creole turn upon him a pleasant look.

"H-my young friend," said the patriarch, turning toward Joseph with a tremendous frown, "when I, Agricola Fusilier, pronounce you a professor, you are a professor. Louisiana will not look to *you* for your credentials; she will look to me!"

He stumbled upon some slight impediment under foot. There were times when it took but little to make Agricola stumble.

Looking to see what it was, Joseph picked up a silken purse. There was a name embroidered on it.

CHAPTER XI

SUDDEN FLASHES OF LIGHT

THE day was nearly gone. The company that had been chatting at the front door, and which in warmer weather would have tarried until bed-time, had wandered off; however, by stepping toward the light the young merchant could decipher the letters on the purse. Citizen Fusilier drew out a pair of spectacles, looked over his junior's shoulder, read aloud, " *Aurore De G. Nanca*——," and uttered an imprecation.

" Do not speak to me ! " he thundered ; " do not approach me ! she did it maliciously ! "

" Sir ! " began Frowenfeld.

But the old man uttered another tremendous malediction and hurried into the street and away.

" Let him pass," said the other Creole calmly.

" What is the matter with him ? " asked Frowenfeld.

" He is getting old." The Creole extended the purse carelessly to the apothecary. " Has it anything inside ? "

" But a single pistareen."

" That is why she wanted the *basilic*, eh ? "

" I do not understand you, sir."

" Do you not know what she was going to do with it ? "

" With the basil ?   No sir."

"May be she was going to make a little *tisane*, eh?" said the Creole, forcing down a smile.

But a portion of the smile would come when Frowenfeld answered, with unnecessary resentment:

"She was going to make some *proper* use of it, which need not concern me."

"Without doubt."

The Creole quietly walked a step or two forward and back and looked idly into the glass case. "Is this young man in love with her?" he asked himself. He turned around.

"Do you know those ladies, Mr. Frowenfeld? Do you visit them at home?"

He drew out his porte-monnaie.

"No, sir."

"I will pay you for the repair of this instrument; have you change for ―― "

"I will see," said the apothecary.

As he spoke he laid the purse on a stool, till he should light his shop, and then went to his till without again taking it.

The Creole sauntered across to the counter and nipped the herb which still lay there.

"Mr. Frowenfeld, you know what some very excellent people do with this? They rub it on the sill of the door to make the money come into the house."

Joseph stopped aghast with the drawer half drawn.

"Not persons of intelligence and ―― "

"All kinds. It is only some of the foolishness

which they take from the slaves. Many of your
best people consult the voudou horses."

" Horses ? "

" Priestesses, you might call them," explained
the Creole, " like Momselle Marcelline or 'Zabeth
Philosophe."

" Witches ! " whispered Frowenfeld.

" Oh no," said the other with a shrug ; " that is
too hard a name ; say fortune-tellers. But Mr.
Frowenfeld, I wish you to lend me your good
offices. Just supposing the possi*bil*ity that that
lady may be in need of money, you know, and will
send back or come back for the purse, you know,
knowing that she most likely lost it here, I ask you
the favor that you will not let her know I have
filled it with gold. In fact, if she mentions my
name ——— "

" To confess the truth, sir, I am not acquainted
with your name."

The Creole smiled a genuine surprise.

" I thought you knew it." He laughed a little
at himself. " We have nevertheless become very
good friends — I believe ? Well, in fact then, Mr.
Frowenfeld, you might say you do not know who
put the money in." He extended his open palm
with the purse hanging across it. Joseph was about
to object to this statement, but the Creole, putting
on an expression of anxious desire, said : " I mean,
not by name. It is somewhat important to me,
Mr. Frowenfeld, that that lady should not know
my present action. If you want to do those two

ladies a favor, you may rest assured the way to do
it is to say you do not know who put this gold."
The Creole in his earnestness slipped in his idiom.
" You will excuse me if I do not tell you my name ;
you can find it out at any time from Agricola. Ah !
I am glad she did not see me ! You must not tell
anybody about this little event, eh ? "

" No, sir," said Joseph, as he finally accepted the
purse. " I shall say nothing to any one else, and
only what I cannot avoid saying to the lady and her
sister."

" *'T is not her sister*," responded the Creole, " *'t is
her daughter.*"

The italics signify, not how the words were said,
but how they sounded to Joseph. As if a dark
lantern were suddenly turned full upon it, he saw
the significance of Citizen Fusilier's transport. The
fair strangers were the widow and daughter of the
man whom Agricola had killed in duel — the ladies
with whom Doctor Keene had desired to make him
acquainted.

" Well, good evening, Mr. Frowenfeld." The
Creole extended his hand (his people are great
hand-shakers). " Ah ―― " and then, for the first
time, he came to the true object of his visit. " The
conversation we had some weeks ago, Mr. Frowenfeld, has started a train of thought in my mind " —
he began to smile as if to convey the idea that
Joseph would find the subject a trivial one —
" which has almost brought me to the ―― "

A light footfall accompanied with the soft sweep

of robes cut short his words. There had been two
or three entrances and exits during the time the
Creole had tarried, but he had not allowed them to
disturb him. Now, however, he had no sooner
turned and fixed his glance upon this last comer,
than without so much as the invariable Creole leave-
taking of "Well, good evening, sir," he hurried
out.

CHAPTER XII

THE PHILOSOPHE

The apothecary felt an inward nervous start as
there advanced into the light of his hanging lamp
and toward the spot where he had halted, just outside the counter, a woman of the quadroon caste, of
superb stature and poise, severely handsome features,
clear, tawny skin and large, passionate black eyes.

"*Bon soi', Miché.*" [Monsieur.] A rather hard,
yet not repellent smile showed her faultless teeth.

Frowenfeld bowed.

"*Mo vien c'erc'er la bourse de Madame.*"

She spoke the best French at her command, but
it was not understood.

The apothecary could only shake his head.

"*La bourse,*" she repeated, softly smiling, but
with a scintillation of the eyes in resentment of his
scrutiny. "*La bourse,*" she reiterated.

"Purse?"

"*Oui, Miché.*"

" You are sent for it ? "

" *Oui, Miché.*"

He drew it from his breast pocket and marked the sudden glisten of her eyes, reflecting the glisten of the gold in the silken mesh.

" *Oui, c'est ça,*" said she, putting her hand out eagerly.

" I am afraid to give you this to-night," said Joseph.

" *Oui,*" ventured she, dubiously, the lightning playing deep back in her eyes.

" You might be robbed," said Frowenfeld. " It is very dangerous for you to be out alone. It will not be long, now, until gun-fire." (Eight o'clock P. M. — the gun to warn slaves to be indoors, under pain of arrest and imprisonment.)

The object of this solicitude shook her head with a smile at its gratuitousness. The smile showed determination also.

" *Mo pas compren',*" she said.

" Tell the lady to send for it to-morrow."

She smiled helplessly and somewhat vexedly, shrugged and again shook her head. As she did so she heard footsteps and voices in the door at her back.

" *C'est ça,*" she said again with a hurried attempt at extreme amiability ; " Dat it ; *oui ;*" and lifting her hand with some rapidity made a sudden eager reach for the purse, but failed.

" No ! " said Frowenfeld, indignantly.

" Hello ! " said Charlie Keene amusedly, as he approached from the door.

The woman turned, and in one or two rapid sentences in the Creole dialect offered her explanation.

"Give her the purse, Joe; I will answer for its being all right."

Frowenfeld handed it to her. She started to pass through the door in the rue Royale by which Doctor Keene had entered; but on seeing on its threshold Agricola frowning upon her, she turned quickly with evident trepidation, and hurried out into the darkness of the other street.

Agricola entered. Doctor Keene looked about the shop.

"I tell you, Agricole, you did n't have it with you; Frowenfeld, you have n't seen a big knotted walking-stick?"

Frowenfeld was sure no walking-stick had been left there.

"Oh, yes, Frowenfeld," said Doctor Keene, with a little laugh, as the three sat down, "I'd a'most as soon trust that woman as if she was white."

The apothecary said nothing.

"How free," said Agricola, beginning with a meditative gaze at the sky without, and ending with a philosopher's smile upon his two companions, — "how free we people are from prejudice against the negro!"

"The white people," said Frowenfeld, half abstractedly, half inquiringly.

"H-my young friend, when we say, 'we people,' we *always* mean we white people. The non-mention of color always implies pure white; and what-

ever is not pure white is to all intents and purposes
pure black. When I say the 'whole community,'
I mean the whole white portion; when I speak of
the 'undivided public sentiment,' I mean the sentiment of the white population. What else could
I mean? Could you suppose, sir, the expression
which you may have heard me use — 'my down-
trodden country' — includes blacks and mulattoes?
What is that up yonder in the sky? The moon.
The new moon, or the old moon, or the moon in
her third quarter, but always the moon! Which
part of it? Why, the shining part — the white
part, always and only! Not that there is a prejudice against the negro. By no means. Wherever
he can be of any service in a strictly menial capacity
we kindly and generously tolerate his presence."

Was the immigrant growing wise, or weak, that
he remained silent?

Agricola rose as he concluded and said he would
go home. Doctor Keene gave him his hand lazily,
without rising.

"Frowenfeld," he said, with a smile and in an
undertone, as Agricola's footsteps died away, "don't
you know who that woman is?"

"No."

"Well, I'll tell you."

He told him.

On that lonely plantation at the Cannes Brulées,
where Aurore Nancanou's childhood had been
passed without brothers or sisters, there had been

given her, according to the well-known custom of plantation life, a little quadroon slave-maid as her constant and only playmate. This maid began early to show herself in many ways remarkable. While yet a child she grew tall, lithe, agile; her eyes were large and black, and rolled and sparkled if she but turned to answer to her name. Her pale yellow forehead, low and shapely, with the jet hair above it, the heavily pencilled eyebrows and long lashes below, the faint red tinge that blushed with a kind of cold passion through the clear yellow skin of the cheek, the fulness of the red, voluptuous lips and the roundness of her perfect neck, gave her, even at fourteen, a barbaric and magnetic beauty, that startled the beholder like an unexpected drawing out of a jewelled sword. Such a type could have sprung only from high Latin ancestry on the one side and — we might venture — Jaloff African on the other. To these charms of person she added mental acuteness, conversational adroitness, concealed cunning, and noiseless but visible strength of will; and to these, that rarest of gifts in one of her tincture, the purity of true womanhood.

At fourteen a necessity which had been parleyed with for two years or more became imperative, and Aurore's maid was taken from her. Explanation is almost superfluous. Aurore was to become a lady and her playmate a lady's maid; but not *her* maid, because the maid had become, of the two, the ruling spirit. It was a question of grave debate in the mind of M. De Grapion what disposition to make of her.

About this time the Grandissimes and De Grapions, through certain efforts of Honoré's father (since dead) were making some feeble pretences of mutual good feeling, and one of those Kentuckian dealers in corn and tobacco whose flatboat fleets were always drifting down the Mississippi, becoming one day M. De Grapion's transient guest, accidentally mentioned a wish of Agricola Fusilier. Agricola, it appeared, had commissioned him to buy the most beautiful lady's maid that in his extended journeyings he might be able to find; he wanted to make her a gift to his niece, Honoré's sister. The Kentuckian saw the demand met in Aurore's playmate. M. De Grapion would not sell her. (Trade with a Grandissime? Let them suspect he needed money?) No; but he would ask Agricola to accept the services of the waiting-maid for, say, ten years. The Kentuckian accepted the proposition on the spot and it was by and by carried out. She was never recalled to the Cannes Brulées, but in subsequent years received her freedom from her master, and in New Orleans became Palmyre la Philosophe, as they say in the corrupt French of the old Creoles, or Palmyre Philosophe, noted for her taste and skill as a hair-dresser, for the efficiency of her spells and the sagacity of her divinations, but most of all for the chaste austerity with which she practised the less baleful rites of the voudous.

"That's the woman," said Doctor Keene, rising to go, as he concluded the narrative, — "that's she, Palmyre Philosophe. Now you get a view of the vastness of Agricole's generosity; he tolerates her even though she does not present herself in the 'strictly menial capacity.' Reason why — *he's afraid of her.*"

Time passed, if that may be called time which we have to measure with a clock. The apothecary of the rue Royale found better ways of measurement. As quietly as a spider he was spinning information into knowledge and knowledge into what is supposed to be wisdom; whether it was or not we shall see. His unidentified merchant friend who had adjured him to become acclimated as "they all did" had also exhorted him to study the human mass of which he had become a unit; but whether that study, if pursued, was sweetening and ripening, or whether it was corrupting him, that friend did not come to see; it was the busy time of year. Certainly so young a solitary, coming among a people whose conventionalities were so at variance with his own door-yard ethics, was in sad danger of being unduly — as we might say — Timonized. His acquaintances continued to be few in number.

During this fermenting period he chronicled much wet and some cold weather. This may in part account for the uneventfulness of its passage; events do not happen rapidly among the Creoles in bad weather. However, trade was good.

But the weather cleared; and when it was getting well on into the Creole spring and approaching the spring of the almanacs, something did occur that extended Frowenfeld's acquaintance without Doctor Keene's assistance.

CHAPTER XIII

A CALL FROM THE RENT-SPECTRE

It is nearly noon of a balmy morning late in February. Aurore Nancanou and her daughter have only this moment ceased sewing, in the small front room of No. 19 rue Bienville. Number 19 is the right-hand half of a single-story, low-roofed tenement, washed with yellow ochre, which it shares generously with whoever leans against it. It sits as fast on the ground as a toad. There is a kitchen belonging to it somewhere among the weeds in the back yard, and besides this room where the ladies are, there is, directly behind it, a sleeping apartment. Somewhere back of this there is a little nook where in pleasant weather they eat. Their cook and housemaid is the plain person who attends them on the street. Her bedchamber is the kitchen and her bed the floor. The house's only other protector is a hound, the aim of whose life is to get thrust out of the ladies' apartments every fifteen minutes.

Yet if you hastily picture to yourself a forlorn-looking establishment, you will be moving straight away from the fact. Neatness, order, excellence, are prevalent qualities in all the details of the main house's inward garniture. The furniture is old-fashioned, rich, French, imported. The carpets, if not new, are not cheap, either. Bits of crystal and silver, visible here and there, are as bright as they are antiquated; and one or two portraits, and the picture of Our Lady of Many Sorrows, are passably good productions. The brass work, of which there is much, is brilliantly burnished, and the front room is bright and cheery.

At the street door of this room somebody has just knocked. Aurore has risen from her seat. The other still sits on a low chair with her hands and sewing dropped into her lap, looking up steadfastly into her mother's face with a mingled expression of fondness and dismayed expectation. Aurore hesitates beside her chair, desirous of resuming her seat, even lifts her sewing from it; but tarries a moment, her alert suspense showing in her eyes. Her daughter still looks up into them. It is not strange that the dwellers round about dispute as to which is the fairer, nor that in the six months during which the two have occupied Number 19 the neighbors have reached no conclusion on this subject. If some young enthusiast compares the daughter — in her eighteenth year — to a bursting blush rosebud full of promise, some older one immediately retorts that the other — in her thirty-fifth — is the red, red, full-blown, faultless joy of the gar-

den.   If one says the maiden has the dew of youth,
—"But!" cry two or three mothers in a breath,
"that other one, child, will never grow old.   With
her it will always be morning.   That woman is
going to last forever; ha-a-a-a! — even longer!"

There was one direction in which the widow evidently had the advantage; you could see from the
street or the opposite windows that she was a wise
householder.   On the day they moved into Number 19 she had been seen to enter in advance of all
her other movables, carrying into the empty house
a new broom, a looking-glass, and a silver coin.
Every morning since, a little watching would have
discovered her at the hour of sunrise sprinkling
water from her side casement, and her opposite
neighbors often had occasion to notice that, sitting
at her sewing by the front window, she never
pricked her finger but she quickly ran it up behind her ear, and then went on with her work.
Would anybody but Joseph Frowenfeld ever have
lived in and moved away from the two-story brick
next them on the right and not have known of the
existence of such a marvel?

"Ha!" they said, "she knows how to keep off
bad luck, that Madame yonder.   And the younger
one seems not to like it.   Girls think themselves so
smart these days."

Ah, there was the knock again, right there on
the street-door, as loud as if it had been given with
a joint of sugar-cane!

The daughter's hand, which had just resumed

the needle, stood still in mid-course with the white thread half-drawn. Aurore tiptoed slowly over the carpeted floor. There came a shuffling sound, and the corner of a folded white paper commenced appearing and disappearing under the door. She mounted a chair and peeped through that odd little *jalousie* which formerly was in almost all New Orleans street-doors; but the missive had meantime found its way across the sill, and she saw only the unpicturesque back of a departing errand-boy. But that was well. She had a pride, to maintain which — and a poverty, to conceal which — she felt to be necessary to her self-respect; and this made her of necessity a trifle unsocial in her own castle. Do you suppose she was going to put on the face of having been born or married to this degraded condition of things?

Who knows? — the knock might have been from 'Sieur Frowenfel' — ha, ha! He might be just silly enough to call so early; or it might have been from that *polisson* of a Grandissime, — which one did n't matter, they were all detestable, — coming to collect the rent. That was her original fear; or, worse still, it might have been, had it been softer, the knock of some possible lady visitor. She had no intention of admitting any feminine eyes to detect this carefully covered up indigence. Besides, it was Monday. There is no sense in trifling with bad luck. The reception of Monday callers is a source of misfortune never known to fail, save in rare cases when good luck has already been secured by smear-

ing the front walk or the banquette with Venetian
red.

Before the daughter could dart up and disengage
herself from her work her mother had pounced
upon the paper.   She was standing and reading,
her rich black lashes curtaining their downcast eyes,
her infant waist and round, close-fitted, childish
arms harmonizing prettily with her mock frown of
infantile perplexity, and her long, limp robe height-
ening the grace of her posture, when the younger
started from her seat with the air of determining
not to be left at a disadvantage.

But what is that on the dark eyelash?   With a
sudden additional energy the daughter dashes the
sewing and chair to right and left, bounds up, and
in a moment has Aurore weeping in her embrace
and has snatched the note from her hand.

"*Ah! maman!   Ah! ma chère mère!*"

The mother forced a laugh.   She was not to be
mothered by her daughter; so she made a dash at
Clotilde's uplifted hand to recover the note, which
was unavailing.   Immediately there arose in colonial French the loveliest of contentions, the issue
of which was that the pair sat down side by side,
like two sisters over one love-letter, and undertook
to decipher the paper.   It read as follows:

"NEW ORLEANS, 20 Feb're, 1804.

"MADAME NANCANOU: I muss oblige to ass you for
rent of that house whare you living, it is at number 19
Bienville street whare I do not received thos rent from you
not since tree mons and I demand you this is mabe thirteen

time.   And I give to you notice of 19 das writen in Ang-
lish as the new law requi.   That witch the law make
necessare only for 15 das, and when you not pay me those
rent in 19 das till the tense of Marh I will rekes you to
move out.   That witch make me to be verry sorry.   I
have the honor to remain, Madam,

" Your humble servant,

" H. Grandissime.

" per Z. F."

There was a short French postscript on the
opposite page signed only by M. Zénon François,
explaining that he, who had allowed them in the
past to address him as their landlord and by his
name, was but the landlord's agent; that the landlord was a far better-dressed man than he could
afford to be; that the writing opposite was a notice
for them to quit the premises they had rented (not
leased), or pay up; that it gave the writer great
pain to send it, although it was but the necessary
legal form and he only an irresponsible drawer of
an inadequate salary, with thirteen children to support; and that he implored them to tear off and
burn up this postscript immediately they had
read it.

" Ah, the miserable ! " was all the comment made
upon it as the two ladies addressed their energies
to the previous English.   They had never suspected him of being M. Grandissime.

Their eyes dragged slowly and ineffectually along
the lines to the signature.

" H. Grandissime !   Loog ad 'im ! " cried the

widow, with a sudden short laugh, that brought the
tears after it like a wind-gust in a rose-tree. She
held the letter out before them as if she was lifting
something alive by the back of the neck, and to
intensify her scorn spoke in the hated tongue pre-
scribed by the new courts. "Loog ad 'im! dad
ridge gen'leman oo give so mudge money to de
'ozpill!"

"Bud, *maman*," said the daughter, laying her
hand appeasingly upon her mother's knee, "*ee* do
nod know 'ow we is poor."

"Ah!" retorted Aurore, "*par example! Non?*
Ee thingue we is ridge, eh? Ligue his oncle, eh?
Ee thing so, too, eh?" She cast upon her daugh-
ter the look of burning scorn intended for Agricola
Fusilier. "You wan' to tague the pard of dose
Grandissime'?"

The daughter returned a look of agony.

"No," she said, "bud a man wad godd some
'ouses to rend, muz ee nod boun' to ged 'is rend?"

"Boun' to ged — ah! yez ee muz do 'is possible
to ged 'is rend. Oh! certain*lee*. Ee is ridge, bud
ee need a lill money, bad, bad. Fo' w'at?" The
excited speaker rose to her feet under a sudden
inspiration. "*Tenez, Mademoiselle!*" She began
to make great show of unfastening her dress.

"*Mais, comment?*" demanded the suffering
daughter.

"Yez!" continued Aurore, keeping up the
demonstration, "you wand 'im to 'ave 'is rend so
bad! An' I godd honely my cloze; so you juz

tague diz to you' fine gen'lemen, 'Sieur Honoré Grandissime."

" Ah-h-h-h ! " cried the martyr.

" An' you is righd," persisted the tormentor, still unfastening; but the daughter's tears gushed forth, and the repentant tease threw herself upon her knees, drew her child's head into her bosom and wept afresh.

Half an hour was passed in council; at the end of which they stood beneath their lofty mantel-shelf, each with a foot on a brazen fire-dog, and no conclusion reached.

" Ah, my child ! " — they had come to themselves now and were speaking in their peculiar French — " if we had here in these hands but the tenth part of what your papa often played away in one night without once getting angry ! But we have not. Ah ! but your father was a fine fellow ; if he could have lived for you to know him ! So accomplished ! Ha, ha, ha ! I can never avoid laughing, when I remember him teaching me to speak English ; I used to enrage him so ! "

The daughter brought the conversation back to the subject of discussion. There were nineteen days yet allowed them. God knows — by the ex-piration of that time they might be able to pay. With the two music scholars whom she then had and three more whom she had some hope to get, she made bold to say they could pay the rent.

" Ah, Clotilde, my child," exclaimed Aurore, with sudden brightness, " you don't need a mask

and costume to resemble your great-grandmother,
the casket-girl!" Aurore felt sure, on her part,
that with the one embroidery scholar then under
her tutelage, and the three others who had declined
to take lessons, they could easily pay the rent —
and how kind it was of Monsieur, the aged father
of that one embroidery scholar, to procure those invi-
tations to the ball! The dear old man! He said
he must see one more ball before he should die.

Aurore looked so pretty in the reverie into which
she fell that her daughter was content to admire her
silently.

"Clotilde," said the mother, presently looking
up, "do you remember the evening you treated me
so ill?"

The daughter smiled at the preposterous charge.

"I did not treat you ill."

"Yes, don't you know — the evening you made
me lose my purse?"

"Certainly, I know!" The daughter took her
foot from the andiron; her eyes lighted up aggres-
sively. "For losing your purse blame yourself.
For the way you found it again — which was far
worse — thank Palmyre. If you had not asked her
to find it and shared the gold with her we could
have returned with it to 'Sieur Frowenfel'; but
now we are ashamed to let him see us. I do not
doubt he filled the purse."

"He? He never knew it was empty. It was
Nobody who filled it. Palmyre says that Papa
Lébat —— "

" Ha ! " exclaimed Clotilde at this superstitious mention.

The mother tossed her head and turned her back, swallowing the unendurable bitterness of being rebuked by her daughter. But the cloud hung over but a moment.

" Clotilde," she said, a minute after, turning with a look of sun-bright resolve, " I am going to see him."

" To see whom ? " asked the other, looking back from the window, whither she had gone to recover from a reactionary trembling.

" To whom, my child ? Why —— "

" You do not expect mercy from Honoré Grandissime ? You would not ask it ? "

" No. There is no mercy in the Grandissime blood ; but cannot I demand justice ? Ha ! it is justice that I shall demand ! "

" And you will really go and see him ? "

" You will see, Mademoiselle," replied Aurore, dropping a broom with which she had begun to sweep up some spilled buttons.

" And I with you ? "

" No ! To a counting-room ? To the presence of the chief of that detestable race ? No ! "

" But you don't know where his office is."

" Anybody can tell me."

Preparation began at once. By and by ——

" Clotilde."

Clotilde was stooping behind her mother, with a ribbon between her lips, arranging a flounce.

" M-m-m."

" You must not watch me go out of sight ; do you hear ? * * But it *is* dangerous. I knew of a gentleman who watched his wife go out of his sight and she never came back ! "

" Hold still ! " said Clotilde.

" But when my hand itches," retorted Aurore in a high key, " have n't I got to put it instantly into my pocket if I want the money to come there ? Well, then ! "

The daughter proposed to go to the kitchen and tell Alphonsina to put on her shoes.

" My child," cried Aurore, " you are crazy ! Do you want Alphonsina to be seized for the rent ? "

" But you cannot go alone — and on foot ! "

" I must go alone ; and — can you lend me your carriage ? Ah, you have none ? Certainly I must go alone and on foot if I am to say I cannot pay the rent. It is no indiscretion of mine. If anything happens to me it is M. Grandissime who is responsible."

Now she is ready for the adventurous errand. She darts to the mirror. The high-water marks are gone from her eyes. She wheels half around and looks over her shoulder. The flaring bonnet and loose ribbons gave her a more girlish look than ever.

" Now which is the older, little old woman ? " she chirrups, and smites her daughter's cheek softly with her palm.

" And you are not afraid to go alone ? "

"No; but remember! look at that dog!"

The brute sinks apologetically to the floor. Clotilde opens the street door, hands Aurore the note, Aurore lays a frantic kiss upon her lips, pressing it on tight so as to get it again when she comes back, and — while Clotilde calls the cook to gather up the buttons and take away the broom, and while the cook, to make one trip of it, gathers the hound into her bosom and carries broom and dog out together — Aurore sallies forth, leaving Clotilde to resume her sewing and await the coming of a guitar scholar.

"It will keep her fully an hour," thought the girl, far from imagining that Aurore had set about a little private business which she proposed to herself to accomplish before she even started in the direction of M. Grandissime's counting-rooms.

CHAPTER XIV

BEFORE SUNSET

In old times, most of the sidewalks of New Orleans not in the heart of town were only a rough, rank turf, lined on the side next the ditch with the gunwales of broken-up flatboats — ugly, narrow, slippery objects. As Aurora — it sounds so much pleasanter to anglicize her name — as Aurora gained a corner where two of these gunwales met, she stopped and looked back to make sure that Clotilde was not watching her. That others had noticed her here and there she did not care ; that was something beauty would have to endure, and it only made her smile to herself.

" Everybody sees I am from the country — walking on the street without a waiting-maid."

A boy passed, hushing his whistle, and gazing at the lone lady until his turning neck could twist no farther. She was so dewy fresh ! After he had got across the street he turned to look again. Where could she have disappeared ?

The only object to be seen on the corner from which she had vanished was a small, yellow-washed house much like the one Aurora occupied, as it was like hundreds that then characterized and still characterize the town, only that now they are of brick instead of adobe. They showed in those days, even more than now, the wide contrast between their homely exteriors and the often elegant apartments within. However, in this house the front room was merely neat. The furniture was of rude, heavy pattern, Creole-made, and the walls were unadorned; the day of cheap pictures had not come. The lofty bedstead which filled one corner was spread and hung with a blue stuff showing through a web of white needlework. The brazen feet of the chairs were brightly burnished, as were the brass mountings of the bedstead and the brass globes on the cold andirons. Curtains of blue and white hung at the single window. The floor, from habitual scrubbing with the common weed which politeness has to call *Helenium autumnale*, was stained a bright, clean yellow. On it were, here and there in places, white mats woven of bleached palmetto-leaf. Such were the room's appointments; there was but one thing more, a singular bit of fantastic carving, — a small table of dark mahogany supported on the upward-writhing images of three scaly serpents.

Aurora sat down beside this table. A dwarf Congo woman, as black as soot, had ushered her in, and, having barred the door, had disappeared, and now the mistress of the house entered.

February though it was, she was dressed — and looked comfortable — in white. That barbaric beauty which had begun to bud twenty years before was now in perfect bloom. The united grace and pride of her movement was inspiring but — what shall we say? — feline? It was a femininity without humanity, — something that made her, with all her superbness, a creature that one would want to find chained. It was the woman who had received the gold from Frowenfeld — Palmyre Philosophe.

The moment her eyes fell upon Aurora her whole appearance changed. A girlish smile lighted up her face, and as Aurora rose up reflecting it back, they simultaneously clapped hands, laughed and advanced joyously toward each other, talking rapidly without regard to each other's words.

"Sit down," said Palmyre, in the plantation French of their childhood, as they shook hands.

They took chairs and drew up face to face as close as they could come, then sighed and smiled a moment, and then looked grave and were silent. For in the nature of things, and notwithstanding the amusing familiarity common between Creole ladies and the menial class, the unprotected little widow should have had a very serious errand to bring her to the voudou's house.

" Palmyre," began the lady, in a sad tone.

" Momselle Aurore."

" I want you to help me." The former mistress not only cast her hands into her lap, lifted her eyes supplicatingly and dropped them again, but actually locked her fingers to keep them from trembling.

" Momselle Aurore —— " began Palmyre, solemnly.

" Now, I know what you are going to say — but it is of no use to say it; do this much for me this one time and then I will let voudou alone as much as you wish — forever!"

" You have not lost your purse *again?* "

" Ah! foolishness, no."

Both laughed a little, the philosophe feebly, and Aurora with an excited tremor.

" Well?" demanded the quadroon, looking grave again.

Aurora did not answer.

" Do you wish me to work a spell for you?"

The widow nodded, with her eyes cast down.

Both sat quite still for some time; then the philosophe gently drew the landlord's letter from between Aurora's hands.

7

"What is this?" She could not read in any language.

"I must pay my rent within nineteen days."

"Have you not paid it?"

The delinquent shook her head.

"Where is the gold that came into your purse? All gone?"

"For rice and potatoes," said Aurora, and for the first time she uttered a genuine laugh, under that condition of mind which Latins usually substitute for fortitude. Palmyre laughed too, very properly.

Another silence followed. The lady could not return the quadroon's searching gaze.

"Momselle Aurore," suddenly said Palmyre, "you want me to work a spell for something else."

Aurora started, looked up for an instant in a frightened way, and then dropped her eyes and let her head droop, murmuring:

"No, I do not."

Palmyre fixed a long look upon her former mistress. She saw that though Aurora might be distressed about the rent, there was something else, — a deeper feeling, — impelling her upon a course the very thought of which drove the color from her lips and made her tremble.

"You are wearing red," said the philosophe.

Aurora's hand went nervously to the red ribbon about her neck.

"It is an accident; I had nothing else convenient."

"Miché Agoussou loves red," persisted Palmyre. (Monsieur Agoussou is the demon upon whom the voudous call in matters of love.)

The color that came into Aurora's cheek ought to have suited Monsieur precisely.

"It is an accident," she feebly insisted.

"Well," presently said Palmyre, with a pretence of abandoning her impression, "then you want me to work you a spell for money, do you?"

Aurora nodded, while she still avoided the quadroon's glance.

"I know better," thought the philosophe. "You shall have the sort you want."

The widow stole an upward glance.

"Oh!" said Palmyre, with the manner of one making a decided digression, "I have been wanting to ask you something. That evening at the pharmacy — was there a tall, handsome gentleman standing by the counter?"

"He was standing on the other side."

"Did you see his face?"

"No; his back was turned."

"Momselle Aurore," said Palmyre, dropping her elbows upon her knees and taking the lady's hand as if the better to secure the truth, "was that the gentleman you met at the ball?"

"My faith!" said Aurora, stretching her eyebrows upward. "I did not think to look. Who was it?"

But Palmyre Philosophe was not going to give more than she got, even to her old-time Momselle;

she merely straightened back into her chair with an amiable face.

"Who do you think he is?" persisted Aurora, after a pause, smiling downward and toying with her rings.

The quadroon shrugged.

They both sat in reverie for a moment — a long moment for such sprightly natures — and Palmyre's mien took on a professional gravity. She presently pushed the landlord's letter under the lady's hands as they lay clasped in her lap, and a moment after drew Aurora's glance with her large, strong eyes and asked:

"What shall we do?"

The lady immediately looked startled and alarmed and again dropped her eyes in silence. The quadroon had to speak again.

"We will burn a candle."

Aurora trembled.

"No," she succeeded in saying.

"Yes," said Palmyre, "you must get your rent money." But the charm which she was meditating had no reference to rent money. "She knows that," thought the voudou.

As she rose and called her Congo slave-woman, Aurora made as if to protest further; but utterance failed her. She clenched her hands and prayed to fate for Clotilde to come and lead her away as she had done at the apothecary's. And well she might.

The articles brought in by the servant were simply a little pound-cake and cordial, a tumbler half-filled with the *sirop naturelle* of the sugar-cane, and a small piece of candle of the kind made from the fragrant green wax of the candleberry myrtle. These were set upon the small table, the bit of candle standing, lighted, in the tumbler of sirup, the cake on a plate, the cordial in a wine-glass. This feeble child's play was all; except that as Palmyre closed out all daylight from the room and received the offering of silver that "paid the floor" and averted *guillons* (interferences of outside imps), Aurora,— alas! alas! — went down upon her knees with her gaze fixed upon the candle's flame, and silently called on Assonquer (the imp of good fortune) to cast his snare in her behalf around the mind and heart of — she knew not whom.

By and by her lips, which had moved at first, were still and she only watched the burning wax. When the flame rose clear and long it was a sign that Assonquer was enlisted in the coveted endeavor. When the wick sputtered, the devotee trembled in fear of failure. Its charred end curled down and twisted away from her and her heart sank; but the tall figure of Palmyre for a moment came between, the wick was snuffed, the flame tapered up again, and for a long time burned, a bright, tremulous cone. Again the wick turned down, but this time toward her,— a propitious omen,— and suddenly fell through the expended wax and went out in the sirup.

The daylight, as Palmyre let it once more into the apartment, showed Aurora sadly agitated. In evidence of the innocence of her fluttering heart, guilt, at least for the moment, lay on it, an appalling burden.

"That is all, Palmyre, is it not? I am sure that is all — it must be all. I cannot stay any longer. I wish I was with Clotilde; I have stayed too long."

"Yes; all for the present," replied the quadroon. "Here, here is some charmed basil; hold it between your lips as you walk ——"

"But I am going to my landlord's office!"

"Office? Nobody is at his office now; it is too late. You would find that your landlord had gone to dinner. I will tell you, though, where you *must* go. First go home; eat your dinner; and this evening [the Creoles never say afternoon], about a half-hour before sunset, walk down Royale to the lower corner of the Place d'Armes, pass entirely around the square and return up Royale. Never look behind until you get into your house again."

Aurora blushed with shame.

"Alone?" she exclaimed, quite unnerved and tremulous.

"You will seem to be alone; but I will follow behind you when you pass here. Nothing shall hurt you. If you do that, the charm will certainly work; if you do not ——"

The quadroon's intentions were good. She was determined to see who it was that could so infatuate her dear little Momselle; and, as on such an evening as the present afternoon promised to merge into all

New Orleans promenaded on the Place d'Armes and the levee, her charm was a very practical one.

" And that will bring the money, will it? " asked Aurora.

" It will bring anything you want."

" Possible ? "

" These things that *you* want, Momselle Aurore, are easy to bring. You have no charms working against you. But, oh, I wish to God I could work the *curse I* want to work!" The woman's eyes blazed, her bosom heaved, she lifted her clenched hand above her head and looked upward, crying: " I would give this right hand off at the wrist to catch Agricola Fusilier where I could work him a curse! But I shall; I shall some day be revenged!" She pitched her voice still higher. " I cannot die till I have been! There is nothing that could kill me, I want my revenge so bad! " As suddenly as she had broken out, she hushed, unbarred the door, and with a stern farewell smile saw Aurora turn homeward.

" Give me something to eat, *chérie*," cried the exhausted lady, dropping into Clotilde's chair and trying to die.

" Ah ! *maman*, what makes you look so sick ? "

Aurora waved her hand contemptuously and gasped.

" Did you see him ? What kept you so long — so long ? "

" Ask me nothing ; I am so enraged with disappointment. He was gone to dinner ! "

"Ah! my poor mother!"

"And I must go back as soon as I can take a little *sieste*.   I am determined to see him this very day."

"Ah! my poor mother!"

CHAPTER XV

ROLLED IN THE DUST

"No, Frowenfeld," said little Doctor Keene, speaking for the after-dinner loungers, "you must take a little human advice.   Go, get the air on the Plaza.   We will keep shop for you.   Stay as long as you like and come home in any condition you think best."   And Joseph, tormented into this course, put on his hat and went out.

"Hard to move as a cow in the moonlight," continued Doctor Keene, "and knows just about as much of the world.   He was n't aware, until I told him to-day, that there are two Honoré Grandissimes."   [Laughter.]

"Why did you tell him?"

"I did n't give him anything but the bare fact. I want to see how long it will take him to find out the rest."

The Place d'Armes offered amusement to every one else rather than to the immigrant.   The family relation, the most noticeable feature of its well-

pleased groups, was to him too painful a reminder
of his late losses, and, after an honest endeavor to
flutter out of the inner twilight of himself into the
outer glare of a moving world, he had given up the
effort and had passed beyond the square and seated
himself upon a rude bench which encircled the trunk
of a willow on the levee.

The negress, who, resting near by with a tray of
cakes before her, has been for some time contemplating the three-quarter face of her unconscious
neighbor, drops her head at last with a small, Ethiopian, feminine laugh.   It is a self-confession that,
pleasant as the study of his countenance is, to resolve that study into knowledge is beyond her
powers ; and very pardonably so it is, she being but
a *marchande des gâteaux* (an itinerant cake-vender),
and he, she concludes, a man of parts.   There is a
purpose, too, as well as an admission, in the laugh.
She would like to engage him in conversation.   But
he does not notice.   Little supposing he is the
object of even a cake-merchant's attention, he is
lost in idle meditation.

One would guess his age to be as much as twenty-
six.   His face is beardless, of course, like almost
everybody's around him, and of a German kind of
seriousness.   A certain diffidence in his look may
tend to render him unattractive to careless eyes, the
more so since he has a slight appearance of self-
neglect.   On a second glance, his refinement shows
out more distinctly, and one also sees that he is not
shabby.   The little that seems lacking is woman's

care, the brush of attentive fingers here and there, the turning of a fold in the high-collared coat, and a mere touch on the neckerchief and shirt-frill. He has a decidedly good forehead. His blue eyes, while they are both strong and modest, are noticeable, too, as betraying fatigue, and the shade of gravity in them is deepened by a certain worn look of excess — in books; a most unusual look in New Orleans in those days, and pointedly out of keeping with the scene which was absorbing his attention.

You might mistake the time for mid-May. Before the view lies the Place d'Armes in its green-breasted uniform of new spring grass crossed diagonally with white shell walks for facings, and dotted with the *élite* of the city for decorations. Over the line of shade-trees which marks its farther boundary, the white-topped twin turrets of St. Louis Cathedral look across it and beyond the bared site of the removed battery (built by the busy Carondelet to protect Louisiana from herself and Kentucky, and razed by his immediate successors) and out upon the Mississippi, the color of whose surface is beginning to change with the changing sky of this beautiful and now departing day. A breeze, which is almost early June, and which has been hovering over the bosom of the great river and above the turf-covered levee, ceases, as if it sank exhausted under its burden of spring odors, and in the profound calm the cathedral bell strikes the sunset hour. From its neighboring garden, the convent of the Ursulines responds in a tone of devoutness,

while from the parapet of the less pious little Fort
St. Charles, the evening gun sends a solemn ejaculation rumbling down the "coast;" a drum rolls, the
air rises again from the water like a flock of birds,
and many in the square and on the levee's crown
turn and accept its gentle blowing. Rising over
the levee willows, and sinking into the streets, —
which are lower than the water, — it flutters among
the balconies and in and out of dim Spanish arcades,
and finally drifts away toward that part of the sky
where the sun is sinking behind the low, unbroken
line of forest.   There is such seduction in the evening air, such sweetness of flowers on its every
motion, such lack of cold, or heat, or dust, or wet,
that the people have no heart to stay in-doors ; nor
is there any reason why they should.   The levee
road is dotted with horsemen, and the willow avenue
on the levee's crown, the whole short mile between
Terre aux Bœufs gate on the right and Tchoupitoulas gate on the left, is bright with promenaders,
although the hour is brief and there will be no twilight ; for, so far from being May, it is merely that
same nineteenth of which we have already spoken,
— the nineteenth of Louisiana's delicious February.

   Among the throng were many whose names were
going to be written large in history.   There was
Casa Calvo, — Sebastian de Casa Calvo de la Puerta
y O'Farril, Marquis of Casa Calvo, — a man then at
the fine age of fifty-three, elegant, fascinating, perfect in Spanish courtesy and Spanish diplomacy,
rolling by in a showy equipage surrounded by a

clanking body-guard of the Catholic king's cavalry. There was young Daniel Clark, already beginning to amass those riches which an age of litigation has not to this day consumed; it was he whom the French colonial prefect, Laussat, in a late letter to France, had extolled as a man whose "talents for intrigue were carried to a rare degree of excellence." There was Laussat himself, in the flower of his years, sour with pride, conscious of great official insignificance and full of petty spites — he yet tarried in a land where his beautiful wife was the "model of taste." There was that convivial old fox, Wilkinson, who had plotted for years with Miro and did not sell himself and his country to Spain because — as we now say — "he found he could do better;" who modestly confessed himself in a traitor's letter to the Spanish king as a man "whose head may err, but whose heart cannot deceive!" and who brought Governor Gayoso to an early death-bed by simply out-drinking him. There also was Edward Livingston, attorney-at-law, inseparably joined to the mention of the famous Batture cases — though that was later. There also was that terror of colonial peculators, the old ex-Intendant Morales, who, having quarrelled with every governor of Louisiana he ever saw, was now snarling at Casa Calvo from force of habit.

And the Creoles — the Knickerbockers of Louisiana — but time would fail us. The Villeres and Destrehans — patriots and patriots' sons; the De La Chaise family in mourning for young Auguste

La Chaise of Kentuckian-Louisianian-San Domingan history; the Livaudaises, *père et fils*, of Haunted House fame, descendants of the first pilot of the Belize; the pirate brothers Lafitte, moving among the best; Marigny de Mandeville, afterwards the marquis member of Congress; the Davezacs, the Mossys, the Boulignys, the Labatuts, the Bringiers, the De Trudeaus, the De Macartys, the De la Houssayes, the De Lavillebœuvres, the Grandprés, the Forstalls; and the proselyted Creoles: Étienne de Boré (he was the father of all such as handle the sugar-kettle); old man Pitot, who became mayor; Madame Pontalba and her unsuccessful suitor, John McDonough; the three Girods, the two Graviers, or the lone Julian Poydras, godfather of orphan girls. Besides these, and among them as shining fractions of the community, the numerous representatives of the not only noble, but noticeable and ubiquitous, family of Grandissime: Grandissimes simple and Grandissimes compound; Brahmins, Mandarins and Fusiliers. One, 'Polyte by name, a light, gay fellow, with classic features, hair turning gray, is standing and conversing with this group here by the mock-cannon inclosure of the grounds. Another, his cousin, Charlie Mandarin, a tall, very slender, bronzed gentleman in a flannel hunting-shirt and buckskin leggings, is walking, in moccasins, with a sweet lady in whose tasteful attire feminine scrutiny, but such only, might detect economy, but whose marked beauty of yesterday is retreating and reappearing in the flock of children who are nois-

ily running round and round them, nominally in
the care of three fat and venerable black nurses.
Another, yonder, Théophile Grandissime, is whipping his stockings with his cane, a lithe youngster
in the height of the fashion (be it understood the
fashion in New Orleans was five years or so behind
Paris), with a joyous, noble face, a merry tongue
and giddy laugh, and a confession of experiences
which these pages, fortunately for their moral tone,
need not recount.   All these were there and many
others.

This throng, shifting like the fragments of colored
glass in the kaleidoscope, had its far-away interest
to the contemplative Joseph. To them he was
of little interest, or none. Of the many passers,
scarcely an occasional one greeted him, and such only
with an extremely polite and silent dignity which
seemed to him like saying something of this sort:
" Most noble alien, give you good-day — stay where
you are.   Profoundly yours ——— "

Two men came through the Place d'Armes on
conspicuously fine horses. One it is not necessary
to describe. The other, a man of perhaps thirty-
three or thirty-four years of age, was extremely
handsome and well dressed, the martial fashion of
the day showing his tall and finely knit figure to
much advantage. He sat his horse with an uncommon grace, and, as he rode beside his companion,
spoke and gave ear by turns with an easy dignity
sufficient of itself to have attracted popular observation. It was the apothecary's unknown friend.

Frowenfeld noticed them while they were yet in the middle of the grounds. He could hardly have failed to do so, for some one close beside his bench in undoubted allusion to one of the approaching figures exclaimed:

"Here comes Honoré Grandissime."

Moreover, at that moment there was a slight unwonted stir on the Place d'Armes. It began at the farther corner of the square, hard by the Principal, and spread so quickly through the groups near about, that in a minute the entire company were quietly made aware of something going notably wrong in their immediate presence. There was no running to see it. There seemed to be not so much as any verbal communication of the matter from mouth to mouth. Rather a consciousness appeared to catch noiselessly from one to another as the knowledge of human intrusion comes to groups of deer in a park. There was the same elevating of the head here and there, the same rounding of beautiful eyes. Some stared, others slowly approached, while others turned and moved away; but a common indignation was in the breast of that thing dreadful everywhere, but terrible in Louisiana, the Majority. For there, in the presence of those good citizens, before the eyes of the proudest and fairest mothers and daughters of New Orleans, glaringly, on the open Plaza, the Creole whom Joseph had met by the graves in the field, Honoré Grandissime, the uttermost flower on the topmost branch of the tallest family tree ever transplanted

from France to Louisiana, Honoré, — the wor-
shiped, the magnificent, — in the broad light of the
sun's going down, rode side by side with the
Yankee governor and was not ashamed !

Joseph, on his bench, sat contemplating the two
parties to this scandal as they came toward him.
Their horses' flanks were damp from some pleasant
gallop, but their present gait was the soft, mettlesome movement of animals who will even submit
to walk if their masters insist. As they wheeled
out of the broad diagonal path that crossed the
square, and turned toward him in the highway, he
fancied that the Creole observed him. He was
not mistaken. As they seemed about to pass the
spot where he sat, M. Grandissime interrupted the
governor with a word and, turning his horse's
head, rode up to the bench, lifting his hat as he
came.

" Good-evening, Mr. Frowenfeld."

Joseph, looking brighter than when he sat unac-
costed, rose and blushed.

" Mr. Frowenfeld, you know my uncle very well,
I believe — Agricole Fusilier — long beard ? "

" Oh ! yes, sir, certainly."

" Well, Mr. Frowenfeld, I shall be much obliged
if you will tell him — that is, should you meet him
this evening — that I wish to see him. If you will
be so kind ? "

" Oh ! yes, sir, certainly."

Frowenfeld's diffidence made itself evident in this
reiterated phrase.

" I do not know that you will see him, but if you should, you know —— "

" Oh, certainly, sir ! "

The two paused a single instant, exchanging a smile of amiable reminder from the horseman and of bashful but pleased acknowledgment from the one who saw his precepts being reduced to practice.

" Well, good-evening, Mr. Frowenfeld."

M. Grandissime lifted his hat and turned. Frowenfeld sat down.

" *Bou zou, Miché Honoré!* " called the *marchande*.

" *Comment to yé, Clemence?* "

The merchant waved his hand as he rode away with his companion.

" *Beau Miché, là,*" said the *marchande*, catching Joseph's eye.

He smiled his ignorance and shook his head.

" Dass one fine gen'leman," she repeated. " *Mo pa'lé Anglé,*" she added with a chuckle.

" You know him ? "

" Oh ! yass, sah ; Mawse Honoré knows me, yass. All de gen'lemens knows me. I sell de *calas*; mawnin's sell *calas*, evenin's sell zinzer-cake. *You* know me " (a fact which Joseph had all along been aware of). " Dat me w'at pass in rue Royale ev'y mawnin' holl'in' ' *Bé calas touts chauds,*' an' singin' ; don't you know? "

The enthusiasm of an artist overcame any timidity she might have been supposed to possess, and, waiving the formality of an invitation, she began, to Frowenfeld's consternation, to sing, in a loud, nasal voice.

But the performance, long familiar, attracted no public attention, and he for whose special delight it was intended had taken an attitude of disclaimer and was again contemplating the quiet groups of the Place d'Armes and the pleasant hurry of the levee road.

"Don't you know?" persisted the woman. "Yass, sah, dass me; I's Clemence."

But Frowenfeld was looking another way.

"You know my boy," suddenly said she.

Frowenfeld looked at her.

"Yass, sah. Dat boy w'at bring you de box of *basilic* lass Chrismus; dass my boy."

She straightened her cakes on the tray and made some changes in their arrangement that possibly were important.

"I learned to speak English in Fijinny. Bawn dah."

She looked steadily into the apothecary's absorbed countenance for a full minute, then let her eyes wander down the highway. The human tide was turning cityward. Presently she spoke again.

"Folks comin' home a'ready, yass."

Her hearer looked down the road.

Suddenly a voice that, once heard, was always known, — deep and pompous, as if a lion roared, — sounded so close behind him as to startle him half from his seat.

" Is this a corporeal man, or must I doubt my eyes ?   Hah !   Professor Frowenfeld ! " it said.

" Mr. Fusilier ! " exclaimed Frowenfeld in a subdued voice, while he blushed again and looked at the new-comer with that sort of awe which children experience in a menagerie.

" *Citizen* Fusilier," said the lion.

Agricola indulged to excess the grim hypocrisy of brandishing the catchwords of newfangled reforms ; they served to spice a breath that was strong with the praise of the " superior liberties of Europe," — those old, cast-iron tyrannies to get rid of which America was settled.

Frowenfeld smiled amusedly and apologetically at the same moment.

" I am glad to meet you.   I —— "

He was going on to give Honoré Grandissime's message, but was interrupted.

" My young friend," rumbled the old man in his deepest key, smiling emotionally and holding and solemning continuing to shake Joseph's hand, " I am sure you are.   You ought to thank God that you have my acquaintance."

Frowenfeld colored to the temples.

" I must acknowledge —— " he began.

" Ah ! " growled the lion, " your beautiful modesty leads you to misconstrue me, sir.   You pay my judgment no compliment.   I know your worth, sir ; I merely meant, sir, that in me — poor, humble me — you have secured a sympathizer in your tastes and plans.   Agricola Fusilier, sir, is not a cock on a dunghill, to find a jewel and then scratch it aside."

The smile of diffidence, but not the flush, passed from the young man's face, and he sat down forcibly.

"You jest," he said.

The reply was a majestic growl.

" I *never* jest!" The speaker half sat down, then straightened up again. "Ah, the Marquis of Caso Calvo!—I must bow to him, though an honest man's bow is more than he deserves."

"More than he deserves?" was Frowenfeld's query.

"More than he deserves!" was the response.

"What has he done? I have never heard——"

The denunciator turned upon Frowenfeld his most royal frown, and retorted with a question which still grows wild in Louisiana:

"What"— he seemed to shake his mane — " what has he *not* done, sir?" and then he withdrew his frown slowly, as if to add, "You'll be careful next time how you cast doubt upon a public official's guilt."

The marquis's cavalcade came briskly jingling by. Frowenfeld saw within the carriage two men, one in citizen's dress, the other in a brilliant uniform. The latter leaned forward, and, with a cordiality which struck the young spectator as delightful, bowed. The immigrant glanced at Citizen Fusilier, expecting to see the greeting returned with great haughtiness; instead of which that person uncov-

ered his leonine head, and, with a solemn sweep
of his cocked hat, bowed half his length. Nay,
he more than bowed, he bowed down — so that the
action hurt Frowenfeld from head to foot.

"What large gentlemen was that sitting on the
other side?" asked the young man, as his companion sat down with the air of having finished an
oration.

"No gentleman at all!" thundered the citizen.
"That fellow" (beetling frown), "that *fellow* is
Edward Livingston."

"The great lawyer?"

"The great villain!"

Frowenfeld himself frowned.

The old man laid a hand upon his junior's
shoulder and growled benignantly:

"My young friend, your displeasure delights
me!"

The patience with which Frowenfeld was bearing
all this forced a chuckle and shake of the head from
the *marchande*.

Citizen Fusilier went on speaking in a manner
that might be construed either as address or solilo-
quy, gesticulating much and occasionally letting out
a fervent word that made passers look around and
Joseph inwardly wince. With eyes closed and
hands folded on the top of the knotted staff which
he carried but never used, he delivered an apos-
trophe to the "spotless soul of youth," enticed by
the "spirit of adventure" to "launch away upon
the unploughed sea of the future!" He lifted one

hand and smote the back of the other solemnly, once, twice, and again, nodding his head faintly several times without opening his eyes, as who should say, "Very impressive; go on," and so resumed; spoke of this spotless soul of youth searching under unknown latitudes for the "sunken treasures of experience"; indulged, as the reporters of our day would say, in "many beautiful flights of rhetoric," and finally depicted the loathing with which the spotless soul of youth "recoils!"— suiting the action to the word so emphatically as to make a pretty little boy who stood gaping at him start back — "on encountering in the holy chambers of public office the vultures hatched in the nests of ambition and avarice!"

Three or four persons lingered carelessly near by with ears wide open. Frowenfeld felt that he must bring this to an end, and, like any young person who has learned neither deceit nor disrespect to seniors, he attempted to reason it down.

"You do not think many of our public men are dishonest!"

"Sir!" replied the rhetorician, with a patronizing smile, "h-you must be thinking of France!"

"No, sir; of Louisiana."

"Louisiana! Dishonest? All, sir, all. They are all as corrupt as Olympus, sir!"

"Well," said Frowenfeld, with more feeling than was called for, "there is one who, I feel sure, is pure. I know it by his face!"

The old man gave a look of stern interrogation.

"Governor Claiborne."

"Ye-e-e g-hods! Claiborne! *Claiborne!* Why, he is a Yankee!"

The lion glowered over the lamb like a thunder-cloud.

"He is a Virginian," said Frowenfeld.

"He is an American, and no American can be honest."

"You are prejudiced," exclaimed the young man.

Citizen Fusilier made himself larger.

"What is prejudice? I do not know."

"I am an American myself," said Frowenfeld, rising up with his face burning.

The citizen rose up also, but unruffled.

"My beloved young friend," laying his hand heavily upon the other's shoulder, "you are not. You were merely born in America."

But Frowenfeld was not appeased.

"Hear me through," persisted the flatterer. "You were merely born in America. I, too, was born in America; but will any man responsible for his opinion mistake me — Agricola Fusilier — for an American?"

He clutched his cane in the middle and glared around, but no person seemed to be making the mistake to which he so scornfully alluded, and he was about to speak again when an outcry of alarm coming simultaneously from Joseph and the *marchande* directed his attention to a lady in danger.

The scene, as afterward recalled to the mind of the un-American citizen, included the figures of his

nephew and the new governor returning up the
road at a canter; but, at the time, he knew only
that a lady of unmistakable gentility, her back
toward him, had just gathered her robes and started
to cross the road, when there was a general cry of
warning, and the *marchande* cried, "*Garde choual!*"
while the lady leaped directly into the danger and
his nephew's horse knocked her to the earth!

Though there was a rush to the rescue from
every direction, she was on her feet before any one
could reach her, her lips compressed, nostrils dilated,
cheek burning, and eyes flashing a lady's wrath
upon a dismounted horseman. It was the governor. As the crowd had rushed in, the startled
horses, from whom the two riders had instantly
leaped, drew violently back, jerking their masters
with them and leaving only the governor in range
of the lady's angry eye.

"Mademoiselle!" he cried, striving to reach her.

She pointed him in gasping indignation to his
empty saddle, and, as the crowd farther separated
them, waved away all permission to apologize and
turned her back.

"Hah!" cried the crowd, echoing her humor.

"Lady," interposed the governor, "do not drive
us to the rudeness of leaving ―――― "

"*Animal, vous!*" cried half a dozen, and the
lady gave him such a look of scorn that he did not
finish his sentence.

"Open the way, there," called a voice in French.
It was Honoré Grandissime. But just then he

saw that the lady had found the best of protectors, and the two horsemen, having no choice, remounted and rode away. As they did so, M. Grandissime called something hurriedly to Frowenfeld, on whose arm the lady hung, concerning the care of her; but his words were lost in the short yell of derision sent after himself and his companion by the crowd.

Old Agricola, meanwhile, was having a trouble of his own. He had followed Joseph's wake as he pushed through the throng; but as the lady turned her face he wheeled abruptly away. This brought again into view the bench he had just left, whereupon he, in turn, cried out, and, dashing through all obstructions, rushed back to it, lifting his ugly staff as he went and flourishing it in the face of Palmyre Philosophe.

She stood beside the seat with the smile of one foiled and intensely conscious of peril, but neither frightened nor suppliant, holding back with her eyes the execution of Agricola's threat against her life.

Presently she drew a short step backward, then another, then a third, and then turned and moved away down the avenue of willows, followed for a few steps by the lion and by the laughing comment of the *marchande*, who stood looking after them with her tray balanced on her head.

"*Ya, ya! ye connais voudou bien!*" [1]

The old man turned to rejoin his companion. The day was rapidly giving place to night and the people were withdrawing to their homes. He

---

[1] "They 're up in the voudou arts."

crossed the levee, passed through the Place d'Armes and on into the city without meeting the object of his search. For Joseph and the lady had hurried off together.

As the populace floated away in knots of three, four and five, those who had witnessed mademoiselle's (?) mishap told it to those who had not; explaining that it was the accursed Yankee governor who had designedly driven his horse at his utmost speed against the fair victim (some of them butted against their hearers by way of illustration); that the fiend had then maliciously laughed; that this was all the Yankees came to New Orleans for, and that there was an understanding among them — " Understanding, indeed ! " exclaimed one, " They have instructions from the President ! " — that unprotected ladies should be run down wherever overtaken. If you did n't believe it you could ask the tyrant, Claiborne, himself; he made no secret of it. One or two — but they were considered by others extravagant — testified that, as the lady fell, they had seen his face distorted with a horrid delight, and had heard him cry : " Daz de way to knog them ! "

" But how came a lady to be out on the levee, at sunset, on foot and alone ? " asked a citizen, and another replied — both using the French of the late province :

" As for being on foot " — a shrug. " But she was not alone ; she had a *milatraisse* behind her."

" Ah ! so ; that was well."

"But — ha, ha ! — the *milatraisse*, seeing her mistress out of danger, takes the opportunity to try to bring the curse upon Agricola Fusilier by sitting down where he had just risen up, and had to get away from him as quickly as possible to save her own skull."

"And left the lady ? "

"Yes ; and who took her to her home at last, but Frowenfeld, the apothecary ! "

"Ho, ho ! the astrologer ! We ought to hang that fellow."

"With his books tied to his feet," suggested a third citizen. "It is no more than we owe to the community to go and smash his show-window. He had better behave himself. Come, gentlemen, a little *taffia* will do us good. When shall we ever get through these exciting times ? "

CHAPTER XVI

STARLIGHT IN THE RUE CHARTRES

"Oh ! M'sieur Frowenfel', tague me ad home !"

It was Aurora, who caught the apothecary's arm vehemently in both her hands with a look of beautiful terror. And whatever Joseph's astronomy might have previously taught him to the contrary, he knew by his senses that the earth thereupon turned entirely over three times in two seconds.

His confused response, though unintelligible,

answered all purposes, as the lady found herself the next moment hurrying across the Place d'Armes close to his side, and as they by-and-by passed its farther limits she began to be conscious that she was clinging to her protector as though she would climb up and hide under his elbow. As they turned up the rue Chartres she broke the silence.

" Oh !–h ! " — breathlessly, — " 'h ! — M'sieur Frowenf' — you walkin' so faz ! "

" Oh ! " echoed Frowenfeld, " I did not know what I was doing."

" Ha, ha, ha ! " laughed the lady, " me, too, juz de sem lag you ! *attendez;* wait."

They halted; a moment's deft manipulation of a veil turned it into a wrapping for her neck.

" 'Sieur Frowenfel', oo dad man was ? You know 'im ? "

She returned her hand to Frowenfeld's arm and they moved on.

" The one who spoke to you, or — you know the one who got near enough to apologize is not the one whose horse struck you ! "

" I din know. But oo dad odder one ? I saw h-only 'is back, bud I thing it is de sem —— "

She identified it with the back that was turned to her during her last visit to Frowenfeld's shop; but finding herself about to mention a matter so nearly connected with the purse of gold, she checked herself; but Frowenfeld, eager to say a good word for his acquaintance, ventured to extol his character while he concealed his name.

"While I have never been introduced to him, I have some acquaintance with him, and esteem him a noble gentleman."

"W'ere you meet him?"

"I met him first," he said, "at the graves of my parents and sisters."

There was a kind of hush after the mention, and the lady made no reply.

"It was some weeks after my loss," resumed Frowenfeld.

"In wad *cimetière* dad was?"

"In no cemetery — being Protestants, you know ——"

"Ah, yes, sir?" with a gentle sigh.

"The physician who attended me procured permission to bury them on some private land below the city."

"Not in de groun'?"[1]

"Yes; that was my father's expressed wish when he died."

"You 'ad de fivver? Oo nurse you w'en you was sick?"

"An old hired negress."

"Dad was all?"

"Yes."

"Hm-m-m!" she said piteously, and laughed in her sleeve.

Who could hope to catch and reproduce the continuous lively thrill which traversed the frame of the escaped book-worm as every moment there was

[1] Only Jews and paupers are buried in the ground in New Orleans.

repeated to his consciousness the knowledge that he was walking across the vault of heaven with the evening star on his arm — at least, that he was, at her instigation, killing time along the dim, ill-lighted *trottoirs* of the rue Chartres, with Aurora listening sympathetically at his side. But let it go; also the sweet broken English with which she now and then interrupted him; also the inward, hidden sparkle of her dancing Gallic blood; her low, merry laugh; the roguish mental reservation that lurked behind her graver speeches; the droll bravados she uttered against the powers that be, as with timid fingers he brushed from her shoulder a little remaining dust of the late encounter — these things, we say, we let go, — as we let butterflies go rather than pin them to paper.

They had turned into the rue Bienville, and were walking toward the river, Frowenfeld in the midst of a long sentence, when a low cry of tearful delight sounded in front of them, some one in long robes glided forward, and he found his arm relieved of its burden and that burden transferred to the bosom and passionate embrace of another — we had almost said a fairer — Creole, amid a bewildering interchange of kisses and a pelting shower of Creole French.

A moment after, Frowenfeld found himself introduced to "my dotter, Clotilde," who all at once ceased her demonstrations of affection and bowed to him with a majestic sweetness, that seemed one instant grateful and the next, distant.

"I can hardly understand that you are not sisters," said Frowenfeld, a little awkwardly.

"Ah! *ecoutez!*" exclaimed the younger.

"Ah! *par exemple!*" cried the elder, and they laughed down each other's throats, while the immigrant blushed.

This encounter was presently followed by a silent surprise when they stopped and turned before the door of Number 19, and Frowenfeld contrasted the women with their painfully humble dwelling. But therein is where your true Creole was, and still continues to be, properly, yea, delightfully un-American; the outside of his house may be as rough as the outside of a bird's nest; it is the inside that is for the birds; and the front room of this house, when the daughter presently threw open the batten shutters of its single street door, looked as bright and happy, with its candelabra glittering on the mantel, and its curtains of snowy lace, as its bright-eyed tenants.

"'Sieur Frowenfel', if you pliz to come in," said Aurora, and the timid apothecary would have bravely accepted the invitation, but for a quick look which he saw the daughter give the mother; whereupon he asked, instead, permission to call at some future day, and received the cordial leave of Aurora and another bow from Clotilde.

CHAPTER XVII

THAT NIGHT

Do we not fail to accord to our nights their true value? We are ever giving to our days the credit and blame of all we do and mis-do, forgetting those silent, glimmering hours when plans — and sometimes plots — are laid ; when resolutions are formed or changed ; when heaven, and sometimes heaven's enemies, are invoked ; when anger and evil thoughts are recalled, and sometimes hate made to inflame and fester ; when problems are solved, riddles guessed, and things made apparent in the dark, which day refused to reveal. Our nights are the keys to our days. They explain them. They are also the day's correctors. Night's leisure untangles the mistakes of day's haste. We should not attempt to comprise our pasts in the phrase, " in those days ; " we should rather say " in those days and nights."

That night was a long-remembered one to the apothecary of the rue Royale. But it was after he had closed his shop, and in his back room sat pondering the unusual experiences of the evening, that it began to be, in a higher degree, a night of events to most of those persons who had a part in its earlier incidents.

That Honoré Grandissime whom Frowenfeld had

only this day learned to know as *the* Honoré Grandissime and the young governor-general were closeted together.

"What can you expect, my-de'-seh?" the Creole was asking, as they confronted each other in the smoke of their choice tobacco. "Remember, they are citizens by compulsion. You say your best and wisest law is that one prohibiting the slave-trade; my-de'-seh, I assure you, privately, I agree with you; but they abhor your law!

"Your principal danger — at least, I mean difficulty — is this: that the Louisianais themselves, some in pure lawlessness, some through loss of office, some in a vague hope of preserving the old condition of things, will not only hold off from all participation in your government, but will make all sympathy with it, all advocacy of its principles, and especially all office-holding under it, odious — disreputable — infamous. You may find yourself constrained to fill your offices with men who can face down the contumely of a whole people. You know what such men generally are. One out of a hundred may be a moral hero — the ninety-nine will be scamps; and the moral hero will most likely get his brains blown out early in the day.

"Count O'Reilly, when he established the Spanish power here thirty-five years ago, cut a similar knot with the executioner's sword; but, my-de'-seh, you are here to establish a *free* government; and how can you make it freer than the people wish it? There is your riddle! They hold off and say,

9

' Make your government as free as you can, but do not ask us to help you; ' and before you know it you have no retainers but a gang of shameless mercenaries, who will desert you whenever the indignation of this people overbalances their indolence; and you will fall the victim of what you may call our mutinous patriotism."

The governor made a very quiet, unappreciative remark about a " patriotism that lets its government get choked up with corruption and then blows it out with gunpowder ! "

The Creole shrugged.

" And repeats the operation indefinitely," he said.

The governor said something often heard, before and since, to the effect that communities will not sacrifice themselves for mere ideas.

" My-de'-seh," replied the Creole, " you speak like a true Anglo-Saxon; but, sir ! how many communities have *committed suicide*.   And this one ? — why, it is *just* the kind to do it ! "

" Well," said the governor, smilingly, " you have pointed out what you consider to be the breakers, now can you point out the channel ? "

" Channel ? There is none ! And you, nor I, cannot dig one.   Two great forces *may* ultimately do it, Religion and Education — as I was telling you I said to my young friend, the apothecary,— but still I am free to say what would be my first and principal step, if I was in your place — as I thank God I am not."

The listener asked him what that was.

" Wherever I could find a Creole that I could venture to trust, my-de'-seh, I would put him in office. Never mind a little political heterodoxy, you know; almost any man can be trusted to shoot away from the uniform he has on. And then —— "

" But," said the other, " I have offered you —— "

" Oh ! " replied the Creole, like a true merchant, "me, I am too busy ; it is impossible ! But, I say, I would *compel*, my-de'-seh, this people to govern themselves ! "

" And pray, how would you give a people a free government and then compel them to administer it ? "

" My-de'-seh, you should not give one poor Creole the puzzle which belongs to your whole Congress ; but you may depend on this, that the worst thing for all parties — and I say it only because it is worst for all — would be a feeble and dilatory punishment of bad faith."

When this interview finally drew to a close the governor had made a memorandum of some fifteen or twenty Grandissimes, scattered through different cantons of Louisiana, who, their kinsman Honoré thought, would not decline appointments.

Certain of the Muses were abroad that night. Faintly audible to the apothecary of the rue Royale through that deserted stillness which is yet the marked peculiarity of New Orleans streets by night, came from a neighboring slave-yard the monotonous chant and machine-like tune-beat of an African

dance.   There our lately met *marchande* (albeit she
was but a guest, fortified against the street-watch
with her master's written "pass") led the ancient
Calinda dance with that well-known song of derision,
in whose ever multiplying stanzas the helpless satire
of a feeble race still continues to celebrate the per-
sonal failings of each newly prominent figure among
the dominant caste.   There was a new distich to
the song to-night, signifying that the pride of the
Grandissimes must find his friends now among the
Yankees :

> " Miché Hon'ré, allé ! h-allé !
>   Trouvé to zamis parmi les Yankis.
> Dancé calinda, bou-joum ! bou-joum !
> Dancé calinda, bou-joum ! bou-joum !

Frowenfeld, as we have already said, had closed
his shop, and was sitting in the room behind it with
one arm on his table and the other on his celestial
globe, watching the flicker of his small fire and
musing upon the unusual experiences of the evening.   Upon every side there seemed to start away
from his turning glance the multiplied shadows of
something wrong.   The melancholy face of that
Honoré Grandissime, his landlord, at whose mention Dr. Keene had thought it fair to laugh without
explaining ; the tall, bright-eyed *milatraisse ;* old
Agricola ; the lady of the basil ; the newly identified
merchant friend, now the more satisfactory Honoré,
— they all came before him in his meditation, pro-
voking among themselves a certain discord, faint
but persistent, to which he strove to close his ear.

For he was brain-weary. Even in the bright recollection of the lady and her talk he became involved among shadows, and going from bad to worse, seemed at length almost to gasp in an atmosphere of hints, allusions, faint unspoken admissions, ill-concealed antipathies, unfinished speeches, mistaken identities and whisperings of hidden strife. The cathedral clock struck twelve and was answered again from the convent belfry; and as the notes died away he suddenly became aware that the weird, drowsy throb of the African song and dance had been swinging drowsily in his brain for an unknown lapse of time.

The apothecary nodded once or twice, and thereupon rose up and prepared for bed, thinking to sleep till morning.

Aurora and her daughter had long ago put out their chamber light. Early in the evening the younger had made favorable mention of retiring, to which the elder replied by asking to be left awhile to her own thoughts. Clotilde, after some tender protestations, consented, and passed through the open door that showed, beyond it, their couch. The air had grown just cool and humid enough to make the warmth of one small brand on the hearth acceptable, and before this the fair widow settled herself to gaze beyond her tiny, slippered feet into its wavering flame, and think. Her thoughts were such as to bestow upon her face that enhancement of beauty that comes of pleasant reverie, and to make it certain that that little city afforded no fairer sight, — unless, indeed, it was the figure of Clotilde just beyond the open door, as in her white night-dress, enriched with the work of a diligent needle, she knelt upon the low *prie-Dieu* before the little family altar, and committed her pure soul to the Divine keeping.

Clotilde could not have been many minutes asleep when Aurora changed her mind and decided to follow. The shade upon her face had deepened for a moment into a look of trouble ; but a bright philosophy, which was part of her paternal birthright, quickly chased it away, and she passed to her room, disrobed, lay softly down beside the beauty already there and smiled herself to sleep, —

> " Blinded alike from sunshine and from rain,
> As though a rose should shut, and be a bud again."

But she also wakened again, and lay beside her unconscious bedmate, occupied with the company of her own thoughts. " Why should these little concealments ruffle my bosom ? Does not even Nature herself practise wiles ? Look at the innocent birds ; do they build where everybody can count their eggs ? And shall a poor human creature try to be better than a bird ? Did n't I say my prayers under the blanket just now ? "

Her companion stirred in her sleep, and she rose upon one elbow to bend upon the sleeper a gaze of ardent admiration. " Ah, beautiful little chick ! how guileless ! indeed, how deficient in that respect ! "

She sat up in the bed and hearkened; the bell
struck for midnight. Was that the hour? The
fates were smiling! Surely M. Assonquer himself
must have wakened her to so choice an opportunity.
She ought not to despise it. Now, by the applica-
tion of another and easily wrought charm, that darkened hour lately spent with Palmyre would have, as
it were, its colors set.

The night had grown much cooler. Stealthily,
by degrees, she rose and left the couch. The openings of the room were a window and two doors, and
these, with much caution, she contrived to open
without noise. None of them exposed her to the
possibility of public view. One door looked into
the dim front room; the window let in only a flood
of moonlight over the top of a high house which
was without openings on that side; the other door
revealed a weed-grown back yard, and that invaluable protector, the cook's hound, lying fast asleep.

In her night-clothes as she was, she stood a
moment in the centre of the chamber, then sank
upon one knee, rapped the floor gently but audibly
thrice, rose, drew a step backward, sank upon the
other knee, rapped thrice, rose again, stepped backward, knelt the third time, the third time rapped,
and then, rising, murmured a vow to pour upon the
ground next day an oblation of champagne — then
closed the doors and window and crept back to bed.
Then she knew how cold she had become. It
seemed as though her very marrow was frozen. She
was seized with such an uncontrollable shivering

that Clotilde presently opened her eyes, threw her arm about her mother's neck, and said :

" Ah ! my sweet mother, are you so cold ? "

" The blanket was all off of me," said the mother, returning the embrace, and the two sank into unconsciousness together.

Into slumber sank almost at the same moment Joseph Frowenfeld. He awoke, not a great while later, to find himself standing in the middle of the floor. Three or four men had shouted at once, and three pistol-shots, almost in one instant, had resounded just outside his shop. He had barely time to throw himself into half his garments when the knocker sounded on his street door, and when he opened it Agricola Fusilier entered, supported by his nephew Honoré on one side and Doctor Keene on the other. The latter's right hand was pressed hard against a bloody place in Agricola's side.

" Give us plenty of light, Frowenfeld," said the doctor, " and a chair and some lint, and some Castile soap, and some towels and sticking-plaster, and anything else you can think of. Agricola's about scared to death —— "

" Professor Frowenfeld," groaned the aged citizen, " I am basely and mortally stabbed ! "

" Right on, Frowenfeld," continued the doctor, " right on into the back room. Fasten that front door. Here, Agricola, sit down here. That 's right, Frow., stir up a little fire. Give me — never mind, I 'll just cut the cloth open."

There was a moment of silent suspense while the wound was being reached, and then the doctor spoke again.

"Just as I thought; only a safe and comfortable gash that will keep you in-doors a while with your arm in a sling. You are more scared than hurt, I think, old gentleman."

"You think an infernal falsehood, sir!"

"See here, sir," said the doctor, without ceasing to ply his dexterous hands in his art, "I'll jab these scissors into your back if you say that again."

"I suppose," growled the "citizen," "it is just the thing your professional researches have qualified you for, sir!"

"Just stand here, Mr. Frowenfeld," said the little doctor, settling down to a professional tone, "and hand me things as I ask for them. Honoré, please hold this arm; so." And so, after a moderate lapse of time, the treatment that medical science of those days dictated was applied—whatever that was. Let those who do not know give thanks.

M. Grandissime explained to Frowenfeld what had occurred.

"You see, I succeeded in meeting my uncle, and we went together to my office. My uncle keeps his accounts with me. Sometimes we look them over. We stayed until midnight; I dismissed my carriage. As we walked homeward we met some friends coming out of the rooms of the Bagatelle Club; five or six of my uncles and cousins, and also Doctor Keene. We all fell a-talking of my grandfather's *fête de grandpère* of next month, and went to have some coffee. When we separated, and my uncle and my cousin Achille Grandissime and Doctor Keene and myself came down Royal street, out from that dark alley behind your shop jumped a little man and stuck my uncle with a knife. If I had not caught his arm he would have killed my uncle."

"And he escaped," said the apothecary.

"No, sir!" said Agricola, with his back turned.

"I think he did.   I do not think he was struck."

"And Mr. ——, your cousin?"

"Achille?   I have sent him for a carriage."

"Why, Agricola," said the doctor, snipping the loose ravellings from his patient's bandages, "an old man like you should not have enemies."

"I am *not* an old man, sir!"

"I said *young* man."

"I am not a *young* man, sir!"

"I wonder who the fellow was," continued Doctor Keene, as he readjusted the ripped sleeve.

"That is *my* affair, sir; I know who it was."

"And yet she insists," M. Grandissime was asking Frowenfeld, standing with his leg thrown across the celestial globe, "that I knocked her down intentionally?"

Frowenfeld, about to answer, was interrupted by a rap on the door.

"That is my cousin, with the carriage," said M. Grandissime, following the apothecary into the shop.

Frowenfeld opened to a young man, — a rather poor specimen of the Grandissime type, deficient in stature but not in stage manner.

" *Est il mort ?* " he cried at the threshold.

" Mr. Frowenfeld, let me make you acquainted with my cousin, Achille Grandissime."

Mr. Achille Grandissime gave Frowenfeld such a bow as we see now only in pictures.

" Ve'y 'appe to meck yo' acquaintenz ! "

Agricola entered, followed by the doctor, and demanded in indignant thunder-tones, as he entered :

" Who — ordered — that — carriage ? "

" I did," said Honoré. " Will you please get into it at once."

" Ah ! dear Honoré ! " exclaimed the old man, " always too kind ! I go in it purely to please you."

Good-night was exchanged ; Honoré entered the vehicle and Agricola was helped in. Achille touched his hat, bowed and waved his hand to Joseph, and shook hands with the doctor, and saying, " Well, good-night, Doctor Keene," he shut himself out of the shop with another low bow. " Think I am going to shake hands with an apothecary ? " thought M. Achille.

Doctor Keene had refused Honoré's invitation to go with them.

" Frowenfeld," he said, as he stood in the middle of the shop wiping a ring with a towel and looking at his delicate, freckled hand, " I propose, before going to bed with you, to eat some of your bread and cheese. Are n't you glad ? "

"I shall be, Doctor," replied the apothecary, "if you will tell me what all this means."

"Indeed I will not, — that is, not to-night. What? Why, it would take until breakfast to tell what 'all this means,' — the story of that pestiferous darky Bras Coupé, with the rest? Oh, no, sir. I would sooner not have any bread and cheese. What on earth has waked your curiosity so suddenly, anyhow?"

"Have you any idea who stabbed Citizen Fusilier?" was Joseph's response.

"Why, at first I thought it was the other Honoré Grandissime; but when I saw how small the fellow was, I was at a loss, completely. But, whoever it is, he has my bullet in him, whatever Honoré may think."

"Will Mr. Fusilier's wound give him much trouble?" asked Joseph, as they sat down to a luncheon at the fire.

"Hardly; he has too much of the blood of Lufki-Humma in him. But I need not say that; for the Grandissime blood is just as strong. A wonderful family, those Grandissimes! They are an old, illustrious line, and the strength that was once in the intellect and will is going down into the muscles. I have an idea that their greatness began, hundreds of years ago, in ponderosity of arm, — of frame, say, — and developed from generation to generation, in a rising scale, first into fineness of sinew, then, we will say, into force of will, then into power of mind, then into subtleties of genius. Now they are going back down the incline. Look at Honoré; he is high up on the scale, intellectual and sagacious. But look at him physically, too. What an exquisite mold! What compact strength! I should not wonder if he gets that from the Indian Queen. What endurance he has! He will probably go to his business by and by and not see his bed for seventeen or eighteen hours. He is the flower of the family, and possibly the last one. Now, old Agricola shows the down- ward grade better. Seventy-five, if he is a day, with, maybe, one-fourth the attain- ments he pretends to have, and still less good sense; but strong — as an orang-outang. Shall we go to bed?"

CHAPTER XVIII

NEW LIGHT UPON DARK PLACES

WHEN the long, wakeful night was over, and the doctor gone, Frowenfeld seated himself to record his usual observations of the weather; but his mind was elsewhere — here, there, yonder. There are understandings that expand, not imperceptibly hour by hour, but as certain flowers do, by little explosive ruptures, with periods of quiescence between. After this night of experiences it was natural that Frowenfeld should find the circumference of his perceptions consciously enlarged. The daylight shone, not into his shop alone, but into his heart as well. The face of Aurora, which had been the dawn to him before, was now a perfect sunrise, while in pleasant timeliness had come in this Apollo of a Honoré

Grandissime. The young immigrant was dazzled.
He felt a longing to rise up and run forward in
this flood of beams. He was unconscious of
fatigue, or nearly so — would have been wholly
so but for the return by and by of that same
dim shadow, or shadows, still rising and darting
across every motion of the fancy that grouped
again the actors in last night's scenes ; not such
shadows as naturally go with sunlight to make it
seem brighter, but a something which qualified the
light's perfection and the air's freshness.

Wherefore, resolved : that he would compound
his life, from this time forward, by a new formula :
books, so much ; observation, so much ; social intercourse, so much ; love — as to that, time enough
for that in the future (if he was in love with anybody, he certainly did not know it) ; of love, therefore, amount not yet necessary to state, but
probably (when it should be introduced), in the
generous proportion in which physicians prescribe
aqua. Resolved, in other words, without ceasing
to be Frowenfeld the studious, to begin at once the
perusal of this newly found book, the Community
of New Orleans. True, he knew he should find
it a difficult task — not only that much of it was
in a strange tongue, but that it was a volume whose
displaced leaves would have to be lifted tenderly,
blown free of much dust, re-arranged, some torn
fragments laid together again with much painstaking, and even the purport of some pages guessed
out. Obviously, the place to commence at was

that brightly illuminated title-page, the ladies Nancanou.

As the sun rose and diffused its beams in an atmosphere whose temperature had just been recorded as 50° F., the apothecary stepped half out of his shop-door to face the bracing air that came blowing upon his tired forehead from the north. As he did so, he said to himself:

"How are these two Honoré Grandissimes related to each other, and why should one be thought capable of attempting the life of Agricola?"

The answer was on its way to him.

There is left to our eyes but a poor vestige of the picturesque view presented to those who looked down the rue Royale before the garish day that changed the rue Enghien into Ingine street, and dropped the 'e' from Royale. It was a long, narrowing perspective of arcades, lattices, balconies, *zaguans*, dormer windows, and blue sky — of low, tiled roofs, red and wrinkled, huddled down into their own shadows; of canvas awnings with fluttering borders, and of grimy lamp-posts twenty feet in height, each reaching out a gaunt iron arm over the narrow street and dangling a lamp from its end. The human life which dotted the view displayed a variety of tints and costumes such as a painter would be glad to take just as he found them: the gayly feathered Indian, the slashed and tinselled Mexican, the leather-breeched raftsmen, the blue- or yellow-turbaned *négresse*, the sugar-planter in white flannel and moccasins, the average townsman

in the last suit of clothes of the lately deceased
century, and now and then a fashionable man in
that costume whose union of tight-buttoned martial severity, swathed throat, and effeminate super-
abundance of fine linen seemed to offer a sort of
state's evidence against the pompous tyrannies and
frivolities of the times.

The *marchande des calas* was out.   She came toward Joseph's shop, singing in a high-pitched nasal
tone this new song :

> " Dé 'tit zozos — yé té assis —
> Dé 'tit zozos — si la barrier.
> Dé 'tit zozos, qui zabotté ;
> Qui ça yé di' mo pas conné.

> " Manzeur-poulet vini simin,
> Croupé si yé et croqué yé ;
> Personn' pli' 'tend' yé zabotté —
> Dé 'tit zozos si la barrier."

" You lak dat song ? " she asked, with a chuckle,
as she let down from her turbaned head a flat
Indian basket of warm rice cakes.

" What does it mean ? "

She laughed again — more than the questioner
could see occasion for.

" Dat mean — two lill birds ; dey was sittin' on
de fence an' gabblin' togeddah, you know, lak you
see two young gals sometime', an' you can't mek
out w'at dey sayin', even ef dey know demself ?
H-ya !   Chicken-hawk come 'long dat road an' jes'
set down an' munch 'em, an' nobody can't no mo'
hea' deir lill gabblin' on de fence, you know."

Here she laughed again.

Joseph looked at her with severe suspicion, but she found refuge in benevolence.

"Honey, you ought to be asleep dis werry minit; look lak folks been a-worr'in' you. I's gwine to pick out de werry bes' *calas* I's got for you."

As she delivered them she courtesied, first to Joseph and then, lower and with hushed gravity, to a person who passed into the shop behind him, bowing and murmuring politely as he passed. She followed the new-comer with her eyes, hastily accepted the price of the cakes, whispered, "Dat's my mawstah," lifted her basket to her head and went away. Her master was Frowenfeld's landlord.

Frowenfeld entered after him, *calas* in hand, and with a grave "Good-morning, sir."

"—— m'sieu'," responded the landlord, with a low bow.

Frowenfeld waited in silence.

The landlord hesitated, looked around him, seemed about to speak, smiled, and said, in his soft, solemn voice, feeling his way word by word through the unfamiliar language:

"Ah lag to teg you apar'."

"See me alone?"

The landlord recognized his error by a fleeting smile.

"Alone," said he.

"Shall we go into my room?"

"*S'il vous plait, m'sieu'.*"

Frowenfeld's breakfast, furnished by contract

from a neighboring kitchen, stood on the table. It was a frugal one, but more comfortable than formerly, and included coffee, that subject of just pride in Creole cookery. Joseph deposited his *calas* with these things and made haste to produce a chair, which his visitor, as usual, declined.

" Idd you' bregfuz, m'sieu'."

" I can do that afterward," said Frowenfeld; but the landlord insisted and turned away from him to look up at the books on the wall, precisely as that other of the same name had done a few weeks before.

Frowenfeld, as he broke his loaf, noticed this, and, as the landlord turned his face to speak, wondered that he had not before seen the common likeness.

" Dez stog," said the sombre man.

" What, sir? Oh! — dead stock? But how can the materials of an education be dead stock ? "

The landlord shrugged. He would not argue the point. One American trait which the Creole is never entirely ready to encounter is this gratuitous Yankee way of going straight to the root of things.

" Dead stock in a mercantile sense, you mean," continued the apothecary; " but are men right in measuring such things only by their present market value ? "

The landlord had no reply. It was little to him, his manner intimated; his contemplation dwelt on deeper flaws in human right and wrong; yet — but it was needless to discuss it. However, he did speak.

"Ah was elevade in Pariz."

"Educated in Paris," exclaimed Joseph, admiringly. "Then you certainly cannot find *your* education dead stock."

The grave, not amused, smile which was the landlord's only rejoinder, though perfectly courteous, intimated that his tenant was sailing over depths of the question that he was little aware of. But the smile in a moment gave way for the look of one who was engrossed with another subject.

"M'sieu'," he began; but just then Joseph made an apologetic gesture and went forward to wait upon an inquirer after "Godfrey's Cordial;" for that comforter was known to be obtainable at "Frowenfeld's." The business of the American drug-store was daily increasing. When Frowenfeld returned his landlord stood ready to address him, with the air of having decided to make short of a matter.

"M'sieu' ——"

"Have a seat, sir," urged the apothecary.

His visitor again declined, with his uniform melancholy grace. He drew close to Frowenfeld.

"Ah wand you mague me one *ouangan*," he said.

Joseph shook his head. He remembered Doctor Keene's expressed suspicion concerning the assault of the night before.

"I do not understand you, sir; what is that?"

"You know."

The landlord offered a heavy, persuading smile.

"An unguent? Is that what you mean — an ointment?"

"M'sieu'," said the applicant, with a not-to-be-deceived expression, "*vous êtes astrologue — magicien* ——"

"God forbid!"

The landlord was grossly incredulous.

"You godd one 'P'tit Albert.'"

He dropped his forefinger upon an iron-clasped book on the table, whose title much use had effaced.

"That is the Bible. I do not know what the Tee Albare is!"

Frowenfeld darted an aroused glance into the ever-courteous eyes of his visitor, who said without a motion:

"You di' n't gave Agricola Fusilier *une ouangan, la nuit passé?*"

"Sir?"

"Ee was yeh? — laz nighd?"

"Mr. Fusilier was here last night — yes. He had been attacked by an assassin and slightly wounded. He was accompanied by his nephew, who, I suppose, is your cousin: he has the same name."

Frowenfeld, hoping he had changed the subject, concluded with a propitiatory smile, which, however, was not reflected.

"Ma bruzzah," said the visitor.

"Your brother!"

"Ma whide bruzzah; ah ham nod whide, m'sieu'."

Joseph said nothing. He was too much awed to speak; the ejaculation that started toward his lips turned back and rushed into his heart, and it was the quadroon who, after a moment, broke the silence:

"Ah ham de holdez son of Numa Grandissime."

"Yes — yes," said Frowenfeld, as if he would wave away something terrible.

"Nod sell me — *ouangan?*" asked the landlord, again.

"Sir," exclaimed Frowenfeld, taking a step backward, "pardon me if I offend you; that mixture of blood which draws upon you the scorn of this community is to me nothing — nothing! And every invidious distinction made against you on that account I despise! But, sir, whatever may be either your private wrongs, or the wrongs you suffer in common with your class, if you have it in your mind to employ any manner of secret art against the interests or person of any one ——"

The landlord was making silent protestations, and his tenant, lost in a wilderness of indignant emotions, stopped.

"M'sieu'," began the quadroon, but ceased and stood with an expression of annoyance every moment deepening on his face, until he finally shook his head slowly, and said with a baffled smile: "Ah can nod spig Engliss."

"Write it," said Frowenfeld, lifting forward a chair.

The landlord, for the first time in their acquaintance, accepted a seat, bowing low as he did so, with a demonstration of profound gratitude that just perceptibly heightened his even dignity. Paper, quills, and ink were handed down from a shelf and Joseph retired into the shop.

Honoré Grandissime, f. m. c. (these initials could hardly have come into use until some months later, but the convenience covers the sin of the slight anachronism), Honoré Grandissime, free man of color, entered from the rear room so silently that Joseph was first made aware of his presence by feeling him at his elbow. He handed the apothecary —— but a few words in time, lest we misjudge.

The father of the two Honorés was that Numa Grandissime — that mere child — whom the Grand Marquis, to the great chagrin of the De Grapions, had so early cadetted. The commission seems not to have been thrown away. While the province was still in first hands, Numa's was a shining name in the annals of Kerlerec's unsatisfactory Indian wars; and in 1768 (when the colonists, ill-informed, inflammable, and long ill-governed, resisted the transfer of Louisiana to Spain), at a time of life when most young men absorb all the political extravagances of their day, he had stood by the side of law and government, though the popular cry was a frenzied one for " liberty." Moreover, he had held back his whole chafing and stamping tribe from a precipice of disaster, and had secured valuable recognition of their office-holding capacities from that really good governor and princely Irishman whose one act of summary vengeance upon a few insurgent office-coveters has branded him in history as Cruel O'Reilly. But the experience of those days turned Numa gray, and withal he was not satisfied with their outcome. In the midst of the struggle he had weakened in one manly resolve — against his will he married. The lady was a Fusilier, Agricola's sister, a person of rare intelligence and beauty, whom, from early childhood, the secret counsels of his seniors had assigned to him. Despite this, he had said he would never marry; he made, he said, no pretensions to severe conscientiousness, or to being better than others, but — as between his Maker and himself — he had forfeited the right to wed, they all knew how. But the Fusiliers had become very angry and Numa, finding strife about to ensue just when without unity he could not bring an undivided clan through the torrent of the revolution, had "nobly sacrificed a little sentimental feeling," as his family defined it, by breaking faith with the mother of the man now standing at Joseph Frowenfeld's elbow, and who was then a little toddling boy. It was necessary to save the party — nay, that was a slip; we should say, to save the family; this is not a parable. Yet Numa loved his wife. She bore him a boy and a girl, twins; and as her son grew in physical, intellectual, and moral symmetry, he indulged the hope that — the ambition and pride of all the various Grandissimes now centering in this lawful son, and all

strife being lulled — he should yet see this Honoré
right the wrongs which he had not quite dared to
uproot. And Honoré inherited the hope and
began to make it an intention and aim even before
his departure (with his half-brother the other
Honoré) for school in Paris, at the early age of
fifteen. Numa soon after died, and Honoré, after
various fortunes in Paris, London, and elsewhere,
in the care, or at least company, of a pious uncle
in holy orders, returned to the ancestral mansion.
The father's will — by the law they might have set
it aside, but that was not their way — left the
darker Honoré the bulk of his fortune, the younger
a competency. The latter — instead of taking office,
as an ancient Grandissime should have done — to
the dismay and mortification of his kindred, established himself in a prosperous commercial business.
The elder bought houses and became a *rentier*.

The landlord handed the apothecary the following writing:

MR. JOSEPH FROWENFELD :

Think not that anybody is to be either poisoned by me
nor yet to be made a sufferer by the exercise of anything
by me of the character of what is generally known as
grigri, otherwise magique. This, sir, I do beg your permission to offer my assurance to you of the same. Ah,
no ! it is not for that ! I am the victim of another entirely and a far differente and dissimilar passion, *i. e.*, Love.
Esteemed sir, speaking or writing to you as unto the only
man of exclusively white blood whom I believe is in Louisi-

ana willing to do my dumb, suffering race the real justice,
I love Palmyre la Philosophe with a madness which is by
the human lips or tongues not possible to be exclaimed (as,
I may add, that I have in the same like manner since ex-
actley nine years and seven months and some days). Alas!
heavens! I can't help it in the least particles at all!
What, what shall I do, for ah! it is pitiful! She loves
me not at all, but, on the other hand, is (if I suspicion not
wrongfully) wrapped up head and ears in devotion of one
who does not love her, either, so cold and incapable of
appreciation is he. I allude to Honoré Grandissime.

Ah! well do I remember the day when we returned —
he and me — from the France. She was there when we
landed on that levee, she was among that throng of kin-
dreds and domestiques, she shind like the evening star as
she stood there (it was the first time I saw her, but she
was known to him when at fifteen he left his home, but
I resided not under my own white father's roof — not at
all — far from that). She cried out '*A la fin to vini!*"
and leap herself with both resplendant arm around his neck
and kist him twice on the one cheek and the other, and
her resplendant eyes shining with a so great beauty.

If you will give me a *poudre d'amour* such as I doubt not
your great knowledge enable you to make of a power that
cannot to be resist, while still at the same time of a harmless character toward the life or the health of such that
I shall succeed in its use to gain the affections of that
emperice of my soul, I hesitate not to give you such price
as it may please you to nominate up as high as to $1,000
— nay, more. Sir, will you do that?

I have the honor to remain, sir,

Very respectfully, your obedient servant,

H. Grandissime.

Frowenfeld slowly transferred his gaze from the paper to his landlord's face. Dejection and hope struggled with each other in the gaze that was returned ; but when Joseph said, with a countenance full of pity, " I have no power to help you," the disappointed lover merely looked fixedly for a moment in the direction of the street, then lifted his hat toward his head, bowed, and departed.

CHAPTER XIX

ART AND COMMERCE

It was some two or three days after the interview just related that the apothecary of the rue Royale found it necessary to ask a friend to sit in the shop a few minutes while he should go on a short errand. He was kept away somewhat longer than he had intended to stay, for, as they were coming out of the cathedral, he met Aurora and Clotilde. Both the ladies greeted him with a cordiality which was almost inebriating, Aurora even extending her hand. He stood but a moment, responding blushingly to two or three trivial questions from her ; yet even in so short a time, and although Clotilde gave ear with the sweetest smiles and loveliest changes of countenance, he experienced a lively renewal of a conviction that this young lady was most unjustly harboring toward him a vague disrelish, if not a positive distrust. That she had some mental reservation was certain.

"'Sieur Frowenfel'," said Aurora, as he raised his hat for good-day, "you din come home yet."

He did not understand until he had crimsoned and answered he knew not what — something about having intended every day. He felt lifted he knew not where, Paradise opened, there was a flood of glory, and then he was alone; the ladies, leaving adieus sweeter than the perfume they carried away with them, floated into the south and were gone. Why was it that the elder, though plainly regarded by the younger with admiration, dependence, and overflowing affection, seemed sometimes to be, one might almost say, watched by her? He liked Aurora the better.

On his return to the shop his friend remarked that if he received many such visitors as the one who had called during his absence, he might be permitted to be vain. It was Honoré Grandissime, and he had left no message.

"Frowenfeld," said his friend, "it would pay you to employ a regular assistant."

Joseph was in an abstracted mood.

"I have some thought of doing so."

Unlucky slip! As he pushed open his door next morning, what was his dismay to find himself confronted by some forty men. Five of them leaped up from the door-sill, and some thirty-five from the edge of the *trottoir*, brushed that part of their wearing-apparel which always fits with great

neatness on a Creole, and trooped into the shop.
The apothecary fell behind his defences, that is to
say, his prescription desk, and explained to them in
a short and spirited address that he did not wish to
employ any of them on any terms. Nine-tenths
of them understood not a word of English; but
his gesture was unmistakable. They bowed grate-
fully, and said good-day.

Now Frowenfeld did these young men an injustice; and though they were far from letting him
know it, some of them felt it and interchanged
expressions of feeling reproachful to him as they
stopped on the next corner to watch a man painting
a sign. He had treated them as if they all wanted
situations. Was this so? Far from it. Only
twenty men were applicants; the other twenty were
friends who had come to see them get the place.
And again, though, as the apothecary had said,
none of them knew anything about the drug business — no, nor about any other business under the
heavens — they were all willing that he should teach
them — except one. A young man of patrician
softness and costly apparel tarried a moment after
the general exodus, and quickly concluded that on
Frowenfeld's account it was probably as well that
he could not qualify, since he was expecting from
France an important government appointment as
soon as these troubles should be settled and Louisiana restored to her former happy condition.
But he had a friend — a cousin — whom he would
recommend, just the man for the position; a

splendid fellow; popular, accomplished — what? the best trainer of dogs that M. Frowenfeld might ever hope to look upon; a "so good fisherman as I never saw!" — the marvel of the ball-room — could handle a partner of twice his weight; the speaker had seen him take a lady so tall that his head hardly came up to her bosom, whirl her in the waltz from right to left — this way! and then, as quick as lightning, turn and whirl her this way, from left to right — "so grezful ligue a peajohn! He could read and write, and knew more comig song!" — the speaker would hasten to secure him before he should take some other situation.

The wonderful waltzer never appeared upon the scene; yet Joseph made shift to get along, and by and by found a man who partially met his requirements. The way of it was this: With his forefinger in a book which he had been reading, he was one day pacing his shop floor in deep thought. There were two loose threads hanging from the web of incident weaving around him which ought to connect somewhere; but where? They were the two visits made to his shop by the young merchant, Honoré Grandissime. He stopped still to think; what "train of thought" could he have started in the mind of such a man?

He was about to resume his walk, when there came in, or more strictly speaking, there shot in, a young, auburn-curled, blue-eyed man, whose adolescent buoyancy, as much as his delicate, silver-buckled feet and clothes of perfect fit, pronounced him all-pure Creole. His name, when it was presently heard, accounted for the blond type by revealing a Franco-Celtic origin.

"'Sieur Frowenfel'," he said, advancing like a boy coming in after recess, " I 'ave somet'ing beauteeful to place into yo' window."

He wheeled half around as he spoke and seized from a naked black boy, who at that instant entered, a rectangular object enveloped in paper.

Frowenfeld's window was fast growing to be a place of art exposition. A pair of statuettes, a golden tobacco-box, a costly jewel-casket, or a pair of richly gemmed horse-pistols — the property of some ancient gentleman or dame of emaciated fortune, and which must be sold to keep up the bravery of good clothes and pomade that hid slow starvation — went into the shop-window of the ever-obliging apothecary, to be disposed of by *tombola*. And it is worthy of note in passing, concerning the moral education of one who proposed to make no conscious compromise with any sort of evil, that in this drivelling species of gambling he saw nothing hurtful or improper. But "in Frowenfeld's window" appeared also articles for simple sale or mere transient exhibition; as, for instance, the wonderful tapestries of a blind widow of ninety; tremulous little bunches of flowers, proudly stated to have been made entirely of the bones of the ordinary catfish; others, large and spreading, the sight of which would make any botanist fall down " and die as mad as the wild waves be," whose ticketed merit was that they were composed exclusively of materials produced upon Creole soil; a picture of the Ursulines' convent and chapel, done in forty-five minutes by a child of ten years, the daughter of the widow Felicie Grandissime; and the siege of Troy, in ordinary ink, done entirely with the pen, the labor of twenty years, by " a citizen of New Orleans." It was natural that these things should come to " Frowenfeld's corner," for there, oftener than elsewhere, the critics were gathered together. Ah! wonderful men, those critics; and, fortunately, we have a few still left.

The young man with auburn curls rested the edge of his burden upon the counter, tore away its wrappings and disclosed a painting.

He said nothing — with his mouth; but stood at arm's length balancing the painting and casting now upon it and now upon Joseph Frowenfeld a look more replete with triumph than Cæsar's three-worded dispatch.

The apothecary fixed upon it long and silently the gaze of a somnambulist. At length he spoke:

" What is it? "

" Louisiana rif-using to hanter de h-Union ! " replied the Creole, with an ecstasy that threatened to burst forth in hip-hurrahs.

Joseph said nothing, but silently wondered at Louisiana's anatomy.

" Gran' subjec' ! " said the Creole.

"Allegorical," replied the hard-pressed apothecary.

" Allegoricon? No, sir ! Allegoricon never saw

dat pigshoe. If you insist to know who make dat pigshoe — de hartis' stan' bif-ore you ! "

" It is your work ? "

" 'T is de work of me, Raoul Innerarity, cousin to de disting-wish Honoré Grandissime. I swear to you, sir, on stack of Bible' as 'igh as yo' head ! "

He smote his breast.

" Do you wish to put it in the window ? "

" Yes, seh."

" For sale ? "

M. Raoul Innerarity hesitated a moment before replying :

" 'Sieur Frowenfel', I think it is a foolishness to be too proud, eh ? I want you to say, ' My frien', 'Sieur Innerarity, never care to sell anything ; 't is for egs-hibby-shun' ; *mais* — when somebody look at it, so," the artist cast upon his work a look of languishing covetousness, " ' you say, *foudre tonnerre !* what de dev' ! — I take dat ris-pon-sibble-ty — you can have her for two hun'red fifty dollah ! ' Better not be too proud, eh, 'Sieur Frowenfel' ? "

" No, sir," said Joseph, proceeding to place it in the window, his new friend following him about spanielwise ; " but you had better let me say plainly that it is for sale."

" Oh — I don't care — *mais* — my rillation' will never forgive me ! *Mais* — go-ahead-I-don't-care ! 'T is for sale."

" ' Sieur Frowenfel'," he resumed, as they came away from the window, " one week ago " — he held up one finger — " what I was doing ? Makin' bill

of ladin', my faith! — for my cousin Honoré! an'
now, I ham a hartis'! So soon I foun' dat, I say,
'Cousin Honoré,'" — the eloquent speaker lifted
his foot and administered to the empty air a soft,
polite kick — "I never goin' to do anoder lick o'
work so long I live; adieu!"

He lifted a kiss from his lips and wafted it in the
direction of his cousin's office.

"Mr. Innerarity," exclaimed the apothecary, "I
fear you are making a great mistake."

"You tink I hass too much?"

"Well, sir, to be candid, I do; but that is not
your greatest mistake."

"What she's worse?"

The apothecary simultaneously smiled and
blushed.

"I would rather not say; it is a passably good
example of Creole art; there is but one way by
which it can ever be worth what you ask for it."

"What dat is?"

The smile faded and the blush deepened as
Frowenfeld replied:

"If it could become the means of reminding this
community that crude ability counts next to nothing
in art, and that nothing else in this world ought to
work so hard as genius, it would be worth thousands
of dollars!"

"You tink she is worse a t'ousand dollah?"
asked the Creole, shadow and sunshine chasing each
other across his face.

"No, sir."

The unwilling critic strove unnecessarily against his smile.

" Ow much you tink ? "

" Mr. Innerarity, as an exercise it is worth whatever truth or skill it has taught you ; to a judge of paintings it is ten dollars' worth of paint thrown away ; but as an article of sale it is worth what it will bring without misrepresentation."

" Two — hun-rade an' — fifty — dollahs or — not'in' ! " said the indignant Creole, clenching one fist, and with the other hand lifting his hat by the front corner and slapping it down upon the counter. " Ha, ha, ha ! a pase of waint — a wase of paint ! 'Sieur Frowenfel', you don' know not'in' 'bout it ! You har a jedge of painting ? " he added cautiously.

" No, sir."

" *Eh, bien! foudre tonnerre !* — look yeh ! you know ? 'Sieur Frowenfel' ? Dat de way de publique halways talk about a hartis's firs' pigshoe. But, I hass you to pardon me, Monsieur Frowenfel', if I 'ave speak a lill too warm."

" Then you must forgive me if, in my desire to set you right, I have spoken with too much liberty. I probably should have said only what I first intended to say, that unless you are a person of independent means ——— "

" You t'ink I would make bill of ladin' ? Ah ! Hm-m ! "

" ——— that you had made a mistake in throwing up your means of support ——— "

" But 'e 'as fill de place an' don' want me no mo'.

You want a clerk? — one what can speak fo' lang-widge — French, Eng-lish, Spanish, an' Italienne? Come! I work for you in de mawnin' an' paint in de evenin'; come!'"

Joseph was taken unaware. He smiled, frowned, passed his hand across his brow, noticed, for the first time since his delivery of the picture, the naked little boy standing against the edge of a door, said, " Why ——," and smiled again.

" I riffer you to my cousin Honoré," said Innerarity.

" Have you any knowledge of this business?"

" I 'ave."

" Can you keep shop in the forenoon or afternoon indifferently, as I may require?"

" Eh? Forenoon — afternoon?" was the reply.

" Can you paint sometimes in the morning and keep shop in the evening?"

" Yes, seh."

Minor details were arranged on the spot. Raoul dismissed the black boy, took off his coat and fell to work decanting something, with the understanding that his salary, a microscopic one, should begin from date if his cousin should recommend him.

" 'Sieur Frowenfel'," he called from under the counter, later in the day, " you t'ink it would be hanny disgrace to paint de pigshoe of a niggah?"

" Certainly not."

" Ah, my soul! what a pigshoe I could paint of Bras-Coupé!"

We have the afflatus in Louisiana, if nothing else.

CHAPTER XX

A VERY NATURAL MISTAKE

Mr. Raoul Innerarity proved a treasure. The fact became patent in a few hours. To a student of the community he was a key, a lamp, a lexicon, a microscope, a tabulated statement, a book of heraldry, a city directory, a glass of wine, a Book of Days, a pair of wings, a comic almanac, a diving bell, a Creole *veritas*. Before the day had had time to cool, his continual stream of words had done more to elucidate the mysteries in which his employer had begun to be befogged than half a year of the apothecary's slow and scrupulous guessing. It was like showing how to carve a strange fowl. The way he dovetailed story into story and drew forward in panoramic procession Lufki-Humma and Epaminondas Fusilier, Zephyr Grandissime and the lady of the *lettre de cachet*, Demosthenes De Grapion and the *fille à l'hôpital*, Georges De Grapion and the *fille à la cassette*, Numa Grandissime, father of the two Honorés, young Nancanou and old Agricola, — the way he made them

> " Knit hands and beat the ground
> In a light, fantastic round,"

would have shamed the skilled volubility of Sheharazade.

"Look!" said the story-teller, summing up; "you take hanny 'istory of France an' see the hage of my familie. Pipple talk about de Boulignys, de Sauvés, de Grandprès, de Lemoynes, de St. Maxents,—bla-a-a! De Grandissimes is as hole as de dev'! What? De mose of de Creole families is not so hold as plenty of my yallah kinfolks!"

The apothecary found very soon that a little salt improved M. Raoul's statements.

But here he was, a perfect treasure, and Frowenfeld, fleeing before his illimitable talking power in order to digest in seclusion the ancestral episodes of the Grandissimes and De Grapions, laid pleasant plans for the immediate future. To-morrow morning he would leave the shop in Raoul's care and call on M. Honoré Grandissime to advise with him concerning the retention of the born artist as a drugclerk. To-morrow evening he would pluck courage and force his large but bashful feet up to the door-step of Number 19 rue Bienville. And the next evening he would go and see what might be the matter with Doctor Keene, who had looked ill on last parting with the evening group that lounged in Frowenfeld's door, some three days before. The intermediate hours were to be devoted, of course, to the prescription desk and his "dead stock."

And yet after this order of movement had been thus compactly planned, there all the more seemed still to be that abroad which, now on this side, and now on that, was urging him in a nervous whisper to make haste. There had escaped into the air, it seemed, and was gliding about, the expectation of a crisis.

Such a feeling would have been natural enough to the tenants of Number 19 rue Bienville, now spending the tenth of the eighteen days of grace allowed them in which to save their little fortress. For Palmyre's assurance that the candle burning would certainly cause the rent-money to be forth-coming in time was to Clotilde unknown, and to Aurora it was poor stuff to make peace of mind of. But there was a degree of impracticability in these ladies, which, if it was unfortunate, was, nevertheless, a part of their Creole beauty, and made the absence of any really brilliant outlook what the galaxy makes a moonless sky. Perhaps they had not been as diligent as they might have been in canvassing all possible ways and means for meeting the pecuniary emergency so fast bearing down upon them. From a Creole standpoint, they were not bad managers. They could dress delightfully on an incredibly small outlay; could wear a well-to-do smile over an inward sigh of stifled hunger; could tell the parents of their one or two scholars to consult their conve-nience, and then come home to a table that would make any kind soul weep; but as to estimating the velocity of bills-payable in their orbits, such trained sagacity was not theirs. Their economy knew how to avoid what the Creole-African apothegm calls *commerce Man Lizon* — *qui asseté pou' trois picaillons et vend' pou' ein escalin* (bought for three picayunes and sold for two); but it was an economy that

made their very hound a Spartan; for, had that
economy been half as wise as it was heroic, his one
meal a day would not always have been the cook's
leavings of cold rice and the lickings of the gumbo
plates.

On the morning fixed by Joseph Frowenfeld for
calling on M. Grandissime, on the banquette of the
rue Toulouse, directly in front of an old Spanish
archway and opposite a blacksmith's shop, — this
blacksmith's shop stood between a jeweller's store
and a large, balconied and dormer-windowed wine-
warehouse — Aurore Nancanou, closely veiled, had
halted in a hesitating way and was inquiring of a
gigantic negro cartman the whereabouts of the
counting-room of M. Honoré Grandissime.

Before he could respond she descried the name
upon a staircase within the archway, and, thanking
the cartman as she would have thanked a prince,
hastened to ascend. An inspiring smell of warm
rusks, coming from a bakery in the paved court
below, rushed through the archway and up the stair
and accompanied her into the cemetery-like silence
of the counting-room. There were in the depart-
ment some fourteen clerks. It was a den of Grandissimes. More than half of them were men
beyond middle life, and some were yet older. One
or two were so handsome, under their noble silvery
locks, that almost any woman — Clotilde, for instance, — would have thought, "No doubt that
one, or that one, is the head of the house." Aurora
approached the railing which shut in the silent

toilers and directed her eyes to the farthest corner
of the room. There sat there at a large desk a
thin, sickly-looking man with very sore eyes and
two pairs of spectacles, plying a quill with a privi-
leged loudness.

"H-h-m-m !" said she, very softly.

A young man laid down his rule and stepped to
the rail with a silent bow. His face showed a jaded
look. Night revelry, rather than care or years, had
wrinkled it; but his bow was high-bred.

"Madame,"—in an undertone.

"Monsieur, it is M. Grandissime whom I wish
to see," she said in French.

But the young man responded in English.

"You har one tenant, ent it?"

"Yes, seh."

"Zen eet ees M. De Brahmin zat you 'ave
to see."

"No, seh; M. Grandissime."

"M. Grandissime nevva see one tenant."

"I muz see M. Grandissime."

Aurora lifted her veil and laid it up on her
bonnet.

The clerk immediately crossed the floor to the
distant desk. The quill of the sore-eyed man
scratched louder — scratch, scratch — as though it
were trying to scratch under the door of Number
19 rue Bienville — for a moment, and then ceased.
The clerk, with one hand behind him and one
touching the desk, murmured a few words, to which
the other, after glancing under his arm at Aurora,

gave a short, low reply and resumed his pen. The
clerk returned, came through a gateway in the railing, led the way into a rich inner room, and turning
with another courtly bow, handed her a cushioned
armchair and retired.

"After eighteen years," thought Aurora, as she
found herself alone. It had been eighteen years
since any representative of the De Grapion line had
met a Grandissime face to face, so far as she knew;
even that representative was only her deceased husband, a mere connection by marriage. How many
years it was since her grandfather, Georges De
Grapion, captain of dragoons, had had his fatal meeting with a Mandarin de Grandissime, she did not
remember. There, opposite her on the wall, was
the portrait of a young man in a corslet who might
have been M. Mandarin himself. She felt the
blood of her race growing warmer in her veins.
"Insolent tribe," she said, without speaking, "we
have no more men left to fight you; but now wait.
See what a woman can do."

These thoughts ran through her mind as her eye
passed from one object to another. Something
reminded her of Frowenfeld, and, with mingled
defiance at her inherited enemies and amusement
at the apothecary, she indulged in a quiet smile.
The smile was still there as her glance in its gradual sweep reached a small mirror.

She almost leaped from her seat.

Not because that mirror revealed a recess which
she had not previously noticed; not because be-

hind a costly desk therein sat a youngish man, reading a letter; not because he might have been observing her, for it was altogether likely that, to avoid premature interruption, he had avoided looking up; nor because this was evidently Honoré Grandissime; but because Honoré Grandissime, if this were he, was the same person whom she had seen only with his back turned in the pharmacy — the rider whose horse ten days ago had knocked her down, the Lieutenant of Dragoons who had unmasked and to whom she had unmasked at the ball! Fly! But where? How? It was too late; she had not even time to lower her veil. M. Grandissime looked up at the glass, dropped the letter with a slight start of consternation and advanced quickly toward her. For an instant her embarrassment showed itself in a mantling blush and a distressful yearning to escape; but the next moment she rose, all a-flutter within, it is true, but with a face as nearly sedate as the inborn witchery of her eyes would allow.

He spoke in Parisian French:

"Please be seated, madame."

She sank down.

"Do you wish to see me?"

"No, sir."

She did not see her way out of this falsehood, but — she couldn't say yes.

Silence followed.

"Whom do —— "

"I wish to see M. Honoré Grandissime."

" That is my name, madame."

" Ah ! " — with an angelic smile ; she had collected her wits now, and was ready for war. " You
are not one of his clerks ? "

M. Grandissime smiled softly, while he said to
himself : " You little honey-bee, you want to sting
me, eh ? " and then he answered her question.

" No, madame ; I am the gentleman you are
looking for."

" The gentleman she was look — " her pride
resented the fact. " Me ! " — thought she — " I
am the lady whom, I have not a doubt, you have
been longing to meet ever since the ball ; " but her
look was unmoved gravity. She touched her handkerchief to her lips and handed him the rent notice.

" I received that from your office the Monday
before last."

There was a slight emphasis in the announcement
of the time ; it was the day of the run-over.

Honoré Grandissime, stopping with the rent-
notice only half unfolded, saw the advisability of
calling up all the resources of his sagacity and wit
in order to answer wisely ; and as they answered
his call a brighter nobility so overspread face and
person that Aurora inwardly exclaimed at it even
while she exulted in her thrust.

" Monday before last ? "

She slightly bowed.

" A serious misfortune befell me that day," said
M. Grandissime.

" Ah ? " replied the lady, raising her brows with

polite distress, " but you have entirely recovered, I suppose."

" It was I, madame, who that evening caused you a mortification for which I fear you will accept no apology."

" On the contrary," said Aurora, with an air of generous protestation, " it is I who should apologize; I fear I injured your horse."

M. Grandissime only smiled, and opening the rent-notice dropped his glance upon it while he said in a preoccupied tone :

" My horse is very well, I thank you."

But as he read the paper, his face assumed a serious air and he seemed to take an unnecessary length of time to reach the bottom of it.

" He is trying to think how he will get rid of me," thought Aurora; " he is making up some pretext with which to dismiss me, and when the tenth of March comes we shall be put into the street."

M. Grandissime extended the letter toward her, but she did not lift her hands.

" I beg to assure you, madame, I could never have permitted this notice to reach you from my office; I am not the Honoré Grandissime for whom this is signed."

Aurora smiled in a way to signify clearly that that was just the subterfuge she had been anticipating. Had she been at home she would have thrown herself, face downward, upon the bed; but she only smiled meditatively upward at the picture of an

East Indian harbor and made an unnecessary re-arrangement of her handkerchief under her folded hands.

"There are, you know," — began Honore, with a smile which changed the meaning to "You know very well there are" — "two Honoré Grandissimes. This one who sent you this letter is a man of color ——"

"Oh!" exclaimed Aurora, with a sudden malicious sparkle.

"If you will entrust this paper to me," said Honoré, quietly, "I will see him and do now engage that you shall have no further trouble about it. Of course, I do not mean that I will pay it, myself; I dare not offer to take such a liberty."

Then he felt that a warm impulse had carried him a step too far.

Aurora rose up with a refusal as firm as it was silent. She neither smiled nor scintillated now, but wore an expression of amiable practicality as she presently said, receiving back the rent-notice as she spoke:

"I thank you, sir, but it might seem strange to him to find his notice in the hands of a person who can claim no interest in the matter. I shall have to attend to it myself."

"Ah! little enchantress," thought her grave-faced listener, as he gave attention, "this, after all — ball and all — is the mood in which you look your very, very best" — a fact which nobody knew better than the enchantress herself.

He walked beside her toward the open door leading back into the counting-room, and the dozen or more clerks, who, each by some ingenuity of his own, managed to secure a glimpse of them, could not fail to feel that they had never before seen quite so fair a couple. But she dropped her veil, bowed M. Grandissime a polite "No farther," and passed out.

M. Grandissime walked once up and down his private office, gave the door a soft push with his foot and lighted a cigar.

The clerk who had before acted as usher came in and handed him a slip of paper with a name written on it. M. Grandissime folded it twice, gazed out the window, and finally nodded. The clerk disappeared, and Joseph Frowenfeld paused an instant in the door and then advanced, with a buoyant good-morning.

"Good-morning," responded M. Grandissime.

He smiled and extended his hand, yet there was a mechanical and preoccupied air that was not what Joseph felt justified in expecting.

"How can I serve you, Mr. Frhowenfeld?" asked the merchant, glancing through into the counting-room. His coldness was almost all in Joseph's imagination, but to the apothecary it seemed such that he was nearly induced to walk away without answering. However, he replied:

"A young man whom I have employed refers to you to recommend him."

"Yes, sir? Prhay, who is that?"

"Your cousin, I believe, Mr. Raoul Innerarity."

M. Grandissime gave a low, short laugh, and took two steps toward his desk.

"Rhaoul? Oh yes, I rhecommend Rhaoul to you. As an assistant in yo' sto'?—the best man you could find."

"Thank you, sir," said Joseph, coldly. "Good-morning!" he added turning to go.

"Mr. Frhowenfeld," said the other, "do you evva rhide?"

"I used to ride," replied the apothecary, turning, hat in hand, and wondering what such a question could mean.

"If I send a saddle-hoss to yo' do' on day aftah to-morrow evening at fo' o'clock, will you rhide out with me for-h about a hour-h and a half—just for a little pleasu'e?"

Joseph was yet more astonished than before. He hesitated, accepted the invitation, and once more said good-morning.

CHAPTER XXI

DOCTOR KEENE RECOVERS HIS BULLET

It early attracted the apothecary's notice, in observing the civilization around him, that it kept the flimsy false bottoms in its social errors only by incessant reiteration. As he re-entered the shop, dissatisfied with himself for accepting M. Grandissime's invitation to ride, he knew by the fervent words which he overheard from the lips of his employee that the f. m. c. had been making one of his reconnoisances, and possibly had ventured in to inquire for his tenant.

"I t'ink, me, dat hanny w'ite man is a gen'leman; but I don't care if a man are good like a h-angel, if 'e har not pu'e w'ite *'ow can* 'e be a gen'leman?"

Raoul's words were addressed to a man who, as he rose up and handed Frowenfeld a note, ratified the Creole's sentiment by a spurt of tobacco juice and an affirmative "Hm-m."

The note was a lead-pencil scrawl, without date.

DEAR JOE: Come and see me some time this evening. I am on my back in bed. Want your help in a little matter.   Yours,   KEENE.
I have found out who —— —— "

Frowenfeld pondered: "I have found out who —— —— " Ah! Doctor Keene had found out who stabbed Agricola.

Some delays occurred in the afternoon, but toward sunset the apothecary dressed and went out. From the doctor's bedside in the rue St. Louis, if not delayed beyond all expectation, he would proceed to visit the ladies at Number 19 rue Bienville. The air was growing cold and threatening bad weather.

He found the Doctor prostrate, wasted, hoarse, cross and almost too weak for speech. He could only whisper, as his friend approached his pillow:

" These vile lungs ! "

" Hemorrhage ? "

The invalid held up three small, freckled fingers.
Joseph dared not show pity in his gaze, but it
seemed savage not to express some feeling, so after
standing a moment he began to say :

" I am very sorry ———— "

" You need n't bother yourself ! " whispered the
doctor, who lay frowning upward. By and by he
whispered again.

Frowenfeld bent his ear, and the little man, so
merry when well, repeated, in a savage hiss :

" Sit down ! "

It was some time before he again broke the
silence.

" Tell you what I want — you to do — for me."

" Well, sir ———— "

" Hold on ! " gasped the invalid, shutting his
eyes with impatience,— " till I get through."

He lay a little while motionless, and then drew
from under his pillow a wallet, and from the wallet
a pistol-ball.

" Took that out — a badly neglected wound —
last day I saw you." Here a pause, an appalling
cough, and by and by a whisper : " Knew the bullet
in an instant." He smiled wearily. " Peculiar
size." He made a feeble motion. Frowenfeld
guessed the meaning of it and handed him a pistol
from a small table. The ball slipped softly home.
" Refused two hundred dollars — those pistols " —
with a sigh and closed eyes. By and by again —

— "Patient had smart fever — but it will be gone — time you get — there. Want you to — take care — t' I get up."

"But, Doctor ———"

The sick man turned away his face with a petulant frown; but presently, with an effort at self-control, brought it back and whispered:

"You mean you — not physician?"

"Yes."

"No. No more are half — doc's. You can do it. Simple gun-shot wound in the shoulder." A rest. "Pretty wound; ranges" — he gave up the effort to describe it. "You'll see it." Another rest. "You see — this matter has been kept quiet so far. I don't want any one — else to know — anything about it." He sighed audibly and looked as though he had gone to sleep, but whispered again, with his eyes closed — "'specially on culprit's own account."

Frowenfeld was silent: but the invalid was waiting for an answer, and, not getting it, stirred peevishly.

"Do you wish me to go to-night?" asked the apothecary.

"To-morrow morning. Will you ———?"

"Certainly, Doctor."

The invalid lay quite still for several minutes, looking steadily at his friend, and finally let a faint smile play about his mouth,— a wan reminder of his habitual roguery.

"Good boy," he whispered.

Frowenfeld rose and straightened the bedclothes,

took a few steps about the room, and finally returned. The Doctor's restless eye had followed him at every movement.

"You'll go?"

"Yes," replied the apothecary, hat in hand; "where is it?"

"Corner Bienville and Bourbon,— upper river corner,— yellow one-story house, door-steps on street. You know the house?"

"I think I do."

"Good-night. Here!— I wish you would send that black girl in here — as you go out — make me better fire — Joe!" the call was a ghostly whisper.

Frowenfeld paused in the door.

"You don't mind my — bad manners, Joe?"

The apothecary gave one of his infrequent smiles.

"No, Doctor."

He started toward Number 19 rue Bienville, but a light, cold sprinkle set in, and he turned back toward his shop. No sooner had the rain got him there than it stopped, as rain sometimes will do.

CHAPTER XXII

WARS WITHIN THE BREAST

The next morning came in frigid and gray. The unseasonable numerals which the meteorologist recorded in his tables might have provoked a super-

stitious lover of better weather to suppose that
Monsieur Danny, the head imp of discord, had
been among the aërial currents. The passionate
southern sky, looking down and seeing some six
thousand to seventy-five hundred of her favorite
children disconcerted and shivering, tried in vain,
for two hours, to smile upon them with a little
frozen sunshine, and finally burst into tears.

In thus giving way to despondency, it is sad to
say, the sky was closely imitating the simultaneous
behavior of Aurora Nancanou. Never was pretty
lady in cheerier mood than that in which she had
come home from Honoré's counting-room. Hard
would it be to find the material with which to build
again the castles-in-air that she founded upon two
or three little discoveries there made. Should she
tell them to Clotilde? Ah! and for what? No,
Clotilde was a dear daughter — ha! few women
were capable of having such a daughter as Clotilde;
but there were things about which she was entirely
too scrupulous. So, when she came in from that
errand profoundly satisfied that she would in future
hear no more about the rent than she might choose
to hear, she had been too shrewd to expose herself
to her daughter's catechising. She would save her
little revelations for disclosure when they might be
used to advantage. As she threw her bonnet upon
the bed, she exclaimed, in a tone of gentle and
wearied reproach :

"Why did you not remind me that M. Honoré
Grandissime, that precious somebody-great, has the

honor to rejoice in a quadroon half-brother of the same illustrious name? Why did you not remind me, eh?"

"Ah! and you know it as well as A, B, C," playfully retorted Clotilde.

"Well, guess which one is our landlord?"

"Which one?"

"*Ma foi!* how do *I* know? I had to wait a shameful long time to see *Monsieur le prince*, — just because I am a De Grapion, I know. When at last I saw him, he says, 'Madame, this is the other Honoré Grandissime.' There, you see we are the victims of a conspiracy; if I go to the other, he will send me back to the first. But, Clotilde, my darling," cried the beautiful speaker, beamingly, "dismiss all fear and care; we shall have no more trouble about it."

"And how, indeed, do you know that?"

"Something tells it to me in my ear. I feel it! Trust in Providence, my child. Look at me, how happy I am; but you — you never trust in Providence. That is why we have so much trouble, — because you don't trust in Providence. Oh! I am so hungry, let us have dinner."

"What sort of a person is M. Grandissime in his appearance?" asked Clotilde, over their feeble excuse for a dinner.

"What sort? Do you imagine I had nothing better to do than notice whether a Grandissime is good-looking or not? For all I know to the contrary, he is —— some more rice, please, my dear."

But this light-heartedness did not last long. It was based on an unutterable secret, all her own, about which she still had trembling doubts; this, too, notwithstanding her consultation of the dark oracles. She was going to stop that. In the long run, these charms and spells themselves bring bad luck. Moreover, the practice, indulged in to excess, was wicked, and she had promised Clotilde, — that droll little saint, — to resort to them no more. Hereafter, she should do nothing of the sort, except, to be sure, to take such ordinary precautions against misfortune as casting upon the floor a little of whatever she might be eating or drinking to propitiate M. Assonquer. She would have liked, could she have done it without fear of detection, to pour upon the front door-sill an oblation of beer sweetened with black molasses to Papa Lébat (who keeps the invisible keys of all the doors that admit suitors), but she dared not; and then, the hound would surely have licked it up. Ah me! was she forgetting that she was a widow?

She was in poor plight to meet the all but icy gray morning; and, to make her misery still greater, she found, on dressing, that an accident had overtaken her, which she knew to be a trustworthy sign of love grown cold. She had lost — alas! how can we communicate it in English! — a small piece of lute-string ribbon, about *so long*, which she used for — not a necktie exactly, but ——

And she hunted and hunted, and could n't bear to give up the search, and sat down to breakfast and ate nothing, and rose up and searched again (not that she cared for the omen), and struck the hound with the broom, and broke the broom, and hunted again, and looked out the front window, and saw the rain beginning to fall, and dropped into a chair — crying, "Oh! Clotilde, my child, my child! the rent collector will be here Saturday and turn us into the street!" and so fell a-weeping.

A little tear-letting lightened her unrevealable burden, and she rose, rejoicing that Clotilde had happened to be out of eye-and-ear-shot. The scanty fire in the fireplace was ample to warm the room; the fire within her made it too insufferably hot! Rain or no rain, she parted the window-curtains and lifted the sash. What a mark for Love's arrow she was, as, at the window, she stretched her two arms upward! And, "right so," who should chance to come cantering by, the big drops of rain pattering after him, but the knightliest man in that old town, and the fittest to perfect the fine old-fashioned poetry of the scene!

"Clotilde," said Aurora, turning from her mirror, whither she had hastened to see if her face showed signs of tears (Clotilde was entering the room), "we shall never be turned out of this house by Honoré Grandissime!"

"Why?" asked Clotilde, stopping short in the floor, forgetting Aurora's trust in Providence, and expecting to hear that M. Grandissime had been found dead in his bed.

"Because I saw him just now; he rode by on

horseback.   A man with that noble face could never *do such a thing !* "

The astonished Clotilde looked at her mother searchingly.   This sort of speech about a Grandissime?   But Aurora was the picture of innocence.

Clotilde uttered a derisive laugh.

" *Impertinente !* " exclaimed the other, laboring not to join in it.

" Ah-h-h ! " cried Clotilde, in the same mood, " and what face had he when he wrote that letter ? "

" What face ? "

" Yes, what face ? "

" I do not know what face you mean," said Aurora.

" What face," repeated Clotilde, " had Monsieur Honoré de Grandissime on the day that he wrote —— "

" Ah, f-fah ! " cried Aurora, and turned away, " you don't know what you are talking about ! You make me wish sometimes that I were dead ! "

Clotilde had gone and shut down the sash, as it began to rain hard and blow.   As she was turning away, her eye was attracted by an object at a distance.

" What is it ? " asked Aurora, from a seat before the fire.

" Nothing," said Clotilde, weary of the sensational, — " a man in the rain."

It was the apothecary of the rue Royale, turning from that street toward the rue Bourbon, and bowing his head against the swirling norther.

CHAPTER XXIII

FROWENFELD KEEPS HIS APPOINTMENT

DOCTOR KEENE, his ill-humor slept off, lay in bed in a quiescent state of great mental enjoyment. At times he would smile and close his eyes, open them again and murmur to himself, and turn his head languidly and smile again.   And when the rain and wind, all tangled together, came against the window with a whirl and a slap, his smile broadened almost to laughter.

" He 's in it," he murmured, " he 's just reaching there.   I would give fifty dollars to see him when he first gets into the house and sees where he is."

As this wish was finding expression on the lips of the little sick man, Joseph Frowenfeld was making room on a narrow door-step for the outward opening of a pair of small batten doors, upon which he had knocked with the vigorous haste of a man in the rain.   As they parted, he hurriedly helped them open, darted within, heedless of the odd black shape which shuffled out of his way, wheeled and clapped them shut again, swung down the bar and then turned, and with the good-natured face that properly goes with a ducking, looked to see where he was.

One object — around which everything else instantly became nothing — set his gaze.   On the high bed, whose hangings of blue we have already described, silently regarding the intruder with a pair of eyes that sent an icy thrill through him and fastened him where he stood, lay Palmyre Philosophe. Her dress was a long, snowy morning-gown, wound loosely about at the waist with a cord and tassel of scarlet silk; a bright-colored woollen shawl covered her from the waist down, and a necklace of red coral heightened to its utmost her untamable beauty.

An instantaneous indignation against Doctor Keene set the face of the speechless apothecary on fire, and this, being as instantaneously comprehended by the philosophe, was the best of introductions. Yet her gaze did not change.

The Congo negress broke the spell with a bristling protest, all in African b's and k's, but hushed and drew off at a single word of command from her mistress.

In Frowenfeld's mind an angry determination was taking shape, to be neither trifled with nor contemned. And this again the quadroon discerned, before he was himself aware of it.

" Doctor Keene " —— he began, but stopped, so uncomfortable were her eyes.

She did not stir or reply.

Then he bethought him with a start, and took off his dripping hat.

At this a perceptible sparkle of imperious approval shot along her glance; it gave the apothecary speech.

" The doctor is sick, and he asked me to dress your wound."

She made the slightest discernible motion of the head, remained for a moment silent, and then, still with the same eye, motioned her hand toward a chair near a comfortable fire.

He sat down. It would be well to dry himself. He drew near the hearth and let his gaze fall into the fire. When he presently lifted his eyes and looked full upon the woman with a steady, candid glance, she was regarding him with apparent coldness, but with secret diligence and scrutiny, and a yet more inward and secret surprise and admiration. Hard rubbing was bringing out the grain of the apothecary. But she presently suppressed the feeling. She hated men.

But Frowenfeld, even while his eyes met hers, could not resent her hostility. This monument of the shame of two races — this poisonous blossom of crime growing out of crime — this final, unanswerable white man's accuser — this would-be murderess — what ranks and companies would have to stand up in the Great Day with her and answer as accessory before the fact ! He looked again into the fire.

The patient spoke :

" *Eh bi'n, Michê ?* " Her look was severe, but less aggressive. The shuffle of the old negress's feet was heard and she appeared bearing warm and cold water and fresh bandages ; after depositing them she tarried.

"Your fever is gone," said Frowenfeld, standing by the bed. He had laid his fingers on her wrist. She brushed them off and once more turned full upon him the cold hostility of her passionate eyes.

The apothecary, instead of blushing, turned pale. "You — " he was going to say, "You insult me;" but his lips came tightly together. Two big cords appeared between his brows, and his blue eyes spoke for him. Then, as the returning blood rushed even to his forehead, he said, speaking his words one by one;

"Please understand that you must trust me."

She may not have understood his English, but she comprehended, nevertheless. She looked up fixedly for a moment, then passively closed her eyes. Then she turned, and Frowenfeld put out one strong arm, helped her to a sitting posture on the side of the bed and drew the shawl about her.

"Zizi," she said, and the negress, who had stood perfectly still since depositing the water and bandages, came forward and proceeded to bare the philosophe's superb shoulder. As Frowenfeld again put forward his hand, she lifted her own as if to prevent him, but he kindly and firmly put it away and addressed himself with silent diligence to his task; and by the time he had finished, his womanly touch, his commanding gentleness, his easy despatch, had inspired Palmyre not only with a sense of safety, comfort, and repose, but with a pleased wonder.

This woman had stood all her life with dagger drawn, on the defensive against what certainly was to her an unmerciful world. With possibly one exception, the man now before her was the only one she had ever encountered whose speech and gesture were clearly keyed to that profound respect which is woman's first, foundation claim on man. And yet, by inexorable decree, she belonged to what we used to call " the happiest people under the sun." We ought to stop saying that.

So far as Palmyre knew, the entire masculine wing of the mighty and exalted race, three-fourths of whose blood bequeathed her none of its prerogatives, regarded her as legitimate prey. The man before her did not. There lay the fundamental difference that, in her sight, as soon as she discovered it, glorified him. Before this assurance the cold fierceness of her eyes gave way, and a friendlier light from them rewarded the apothecary's final touch. He called for more pillows, made a nest of them, and, as she let herself softly into it, directed his next consideration toward his hat and the door.

It was many an hour after he had backed out into the trivial remains of the rain-storm before he could replace with more tranquillizing images the vision of the philosophe reclining among her pillows, in the act of making that uneasy movement of her fingers upon the collar button of her robe, which women make when they are uncertain about the perfection of their dishabille, and giving her inaudible adieu with the majesty of an empress.

CHAPTER XXIV

FROWENFELD MAKES AN ARGUMENT

On the afternoon of the same day on which Frowenfeld visited the house of the philosophe, the weather, which had been so unfavorable to his late plans, changed; the rain ceased, the wind drew around to the south, and the barometer promised a clear sky. Wherefore he decided to leave his business, when he should have made his evening weather notes, to the care of M. Raoul Innerarity, and venture to test both Mademoiselle Clotilde's repellent attitude and Aurora's seeming cordiality at Number 19 rue Bienville.

Why he should go was a question which the apothecary felt himself but partially prepared to answer. What necessity called him, what good was to be effected, what was to happen next, were points he would have liked to be clear upon. That he should be going merely because he was invited to come — merely for the pleasure of breathing their atmosphere — that he should be supinely gravitating toward them — this conclusion he positively could not allow; no, no; the love of books and the fear of women alike protested.

True, they were a part of that book which is pronounced "the proper study of mankind," — indeed, that was probably the reason which he sought: he was going to contemplate them as a frontispiece to that unwriteable volume which he had undertaken to con. Also, there was a charitable motive. Doctor Keene, months before, had expressed a deep concern regarding their lack of protection and even of daily provision; he must quietly look into that. Would some unforeseen circumstance shut him off this evening again from this very proper use of time and opportunity?

As he was sitting at the table in his back room, registering his sunset observations, and wondering what would become of him if Aurora should be out and that other in, he was startled by a loud, deep voice exclaiming, close behind him:

" *Eh, bien! Monsieur le Professeur!* "

Frowenfeld knew by the tone, before he looked behind him, that he would find M. Agricola Fusilier very red in the face; and when he looked, the only qualification he could make was that the citizen's countenance was not so ruddy as the red handkerchief in which his arm was hanging.

" What have you there?" slowly continued the patriarch, taking his free hand off his fettered arm and laying it upon the page as Frowenfeld hurriedly rose, and endeavored to shut the book.

" Some private memoranda," answered the meteorologist, managing to get one page turned backward, reddening with confusion and indignation, and noticing that Agricola's spectacles were upside down.

" Private! Eh? No such thing, sir! Professor Frowenfeld, allow me " (a classic oath) " to say to your face, sir, that you are the most brilliant and the most valuable man — of your years — in afflicted Louisiana! Ha!" (reading:) "'Morning observation; Cathedral clock, 7 A. M. Thermometer 70 degrees.' Ha! 'Hygrometer 15' — but this is not to-day's weather? Ah! no. Ha! 'Barometer 30.380.' Ha! 'Sky cloudy, dark; wind, south, light.' Ha! 'River rising.' Ha! Professor Frowenfeld, when will you give your splendid services to your section? You must tell me, my son, for I ask you, my son, not from curiosity, but out of impatient interest."

"I cannot say that I shall ever publish my tables," replied the "son," pulling at the book.

"Then, sir, in the name of Louisiana," thundered the old man, clinging to the book, "I can! They shall be published! Ah! yes, dear Frowenfeld. The book, of course, will be in French, eh? You would not so affront the most sacred prejudices of the noble people to whom you owe everything as to publish it in English? You — ah! have we torn it?"

"I do not write French," said the apothecary, laying the torn edges together.

"Professor Frowenfeld, men are born for each other. What do I behold before me? I behold before me, in the person of my gifted young friend, a supplement to myself! Why has Nature strengthened the soul of Agricola to hold the crumbling fortress of this body until these eyes — which were once, my dear boy, as proud and piercing as the battle-steed's — have become dim?"

Joseph's insurmountable respect for gray hairs kept him standing, but he did not respond with any conjecture as to Nature's intentions, and there was a stern silence.

The crumbling fortress resumed, his voice pitched low like the beginning of the long roll.   He knew Nature's design.

" It was in order that you, Professor Frowenfeld, might become my vicar !   Your book shall be in French !   We must give it a wide scope !   It shall contain valuable geographical, topographical, biographical, and historical notes.   It shall contain complete lists of all the officials in the province (I don't say territory, I say province) with their salaries and perquisites ; ah ! we will expose that ! And — ha ! I will write some political essays for it. Raoul shall illustrate it.   Honoré shall give you money to publish it.   Ah !   Professor Frowenfeld, the star of your fame is rising out of the waves of oblivion !   Come — I dropped in purposely to ask you — come across the street and take a glass of *taffia* with Agricola Fusilier."

This crowning honor the apothecary was insane enough to decline, and Agricola went away with many professions of endearment, but secretly offended because Joseph had not asked about his wound.

All the same the apothecary, without loss of time, departed for the yellow-washed cottage, Number 19 rue Bienville.

" To-morrow, at four P. M.," he said to himself,

" if the weather is favorable, I ride with M. Grandissime."

He almost saw his books and instruments look up at him reproachfully.

The ladies were at home. Aurora herself opened the door, and Clotilde came forward from the bright fire-place with a cordiality never before so unqualified. There was something about these ladies — in their simple, but noble grace, in their half-Gallic, half-classic beauty, in a jocund buoyancy mated to an amiable dignity — that made them appear to the scholar as though they had just bounded into life from the garlanded procession of some old fresco. The resemblance was not a little helped on by the costume of the late Revolution (most acceptably chastened and belated by the distance from Paris). Their black hair, somewhat heavier on Clotilde's head, where it rippled once or twice, was knotted *en Grecque*, and adorned only with the spoils of a nosegay given to Clotilde by a chivalric small boy in the home of her music scholar.

" We was expectin' you since several days," said Clotilde, as the three sat down before the fire, Frowenfeld in a cushioned chair whose moth-holes had been carefully darned.

Frowenfeld intimated, with tolerable composure, that matters beyond his control had delayed his coming, beyond his intention.

"You gedd'n' ridge," said Aurora, dropping her wrists across each other.

Frowenfeld, for once, laughed outright, and it seemed so odd in him to do so that both the ladies followed his example. The ambition to be rich had never entered his thought, although in an unemotional, German way, he was prospering in a little city where wealth was daily pouring in, and a man had only to keep step, so to say, to march into possessions.

" You hought to 'ave a mo' larger sto' an' some clerque," pursued Aurora.

The apothecary answered that he was contemplating the enlargement of his present place or removal to a roomier, and that he had already employed an assistant.

" Oo it is, 'Sieur Frowenfel' ? "

Clotilde turned toward the questioner a remonstrative glance.

" His name," replied Frowenfeld, betraying a slight embarrassment, " is — Innerarity ; Mr. Raoul Innerarity ; he is —— "

" Ee pain' dad pigtu' w'at 'angin' in yo' window ? "

Clotilde's remonstrance rose to a slight movement and a murmur.

Frowenfeld answered in the affirmative, and possibly betrayed the faint shadow of a smile. The response was a peal of laughter from both ladies.

" He is an excellent drug clerk," said Frowenfeld defensively.

Whereat Aurora laughed again, leaning over and touching Clotilde's knee with one finger.

"An' excellen' drug cl' — ha, ha, ha ! oh ! "

"You muz podden uz, M'sieu' Frowenfel'," said Clotilde, with forced gravity.

Aurora sighed her participation in the apology; and, a few moments later, the apothecary and both ladies (the one as fond of the abstract as the other two were ignorant of the concrete) were engaged in an animated, running discussion on art, society, climate, education,— all those large, secondary *desiderata* which seem of first importance to young ambition and secluded beauty, flying to and fro among these subjects with all the liveliness and uncertainty of a game of pussy-wants-a-corner.

Frowenfeld had never before spent such an hour. At its expiration, he had so well held his own against both the others, that the three had settled down to this sort of entertainment: Aurora would make an assertion, or Clotilde would ask a question; and Frowenfeld, moved by that frankness and ardent zeal for truth which had enlisted the early friendship of Dr. Keene, amused and attracted Honoré Grandissime, won the confidence of the f. m. c., and tamed the fiery distrust and enmity of Palmyre, would present his opinions without the thought of a reservation either in himself or his hearers. On their part, they would sit in deep attention, shielding their faces from the fire, and responding to enunciations directly contrary to their convictions with an occasional "yes-seh," or "ceddenly," or "of coze," or,— prettier affirmation still,— a solemn drooping of the eyelids, a slight compression of the lips, and a low, slow declination of the head.

"The bane of all Creole art-effort" — (we take up the apothecary's words at a point where Clotilde was leaning forward and slightly frowning in an honest attempt to comprehend his condensed English) — "the bane of all Creole art-effort, so far as I have seen it, is amateurism."

"Amateu —" murmured Clotilde, a little beclouded on the main word and distracted by a French difference of meaning, but planting an elbow on one knee in the genuineness of her attention, and responding with a bow.

"That is to say," said Frowenfeld, apologizing for the homeliness of his further explanation by a smile, "a kind of ambitious indolence that lays very large eggs, but can neither see the necessity for building a nest beforehand, nor command the patience to hatch the eggs afterward."

"Of coze," said Aurora.

"It is a great pity," said the sermonizer, looking at the face of Clotilde, elongated in the brass and-iron; and, after a pause: "Nothing on earth can take the place of hard and patient labor. But that, in this community, is not esteemed; most sorts of it are contemned; the humbler sorts are despised, and the higher are regarded with mingled patronage and commiseration. Most of those who come to my shop with their efforts at art hasten to explain, either that they are merely seeking pastime, or else that they are driven to their course by want; and

if I advise them to take their work back and finish
it, they take it back and never return.   Industry is
not only despised, but has been degraded and disgraced, handed over into the hands of African
savages."

"Doze Creole' is *lezzy*," said Aurora.

"That is a hard word to apply to those who do
not *consciously* deserve it," said Frowenfeld; "but if
they could only wake up to the fact, — find it out
themselves —— "

"Ceddenly," said Clotilde.

"'Sieur Frowenfel'," said Aurora, leaning her
head on one side, "some pipple thing it is doze
climade; 'ow you lag doze climade?"

"I do not suppose," replied the visitor, "there
is a more delightful climate in the world."

"Ah-h-h!" — both ladies at once, in a low, gracious tone of acknowledgment.

"I thing Louisiana is a paradize-me!" said
Aurora.   "W'ere you goin' fin' sudge a h-air?"
She respired a sample of it.   "W'ere you goin' fin'
sudge a so ridge groun'?   De weed' in my bag yard
is twenny-five feet 'igh!"

"Ah! maman!"

"Twenty-six!" said Aurora, correcting herself.
"W'ere you fin' sudge a reever lag dad Mississippi?
On dit," she said, turning to Clotilde, "*que ses eaux
ont la propriété de contribuer même à multiplier l'espèce
humaine* — ha, ha, ha!"

Clotilde turned away an unmoved countenance to
hear Frowenfeld.

Frowenfeld had contracted a habit of falling into meditation whenever the French language left him out of the conversation.

"Yes," he said, breaking a contemplative pause, "the climate is *too* comfortable and the soil too rich, — though I do not think it is entirely on their account that the people who enjoy them are so sadly in arrears to the civilized world." He blushed with the fear that his talk was bookish, and felt grateful to Clotilde for seeming to understand his speech.

"W'ad you fin' de rizzon is, 'Sieur Frowenfel'?" she asked.

"I do not wish to philosophize," he answered.

"*Mais*, go hon." "*Mais*, go ahade," said both ladies, settling themselves.

"It is largely owing," exclaimed Frowenfeld, with sudden fervor, "to a defective organization of society, which keeps this community, and will continue to keep it for an indefinite time to come, entirely unprepared and disinclined to follow the course of modern thought."

"Of coze," murmured Aurora, who had lost her bearings almost at the first word.

"One great general subject of thought now is human rights, — universal human rights. The entire literature of the world is becoming tinctured with contradictions of the dogmas upon which society in this section is built. Human rights is, of all subjects, the one upon which this community is most violently determined to hear no discussion.

It has pronounced that slavery and caste are right, and sealed up the whole subject. What, then, will they do with the world's literature? They will coldly decline to look at it, and will become, more and more as the world moves on, a comparatively illiterate people."

"Bud, 'Sieur Frowenfel'," said Clotilde, as Frowenfeld paused — Aurora was stunned to silence, — "de Unitee State' goin' pud doze nigga' free, aind it?"

Frowenfeld pushed his hair hard back. He was in the stream now, and might as well go through.

"I have heard that charge made, even by some Americans. I do not know. But there is a slavery that no legislation can abolish, — the slavery of caste. That, like all the slaveries on earth, is a double bondage. And what a bondage it is which compels a community, in order to preserve its established tyrannies, to walk behind the rest of the intelligent world! What a bondage is that which incites a people to adopt a system of social and civil distinctions, possessing all the enormities and none of the advantages of those systems which Europe is learning to despise! This system, moreover, is only kept up by a flourish of weapons. We have here what you may call an armed aristocracy. The class over which these instruments of main force are held is chosen for its servility, ignorance, and cowardice; hence, indolence in the ruling class. When a man's social or civil standing is not dependent on his knowing how to read, he is not likely to become a scholar."

"Of coze," said Aurora, with a pensive respiration, "I thing id is doze climade," and the apothecary stopped, as a man should who finds himself unloading large philosophy in a little parlor.

"I thing, me, dey hought to pud doze quadroon' free?" It was Clotilde who spoke, ending with the rising inflection to indicate the tentative character of this daringly premature declaration.

Frowenfeld did not answer hastily.

"The quadroons," said he, "want a great deal more than mere free papers can secure them. Emancipation before the law, though it may be a right which man has no right to withhold, is to them little more than a mockery until they achieve emancipation in the minds and good will of the people — 'the people,' did I say? I mean the ruling class." He stopped again. One must inevitably feel a little silly, setting up tenpins for ladies who are too polite, even if able, to bowl them down.

Aurora and the visitor began to speak simultaneously; both apologized, and Aurora said:

"'Sieur Frowenfel', w'en I was a lill girl," — and Frowenfeld knew that he was going to hear the story of Palmyre. Clotilde moved, with the obvious intention to mend the fire. Aurora asked, in French, why she did not call the cook to do it, and Frowenfeld said, "Let me," — threw on some wood, and took a seat nearer Clotilde. Aurora had the floor.

CHAPTER XXV

AURORA AS A HISTORIAN

Alas! the phonograph was invented three-quarters of a century too late. If type could entrap one-half the pretty oddities of Aurora's speech, — the arch, the pathetic, the grave, the earnest, the matter-of-fact, the ecstatic tones of her voice, — nay, could it but reproduce the movement of her hands, the eloquence of her eyes, or the shapings of her mouth, — ah! but type — even the phonograph — is such an inadequate thing! Sometimes she laughed; sometimes Clotilde, unexpectedly to herself, joined her; and twice or thrice she provoked a similar demonstration from the ox-like apothecary, — to her own intense amusement. Sometimes she shook her head in solemn scorn; and, when Frowenfeld, at a certain point where Palmyre's fate locked hands for a time with that of Bras-Coupé, asked a fervid question concerning that strange personage, tears leaped into her eyes, as she said:

"Ah! 'Sieur Frowenfel', iv I tra to tell de sto'y of Bras-Coupé, I goin' to cry lag a lill bebby."

The account of the childhood days upon the plantation at Cannes Brulées may be passed by. It was early in Palmyre's fifteenth year that that Kentuckian, 'mutual friend' of her master and Agricola, prevailed with M. de Grapion to send her to the paternal Grandissime mansion, — a complimentary gift, through Agricola, to Mademoiselle, his niece, — returnable ten years after date.

The journey was made in safety; and, by and by, Palmyre was presented to her new mistress. The occasion was notable. In a great chair in the centre sat the *grandpère*, a Chevalier de Grandissime, whose business had narrowed down to sitting on the front veranda and wearing his decorations, — the cross of St. Louis being one; on his right, Colonel Numa Grandissime, with one arm dropped around Honoré, then a boy of Palmyre's age, expecting to be off in sixty days for France; and on the left, with Honoré's fair sister nestled against her, " Madame Numa," as the Creoles would call her, a stately woman and beautiful, a great admirer of her brother Agricola. (Aurora took pains to explain that she received these minutiæ from Palmyre herself in later years.) One other member of the group was a young don of some twenty years' age, not an inmate of the house, but only a cousin of Aurora on her deceased mother's side. To make the affair complete, and as a seal to this tacit Grandissime-de-Grapion treaty, this sole available representative of the " other side " was made a guest for the evening. Like the true Spaniard that he was, Don José Martinez fell deeply in love with Honoré's sister. Then there came Agricola leading in Palmyre. There were others, for the Grandissime mansion was always full of Grandissimes; but this was the central group.

In this house Palmyre grew to womanhood, retaining without interruption the place into which she seemed to enter by right of indisputable superiority over all competitors, — the place of favorite attendant to the sister of Honoré. Attendant, we say, for servant she never seemed. She grew tall, arrowy, lithe, imperial, diligent, neat, thorough, silent. Her new mistress, though scarcely at all her senior, was yet distinctly her mistress; she had that through her Fusilier blood; experience was just then beginning to show that the Fusilier Grandissime was a superb variety; she was a mistress one could wish to obey. Palmyre loved her, and through her contact ceased, for a time, at least, to be the pet leopard she had been at the Cannes Brulées.

Honoré went away to Paris only sixty days after Palmyre entered the house. But even that was not soon enough.

"'Sieur Frowenfel'," said Aurora, in her recital, "Palmyre, she never tole me dad, *mais* I am shoe, *shoe* dad she fall in love wid Honoré Grandissime. 'Sieur Frowenfel', I thing dad Honoré Grandissime is one bad man, ent it? Whad you thing, 'Sieur Frowenfel'?"

"I think, as I said to you the last time, that he is one of the best, as I know that he is one of the kindest and most enlightened gentlemen in the city," said the apothecary.

"Ah, 'Sieur Frowenfel'! ha, ha!"

"That is my conviction."

The lady went on with her story.

" Hanny'ow, I know she *con*tinue in love wid 'im all doze ten year' w'at 'e been gone.   She baig Mademoiselle Grandissime to wrad dad ledder to my papa to ass to kip her two years mo'."

Here Aurora carefully omitted that episode which Doctor Keene had related to Frowenfeld, — her own marriage and removal to Fausse Rivière, the visit of her husband to the city, his unfortunate and finally fatal affair with Agricola, and the surrender of all her land and slaves to that successful duellist.

M. de Grapion, through all that, stood by his engagement concerning Palmyre; and, at the end of ten years, to his own astonishment, responded favorably to a letter from Honoré's sister, irresistible for its goodness, good sense, and eloquent pleading, asking leave to detain Palmyre two years longer; but this response came only after the old master and his pretty, stricken Aurora had wept over it until they were weak and gentle, — and was not a response either, but only a silent consent.

Shortly before the return of Honoré — and here it was that Aurora took up again the thread of her account — while his mother, long-widowed, reigned in the paternal mansion, with Agricola for her manager, Bras-Coupé appeared.   From that advent, and the long and varied mental sufferings which its consequences brought upon her, sprang that second change in Palmyre, which made her finally untamable, and ended in a manumission, granted her more for fear than for conscience' sake.   When Aurora attempted to tell those experiences, even leaving Bras-Coupé as much as might be out of the recital, she choked with tears at the very start, stopped, laughed, and said:

"*C'est tout* — daz all. 'Sieur Frowenfel', oo you fine dad pigtu' to loog lag, yonnah, hon de wall?"

She spoke as if he might have overlooked it, though twenty times, at least, in the last hour, she had seen him glance at it.

"It is a good likeness," said the apothecary, turning to Clotilde, yet showing himself somewhat puzzled in the matter of the costume.

The ladies laughed.

"Daz ma grade-gran'-mamma," said Clotilde.

"Dass one *fille à la cassette*," said Aurora, "my gran'-muzzah; *mais*, ad de sem tam id is Clotilde." She touched her daughter under the chin with a ringed finger. "Clotilde is my gran'-mamma."

Frowenfeld rose to go.

"You muz come again, 'Sieur Frowenfel'," said both ladies, in a breath.

What could he say?

CHAPTER XXVI

A RIDE AND A RESCUE

"Douane or Bienville?"

Such was the choice presented by Honoré Grandissime to Joseph Frowenfeld, as the former on a lively brown colt and the apothecary on a nervy chestnut fell into a gentle, preliminary trot while yet in the rue Royale, looked after by that great admirer of both, Raoul Innerarity.

"Douane?" said Frowenfeld. (It was the street we call Custom-house.)

"It has mud-holes," objected Honoré.

"Well, then, the rue du Canal?"

"The canal — I can smell it from here. Why not rue Bienville?"

Frowenfeld said he did not know. (We give the statement for what it is worth.)

Notice their route. A spirit of perversity seems to have entered into the very topography of this quarter. They turned up the rue Bienville (up is toward the river); reaching the levee, they took their course up the shore of the Mississippi (almost due south), and broke into a lively gallop on the Tchoupitoulas road, which in those days skirted that margin of the river nearest the sunsetting, namely, the *eastern* bank.

Conversation moved sluggishly for a time, halting upon trite topics or swinging easily from polite inquiry to mild affirmation, and back again. They were men of thought, these two, and one of them did not fully understand why he was in his present position; hence some reticence. It was one of those afternoons in early March that make one wonder how the rest of the world avoids emigrating to Louisiana in a body.

"Is not the season early?" asked Frowenfeld.

M. Grandissime believed it was; but then the Creole spring always seemed so, he said.

The land was an inverted firmament of flowers. The birds were an innumerable, busy, joy-compelling multitude, darting and fluttering hither and thither, as one might imagine the babes do in heaven. The orange-groves were in blossom; their dark-green boughs seemed snowed upon from a cloud of incense, and a listening ear might catch an incessant, whispered trickle of falling petals, dropping "as the honey-comb." The magnolia was beginning to add to its dark and shining evergreen foliage frequent sprays of pale new leaves and long, slender, buff buds of others yet to come. The oaks, both the bare-armed and the "green-robed senators," the willows, and the plaqueminiers, were putting out their subdued florescence as if they smiled in grave participation with the laughing gardens. The homes that gave perfection to this beauty were those old, large, belvidered colonial villas, of which you may still here and there see one standing, battered into half ruin, high and broad, among foundries, cotton- and tobacco-sheds, junk-yards, and longshoremen's hovels, like one unconquered elephant in a wreck of artillery. In Frowenfeld's day the "smell of their garments was like Lebanon." They were seen by glimpses through chance openings in lofty hedges of Chero-kee-rose or bois-d'arc, under boughs of cedar or pride-of-China, above their groves of orange or down their long, overarched avenues of oleander; and the lemon and the pomegranate, the banana, the fig, the shaddock, and at times even the mango

and the guava, joined "hands around" and tossed
their fragrant locks above the lilies and roses.
Frowenfeld forgot to ask himself further concerning the probable intent of M. Grandissime's invitation to ride; these beauties seemed rich enough
in good reasons.   He felt glad and grateful.

At a certain point the two horses turned of their
own impulse, as by force of habit, and with a few
clambering strides mounted to the top of the levee
and stood still, facing the broad, dancing, hurrying,
brimming river.

The Creole stole an amused glance at the elated,
self-forgetful look of his immigrant friend.

"Mr. Frowenfeld," he said, as the delighted
apothecary turned with unwonted suddenness and
saw his smile, "I believe you like this better than
discussion.   You find it easier to be in harmony
with Louisiana than with Louisianians, eh?"

Frowenfeld colored with surprise.   Something
unpleasant had lately occurred in his shop.   Was
this to signify that M. Grandissime had heard of it?

"I am a Louisianian," replied he, as if this were
a point assailed.

"I would not insinuate otherwise," said M.
Grandissime, with a kindly gesture.   "I would like
you to feel so.   We are citizens now of a different
government from that under which we lived the
morning we first met.   Yet"—the Creole paused
and smiled—"you are not, and I am glad you are
not, what we call a Louisianian."

Frowenfeld's color increased.   He turned quickly

in his saddle as if to say something very positive, but hesitated, restrained himself and asked:

"Mr. Grandissime, is not your Creole 'we' a word that does much damage?"

The Creole's response was at first only a smile, followed by a thoughtful countenance; but he presently said, with some suddenness:

"My-de'-seh, yes. Yet you see I am, even this moment, forgetting we are not a separate people. Yes, our Creole 'we' does damage, and our Creole 'you' does more. I assure you, sir, I try hard to get my people to understand that it is time to stop calling those who come and add themselves to the community, aliens, interlopers, invaders. That is what I hear my cousins, 'Polyte and Sylvestre, in the heat of discussion, called you the other evening; is it so?"

"I brought it upon myself," said Frowenfeld. "I brought it upon myself."

"Ah!" interrupted M. Grandissime, with a broad smile, "excuse me — I am fully prepared to believe it. But the charge is a false one. I told them so. My-de'-seh — I know that a citizen of the United States in the United States has a right to become, and to be called, under the laws governing the case, a Louisianian, a Vermonter, or a Virginian, as it may suit his whim; and even if he should be found dishonest or dangerous, he has a right to be treated just exactly as we treat the knaves and ruffians who are native born! Every discreet man must admit that."

"But if they do not enforce it, Mr. Grandissime," quickly responded the sore apothecary, "if they continually forget it — if one must surrender himself to the errors and crimes of the community as he finds it —— "

The Creole uttered a low laugh.

"Party differences, Mr. Frowenfeld; they have them in all countries."

"So your cousins said," said Frowenfeld.

"And how did you answer them?"

"Offensively," said the apothecary, with sincere mortification.

"Oh! that was easy," replied the other, amusedly; "but how?"

"I said that, having here only such party differences as are common elsewhere, we do not behave as they elsewhere do; that in most civilized countries the immigrant is welcome, but here he is not. I am afraid I have not learned the art of courteous debate," said Frowenfeld, with a smile of apology.

"'T is a great art," said the Creole, quietly, stroking his horse's neck. "I suppose my cousins denied your statement with indignation, eh?"

"Yes; they said the honest immigrant is always welcome."

"Well, do you not find that true?"

"But, Mr. Grandissime, that is requiring the immigrant to prove his innocence!" Frowenfeld spoke from the heart. "And even the honest immigrant is welcome only when he leaves his peculiar opinions behind him.   Is that right, sir?"

The Creole smiled at Frowenfeld's heat.

"My-de'-seh, my cousins complain that you advocate measures fatal to the prevailing order of society."

"But," replied the unyielding Frowenfeld, turning redder than ever, "that is the very thing that American liberty gives me the right — peaceably — to do!   Here is a structure of society defective, dangerous, erected on views of human relations which the world is abandoning as false; yet the immigrant's welcome is modified with the warning not to touch these false foundations with one of his fingers."

"Did you tell my cousins the foundations of society here are false?"

"I regret to say I did, very abruptly.   I told them they were privately aware of the fact."

"You may say," said the ever-amiable Creole, "that you allowed debate to run into controversy, eh?"

Frowenfeld was silent; he compared the gentleness of this Creole's rebukes with the asperity of his advocacy of right, and felt humiliated.   But M. Grandissime spoke with a rallying smile.

"Mr. Frowenfeld, you never make pills with eight corners eh?"

"No, sir."   The apothecary smiled.

"No, you make them round; cannot you make your doctrines the same way?   My-de'-seh, you will think me impertinent; but the reason I speak is because I wish very much that you and my cousins would not be offended with each other. To tell you the truth, my-de'-seh, I hoped to use you with them — pardon my frankness."

"If Louisiana had more men like you, M. Grandissime," cried the untrained Frowenfeld, "society would be less sore to the touch."

"My-de'-seh," said the Creole, laying his hand out toward his companion and turning his horse in such a way as to turn the other also, "do me one favor; remember that it *is* sore to the touch."

The animals picked their steps down the inner face of the levee and resumed their course up the road at a walk.

"Did you see that man just turn the bend of the road, away yonder?" the Creole asked.

"Yes."

"Did you recognize him?"

"It was — my landlord, was n't it?"

"Yes. Did he not have a conversation with you lately, too?"

"Yes, sir; why do you ask?"

"It has had a bad effect on him. I wonder why he is out here on foot?"

The horses quickened their paces. The two friends rode along in silence. Frowenfeld noticed his companion frequently cast an eye up along the distant sunset shadows of the road with a new anxiety. Yet, when M. Grandissime broke the silence it was only to say:

"I suppose you find the blemishes in our state of society can all be attributed to one main defect, Mr. Frowenfeld ? "

Frowenfeld was glad of the chance to answer :

"I have not overlooked that this society has disadvantages as well as blemishes; it is distant from enlightened centres; it has a language and religion different from that of the great people of which it is now called to be a part. That it has also positive blemishes of organism ——"

"Yes," interrupted the Creole, smiling at the immigrant's sudden magnanimity, "its positive blemishes; do they all spring from one main defect ? "

"I think not. The climate has its influence, the soil has its influence — dwellers in swamps cannot be mountaineers."

"But after all," persisted the Creole, "the greater part of our troubles comes from ——"

"Slavery," said Frowenfeld, "or rather caste."

"Exactly," said M. Grandissime.

"You surprise me, sir," said the simple apothecary. "I supposed you were ——"

"My-de'-seh," exclaimed M. Grandissime, suddenly becoming very earnest, "I am nothing, nothing! There is where you have the advantage of me. I am but a *dilettante*, whether in politics, in philosophy, morals, or religion. I am afraid to go deeply into anything, lest it should make ruin in my name, my family, my property."

He laughed unpleasantly.

The question darted into Frowenfeld's mind, whether this might not be a hint of the matter that M. Grandissime had been trying to see him about.

"Mr. Grandissime," he said, "I can hardly believe you would neglect a duty either for family, property, or society."

"Well, you mistake," said the Creole, so coldly that Frowenfeld colored.

They galloped on. M. Grandissime brightened again, almost to the degree of vivacity. By and by they slackened to a slow trot and were silent. The gardens had been long left behind, and they were passing between continuous Cherokee-rose hedges on the right and on the left, along that bend of the Mississippi where its waters, glancing off three miles above from the old De Macarty levee (now Carrollton), at the slightest opposition in the breeze go whirling and leaping like a herd of dervishes across to the ever-crumbling shore, now marked by the little yellow depot-house of Westwego. Miles up the broad flood the sun was disappearing gorgeously. From their saddles, the two horsemen feasted on the scene without comment.

But presently, M. Grandissime uttered a low ejaculation and spurred his horse toward a tree hard by, preparing, as he went, to fasten his rein to an overhanging branch. Frowenfeld, agreeable to his beckon, imitated the movement.

"I fear he intends to drown himself," whispered M. Grandissime, as they hurriedly dismounted.

"Who? Not——"

" Yes, your landlord, as you call him. He is on the flatboat; I saw his hat over the levee. When we get on top the levee, we must get right into it. But do not follow him into the water in front of the flat; it is certain death; no power of man could keep you from going under it."

The words were quickly spoken; they scrambled to the levee's crown. Just abreast of them lay a flatboat, emptied of its cargo and moored to the levee. They leaped into it. A human figure swerved from the onset of the Creole and ran toward the bow of the boat, and in an instant more would have been in the river.

" Stop ! " said Frowenfeld, seizing the unresisting f. m. c. firmly by the collar.

Honoré Grandissime smiled, partly at the apothecary's brief speech, but much more at his success.

" Let him go, Mr. Frowenfeld," he said, as he came near.

The silent man turned away his face with a gesture of shame.

M. Grandissime, in a gentle voice, exchanged a few words with him, and he turned and walked away, gained the shore, descended the levee, and took a foot-path which soon hid him behind a hedge.

" He gives his pledge not to try again," said the Creole, as the two companions proceeded to resume the saddle. " Do not look after him." (Joseph had cast a searching look over the hedge.)

They turned homeward.

"Ah! Mr. Frowenfeld," said the Creole, suddenly, "if the *immygrant* has cause of complaint, how much more has *that* man! True, it is only love for which he would have just now drowned himself; yet what an accusation, my-de'-seh, is his whole life against that 'caste' which shuts him up within its narrow and almost solitary limits! And yet, Mr. Frowenfeld, this people esteem this very same crime of caste the holiest and most precious of their virtues. My-de'-seh, it never occurs to us that in this matter we are interested, and therefore disqualified, witnesses. We say we are not understood; that the jury (the civilized world) renders its decision without viewing the body; that we are judged from a distance. We forget that we ourselves are too *close* to see distinctly, and so continue, a spectacle to civilization, sitting in a horrible darkness, my-de'-seh!" He frowned.

"The shadow of the Ethiopian," said the grave apothecary.

M. Grandissime's quick gesture implied that Frowenfeld had said the very word.

"Ah! my-de'-seh, when I try sometimes to stand outside and look at it, I am *ama-aze* at the length, the blackness of that shadow!" (He was so deeply in earnest that he took no care of his English.) "It is the *Némésis* w'ich, instead of coming afteh, glides along by the side of this morhal, political, commercial, social mistake! It blanches, my-de'-seh, ow whole civilization! It drhags us a centurhy behind the rhes' of the world! It rhetahds and

poisons everhy industrhy we got! — mos' of all
our-h immense agrhicultu'e! It brheeds a thousan'
cusses that nevva leave home but jus' flutter-h up
an' rhoost, my-de'-seh, on ow *heads*; an' we nevva
know it! — yes, sometimes some of us know it."

He changed the subject.

They had repassed the ruins of Fort St. Louis,
and were well within the precincts of the little city,
when, as they pulled up from a final gallop, mention
was made of Doctor Keene. He was improving;
Honoré had seen him that morning; so, at another
hour, had Frowenfeld. Doctor Keene had told
Honoré about Palmyre's wound.

"You was at her house again this morning?"
asked the Creole.

"Yes," said Frowenfeld.

M. Grandissime shook his head warningly.

"'T is a dangerous business. You are almost
sure to become the object of slander. You ought
to tell Doctor Keene to make some other arrangement, or presently you, too, will be under the — "
he lowered his voice, for Frowenfeld was dismounting at the shop door, and three or four acquaintances stood around — "under the 'shadow of the
Ethiopian.'"

CHAPTER XXVII

THE FÊTE DE GRANDPÈRE

SOJOURNERS in New Orleans who take their afternoon drive down Esplanade street will notice, across
on the right, between it and that sorry streak once
fondly known as Champs Élysées, two or three
large, old houses, rising above the general surroundings and displaying architectural features which
identify them with an irrevocable past — a past
when the faithful and true Creole could, without
fear of contradiction, express his religious belief that
the antipathy he felt for the Américain invader was
an inborn horror laid lengthwise in his ante-natal
bones by a discriminating and appreciative Providence.   There is, for instance, or was until lately,
one house which some hundred and fifteen years
ago was the suburban residence of the old sea-captain
governor, Kerlerec.   It stands up among the
oranges as silent and gray as a pelican, and, so far
as we know, has never had one cypress plank added
or subtracted since its master was called to France
and thrown into the Bastile.   Another has two
dormer windows looking out westward, and, when
the setting sun strikes the panes, reminds one of a
man with spectacles standing up in an audience,
searching for a friend who is not there and will
never come back.   These houses are the last remaining — if, indeed, they were not pulled down

yesterday — of a group that once marked from afar
the direction of the old highway between the city's
walls and the suburb St. Jean. Here clustered the
earlier aristocracy of the colony ; all that pretty
crew of counts, chevaliers, marquises, colonels,
dons, etc., who loved their kings, and especially
their kings' moneys, with an *abandon* which affected
the accuracy of nearly all their accounts.

Among these stood the great mother-mansion of
the Grandissimes. Do not look for it now ; it is
quite gone. The round, white-plastered brick pil-
lars which held the house fifteen feet up from the
reeking ground and rose on loftily to sustain the
great overspreading roof, or clustered in the cool,
paved basement ; the lofty halls, with their multitudinous glitter of gilded brass and twinkle of sweet-
smelling wax-candles ;   the   immense   encircling
veranda, where twenty Creole girls might walk
abreast ; the great front stairs, descending from the
veranda to the garden, with a lofty palm on either
side, on whose broad steps forty Grandissimes could
gather on a birthday afternoon ; and the belvidere,
whence you could see the cathedral, the Ursulines',
the governor's mansion, and the river, far away,
shining between the villas of Tchoupitoulas Coast
— all have disappeared as entirely beyond recall as
the flowers that bloomed in the gardens on the day
of this *fête de grandpère.*

Odd to say, it was not the grandpère's birthday
that had passed. For weeks the happy children of
the many Grandissime branches — the Mandarins,

the St. Blancards, the Brahmins — had been standing with their uplifted arms apart, awaiting the signal
to clap hands and jump, and still, from week to
week, the appointed day had been made to fall back,
and fall back before — what think you ? — an inability to understand Honoré.

It was a sad paradox in the history of this majestic old house that her best child gave her the most
annoyance; but it had long been so. Even in
Honoré's early youth, a scant two years after she
had watched him, over the tops of her green myrtles
and white and crimson oleanders, go away, a lad of
fifteen, supposing he would of course come back a
Grandissime of the Grandissimes — an inflexible of
the inflexibles — he was found "inciting" (so the
stately dames and officials who graced her front
veranda called it) a Grandissime-De Grapion recon-
ciliation by means of transatlantic letters, and re-
ducing the flames of the old feud, rekindled by the
Fusilier-Nancanou duel, to a little foul smoke.
The main difficulty seemed to be that Honoré could
not be satisfied with a clean conscience as to his
own deeds and the peace and fellowships of single
households; his longing was, and had ever been —
he had inherited it from his father — to see one
unbroken and harmonious Grandissime family gathering yearly under this venerated roof without reproach before all persons, classes, and races with
whom they had ever had to do. It was not hard
for the old mansion to forgive him once or twice;
but she had had to do it often. It seems no over-

stretch of fancy to say she sometimes gazed down upon his erring ways with a look of patient sadness in her large and beautiful windows.

And how had that forbearance been rewarded? Take one short instance : when, seven years before this present *fête de grandpère*, he came back from Europe, and she (this old home which we cannot help but personify), though in trouble then — a trouble that sent up the old feud flames again — opened her halls to rejoice in him with the joy of all her gathered families, he presently said such strange things in favor of indiscriminate human freedom that for very shame's sake she hushed them up, in the fond hope that he would outgrow such heresies. But he? On top of all the rest, he declined a military commission and engaged in commerce — " shop-keeping, *parbleu !* "

However, therein was developed a grain of consolation. Honoré became — as he chose to call it — more prudent. With much tact, Agricola was amiably crowded off the dictator's chair, to become, instead, a sort of seneschal. For a time the family peace was perfect, and Honoré, by a touch here to-day and a word there to-morrow, was ever lifting the name, and all who bore it, a little and a little higher ; when suddenly, as in his father's day — that dear Numa who knew how to sacrifice his very soul, as a sort of Iphigenia for the propitiation of the family gods — as in Numa's day came the cession to Spain, so now fell this other cession, like an unexpected tornado, threatening the wreck of

her children's slave-schooners and the prostration
alike of their slave-made crops and their Spanish
liberties ; and just in the fateful moment where
Numa would have stood by her, Honoré had let
go.   Ah, it was bitter !

"See what foreign education does !" cried a
Mandarin de Grandissime of the Baton Rouge
Coast.   "I am sorry now" — derisively — "that
I never sent *my* boy to France, am I not ?   No !
No-o-o !   I would rather my son should never
know how to read, than that he should come back
from Paris repudiating the sentiments and prejudices of his own father.   Is education better than
family peace ?   Ah, bah !   My son make friends
with Américains and tell me they — that call a
negro 'monsieur' — are as good as his father ?
But that is what we get for letting Honoré become a merchant.   Ha ! the degradation !   Shaking hands with men who do not believe in the
slave trade !   Shake hands ?   Yes ; associate —
fraternize ! with apothecaries and negrophiles.   And
now we are invited to meet at the *fête de grandpère*, in the house where he is really the chief — the
caçique ! "

No !   The family would not come together on
the first appointment ; no, nor on the second ; no,
not if the grandpapa did express his wish ; no, nor
on the third — nor on the fourth.

"*Non, Messieurs* !" cried both youth and reckless
age ; and, sometimes, also, the stronger heads of
the family, the men of means, of force and of in-

fluence, urged on from behind by their proud and beautiful wives and daughters.

Arms, generally, rather than heads, ruled there in those days. Sentiments (which are the real laws) took shape in accordance with the poetry, rather than the reason, of things, and the community recognized the supreme domination of " the gentleman " in questions of right and of " the ladies " in matters of sentiment. Under such conditions strength establishes over weakness a showy protection which is the subtlest of tyrannies, yet which, in the very moment of extending its arm over woman, confers upon her a power which a truer freedom would only diminish ; constitutes her in a large degree an autocrat of public sentiment and thus accepts her narrowest prejudices and most belated errors as veriest need-be's of social life.

The clans classified easily into three groups ; there were those who boiled, those who stewed, and those who merely steamed under a close cover. The men in the first two groups were, for the most part, those who were holding office under old Spanish commissions, and were daily expecting themselves to be displaced and Louisiana thereby ruined. The steaming ones were a goodly fraction of the family — the timid, the apathetic, the " conservative." The conservatives found ease better than exactitude, the trouble of thinking great, the agony of deciding harrowing, and the alternative of smiling cynically and being liberal so much easier

— and the warm weather coming on with a rapidity wearying to contemplate.

" The Yankee was an inferior animal."

" Certainly."

" But Honoré had a right to his convictions."

" Yes, that was so, too."

" It looked very traitorous, however."

" Yes, so it did."

" Nevertheless, it might turn out that Honoré was advancing the true interests of his people."

" Very likely."

" It would not do to accept office under the Yankee government."

" Of course not."

" Yet it would never do to let the Yankees get the offices, either."

" That was true ; nobody could deny that."

" If Spain or France got the country back, they would certainly remember and reward those who had held out faithfully."

" Certainly ! That was an old habit with France and Spain."

" But if they did not get the country back —— "

" Yes, that is so; Honoré is a very good fellow, and —— "

And, one after another, under the mild coolness of Honoré's amiable disregard, their indignation trickled back from steam to water, and they went on drawing their stipends, some in Honoré's counting-room, where they held positions, some from the provisional government, which had as yet made but few changes, and some, secretly, from the cunning Casa-Calvo; for, blow the wind east or blow the wind west, the affinity of the average Grandissime for a salary abideth forever.

Then, at the right moment, Honoré made a single happy stroke, and even the hot Grandissimes, they of the interior parishes and they of Agricola's squadron, slaked and crumbled when he wrote each a letter saying that the governor was about to send them appointments, and that it would be well, if they wished to *evade* them, to write the governor at once, surrendering their present commissions. Well! Evade? They would evade nothing! Do you think they would so belittle themselves as to write to the usurper? They would submit to keep the positions first.

But the next move was Honoré's making the whole town aware of his apostasy. The great mansion, with the old grandpère sitting out in front, shivered. As we have seen, he had ridden through the Place d'Armes with the arch-usurper himself. Yet, after all, a Grandissime would be a Grandissime still; whatever he did he did openly. And wasn't that glorious — never to be ashamed of anything, no matter how bad? It was not everyone who could ride with the governor.

And blood was so much thicker than vinegar that the family, that would not meet either in January or February, met in the first week of March, every constituent one of them.

The feast has been eaten. The garden now is

joyous with children and the veranda resplendent
with ladies.   From among the latter the eye quickly
selects one.   She is perceptibly taller than the
others; she sits in their midst near the great hall
entrance; and as you look at her there is no claim
of ancestry the Grandissimes can make which you
would not allow.   Her hair, once black, now lifted
up into a glistening snow-drift, augments the
majesty of a still beautiful face, while her full stature and stately bearing suggest the finer parts of
Agricola, her brother.   It is Madame Grandissime,
the mother of Honoré.

One who sits at her left, and is very small, is a
favorite cousin.   On her right is her daughter, the
widowed señora of José Martinez; she has wonderful black hair and a white brow as wonderful.
The commanding carriage of the mother is tem-
pered in her to a gentle dignity and calm, contrasting pointedly with the animated manners of the
courtly matrons among whom she sits, and whose
continuous conversation takes this direction or
that, at the pleasure of Madame Grandissime.

But if you can command your powers of attention, despite those children who are shouting Creole
French and sliding down the rails of the front stair,
turn the eye to the laughing squadron of beautiful
girls, which every few minutes, at an end of the
veranda, appears, wheels and disappears, and you
note, as it were by flashes, the characteristics of
face and figure that mark the Louisianaises in the
perfection of the new-blown flower.   You see that

blondes are not impossible; there, indeed, are two sisters who might be undistinguishable twins but that one has blue eyes and golden hair. You note the exquisite pencilling of their eyebrows, here and there some heavier and more velvety, where a less vivacious expression betrays a share of Spanish blood. As Grandissimes, you mark their tendency to exceed the medium Creole stature, an appearance heightened by the fashion of their robes. There is scarcely a rose in all their cheeks, and a full red-ripeness of the lips would hardly be in keeping; but there is plenty of life in their eyes, which glance out between the curtains of their long lashes with a merry dancing that keeps time to the prattle of tongues. You are not able to get a straight look into them, and if you could you would see only your own image cast back in pitiful miniature; but you turn away and feel, as you fortify yourself with an inward smile, that they know you, you man, through and through, like a little song. And in turning, your sight is glad to rest again on the face of Honoré's mother. You see, this time, that she *is* his mother, by a charm you had overlooked, a candid, serene and lovable smile. It is the wonder of those who see that smile that she can ever be harsh.

The playful, mock-martial tread of the delicate Creole feet is all at once swallowed up by the sound of many heavier steps in the hall, and the fathers, grandfathers, sons, brothers, uncles and nephews of the great family come out, not a man of them

that cannot, with a little care, keep on his feet.
Their descendants of the present day sip from
shallower glasses and with less marked results.

The matrons, rising, offer the chief seat to the
first comer, the great-grandsire — the oldest living
Grandissime — Alcibiade, a shaken but unfallen
monument of early colonial days, a browned and
corrugated souvenir of De Vaudreuil's pomps, of
O'Reilly's iron rule, of Galvez' brilliant wars — a
man who had seen Bienville and Zephyr Grandissime.   With what splendor of manner Madame
Fusilier de Grandissime offers, and he accepts, the
place of honor!   Before he sits down he pauses
a moment to hear out the companion on whose
arm he had been leaning.   But Théophile, a dark,
graceful youth of eighteen, though he is recounting
something with all the oblivious ardor of his kind,
becomes instantly silent, bows with grave deference
to the ladies, hands the aged forefather gracefully to
his seat, and turning, recommences the recital before
one who hears all with the same perfect courtesy —
his beloved cousin Honoré.

Meanwhile, the gentlemen throng out.   Gallant
crew!   These are they who have been pausing
proudly week after week in an endeavor (?) to understand the opaque motives of Numa's son.

In the middle of the veranda pauses a tall, muscular man of fifty, with the usual smooth face and
an iron-gray queue.   That is Colonel Agamemnon
Brahmin de Grandissime, purveyor to the family's
military pride, conservator of its military glory,

and, after Honoré, the most admired of the name. Achille Grandissime, he who took Agricola away from Frowenfeld's shop in the carriage, essays to engage Agamemnon in conversation, and the colonel, with a glance at his kinsman's nether limbs and another at his own, and with that placid facility with which the graver sort of Creoles take up the trivial topics of the lighter, grapples the subject of boots. A tall, bronzed, slender young man, who prefixes to Grandissime the maternal St. Blancard, asks where his wife is, is answered from a distance, throws her a kiss and sits down on a step, with Jean Baptiste de Grandissime, a piratical-looking black-beard, above him, and Alphonse Mandarin, an olive-skinned boy, below. Valentine Grandissime, of Tchoupitoulas, goes quite down to the bottom of the steps and leans against the balustrade. He is a large, broad-shouldered, well-built man, and, as he stands smoking a cigar, with his black-stockinged legs crossed, he glances at the sky with the eye of a hunter—or, it may be, of a sailor.

"Valentine will not marry," says one of two ladies who lean over the rail of the veranda above. "I wonder why."

The other fixes on her a meaning look, and she twitches her shoulders and pouts, seeing she has asked a foolish question, the answer to which would only put Valentine in a numerous class and do him no credit.

Such were the choice spirits of the family. Agricola had retired. Raoul was there; his pretty auburn head might have been seen about half-way up the steps, close to one well sprinkled with premature gray.

" No such thing ! " exclaimed his companion.

(The conversation was entirely in Creole French.)

" I give you my sacred word of honor ! " cried Raoul.

" That Honoré is having all his business carried on in English ? " asked the incredulous Sylvestre. (Such was his name.)

" I swear — " replied Raoul, resorting to his favorite pledge — " on a stack of Bibles that high ! "

" Ah-h-h-h, pf-f-f-f-f ! "

This polite expression of unbelief was further emphasized by a spasmodic flirt of one hand, with the thumb pointed outward.

" Ask him ! ask him ! " cried Raoul.

" Honoré ! " called Sylvestre, rising up. Two or three persons passed the call around the corner of the veranda.

Honoré came with a chain of six girls on either arm. By the time he arrived, there was a Babel of discussion.

" Raoul says you have ordered all your books and accounts to be written in English," said Sylvestre.

" Well ? "

" It is not true, is it ? "

" Yes."

The entire veranda of ladies raised one long-

drawn, deprecatory " Ah ! " except Honoré's
mother. She turned upon him a look of silent
but intense and indignant disappointment.

" Honoré ! " cried Sylvestre, desirous of repairing
his defeat, " Honoré ! "

But Honoré was receiving the clamorous abuse
of the two half dozens of girls.

" Honoré ! " cried Sylvestre again, holding up a
torn scrap of writing-paper which bore the marks
of the counting-room floor and of a boot-heel,
" how do you spell ' la-dee ? ' "

There was a moment's hush to hear the answer.

" Ask Valentine," said Honoré.

Everybody laughed aloud. That taciturn man's
only retort was to survey the company above him
with an unmoved countenance, and to push the
ashes slowly from his cigar with his little finger.
M. Valentine Grandissime, of Tchoupitoulas, could
not read.

" Show it to Agricola," cried two or three, as
that great man came out upon the veranda, heavy-
eyed, and with tumbled hair.

Sylvestre, spying Agricola's head beyond the
ladies, put the question.

" How is it spelled on that paper ? " retorted the
king of beasts.

" L-a-y —— "

" Ignoramus ! " growled the old man.

" I did not spell it," cried Raoul, and attempted
to seize the paper. But Sylvestre throwing his
hand behind him, a lady snatched the paper, two

or three cried " Give it to Agricola ! " and a pretty
boy, whom the laughter and excitement had lured
from the garden, scampered up the steps and
handed it to the old man.

" Honoré ! " cried Raoul, " it must not be read.
It is one of your private matters."

But Raoul's insinuation that anybody would
entrust him with a private matter brought another
laugh.

Honoré nodded to his uncle to read it out,
and those who could not understand English, as
well as those who could, listened. It was a paper
Sylvestre had picked out of a waste-basket on the
day of Aurore's visit to the counting-room. Agricola read :

" What is that layde want in thare with Honoré ? "

" Honoré is goin giv her bac that proprety — that is
Aurore De Grapion what Agricola kill the husband."

That was the whole writing, but Agricola never
finished. He was reading aloud — " that is Aurore
De Grap ——— "

At that moment he dropped the paper and
blackened with wrath ; a sharp flash of astonishment ran through the company ; an instant of
silence followed and Agricola's thundering voice
rolled down upon Sylvestre in a succession of
terrible imprecations.

It was painful to see the young man's face as,
speechless, he received this abuse. He stood pale
and frightened, with a smile playing about his

mouth, half of distress and half of defiance, that said as plain as a smile could say, "Uncle Agricola, you will have to pay for this mistake."

As the old man ceased, Sylvestre turned and cast a look downward to Valentine Grandissime, then walked up the steps, and passing with a courteous bow through the group that surrounded Agricola, went into the house. Valentine looked at the zenith, then at his shoe-buckles, tossed his cigar quietly into the grass and passed around a corner of the house to meet Sylvestre in the rear.

Honoré had already nodded to his uncle to come aside with him, and Agricola had done so. The rest of the company, save a few male figures down in the garden, after some feeble efforts to keep up their spirits on the veranda, remarked the growing coolness or the waning daylight, and singly or in pairs withdrew. It was not long before Raoul, who had come up upon the veranda, was left alone. He seemed to wait for something, as, leaning over the rail while the stars came out, he sang to himself, in a soft undertone, a snatch of a Creole song:

> " La pluie — la pluie tombait,
>   Crapaud criait,
>   Moustique chantait —— "

The moon shone so brightly that the children in the garden did not break off their hide-and-seek, and now and then Raoul suspended the murmur of his song, absorbed in the fate of some little elf gliding from one black shadow to crouch in another.

He was himself in the deep shade of a magnolia,
over whose outer boughs the moonlight was trick-
ling, as if the whole tree had been dipped in
quicksilver.

In the broad walk running down to the garden
gate some six or seven dark forms sat in chairs, not
too far away for the light of their cigars to be
occasionally seen and their voices to reach his ear;
but he did not listen.   In a little while there came
a light footstep, and a soft, mock-startled " Who is
that ? " and one of that same sparkling group of
girls that had lately hung upon Honoré came so
close to Raoul, in her attempt to discern his linea-
ments, that their lips accidentally met.   They had
but a moment of hand-in-hand converse before
they were hustled forth by a feminine scouting
party and thrust along into one of the great rooms
of the house, where the youth and beauty of the
Grandissimes were gathered in an expansive semicircle around a languishing fire, waiting to hear a
story, or a song, or both, or half a dozen of each,
from that master of narrative and melody, Raoul
Innerarity.

" But mark," they cried unitedly, " you have got
to wind up with the story of Bras-Coupé ! "

" A song ! A song ! "

" *Une chanson Créole ! Une chanson des nègres !* "

" Sing ' yé tolé dancé la doung y doung doung ! ' "
cried a black-eyed girl.

Raoul explained that it had too many objectionable phrases.

"Oh, just hum the objectionable phrases and go right on."

But instead he sang them this:

> " *La prémier' fois mo té 'oir li,*
> *Li té posé au bord so lit ;*
> *Mo di', Bouzon, bel n'amourèse !*
> *L'aut' fois li té si' so la saise*
> *Comme viê Madam dans so fauteil,*
> *Quand li vivé côté soleil.*
>
> *So giés yé té plis noir passé la nouitte,*
> *So dé la lev' plis doux passe la quitte !*
> *Tou' mo la vie, zamein mo oir*
> *Ein n'amourèse zoli comme ça !*
>   *Mo' bliê manzé — mo' bliê boir' —*
>   *Mo' bliê tout dipi ç' temps-là —*
>   *Mo' bliê parlé — mo' bliê dormi,*
>   *Quand mo pensé aprés zami !* "

"And you have heard Bras-Coupé sing that, yourself?"

"Once upon a time," said Raoul, warming with his subject, "we were coming down from Pointe Macarty in three pirogues. We had been three days fishing and hunting in Lake Salvador. Bras-Coupé had one pirogue with six paddles —— "

"Oh, yes!" cried a youth named Baltazar; "sing that, Raoul!"

And he sang that.

"But oh, Raoul, sing that song the negroes sing when they go out in the bayous at night, stealing pigs and chickens!"

"That boat song, do you mean, which they sing as a signal to those on shore?"   He hummed.

"Dé zabs, dé zabs, dé counou ouaïe ouaïe,
    Dé zabs, dé zabs, dé counou ouaïe ouaïe,
    Counou ouaïe ouaïe ouaïe ouaïe,
    Counou ouaïe ouaïe ouaïe ouaïe,
    Counou ouaïe, ouaïe ouaïe, momza ;
    Momza, momza, momza, momza,
    Roza, roza, roza-et — momza."

This was followed by another and still another, until the hour began to grow late.   And then they gathered closer around him and heard the promised story.   At the same hour Honoré Grandissime, wrapping himself in a greatcoat and giving himself up to sad and somewhat bitter reflections, had wandered from the paternal house, and by and by from the grounds, not knowing why or whither, but after a time soliciting, at Frowenfeld's closing door, the favor of his company.   He had been feeling a kind of suffocation.   This it was that made him seek and prize the presence and hand-grasp of the inexperienced apothecary. He led him out to the edge of the river. Here they sat down, and with a laborious attempt at a hard and jesting mood, Honoré told the same dark story.

CHAPTER XXVIII

THE STORY OF BRAS-COUPÉ

"A very little more than eight years ago," began Honoré — but not only Honoré, but Raoul also; and not only they, but another, earlier on the same day, — Honoré, the f. m. c. But we shall not exactly follow the words of any one of these.

Bras-Coupé, they said, had been, in Africa and under another name, a prince among his people. In a certain war of conquest, to which he had been driven by *ennui*, he was captured, stripped of his royalty, marched down upon the beach of the Atlantic, and, attired as a true son of Adam, with two goodly arms intact, became a commodity. Passing out of first hands in barter for a looking-glass, he was shipped in good order and condition on board the good schooner *Égalité*, whereof Blank was master, to be delivered without delay at the port of Nouvelle Orléans (the dangers of fire and navigation excepted), unto Blank Blank. In witness whereof, He that made men's skins of different colors, but all blood of one, hath entered the same upon His book, and sealed it to the day of judgment.

Of the voyage little is recorded — here below; the less the better. Part of the living merchandise failed to keep; the weather was rough, the cargo large, the vessel small. However, the captain discovered there was room over the side, and there — all flesh is grass — from time to time during the voyage he jettisoned the unmerchantable.

Yet, when the reopened hatches let in the sweet smell of the land, Bras-Coupé had come to the upper — the favored — the buttered side of the world; the anchor slid with a rumble of relief down through the muddy fathoms of the Mississippi, and the prince could hear through the schooner's side the savage current of the river, leaping and licking about the bows, and whimpering low welcomes home. A splendid picture to the eyes of the royal captive, as his head came up out of the hatchway, was the little Franco-Spanish-American city that lay on the low, brimming bank. There were little forts that showed their whitewashed teeth; there was a green parade-ground, and yellow barracks, and cabildo, and hospital, and cavalry stables, and custom-house, and a most inviting jail, convenient to the cathedral — all of dazzling white and yellow, with a black stripe marking the track of the conflagration of 1794, and here and there among the low roofs a lofty one with round-topped dormer windows and a breezy belvidere looking out upon the plantations of coffee and indigo beyond the town.

When Bras-Coupé staggered ashore, he stood but a moment among a drove of "likely boys," before Agricola Fusilier, managing the business adventures of the Grandissime estate, as well as the residents thereon, and struck with admiration for the physical beauties of the chieftain (a man may even fancy a negro—as a negro), bought the lot, and, loth to resell him with the rest to some unappreciative 'Cadian, induced Don José Martinez' overseer to become his purchaser.

Down in the rich parish of St. Bernard (whose boundary line now touches that of the distended city) lay the plantation, known before Bras-Coupé passed away as La Renaissance. Here it was that he entered at once upon a chapter of agreeable surprises. He was humanely met, presented with a clean garment, lifted into a cart drawn by oxen, taken to a whitewashed cabin of logs, finer than his palace at home, and made to comprehend that it was a free gift. He was also given some clean food, whereupon he fell sick. At home it would have been the part of piety for the magnate next the throne to launch him heavenward at once; but now, healing doses were administered, and to his amazement he recovered. It reminded him that he was no longer king.

His name, he replied to an inquiry touching that subject, was —— ——, something in the Jaloff tongue, which he by and by condescended to render into Congo: Mioko-Koanga; in French Bras-Coupé; the Arm Cut Off. Truly it would have been easy to admit, had this been his meaning, that his tribe, in losing him, had lost its strong right arm close off at the shoulder; not so easy for his high-paying purchaser to allow, if this other was his intent: that the arm which might no longer shake the spear or swing the wooden sword was no better than a useless stump never to be lifted for aught else. But whether easy to allow or not, that was his meaning. He made himself a type of all Slavery, turning into flesh and blood the truth that all Slavery is maiming.

He beheld more luxury in a week than all his subjects had seen in a century. Here Congo girls were dressed in cottons and flannels worth, where he came from, an elephant's tusk apiece. Everybody wore clothes — children and lads alone excepted. Not a lion had invaded the settlement since his immigration. The serpents were as nothing; an occasional one coming up through the floor — that was all. True, there was more emaciation than unassisted conjecture could explain — a profusion of enlarged joints and diminished muscles, which, thank God, was even then confined to a narrow section and disappeared with Spanish rule. He had no experimental knowledge of it; nay, regular meals, on the contrary, gave him anxious concern, yet had the effect — spite of his apprehension that he was being fattened for a purpose — of restoring the herculean puissance which formerly in Africa had made him the terror of the battle.

When one day he had come to be quite himself, he was invited out into the sunshine, and escorted by the driver (a sort of foreman to the overseer), went forth dimly wondering. They reached a field where some men and women were hoeing. He had seen men and women — subjects of his — labor — a little — in Africa. The driver handed him a hoe ; he examined it with silent interest — until by signs he was requested to join the pastime.

"What ? "

He spoke, not with his lips, but with the recoil of his splendid frame and the ferocious expansion of his eyes. This invitation was a cataract of lightning leaping down an ink-black sky. In one instant of all-pervading clearness he read his sentence — WORK.

Bras-Coupé was six feet five. With a sweep as quick as instinct the back of the hoe smote the driver full in the head. Next, the prince lifted the nearest Congo crosswise, brought thirty-two teeth together in his wildly kicking leg and cast him away as a bad morsel ; then, throwing another into the branches of a willow, and a woman over his head into a draining-ditch, he made one bound for freedom, and fell to his knees, rocking from side to side under the effect of a pistol-ball from the overseer. It had struck him in the forehead, and running around the skull in search of a penetrable spot, tradition — which sometimes jests— says came out despairingly, exactly where it had entered.

It so happened that, except the overseer, the

whole company were black. Why should the trivial scandal be blabbed? A plaster or two made everything even in a short time, except in the driver's case — for the driver died. The woman whom Bras-Coupé had thrown over his head lived to sell *calas* to Joseph Frowenfeld.

Don José, young and austere, knew nothing about agriculture and cared as much about human nature. The overseer often thought this, but never said it; he would not trust even himself with the dangerous criticism. When he ventured to reveal the foregoing incidents to the señor he laid all the blame possible upon the man whom death had removed beyond the reach of correction, and brought his account to a climax by hazarding the asserting that Bras-Coupé was an animal that could not be whipped.

"Caramba!" exclaimed the master, with gentle emphasis, "how so?"

"Perhaps señor had better ride down to the quarters," replied the overseer.

It was a great sacrifice of dignity, but the master made it.

"Bring him out."

They brought him out — chains on his feet, chains on his wrists, an iron yoke on his neck. The Spanish Creole master had often seen the bull, with his long, keen horns and blazing eye, standing in the arena; but this was as though he had come face to face with a rhinoceros.

"This man is not a Congo," he said.

" He is a Jaloff," replied the encouraged overseer. " See his fine, straight nose; moreover, he is
a *candio* — a prince.   If I whip him he will die."

The dauntless captive and fearless master stood
looking into each other's eyes until each recognized
in the other his peer in physical courage, and each
was struck with an admiration for the other which
no after difference was sufficient entirely to destroy.
Had Bras-Coupé's eye quailed but once — just for
one little instant— he would have got the lash ;
but, as it was ——

" Get an interpreter," said Don José; then, more
privately, " and come to an understanding.   I shall
require it of you."

Where might one find an interpreter — one not
merely able to render a Jaloff's meaning into Creole
French, or Spanish, but with such a turn for dip-
lomatic correspondence as would bring about an
" understanding" with this African buffalo?   The
overseer was left standing and thinking, and Clemence, who had not forgotten who threw her into
the draining-ditch, cunningly passed by.

" Ah, Clemence —— "

" *Mo pas capabe !   Mo pas capabe !*   (I cannot,
I cannot !)   *Ya, ya, ya! 'oir Miché Agricol' Fusilier ! ouala yune bon monture, oui !* " — which was to
signify that Agricola could interpret the very Papa
Lébat.

" Agricola Fusilier !   The last man on earth to
make peace."

But there seemed to be no choice, and to Agricola the overseer went.   It was but a little ride to the Grandissime place.

"I, Agricola Fusilier, stand as an interpreter to a negro?   H-sir!"

"But I thought you might know of some person," said the weakening applicant, rubbing his ear with his hand.

"Ah!" replied Agricola, addressing the surrounding scenery, "if I did not — who would? You may take Palmyre."

The overseer softly smote his hands together at the happy thought.

"Yes," said Agricola, "take Palmyre; she has picked up as many negro dialects as I know European languages."

And she went to the don's plantation as interpreter, followed by Agricola's prayer to Fate that she might in some way be overtaken by disaster. The two hated each other with all the strength they had.   He knew not only her pride, but her passion for the absent Honoré.   He hated her, also, for her intelligence, for the high favor in which she stood with her mistress, and for her invincible spirit, which was more offensively patent to him than to others, since he was himself the chief object of her silent detestation.

It was Palmyre's habit to do nothing without painstaking.   "When Mademoiselle comes to be Señora," thought she — she knew that her mistress and the don were affianced — "it will be well to have a Señor's esteem.   I shall endeavor to succeed." It was from this motive, then, that with the aid of her mistress she attired herself in a resplendence of scarlet and beads and feathers that could not fail the double purpose of connecting her with the children of Ethiopia and commanding the captive's instant admiration.

Alas for those who succeed too well! No sooner did the African turn his tiger glance upon her than the fire of his eyes died out; and when she spoke to him in the dear accents of his native tongue, the matter of strife vanished from his mind. He loved.

He sat down tamely in his irons and listened to Palmyre's argument as a wrecked mariner would listen to ghostly church-bells. He would give a short assent, feast his eyes, again assent, and feast his ears; but when at length she made bold to approach the actual issue, and finally uttered the loathed word, *Work*, he rose up, six feet five, a statue of indignation in black marble.

And then Palmyre, too, rose up, glorying in him, and went to explain to master and overseer. Bras-Coupé understood, she said, that he was a slave—it was the fortune of war, and he was a warrior; but, according to a generally recognized principle in African international law, he could not reasonably be expected to work.

"As Señor will remember I told him," remarked the overseer; "how can a man expect to plow with a zebra?"

Here he recalled a fact in his earlier experience.

An African of this stripe had been found to answer admirably as a " driver " to make others work. A second and third parley, extending through two or three days, were held with the prince, looking to his appointment to the vacant office of driver; yet what was the master's amazement to learn at length that his Highness declined the proffered honor.

" Stop ! " spoke the overseer again, detecting a look of alarm in Palmyre's face as she turned away, " he does n't do any such thing. If Señor will let me take the man to Agricola —— "

" No ! " cried Palmyre, with an agonized look, " I will tell. He will take the place and fill it if you will give me to him for his own — but oh, messieurs, for the love of God — I do not want to be his wife ! "

The overseer looked at the Señor, ready to approve whatever he should decide. Bras-Coupé's intrepid audacity took the Spaniard's heart by irresistible assault.

" I leave it entirely with Señor Fusilier," he said.

" But he is not my master; he has no right—— "

" Silence ! "

And she was silent; and so, sometimes, is fire in the wall.

Agricola's consent was given with malicious promptness, and as Bras-Coupé's fetters fell off it was decreed that, should he fill his office efficiently, there should be a wedding on the rear veranda of the Grandissime mansion simultaneously with the one already appointed to take place in the grand hall of the same house six months from that present day. In the meanwhile Palmyre should remain with Mademoiselle, who had promptly but quietly made up her mind that Palmyre should not be wed unless she wished to be. Bras-Coupé made no objection, was royally worthless for a time, but learned fast, mastered the "gumbo" dialect in a few weeks, and in six months was the most valuable man ever bought for gourde dollars. Nevertheless, there were but three persons within as many square miles who were not most vividly afraid of him.

The first was Palmyre. His bearing in her presence was ever one of solemn, exalted respect, which, whether from pure magnanimity in himself, or by reason of her magnetic eye, was something worth being there to see. "It was royal!" said the overseer.

The second was not that official. When Bras-Coupé said — as, at stated intervals, he did say — "*Mo courri c'ez Agricole Fusilier pou' 'oir 'namourouse* (I go to Agricole Fusilier to see my betrothed,)" the overseer would sooner have intercepted a score of painted Chickasaws than that one lover. He would look after him and shake a prophetic head. "Trouble coming; better not deceive that fellow;" yet that was the very thing Palmyre dared do. Her admiration for Bras-Coupé was almost boundless. She rejoiced in his stature; she revelled in the contemplation of his untamable spirit; he seemed to her the gigantic embodiment of her own dark, fierce will, the expanded realization of her lifetime longing for terrible strength. But the single deficiency in all this impassioned regard was — what so many fairer loves have found impossible to explain to so many gentler lovers — an entire absence of preference ; her heart she could not give him — she did not have it. Yet after her first prayer to the Spaniard and his overseer for deliverance, to the secret surprise and chagrin of her young mistress, she simulated content. It was artifice ; she knew Agricola's power, and to seem to consent was her one chance with him. He might thus be beguiled into withdrawing his own consent. That failing, she had Mademoiselle's promise to come to the rescue, which she could use at the last moment ; and that failing, there was a dirk in her bosom, for which a certain hard breast was not too hard. Another element of safety, of which she knew nothing, was a letter from the Cannes Brulée. The word had reached there that love had conquered — that, despite all hard words, and rancor, and positive injury, the Grandissime hand — the fairest of Grandissime hands — was about to be laid into that of one who without much stretch might be called a De Grapion ; that there was, moreover, positive effort being made to induce a restitution of old gaming-table spoils. Honoré and Mademoiselle, his sister, one on each side of the Atlantic, were striving for this end. Don José sent this intelligence to his kinsman as glad tidings (a lover never imagines there are two sides to that which makes him happy), and, to add a touch of humor, told how Palmyre, also, was given to the chieftain. The letter that came back to the young Spaniard did not blame him so much : *he* was ignorant of all the facts ; but a very formal one to Agricola begged to notify him that if Palmyre's union with Bras-Coupé should be completed, as sure as there was a God in heaven, the writer would have the life of the man who knowingly had thus endeavored to dishonor one who *shared the blood of the De Grapions.* Thereupon Agricola, contrary to his general character, began to drop hints to Don José that the engagement of Bras-Coupé and Palmyre need not be considered irreversible ; but the don was not desirous of disappointing his terrible pet. Palmyre, unluckily, played her game a little too deeply. She thought the moment had come for herself to insist on the match, and thus provoke Agricola to forbid it. To her incalculable dismay she saw him a second time reconsider and become silent.

The second person who did not fear Bras-Coupé was Mademoiselle. On one of the giant's earliest visits to see Palmyre he obeyed the summons which she brought him, to appear before the lady. A more artificial man might have objected on the score of dress, his attire being a single gaudy garment tightly enveloping the waist and thighs. As his eyes fell upon the beautiful white lady he prostrated himself upon the ground, his arms outstretched before him. He would not move till she was gone. Then he arose like a hermit who has

seen a vision. "*Bras-Coupé n' pas oulé oir zombis*
(Bras-Coupé dares not look upon a spirit)." From
that hour he worshipped. He saw her often;
every time, after one glance at her countenance, he
would prostrate his gigantic length with his face in
the dust.

The third person who did not fear him was —
Agricola? Nay, it was the Spaniard — a man
whose capability to fear anything in nature or beyond had never been discovered.

Long before the end of his probation Bras-Coupé
would have slipped the entanglements of bondage,
though as yet he felt them only as one feels a
spider's web across the face, had not the master,
according to a little affectation of the times, pro-
moted him to be his game-keeper. Many a day
did these two living magazines of wrath spend
together in the dismal swamps and on the meagre
intersecting ridges, making war upon deer and bear
and wildcat; or on the Mississippi after wild goose
and pelican; when even a word misplaced would
have made either the slayer of the other. Yet the
months ran smoothly round and the wedding night
drew nigh.[1] A goodly company had assembled.
All things were ready. The bride was dressed, the
bridegroom had come. On the great back piazza,

[1] An over-zealous Franciscan once complained bitterly to the
bishop of Havana, that people were being married in Louisiana in their
own houses after dark and thinking nothing of it. It is not certain
that he had reference to the Grandissime mansion; at any rate he was
tittered down by the whole community.

which had been inclosed with sail-cloth and lighted
with lanterns, was Palmyre, full of a new and deep
design and playing her deceit to the last, robed in
costly garments to whose beauty was added the
charm of their having been worn once, and once
only, by her beloved Mademoiselle.

But where was Bras-Coupé?

The question was asked of Palmyre by Agricola
with a gaze that meant in English, " No tricks, girl ! "

Among the servants who huddled at the windows
and door to see the inner magnificence a frightened
whisper was already going round.

" We have made a sad discovery, Miché Fusilier,"
said the overseer. " Bras-Coupé is here ; we have
him in a room just yonder.   But — the truth is, sir,
Bras-Coupé is a voudou."

" Well, and suppose he is ; what of it?   Only
hush ; do not let his master know it. It is nothing ; all the blacks are voudous, more or less."

" But he declines to dress himself — has painted
himself all rings and stripes, antelope fashion."

" Tell him Agricola Fusilier says, ' dress immediately ! ' "

" Oh, Miché, we have said that five times already,
and his answer — you will pardon me — his answer
is — spitting on the ground — that you are a con-
temptible *dotchian* (white trash)."

There is nothing to do but privily to call the
very bride — the lady herself. She comes forth in
all her glory, small, but oh, so beautiful ! Slam !
Bras-Coupé is upon his face, his finger-tips touching

the tips of her snowy slippers. She gently bids him go and dress, and at once he goes.

Ah! now the question may be answered without whispering. There is Bras-Coupé, towering above all heads, in ridiculous red and blue regimentals, but with a look of savage dignity upon him that keeps every one from laughing. The murmur of admiration that passed along the thronged gallery leaped up into a shout in the bosom of Palmyre. Oh, Bras-Coupé — heroic soul! She would not falter. She would let the silly priest say his say — then her cunning should help her *not to be* his wife, yet to show his mighty arm how and when to strike.

"He is looking for Palmyre," said some, and at that moment he saw her.

"Ho-o-o-o-o!"

Agricola's best roar was a penny trumpet to Bras-Coupé's note of joy. The whole masculine half of the indoor company flocked out to see what the matter was. Bras-Coupé was taking her hand in one of his and laying his other upon her head; and as some one made an unnecessary gesture for silence, he sang, beating slow and solemn time with his naked foot and with the hand that dropped hers to smite his breast:

> " ' *En haut la montagne, zami,*
> *Mo pé coupé canne, zami,*
> *Pou' fé l' a' zen' zami,*
> *Pou' mo baille Palmyre.*
> *Ah! Palmyre, Palmyre mo c'ere,*
> *Mo l' aimé 'ou' — mo l' aimé 'ou'.* ' "

" *Montagne?* " asked one slave of another, " *qui est çà, montagne? gnia pas quiç 'ose comme çà dans la Louisiana?* (What's a mountain? We have n't such things in Louisiana.)"

" *Mein ye gagnein plein montagnes dans l'Afrique,* listen ! "

> " ' *Ah! Palmyre, Palmyre, mo' piti zozo,*
> *Mo l'aimé 'ou' — mo l'aimé, l'aimé 'ou'.* ' "

" Bravissimo ! — " but just then a counter-attraction drew the white company back into the house. An old French priest with sandalled feet and a dirty face had arrived. There was a moment of hand-shaking with the good father, then a moment of palpitation and holding of the breath, and then — you would have known it by the turning away of two or three feminine heads in tears — the lily hand became the don's, to have and to hold, by authority of the Church and the Spanish king. And all was merry, save that outside there was coming up as villanous a night as ever cast black looks in through snug windows.

It was just as the newly-wed Spaniard, with Agricola and all the guests, were concluding the by-play of marrying the darker couple, that the hurricane struck the dwelling. The holy and jovial father had made faint pretence of kissing this second bride; the ladies, colonels, dons, etc., — though the joke struck them as a trifle coarse — were beginning to laugh and clap hands again and the gowned jester to bow to right and left, when Bras-Coupé, tardily realizing the consummation of his hopes, stepped forward to embrace his wife.

" Bras-Coupé ! "

The voice was that of Palmyre's mistress. She had not been able to comprehend her maid's behavior, but now Palmyre had darted upon her an appealing look.

The warrior stopped as if a javelin had flashed over his head and stuck in the wall.

" Bras-Coupé must wait till I give him his wife."

He sank, with hidden face, slowly to the floor.

" Bras-Coupé hears the voice of zombis ; the voice is sweet, but the words are very strong ; from the same sugar-cane comes *sirop* and *tafia ;* Bras-Coupé says to zombis, ' Bras-Coupé will wait ; but if the *dotchians* deceive Bras-Coupé — " he rose to his feet with his eyes closed and his great black fist lifted over his head — " Bras-Coupé will call Voudou-Magnan ! "

The crowd retreated and the storm fell like a burst of infernal applause. A whiff like fifty witches flouted up the canvas curtain of the gallery and a fierce black cloud, drawing the moon under its cloak, belched forth a stream of fire that seemed to flood the ground ; a peal of thunder followed as if the sky had fallen in, the house quivered, the great oaks groaned, and every lesser thing bowed down before the awful blast. Every lip held its breath for a minute — or an hour, no one knew — there was a sudden lull of the wind, and the floods came down. Have you heard it thunder and rain in those Louisiana lowlands? Every clap seems to crack the world. It has rained a moment; you peer through the black pane — your house is an island, all the land is sea.

However, the supper was spread in the hall and in due time the guests were filled. Then a supper was spread in the big hall in the basement, below stairs, the sons and daughters of Ham came down like the fowls of the air upon a rice-field, and Bras-Coupé, throwing his heels about with the joyous carelessness of a smutted Mercury, for the first time in his life tasted the blood of the grape. A second, a fifth, a tenth time he tasted it, drinking more deeply each time, and would have taken it ten times more had not his bride cunningly concealed it. It was like stealing a tiger's kittens.

The moment quickly came when he wanted his eleventh bumper. As he presented his request a silent shiver of consternation ran through the dark company; and when, in what the prince meant as a remonstrative tone, he repeated the petition — splitting the table with his fist by way of punctuation — there ensued a hustling up staircases and a cramming into dim corners that left him alone at the banquet.

Leaving the table, he strode upstairs and into the chirruping and dancing of the grand salon. There was a halt in the cotillion and a hush of amazement like the shutting off of steam. Bras-Coupé strode straight to his master, laid his paw upon his fellow-bridegroom's shoulder and in a thunder-tone demanded:

" More ! "

The master swore a Spanish oath, lifted his hand
and — fell, beneath the terrific fist of his slave, with
a bang that jingled the candelabra.   Dolorous
stroke ! — for the dealer of it.   Given, apparently
to him — poor, tipsy savage — in self-defence, pun-
ishable, in a white offender, by a small fine or a few
days' imprisonment, it assured Bras-Coupé the death
of a felon ; such was the old *Code Noir*.   (We have
a *Code Noir* now, but the new one is a mental reservation, not an enactment.)

The guests stood for an instant as if frozen,
smitten stiff with the instant expectation of insurrection, conflagration and rapine (just as we do to-
day whenever some poor swaggering Pompey rolls
up his fist and gets a ball through his body), while,
single-handed and naked-fisted in a room full of
swords, the giant stood over his master, making
strange signs and passes and rolling out in wrathful
words of his mother tongue what it needed no interpreter to tell his swarming enemies was a voudou
malediction.

" *Nous sommes grigis !* " screamed two or three
ladies, " we are bewitched ! "

" Look to your wives and daughters ! " shouted
a Brahmin-Mandarin.

" Shoot the black devils without mercy ! " cried a
Mandarin-Fusilier, unconsciously putting into a
single outflash of words the whole Creole treatment
of race troubles.

With a single bound Bras-Coupé reached the

drawing-room door; his gaudy regimentals made a red and blue streak down the hall; there was a rush of frilled and powdered gentlemen to the rear veranda, an avalanche of lightning with Bras-Coupé in the midst making for the swamp, and then all without was blackness of darkness and all within was a wild commingled chatter of Creole, French, and Spanish tongues, — in the midst of which the reluctant Agricola returned his dresssword to its scabbard.

While the wet lanterns swung on crazily in the trees along the way by which the bridegroom was to have borne his bride; while Madame Grandissime prepared an impromptu bridalchamber; while the Spaniard bathed his eye and the blue gash on his cheek-bone; while Palmyre paced her room in a fever and wild tremor of conflicting emotions throughout the night, and the guests splashed home after the storm as best they could, Bras-Coupé was practically declaring his independence on a slight rise of ground hardly sixty feet in circumference and lifted scarce above the water in the inmost depths of the swamp.

And amid what surroundings! Endless colonnades of cypresses; long, motionless drapings of gray moss; broad sheets of noisome waters, pitchy black, resting on bottomless ooze; cypress knees studding the surface; patches of floating green, gleaming brilliantly here and there; yonder where the sunbeams wedge themselves in, constellations of water-lilies, the many-hued iris, and a multitude of flowers

ALBERT HERTER

that no man had named; here, too, serpents great and small, of wonderful colorings, and the dull and loathsome moccasin sliding warily off the dead tree; in dimmer recesses the cow alligator, with her nest hard by; turtles a century old; owls and bats, raccoons, opossums, rats, centipedes and creatures of like vileness; great vines of beautiful leaf and scarlet fruit in deadly clusters; maddening mosquitoes, parasitic insects, gorgeous dragon-flies and pretty water-lizards: the blue heron, the snowy crane, the red-bird, the moss-bird, the night-hawk and the chuckwill's-widow; a solemn stillness and stifled air only now and then disturbed by the call or whir of the summer duck, the dismal ventriloquous note of the rain-crow, or the splash of a dead branch falling into the clear but lifeless bayou.

The pack of Cuban hounds that howl from Don José's kennels cannot snuff the trail of the stolen canoe that glides through the sombre blue vapors of the African's fastnesses. His arrows send no telltale reverberations to the distant clearing. Many a wretch in his native wilderness has Bras-Coupé himself, in palmier days, driven to just such an existence, to escape the chains and horrors of the barracoons; therefore not a whit broods he over man's inhumanity, but, taking the affair as a matter of course, casts about him for a future.

CHAPTER XXIX

THE STORY OF BRAS-COUPÉ, CONTINUED

BRAS-COUPÉ let the autumn pass, and wintered in his den.

Don José, in a majestic way, endeavored to be happy. He took his señora to his hall, and under her rule it took on for a while a look and feeling which turned it from a hunting-lodge into a home. Wherever the lady's steps turned — or it is as correct to say wherever the proud tread of Palmyre turned — the features of bachelor's-hall disappeared; guns, dogs, oars, saddles, nets, went their way into proper banishment, and the broad halls and lofty chambers — the floors now muffled with mats of palmetto-leaf — no longer re-echoed the tread of a lonely master, but breathed a redolence of flowers and a rippling murmur of well-contented song.

But the song was not from the throat of Bras-Coupé's "*piti zozo.*" Silent and severe by day, she moaned away whole nights heaping reproaches upon herself for the impulse — now to her, because it had failed, inexplicable in its folly — which had permitted her hand to lie in Bras-Coupé's and the priest to bind them together.

For in the audacity of her pride, or, as Agricola would have said, in the immensity of her impudence, she had held herself consecrate to a hopeless love.

But now she was a black man's wife! and even he
unable to sit at her feet and learn the lesson she
had hoped to teach him. She had heard of San
Domingo; for months the fierce heart within her
silent bosom had been leaping and shouting and
seeing visions of fire and blood, and when she
brooded over the nearness of Agricola and the
remoteness of Honoré these visions got from her a
sort of mad consent. The lesson she would have
taught the giant was Insurrection. But it was too
late. Letting her dagger sleep in her bosom, and
with an undefined belief in imaginary resources, she
had consented to join hands with her giant hero
before the priest; and when the wedding had come
and gone like a white sail, she was seized with a
lasting, fierce despair. A wild aggressiveness that
had formerly characterized her glance in moments
of anger — moments which had grown more and
more infrequent under the softening influence of
her Mademoiselle's nature — now came back intensified, and blazed in her eye perpetually. Whatever
her secret love may have been in kind, its sinking
beyond hope below the horizon had left her fifty
times the mutineer she had been before — the
mutineer who has nothing to lose.

"She loves her *candio*," said the negroes.

"Simple creatures!" said the overseer, who prided
himself on his discernment, "she loves nothing;
she hates Agricola; it's a case of hate at first sight
— the strongest kind."

Both were partly right; her feelings were wonderfully knit to the African; and she now dedicated herself to Agricola's ruin.

The señor, it has been said, endeavored to be happy; but now his heart conceived and brought forth its first-born fear, sired by superstition — the fear that he was bewitched. The negroes said that Bras-Coupé had cursed the land. Morning after morning the master looked out with apprehension toward the fields, until one night the worm came upon the indigo, and between sunset and sunrise every green leaf had been eaten up and there was nothing left for either insect or apprehension to feed upon.

And then he said — and the echo came back from the Cannes Brulées — that the very bottom culpability of this thing rested on the Grandissimes, and specifically on their fugleman Agricola, through his putting the hellish African upon him. Moreover, fever and death, to a degree unknown before, fell upon his slaves. Those to whom life was spared — but to whom strength did not return — wandered about the place like scarecrows, looking for shelter, and made the very air dismal with the reiteration, "*No' ouanga* (we are bewitched), *Bras-Coupé fé moi des grigis* (the voudou's spells are on me)." The ripple of song was hushed and the flowers fell upon the floor.

"I have heard an English maxim," wrote Colonel De Grapion to his kinsman, "which I would recommend you to put into practice — 'Fight the devil with fire.'"

No, he would not recognize devils as belligerents.

But if Rome commissioned exorcists, could not he employ one?

No, he would not! If his hounds could not catch Bras-Coupé, why, let him go. The overseer tried the hounds once more and came home with the best one across his saddle-bow, an arrow run half through its side.

Once the blacks attempted by certain familiar rum-pourings and nocturnal charm-singing to lift the curse; but the moment the master heard the wild monotone of their infernal worship, he stopped it with a word.

Early in February came the spring, and with it some resurrection of hope and courage. It may have been — it certainly was, in part — because young Honoré Grandissime had returned. He was like the sun's warmth wherever he went; and the other Honoré was like his shadow. The fairer one quickly saw the meaning of these things, hastened to cheer the young don with hopes of a better future, and to effect, if he could, the restoration of Bras-Coupé to his master's favor. But this latter effort was an idle one. He had long sittings with his uncle Agricola to the same end, but they always ended fruitless and often angrily.

His dark half-brother had seen Palmyre and loved her. Honoré would gladly have solved one or two riddles by effecting their honorable union in marriage. The previous ceremony on the Grandissime back piazza need be no impediment;

all slave-owners understood those things. Following Honoré's advice, the f. m. c., who had come into possession of his paternal portion, sent to Cannes Brulées a written offer, to buy Palmyre at any price that her master might name, stating his intention to free her and make her his wife. Colonel De Grapion could hardly hope to settle Palmyre's fate more satisfactorily, yet he could not forego an opportunity to indulge his pride by following up the threat he had hung over Agricola to kill whosoever should give Palmyre to a black man. He referred the subject and the would-be purchaser to him. It would open up to the old braggart a line of retreat, thought the planter of the Cannes Brulées.

But the idea of retreat had left Citizen Fusilier.

"She is already married," said he to M. Honoré Grandissime, f. m. c. "She is the lawful wife of Bras-Coupé; and what God has joined together let no man put asunder. You know it, sirrah. You did this for impudence, to make a show of your wealth. You intended it as an insinuation of equality. I overlook the impertinence for the sake of the man whose white blood you carry; but h-mark you, if ever you bring your Parisian airs and self-sufficient face on a level with mine again, h-I will slap it."

The quadroon, three nights after, was so indiscreet as to give him the opportunity, and he did it — at that quadroon ball to which Dr. Keene alluded in talking to Frowenfeld.

But Don José, we say, plucked up new spirit.

"Last year's disasters were but fortune's freaks," he said. "See, others' crops have failed all about us."

The overseer shook his head.

"*C'est ce maudit cocodri' là bas* (It is that accursed alligator, Bras-Coupé, down yonder in the swamp)."

And by and by the master was again smitten with the same belief. He and his neighbors put in their crops afresh. The spring waned, summer passed, the fevers returned, the year wore round, but no harvest smiled. "Alas!" cried the planters, "we are all poor men!" The worst among the worst were the fields of Bras-Coupé's master — parched and shrivelled. "He does not understand planting," said his neighbors; "neither does his overseer. Maybe, too, it is true as he says, that he is voudoued."

One day at high noon the master was taken sick with fever.

The third noon after — the sad wife sitting by the bedside — suddenly, right in the centre of the room, with the door open behind him, stood the magnificent, half-nude form of Bras-Coupé. He did not fall down as the mistress's eyes met his, though all his flesh quivered. The master was lying with his eyes closed. The fever had done a fearful three days' work.

"*Mioko-Koanga oulé so' femme* (Bras-Coupé wants his wife)."

The master started wildly and stared upon his slave.

"*Bras-Coupé oulé so' femme!*" repeated the black.

"Seize him!" cried the sick man, trying to rise.

But, though several servants had ventured in with frightened faces, none dared molest the giant. The master turned his entreating eyes upon his wife, but she seemed stunned, and only covered her face with her hands and sat as if paralyzed by a foreknowledge of what was coming.

Bras-Coupé lifted his great black palm and commenced:

"*Mo cé voudrai que la maison ci là, et tout ça qui pas femme' ici, s'raient encore maudits!* (May this house, and all in it who are not women, be accursed)."

The master fell back upon his pillow with a groan of helpless wrath.

The African pointed his finger through the open window.

"May its fields not know the plough nor nourish the herds that overrun it."

The domestics, who had thus far stood their ground, suddenly rushed from the room like stampeded cattle, and at that moment appeared Palmyre.

"Speak to him," faintly cried the panting invalid.

She went firmly up to her husband and lifted her hand. With an easy motion, but quick as lightning, as a lion sets foot on a dog, he caught her by the arm.

"*Bras-Coupé oulé so' femme,*" he said, and just then Palmyre would have gone with him to the equator.

"You shall not have her!" gasped the master.

The African seemed to rise in height, and still holding his wife at arm's length, resumed his malediction:

"May weeds cover the ground until the air is full of their odor and the wild beasts of the forest come and lie down under their cover."

With a frantic effort the master lifted himself upon his elbow and extended his clenched fist in speechless defiance; but his brain reeled, his sight went out, and when again he saw, Palmyre and her mistress were bending over him, the overseer stood awkwardly by, and Bras-Coupé was gone.

The plantation became an invalid camp. The words of the voudou found fulfilment on every side. The plough went not out; the herds wandered through broken hedges from field to field and came up with staring bones and shrunken sides; a frenzied mob of weeds and thorns wrestled and throttled each other in a struggle for standing-room — rag-weed, smart-weed, sneeze-weed, bind-weed, iron-weed — until the burning skies of mid-summer checked their growth and crowned their unshorn tops with rank and dingy flowers.

"Why in the name of — St. Francis," asked the priest of the overseer, "did n't the señora use her power over the black scoundrel when he stood and cursed, that day?"

"Why, to tell you the truth, father," said the overseer, in a discreet whisper, "I can only suppose she thought Bras-Coupé had half a right to do it."

"Ah, ah, I see; like her brother Honoré ——
—looks at both sides of a question—a miserable
practice; but why couldn't Palmyre use *her* eyes?
They would have stopped him."

"Palmyre? Why Palmyre has become the best
monture (Plutonian medium) in the parish. Agricola Fusilier himself is afraid of her. Sir, I think
sometimes Bras-Coupé is dead and his spirit has
gone into Palmyre. She would rather add to his
curse than take from it."

"Ah!" said the jovial divine, with a fat smile,
"castigation would help her case; the whip is a
great sanctifier. I fancy it would even make a
Christian of the inexpugnable Bras-Coupé."

But Bras-Coupé kept beyond the reach alike of
the lash and of the Latin Bible.

By and by came a man with a rumor, whom the
overseer brought to the master's sick-room, to tell
that an enterprising Frenchman was attempting to
produce a new staple in Louisiana, one that worms
would not annihilate. It was that year of history
when the despairing planters saw ruin hovering so
close over them that they cried to heaven for succor.
Providence raised up Étienne de Boré. "And if
Étienne is successful," cried the news-bearer, "and
gets the juice of the sugar-cane to crystallize, so
shall all of us, after him, and shall yet save our
lands and homes. Oh, Señor, it will make you
strong again to see these fields all cane and the long
rows of negroes and negresses cutting it, while they
sing their song of those droll African numerals,

counting the canes they cut," and the bearer of good tidings sang them for very joy :

An - o - qué, An - o - bia,   Bia-tail - la,   Qué - re - qué, Nal - le - oua,

Au-mon-dé, Au-tap - o - té, Au - pé - to - té, Au-qué-ré-qué, Bo.

"And Honoré Grandissime is going to introduce it on his lands," said Don José.

"That is true," said Agricola Fusilier, coming in. Honoré, the indefatigable peacemaker, had brought his uncle and his brother-in-law for the moment not only to speaking, but to friendly, terms.

The señor smiled.

"I have some good tidings, too," he said; "my beloved lady has borne me a son."

"Another scion of the house of Grand—— I mean Martinez!" exclaimed Agricola.   'And now, Don José, let me say that *I* have an item of rare intelligence!"

The don lifted his feeble head and opened his inquiring eyes with a sudden, savage light in them.

"No," said Agricola, "he is not exactly taken yet, but they are on his track."

"Who?"

"The police.   We may say he is virtually in our grasp."

It was on a Sabbath afternoon that a band of Choctaws having just played a game of racquette

behind the city and a similar game being about to
end between the white champions of two rival faubourgs, the beating of tom-toms, rattling of mules'
jawbones and sounding of wooden horns drew the
populace across the fields to a spot whose present
name of Congo Square still preserves a reminder of
its old barbaric pastimes. On a grassy plain under
the ramparts, the performers of these hideous dis-
cords sat upon the ground facing each other, and in
their midst the dancers danced. They gyrated in
couples, a few at a time, throwing their bodies into
the most startling attitudes and the wildest contor-
tions, while the whole company of black lookers-on,
incited by the tones of the weird music and the violent posturing of the dancers, swayed and writhed
in passionate sympathy, beating their breasts, palms
and thighs in time with the bones and drums, and
at frequent intervals lifting, in that wild African
unison no more to be described than forgotten, the
unutterable songs of the Babouille and Counjaille
dances, with their ejaculatory burdens of "*Aie!
Aie! Voudou Magnan!*" and "*Aie Calinda! Dancé
Calinda!*" The volume of sound rose and fell
with the augmentation or diminution of the dancers'
extravagances. Now a fresh man, young and
supple, bounding into the ring, revived the flagging
rattlers, drummers and trumpeters; now a wearied
dancer, finding his strength going, gathered all his
force at the cry of "*Dancé zisqu'a mort!*" rallied to
a grand finale and with one magnificent antic fell,
foaming at the mouth.

The amusement had reached its height. Many participants had been lugged out by the neck to avoid their being danced on, and the enthusiasm had risen to a frenzy, when there bounded into the ring the blackest of black men, an athlete of superb figure, in breeches of " Indienne " — the stuff used for slave women's best dresses — jingling with bells, his feet in moccasins, his tight, crisp hair decked out with feathers, a necklace of alligator's teeth rattling on his breast and a living serpent twined about his neck.

It chanced that but one couple was dancing. Whether they had been sent there by advice of Agricola is not certain. Snatching a tambourine from a bystander as he entered, the stranger thrust the male dancer aside, faced the woman and began a series of saturnalian antics, compared with which all that had gone before was tame and sluggish ; and as he finally leaped, with tinkling heels, clean over his bewildered partner's head, the multitude howled with rapture.

Ill-starred Bras-Coupé. He was in that extra-hazardous and irresponsible condition of mind and body known in the undignified present as " drunk again."

By the strangest fortune, if not, as we have just hinted, by some design, the man whom he had once deposited in the willow bushes, and the woman Clemence, were the very two dancers, and no other, whom he had interrupted. The man first stupidly regarded, next admiringly gazed upon, and then

distinctly recognized, his whilom driver. Five
minutes later the Spanish police were putting their
heads together to devise a quick and permanent
capture; and in the midst of the sixth minute, as
the wonderful fellow was rising in a yet more
astounding leap than his last, a lasso fell about his
neck and brought him, crashing like a burnt tree,
face upward upon the turf.

" The runaway slave," said the old French code,
continued in force by the Spaniards, "the runaway
slave who shall continue to be so for one month
from the day of his being denounced to the officers
of justice shall have his ears cut off and shall be
branded with the flower de luce on the shoulder;
and on a second offence of the same nature, persisted in during one month of his being denounced,
he shall be hamstrung, and be marked with the
flower de luce on the other shoulder. On the third
offence he shall die." Bras-Coupé had run away
only twice. " But," said Agricola, " these ' bossals '
must be taught their place. Besides, there is Article
27 of the same code : ' The slave who, having struck
his master, shall have produced a bruise, shall suffer
capital punishment ' — a very necessary law ! " He
concluded with a scowl upon Palmyre, who shot
back a glance which he never forgot.

The Spaniard showed himself very merciful —
for a Spaniard; he spared the captive's life. He
might have been more merciful still; but Honoré
Grandissime said some indignant things in the
African's favor, and as much to teach the Gran-

dissimes a lesson as to punish the runaway, he would have repented his clemency, as he repented the momentary truce with Agricola, but for the tearful pleading of the señora and the hot, dry eyes of her maid. Because of these he overlooked the offence against his person and estate, and delivered Bras-Coupé to the law to suffer only the penalties of the crime he had committed against society by attempting to be a free man.

We repeat it for the credit of Palmyre, that she pleaded for Bras-Coupé. But what it cost her to make that intercession, knowing that his death would leave her free, and that if he lived she must be his wife, let us not attempt to say.

In the midst of the ancient town, in a part which is now crumbling away, stood the Calaboza, with its humid vaults and grated cells, its iron cages and its whips; and there, soon enough, they strapped Bras-Coupé face downward and laid on the lash. And yet not a sound came from the mutilated but unconquered African to annoy the ear of the sleeping city.

("And you suffered this thing to take place?" asked Joseph Frowenfeld of Honoré Grandissime.

"My-de'-seh!" exclaimed the Creole, "they lied to me — said they would not harm him!")

He was brought at sunrise to the plantation. The air was sweet with the smell of the weed-grown fields. The long-horned oxen that drew him and the naked boy that drove the team stopped before his cabin.

" You cannot put that creature in there," said the thoughtful overseer. " He would suffocate under a roof— he has been too long out-of-doors for that. Put him on my cottage porch." There, at last, Palmyre burst into tears and sank down, while before her, on a soft bed of dry grass, rested the helpless form of the captive giant, a cloth thrown over his galled back, his ears shorn from his head, and the tendons behind his knees severed. His eyes were dry, but there was in them that unspeakable despair that fills the eye of the charger when, fallen in battle, he gazes with sidewise-bended neck on the ruin wrought upon him. His eye turned sometimes slowly to his wife. He need not demand her now — she was always by him.

There was much talk over him — much idle talk. He merely lay still under it with a fixed frown ; but once some incautious tongue dropped the name of Agricola. The black man's eyes came so quickly round to Palmyre that she thought he would speak ; but no; his words were all in his eyes. She answered their gleam with a fierce affirmative glance, whereupon he slowly bent his head and spat upon the floor.

There was yet one more trial of his wild nature. The mandate came from his master's sick-bed that he must lift the curse.

Bras-Coupé merely smiled. God keep thy enemy from such a smile !

The overseer, with a policy less Spanish than his master's, endeavored to use persuasion. But the fallen prince would not so much as turn one glance from his parted hamstrings. Palmyre was then besought to intercede. She made one poor attempt, but her husband was nearer doing her an unkindness than ever he had been before ; he made a slow sign for silence — with his fist ; and every mouth was stopped.

At midnight following, there came, on the breeze that blew from the mansion, a sound of running here and there, of wailing and sobbing— another Bridegroom was coming, and the Spaniard, with much such a lamp in hand as most of us shall be found with, neither burning brightly nor wholly gone out, went forth to meet Him.

"Bras-Coupé," said Palmyre, next evening, speaking low in his mangled ear, "the master is dead ; he is just buried. As he was dying, Bras-Coupé, he asked that you would forgive him."

The maimed man looked steadfastly at his wife. He had not spoken since the lash struck him, and he spoke not now ; but in those large, clear eyes, where his remaining strength seemed to have taken refuge as in a citadel, the old fierceness flared up for a moment, and then, like an expiring beacon, went out.

"Is your mistress well enough by this time to venture here ? " whispered the overseer to Palmyre. "Let her come. Tell her not to fear, but to bring the babe — in her own arms, tell her— quickly ! "

The lady came, her infant boy in her arms, knelt down beside the bed of sweet grass and set the child within the hollow of the African's arm. Bras-

Coupé turned his gaze upon it; it smiled, its
mother's smile, and put its hand upon the runaway's face, and the first tears of Bras-Coupé's life,
the dying testimony of his humanity, gushed from
his eyes and rolled down his cheek upon the infant's hand. He laid his own tenderly upon the
babe's forehead, then removing it, waved it abroad,
inaudibly moved his lips, dropped his arm, and
closed his eyes. The curse was lifted.

" *Le pauv' dgiab'!* " said the overseer, wiping his
eyes and looking fieldward. " Palmyre, you must
get the priest."

The priest came, in the identical gown in which
he had appeared the night of the two weddings.
To the good father's many tender questions Bras-
Coupé turned a failing eye that gave no answers;
until, at length:

" Do you know where you are going? " asked
the holy man.

" Yes," answered his eyes, brightening.

" Where? "

He did not reply; he was lost in contemplation,
and seemed looking far away.

So the question was repeated.

" Do you know where you are going? "

And again the answer of the eyes. He knew.

" Where? "

The overseer at the edge of the porch, the widow
with her babe, and Palmyre and the priest bending
over the dying bed, turned an eager ear to catch the
answer.

"To —" the voice failed a moment; the departing hero essayed again; again it failed; he tried
once more, lifted his hand, and with an ecstatic, upward smile, whispered, "To — Africa" — and was
gone.

CHAPTER XXX

PARALYSIS

AS we have said, the story of Bras-Coupé was told that day three times: to the Grandissime beauties once, to Frowenfeld twice. The fair Grandissimes all agreed, at the close, that it was pitiful. Specially, that it was a great pity to have hamstrung Bras-Coupé, a man who even in his cursing had made an exception in favor of the ladies. True, they could suggest no alternative; it was undeniable that he had deserved his fate; still, it seemed a pity. They dispersed, retired and went to sleep confirmed in this sentiment. In Frowenfeld the story stirred deeper feelings.

On this same day, while it was still early morning, Honoré Grandissime, f. m. c., with more than even his wonted slowness of step and propriety of rich attire, had reappeared in the shop of the rue

Royale.   He did not need to say he desired another
private interview.   Frowenfeld ushered him silently
and at once into his rear room, offered him a chair
(which he accepted), and sat down before him.

In his labored way the quadroon stated his
knowledge that Frowenfeld had been three times to
the dwelling of Palmyre Philosophe.   Why, he
further intimated, he knew not, nor would he ask ;
but *he* — when *he* had applied for admission — had
been refused.   He had laid open his heart to
the apothecary's eyes — " It may have been un-
wisely —— "

Frowenfeld interrupted him ; Palmyre had been
ill for several days ; Doctor Keene — who, Mr.
Grandissime probably knew, was her physician ——

The landlord bowed, and Frowenfeld went on to
explain that Doctor Keene, while attending her,
had also fallen sick and had asked him to take the
care of this one case until he could himself resume it.
So there, in a word, was the reason why Joseph had,
and others had not, been admitted to her presence.

As obviously to the apothecary's eyes as anything intangible could be, a load of suffering was
lifted from the quadroon's mind, as this explanation
was concluded.   Yet he only sat in meditation
before his tenant, who regarded him long and sadly.
Then, seized with one of his energetic impulses, he
suddenly said :

" Mr. Grandissime, you are a man of intelligence,
accomplishments, leisure and wealth ; why " (clench-

ings his fists and frowning), "why do you not give
yourself — your time — wealth — attainments —
energies — everything — to the cause of the down-
trodden race with which this community's scorn
unjustly compels you to rank yourself?"

The quadroon did not meet Frowenfeld's kindled
eyes for a moment, and when he did, it was slowly
and dejectedly.

"He canno' be," he said, and then, seeing his
words were not understood, he added: "He 'ave
no Cause. Dad peop' 'ave no Cause." He went
on from this with many pauses and gropings after
words and idiom, to tell, with a plaintiveness that
seemed to Frowenfeld almost unmanly, the reasons
why the people, a little of whose blood had been
enough to blast his life, would never be free by the
force of their own arm. Reduced to the meanings
which he vainly tried to convey in words, his statement was this: that that people was not a people.
Their cause — was in Africa. They upheld it there
— they lost it there — and to those that are here
the struggle was over; they were, one and all, prisoners of war.

"You speak of them in the third person," said
Frowenfeld.

"Ah ham nod a slev."

"Are you certain of that?" asked the tenant.

His landlord looked at him.

"It seems to me," said Frowenfeld, "that you —
your class — the free quadroons — are the saddest

slaves of all. Your men, for a little property, and your women, for a little amorous attention, let themselves be shorn even of the virtue of discontent, and for a paltry bait of sham freedom have consented to endure a tyrannous contumely which flattens them into the dirt like grass under a slab. I would rather be a runaway in the swamps than content myself with such a freedom. As your class stands before the world to-day — free in form but slaves in spirit — you are — I do not know but I was almost ready to say — a warning to philanthropists ! "

The free man of color slowly arose.

" I trust you know," said Frowenfeld, " that I say nothing in offence."

" Havery word is tru'," replied the sad man.

" Mr. Grandissime," said the apothecary, as his landlord sank back again into his seat, " I know you are a broken-hearted man."

The quadroon laid his fist upon his heart and looked up.

" And being broken-hearted, you are thus specially fitted for a work of patient and sustained self-sacrifice. You have only those things to lose which grief has taught you to despise — ease, money, display. Give yourself to your people — to those, I mean, who groan, or should groan, under the degraded lot which is theirs and yours in common."

The quadroon shook his head, and after a moment's silence, answered :

" Ah cannod be one Toussaint l'Ouverture. Ah

cannod trah to be. Hiv I trah, I h-only s'all soog-
ceed to be one Bras-Coupé."

"You entirely misunderstand me," said Frowenfeld in quick response. "I have no stronger disbelief than my disbelief in insurrection. I believe
that to every desirable end there are two roads, the
way of strife and the way of peace. I can imagine
a man in your place, going about among his people,
stirring up their minds to a noble discontent, laying
out his means, sparingly here and bountifully there,
as in each case might seem wisest, for their enlight-
enment, their moral elevation, their training in
skilled work; going, too, among the men of the
prouder caste, among such as have a spirit of fair-
ness, and seeking to prevail with them for a public
recognition of the rights of all; using all his cunning
to show them the double damage of all oppression,
both great and petty ——"

The quadroon motioned "enough." There was
a heat in his eyes which Frowenfeld had never seen
before.

"M'sieu'," he said, "waid till Agricola Fusilier
ees keel."

"Do you mean 'dies'?"

"No," insisted the quadroon; "listen." And
with slow, painstaking phrase this man of strong
feeling and feeble will (the trait of his caste) told
—as Frowenfeld felt he would do the moment he
said "listen"— such part of the story of Bras-
Coupé as showed how he came by his deadly hatred
of Agricola.

"Tale me," said the landlord, as he concluded the recital, "w'y deen Bras Coupé mague dad curze on Agricola Fusilier? Becoze Agricola ees one sorcier! Elz 'e bin dade sinz long tamm."

The speaker's gestures seemed to imply that his own hand, if need be, would have brought the event to pass.

As he rose to say adieu, Frowenfeld, without previous intention, laid a hand upon his visitor's arm.

"Is there no one who can make peace between you?"

The landlord shook his head.

"'T is impossib'. We don' wand."

"I mean," insisted Frowenfeld, "Is there no man who can stand between you and those who wrong you, and effect a peaceful reparation?"

The landlord slowly moved away, neither he nor his tenant speaking, but each knowing that the one man in the minds of both, as a possible peace-maker, was Honoré Grandissime.

"Should the opportunity offer," continued Joseph, "may I speak a word for you myself?"

The quadroon paused a moment, smiled politely though bitterly, and departed repeating again:

"'Tis impossib'. We don' wand."

"Palsied," murmured Frowenfeld, looking after him, regretfully,—"like all of them."

Frowenfeld's thoughts were still on the same theme when, the day having passed, the hour was approaching wherein Innerarity was exhorted to tell his good-night story in the merry circle at the distant Grandissime mansion. As the apothecary was closing his last door for the night, the fairer Honoré called him out into the moonlight.

"Withered," the student was saying audibly to himself, "not in the shadow of the Ethiopian, but in the glare of the white man."

"Who is withered?" pleasantly demanded Honoré. The apothecary started slightly.

"Did I speak? How do you do, sir? I meant the free quadroons."

"Including the gentleman from whom you rent your store?"

"Yes, him especially; he told me this morning the story of Bras-Coupé."

M. Grandissime laughed. Joseph did not see why, nor did the laugh sound entirely genuine.

"Do not open the door, Mr Frowenfeld," said the Creole, "Get your great-coat and cane and come take a walk with me; I will tell you the same story."

It was two hours before they approached this door again on their return. Just before they reached it, Honoré stopped under the huge street-lamp, whose light had gone out, where a large stone lay before him on the ground in the narrow, moonlit street. There was a tall, unfinished building at his back.

"Mr Frowenfeld," — he struck the stone with his cane, — "this stone is Bras-Coupé — we cast it aside because it turns the edge of our tools."

He laughed. He had laughed to-night more than was comfortable to a man of Frowenfeld's quiet mind.

As the apothecary thrust his shopkey into the lock and so paused to hear his companion, who had begun again to speak, he wondered what it could be — for M. Grandissime had not disclosed it — that induced such a man as he to roam aimlessly, as it seemed, in deserted streets at such chill and dangerous hours. "What does he want with me?" The thought was so natural that it was no miracle the Creole read it.

"Well," said he, smiling and taking an attitude, "you are a great man for causes, Mr. Frowenfeld; but me, I am for results, ha, ha! You may ponder the philosophy of Bras-Coupé in your study, but *I* have got to get rid of his results, me. You know them."

"You tell me it revived a war where you had made a peace," said Frowenfeld.

"Yes — yes — that is his results; but good night, Mr. Frowenfeld."

"Good night, sir."

CHAPTER XXXI

ANOTHER WOUND IN A NEW PLACE

Each day found Doctor Keene's strength increasing, and on the morning following the incidents last recorded he was imprudently projecting an outdoor promenade.   An announcement from Honoré Grandissime, who had paid an early call, had, to that gentleman's no small surprise, produced a sudden and violent effect on the little man's temper.

He was sitting alone by his window, looking out upon the levee, when the apothecary entered the apartment.

"Frowenfeld," he instantly began, with evident displeasure most unaccountable to Joseph, "I hear you have been visiting the Nancanous."

"Yes, I have been there."

"Well, you had no business to go!"

Doctor Keene smote the arm of his chair with his fist.

Frowenfeld reddened with indignation, but suppressed his retort.   He stood still in the middle of the floor, and Doctor Keene looked out of the window.

"Doctor Keene," said the visitor, when his attitude was no longer tolerable, "have you anything more to say to me before I leave you?"

"No, sir."

"It is necessary for me, then, to say that in fulfilment of my promise, I am going from here to the house of Palmyre, and that she will need no further attention after to-day.   As to your present manner toward me, I shall endeavor to suspend judgment until I have some knowledge of its cause."

The doctor made no reply, but went on looking

out of the window, and Frowenfeld turned and left him.

As he arrived in the philosophe's sick-chamber — where he found her sitting in a chair set well back from a small fire — she half-whispered "Miché" with a fine, greeting smile, as if to a brother after a week's absence. To a person forced to lie abed, shut away from occupation and events, a day is ten, three are a month : not merely in the wear and tear upon the patience, but also in the amount of thinking and recollecting done. It was to be expected, then, that on this, the apothecary's fourth visit, Palmyre would have learned to take pleasure in his coming.

But the smile was followed by a faint, momentary frown, as if Frowenfeld had hardly returned it in kind. Likely enough, he had not. He was not distinctively a man of smiles ; and as he engaged in his appointed task she presently thought of this.

"This wound is doing so well," said Joseph, still engaged with the bandages, "that I shall not need to come again." He was not looking at her as he spoke, but he felt her give a sudden start. "What is this ?" he thought, but presently said very quietly : "With the assistance of your slave woman, you can now attend to it yourself."

She made no answer.

When, with a bow, he would have bade her good morning, she held out her hand for his. After a barely perceptible hesitation, he gave it, whereupon she held it fast, in a way to indicate that there was something to be said which he must stay and hear.

She looked up into his face. She may have been merely framing in her mind the word or two of English she was about to utter; but an excitement shone through her eyes and reddened her lips, and something sent out from her countenance a look of wild distress.

" You goin' tell 'im? " she asked.

" Who? Agricola? "

" *Non!* "

He spoke the next name more softly.

" Honoré? "

Her eyes looked deeply into his for a moment, then dropped, and she made a sign of assent.

He was about to say that Honoré knew already, but saw no necessity for doing so, and changed his answer.

" I will never tell any one."

" You know? " she asked, lifting her eyes for an instant. She meant to ask if he knew the motive that had prompted her murderous intent.

" I know your whole sad history."

She looked at him for a moment, fixedly; then, still holding his hand with one of hers, she threw the other to her face and turned away her head. He thought she moaned.

Thus she remained for a few moments, then suddenly she turned, clasped both hands about his, her face flamed up and she opened her lips to speak, but speech failed. An expression of pain and sup-

plication came upon her countenance, and the cry
burst from her :

"Meg 'im to love me !"

He tried to withdraw his hand, but she held it
fast, and, looking up imploringly with her wide,
electric eyes, cried :

"*Vous pouvez le faire, vous pouvez le faire* (You
can do it, you can do it); *vous êtes sorcier, mo
conné bien vous êtes sorcier* (you are a sorcerer, I
know)."

However harmless or healthful Joseph's touch
might be to the philosophe, he felt now that hers,
to him, was poisonous. He dared encounter her
eyes, her touch, her voice, no longer. The better
man in him was suffocating. He scarce had power
left to liberate his right hand with his left, to seize
his hat and go.

Instantly she rose from her chair, threw herself
on her knees in his path, and found command of
his language sufficient to cry as she lifted her arms,
bared of their drapery :

"Oh, my God ! don' rif-used me — don' rif-used
me !"

There was no time to know whether Frowenfeld
wavered or not. The thought flashed into his
mind that in all probability all the care and skill
he had spent upon the wound was being brought
to naught in this moment of wild posturing and
excitement ; but before it could have effect upon
his movements, a stunning blow fell upon the back
of his head, and Palmyre's slave woman, the Congo

dwarf, under the impression that it was the most timely of strokes, stood brandishing a billet of pine and preparing to repeat the blow.

He hurled her, snarling and gnashing like an ape, against the farther wall, cast the bar from the street door and plunged out, hatless, bleeding and stunned.

CHAPTER XXXII

INTERRUPTED PRELIMINARIES

ABOUT the same time of day, three gentlemen (we use the term gentlemen in its petrified state) were walking down the rue Royale from the direction of the Faubourg Ste. Marie.

They were coming down toward Palmyre's corner. The middle one, tall and shapely, might have been mistaken at first glance for Honoré Grandissime, but was taller and broader, and wore a cocked hat, which Honoré did not. It was Valentine. The short, black-bearded man in buckskin breeches on his right was Jean-Baptiste Grandissime, and the slight one on the left, who, with the prettiest and most graceful gestures and balancings, was leading the conversation, was Hippolyte Brahmin-Mandarin, a cousin and counterpart of that sturdy-hearted challenger of Agricola, Sylvestre.

"But after all," he was saying in Louisiana French, "there is no spot comparable, for comfortable seclusion, to the old orange grove under the levee on the Point; twenty minutes in a skiff, five minutes for preliminaries — you would not want more, the ground has been measured off five hundred times — ' are you ready ? ' —— "

" Ah, bah ! " said Valentine, tossing his head, " the Yankees would be down on us before you could count one."

" Well, then, behind the Jesuits' warehouses, if you insist. I don't care. Perdition take such a government ! I am almost sorry I went to the governor's reception."

" It was quiet, I hear; a sort of quiet ball, all promenading and no contra-dances. One quadroon ball is worth five of such."

This was the opinion of Jean-Baptiste.

" No, it was fine, anyhow. There was a contra-dance. The music was — tárata joonc, tará, tará — tárata joonc, tarárata joonc, tará — oh ! it was the finest thing — and composed here. They compose as fine things here as they do anywhere in the —— look there ! That man came out of Palmyre's house ; see how he staggered just then ! "

" Drunk," said Jean-Baptiste.

" No, he seems to be hurt. He has been struck on the head. Oho, I tell you, gentlemen, that same Palmyre is a wonderful animal ! Do you see ? She not only defends herself and ejects the wretch, but she puts her mark upon him ; she identifies him, ha, ha, ha ! Look at the high art of the thing ; she keeps his hat as a small souvenir and gives him a receipt for it on the back of his head.

Ah! but has n't she taught him a lesson? Why, gentlemen,— it is — if it is n't that sorcerer of an apothecary!"

"What?" exclaimed the other two; "well, well, but this is too good! Caught at last, ha, ha, ha, the saintly villain! Ah, ha, ha! Will not Honoré be proud of him now? *Ah! voilà un joli Joseph!* What did I tell you? Did n't I *always* tell you so?"

"But the beauty of it is, he is caught so cleverly. No escape — no possible explanation. There he is, gentlemen, as plain as a rat in a barrel, and with as plain a case. Ha, ha, ha! Is n't it just glorious?"

And all three laughed in such an ecstasy of glee that Frowenfeld looked back, saw them, and knew forthwith that his good name was gone. The three gentlemen, with tears of merriment still in their eyes, reached a corner and disappeared.

"Mister," said a child, trotting along under Frowenfeld's elbow, — the odd English of the New Orleans street-urchin was at that day just beginning to be heard — "Mister, dey got some blood on de back of you' hade!"

But Frowenfeld hurried on groaning with mental anguish.

CHAPTER XXXIII

UNKINDEST CUT OF ALL

IT was the year 1804. The world was trembling under the tread of the dread Corsican. It was but now that he had tossed away the whole Valley of the Mississippi, dropping it overboard as a little sand from a balloon, and Christendom in a pale agony of suspense was watching the turn of his eye; yet when a gibbering black fool here on the edge of civilization merely swings a pine-knot, the swinging of that pine-knot becomes to Joseph Frowenfeld, student of man, a matter of greater moment than the destination of the Boulogne Flotilla. For it now became for the moment the foremost necessity of his life to show, to that minute fraction of the earth's population which our terror misnames "the world," that a man may leap forth hatless and bleeding from the house of a New Orleans quadroon into the open street and yet be pure white within. Would it answer to tell the truth? Parts of that truth he was pledged not to tell; and even if he could tell it all it was incredible — bore all the features of a flimsy lie.

"Mister," repeated the same child who had spoken before, reinforced by another under the other elbow, "dey got some *blood* on de back of you' hade."

And the other added the suggestion:

" Dey got one drug-sto', yondah."

Frowenfeld groaned again. The knock had been a hard one, the ground and sky went round not a little, but he retained withal a white-hot process of thought that kept before him his hopeless inability to explain. He was coffined alive. The world (so-called) would bury him in utter loathing, and write on his headstone the one word — hypocrite. And he should lie there and helplessly contemplate Honoré pushing forward those purposes which he had begun to hope he was to have had the honor of furthering. But instead of so doing he would now be the by-word of the street.

" Mister," interposed the child once more, spokesman this time for a dozen blacks and whites of all sizes trailing along before and behind, " *dey got some blood* on de back of you' *hade*."

That same morning Clotilde had given a music-scholar her appointed lesson, and at its conclusion had borrowed of her patroness (how pleasant it must have been to have such things to lend !) a little yellow maid, in order that, with more pro-priety, she might make a business call. It was that matter of the rent — one that had of late occasioned her great secret distress. " It is plain," she had begun to say to herself, unable to comprehend Aurora's peculiar trust in Providence, " that if the money is to be got I must get it." A possibility had flashed upon her mind ; she had nurtured it into a project, had submitted it to her father-confessor in the cathedral, and received his unqualified approval of it, and was ready this morning to put it into execution. A great merit of the plan was its simplicity. It was merely to find for her heaviest bracelet a purchaser in time, and a price sufficient, to pay to-morrow's " maturities." See there again ! — to her, her little secret was of greater import than the collision of almost any pine-knot with almost any head.

It must not be accepted as evidence either of her unwillingness to sell or of the amount of gold in the bracelet, that it took the total of Clotilde's moral and physical strength to carry it to the shop where she hoped — against hope — to dispose of it.

'Sieur Frowenfeld, M. Innerarity said, was out, but would certainly be in in a few minutes, and she was persuaded to take a chair against the half-hidden door at the bottom of the shop with the little borrowed maid crouched at her feet.

She had twice or thrice felt a regret that she had undertaken to wait, and was about to rise and go, when suddenly she saw before her Joseph Frowenfeld, wiping the sweat of anguish from his brow and smeared with blood from his forehead down. She rose quickly and silently, turned sick and blind, and laid her hand upon the back of the chair for support. Frowenfeld stood an instant before her, groaned, and disappeared through the door. The little maid, retreating backward against her from the direction of the street-door, drew to her attention a crowd of sight-seers which had rushed up to the doors and against which Raoul was hurriedly closing the shop.

CHAPTER XXXIV

CLOTILDE AS A SURGEON

WAS it worse to stay, or to fly? The decision must be instantaneous. But Raoul made it easy by crying in their common tongue, as he slammed a massive shutter and shot its bolt:

"Go to him! he is down — I heard him fall. Go to him!"

At this rallying cry she seized her shield — that is to say, the little yellow attendant — and hurried into the room. Joseph lay just beyond the middle of the apartment, face downward. She found water and a basin, wet her own handkerchief, and dropped to her knees beside his head; but the moment he felt the small feminine hands he stood up. She took him by the arm.

" *Asseyez-vous, Monsieu'* — pliz to give you'sev de pens to seet down, 'Sieu' Frowenfel'. "

She spoke with a nervous tenderness in contrast with her alarmed and entreating expression of face, and gently pushed him into a chair.

The child ran behind the bed and burst into frightened sobs, but ceased when Clotilde turned for an instant and glared at her.

" Mague yo' 'ead back," said Clotilde, and with

tremulous tenderness she softly pressed back his brow and began wiping off the blood. " W'ere you is 'urted ? "

But while she was asking her question she had found the gash and was growing alarmed at its ugliness, when Raoul, having made everything fast, came in with :

" W'at 's de mattah, 'Sieur Frowenfel' ? w'at 's de mattah wid you ? Oo done dat, 'Sieur Frowen fel' ? "

Joseph lifted his head and drew away from it the small hand and wet handkerchief, and without letting go the hand, looked again into Clotilde's eyes, and said :

" Go home ; oh, go home ! "

" Oh ! no," protested Raoul, whereupon Clotilde turned upon him with a perfectly amiable, nurse's grimace for silence.

" I goin' rad now," she said.

Raoul's silence was only momentary.

" W'ere you lef' you' hat, 'Sieur Frowenfel' ? " he asked, and stole an artist's glance at Clotilde, while Joseph straightened up, and nerving himself to a tolerable calmness of speech, said :

" I have been struck with a stick of wood by a half-witted person under a misunderstanding of my intentions ; but the circumstances are such as to blacken my character hopelessly ; but I am inno-cent ! " he cried, stretching forward both arms and quite losing his momentary self-control.

" 'Sieu' Frowenfel' ! " cried Clotilde, tears leaping to her eyes, " I am shoe of it ! "

" I believe you ! I believe you, 'Sieur Frowen-fel' ! " exclaimed Raoul with sincerity.

" You will not believe me," said Joseph. " You will not; it will be impossible."

" *Mais*," cried Clotilde, " id shall nod be impossib' ! "

But the apothecary shook his head.

" All I can be suspected of will seem probable ; the truth only is incredible."

His head began to sink and a pallor to overspread his face.

" *Allez, Monsieur, allez*," cried Clotilde to Raoul, a picture of beautiful terror which he tried afterward to paint from memory, " *appelez* Doctah Kin ! "

Raoul made a dash for his hat, and the next moment she heard, with unpleasant distinctness, his impetuous hand slam the shop door and lock her in.

" *Baille ma do l'eau*," she called to the little mulattress, who responded by searching wildly for a cup and presently bringing a measuring-glass full of water.

Clotilde gave it to the wounded man, and he rose at once and stood on his feet.

" Raoul."

" 'E gone at Doctah Kin."

" I do not need Doctor Keene ; I am not badly hurt. Raoul should not have left you here in this manner. You must not stay."

" Bud, 'Sieur Frowenfel', I am afred to paz dad gangue ! "

A new distress seized Joseph in view of this additional complication. But, unmindful of this suggestion, the fair Creole suddenly exclaimed:

" 'Sieu' Frowenfel', you har a hinnocen' man! Go, hopen yo' do's an' stan juz as you har ub biffo dad crowd and sesso! My God! 'Sieu' Frowenfel', iv you cannod stan' ub by you'sev —— "

She ceased suddenly with a wild look, as if another word would have broken the levees of her eyes, and in that instant Frowenfeld recovered the full stature of a man.

" God bless you!" he cried. " I will do it!" He started, then turned again toward her, dumb for an instant, and said: " And God reward you! You believe in me, and you do not even know me."

Her eyes became wilder still as she looked up into his face with the words:

" *Mais*, I does know you — betteh 'n you know annyt'in' boud it!" and turned away, blushing violently.

Frowenfeld gave a start. She had given him too much light. He recognized her, and she knew it. For another instant he gazed at her averted face, and then with forced quietness said:

" Please go into the shop."

The whole time that had elapsed since the shutting of the doors had not exceeded five minutes; a sixth sufficed for Clotilde and her attendant to resume their original position in the nook by the private door and for Frowenfeld to wash his face

and hands. Then the alert and numerous ears
without heard a drawing of bolts at the door next
to that which Raoul had issued, its leaves opened
outward, and first the pale hands and then the white,
weakened face and still bloody hair and apparel of
the apothecary made their appearance. He opened
a window and another door. The one locked by
Raoul, when unbolted, yielded without a key, and
the shop stood open.

"My friends," said the trembling proprietor, "if
any of you wishes to buy anything, I am ready to
serve him. The rest will please move away."

The invitation, though probably understood, was
responded to by only a few at the banquette's edge,
where a respectable face or two wore scrutinizing
frowns. The remainder persisted in silently standing and gazing in at the bloody man.

Frowenfeld bore the gaze. There was one element of emphatic satisfaction in it — it drew their
observation from Clotilde at the other end of the
shop. He stole a glance backward; she was not
there. She had watched her chance, safely escaped
through the side door, and was gone.

Raoul returned.

"'Sieur Frowenfel', Doctor Keene is took worse
ag'in. 'E is in bed; but 'e say to tell you in dat
lill troubl' of dis mawnin' it is himseff w'at is inti'lie
wrong, an' 'e hass you poddon. 'E says sen' fo'
Doctor Conrotte, but I din go fo' him; dat ole
scoun'rel — he believe in puttin' de niggas fre'."

Frowenfeld said he would not consult professional

advisers; with a little assistance from Raoul, he could give the cut the slight attention it needed. He went back into his room, while Raoul turned back to the door and addressed the public.

"Pray, Messieurs, come in and be seated." He spoke in the Creole French of the gutters. "Come in. M. Frowenfeld is dressing, and desires that you will have a little patience. Come in. Take chairs. You will not come in? No? Nor you, Monsieur? No? I will set some chairs outside, eh? No?"

They moved by twos and threes away, and Raoul, retiring, gave his employer such momentary aid as was required. When Joseph, in changed dress, once more appeared, only a child or two lingered to see him, and he had nothing to do but sit down and, as far as he felt at liberty to do so, answer his assistant's questions.

During the recital, Raoul was obliged to exercise the severest self-restraint to avoid laughing,—a feeling which was modified by the desire to assure his employer that he understood this sort of thing perfectly, had run the same risks himself, and thought no less of a man, *providing he was a gentleman*, because of an unlucky retributive knock on the head. But he feared laughter would overclimb speech; and, indeed, with all expression of sympathy stifled, he did not succeed so completely in hiding the conflicting emotion but that Joseph did once turn his pale, grave face surprisedly, hearing a snuffling sound, suddenly stifled in a drawer of corks.

Said Raoul, with an unsteady utterance, as he slammed the drawer :

"H-h-dat makes me dat I can't 'elp to laugh w'en I t'ink of dat fool yesse'dy w'at want to buy my pigshoe for honly one 'undred dolla' — ha, ha ha, ha ! "

He laughed almost indecorously.

"Raoul," said Frowenfeld, rising and closing his eyes, "I am going back for my hat. It would make matters worse for that person to send it to me, and it would be something like a vindication for me to go back to the house and get it."

Mr. Innerarity was about to make strenuous objection, when there came in one whom he recognized as an attaché of his cousin Honoré's counting-room, and handed the apothecary a note. It contained Honoré's request that if Frowenfeld was in his shop he would have the goodness to wait there until the writer could call and see him.

"I will wait," was the reply.

XXXV

" FO' WAD YOU CRYNE ? "

CLOTILDE, a step or two from home, dismissed her attendant, and as Aurora, with anxious haste, opened to her familiar knock, appeared before her pale and trembling.

" *Ah, ma fille* —— "

The overwrought girl dropped her head and wept without restraint upon her mother's neck. She let herself be guided to a chair, and there, while Aurora nestled close to her side, yielded a few moments to reverie before she was called upon to speak. Then Aurora first quietly took possession of her hands, and after another tender pause asked in English, which was equivalent to whispering:

"W'ere you was, *chérie ?* "

"'Sieur Frowenfel' —— "

Aurora straightened up with angry astonishment and drew in her breath for an emphatic speech, but Clotilde, liberating her own hands, took Aurora's, and hurriedly said, turning still paler as she spoke:

"'E godd his 'ead strigue ! 'T is all knog in be'ine ! 'E come in blidding —— "

" In w'ere ? " cried Aurora.

" In 'is shob."

" You was in dad shob of 'Sieur Frowenfel' ? "

" I wend ad 'is shob to pay doze rend."

" How — you wend ad 'is shob to pay —— "

Clotilde produced the bracelet. The two looked at each other in silence for a moment, while Aurora took in without further explanation Clotilde's project and its failure.

" An' 'Sieur Frowenfel' — dey kill 'im ? Ah ! *Ma chère,* fo' wad you mague me to hass all dose question ? "

Clotilde gave a brief account of the matter, omitting only her conversation with Frowenfeld.

" *Mais*, oo strigue 'im ? " demanded Aurora, impatiently.

" Addunno ! " replied the other.   " Bud I does know 'e is hinnocen' ! "

A small scouting-party of tears reappeared on the edge of her eyes.

" Innocen' from wad ? "

Aurora betrayed a twinkle of amusement.

" Hev'ryt'in', iv you pliz ! " exclaimed Clotilde, with most uncalled-for warmth.

" An' you crah bic-ause 'e is nod guiltie ? "

" Ah ! foolish ! "

" Ah, non, my chile, I know fo' wad you cryne : 't is h-only de sighd of de blood."

" Oh, sighd of blood ! "

Clotilde let a little nervous laugh escape through her dejection.

" Well, then," — Aurora's eyes twinkled like stars, — " id muz be bic-ause 'Sieur Frowenfel' bump 'is 'ead — ha, ha, ha ! "

" 'T is nod tru' ! " cried Clotilde ; but, instead of laughing, as Aurora had supposed she would, she sent a double flash of light from her eyes, crimsoned, and retorted, as the tears again sprang from their lurking-place, " You wand to mague ligue you don't kyah ! But *I* know ! I know verrie well ! You kyah fifty time' as mudge as me ! I know you ! I know you ! I bin wadge you ! "

Aurora was quite dumb for a moment, and gazed at Clotilde, wondering what could have made her

so unlike herself. Then she half rose up, and, as
she reached forward an arm, and laid it tenderly
about her daughter's neck, said :

"Ma lill dotter, wad dad meggin you cry ? Iv
you will tell me wad dad mague you cry, I will tell
you — on ma *second word of honor* " — she rolled
up her fist — "juz wad I thing about dad 'Sieur
Frowenfel' ! "

" I don't kyah wad de whole worl' thing aboud
'im ! "

" *Mais*, anny'ow, tell me fo' wad you cryne ! "

Clotilde gazed aside for a moment and then confronted her questioner consentingly.

" I tole 'im I knowed 'e was h-innocen'."

" *Eh, bien*, dad was h-only de poli-i-idenez.
Wad 'e said ? "

" E said I din knowed 'im 'tall."

" An' you," exclaimed Aurora, "it is nod poz-
zyble dad you —— "

" I tole 'im I know 'im bette'n 'e know annyt'in'
'boud id ! "

The speaker dropped her face into her mother's
lap.

" Ha, ha ! " laughed Aurora, "an' wad of dad ? I
would say dad, me, fo' time' a day. I gi'e you my
word 'e don godd dad sens' to know wad dad mean."

" Ah ! don godd sens' ! " cried Clotilde, lifting
her head up suddenly with a face of agony.
" 'E reg — 'e reggo-ni-i-ize me ! "

Aurora caught her daughter's cheeks between her
hands and laughed all over them.

"*Mais*, don you see 'ow dad was luggy? Now, you know?—'e goin' fall in love wid you an' you goin' 'ave dad sadizfagzion to rif-use de biggis' hand in Noo-'leans. An' you will be h-even, ha, ha! Bud me—you wand to know wad I thing aboud 'im? I thing 'e is one—egcellen' drug-cl—ah, ha, ha!"

Clotilde replied with a smile of grieved incredulity.

"De bez in de ciddy!" insisted the other. She crossed the forefinger of one hand upon that of the other and kissed them, reversed the cross and kissed them again. "*Mais*, ad de sem tam," she added, giving her daughter time to smile, "I thing 'e is one *noble gen'leman*. Nod to sood me, of coze, *mais, çà fait rien*—daz nott'n; me, I am now a h'ole woman, you know, eh? Noboddie can' nevva sood me no mo', nod ivven dad Govenno' Cleb-orne."

She tried to look old and jaded.

"Ah, Govenno' Cleb-orne!" exclaimed Clotilde.

"Yass!—Ah, you!—you thing iv a man is nod a Creole 'e bown to be no 'coun'! I assu' you dey don' godd no boddy wad I fine a so nize gen-'leman lag Govenno' Cleb-orne! Ah! Clotilde, you godd no lib'ral'ty!"

The speaker rose, cast a discouraged parting look upon her narrow-minded companion and went to investigate the slumbrous silence of the kitchen.

CHAPTER XXXVI

AURORA'S LAST PICAYUNE

NOT often in Aurora's life had joy and trembling so been mingled in one cup as on this day. Clotilde wept; and certainly the mother's heart could but respond; yet Clotilde's tears filled her with a secret pleasure which fought its way up into the beams of her eyes and asserted itself in the frequency and heartiness of her laugh despite her sincere participation in her companion's distresses and a fearful looking forward to to-morrow.

Why these flashes of gladness? If we do not know, it is because we have overlooked one of her sources of trouble. From the night of the *bal masqué* she had — we dare say no more than that she had been haunted; she certainly would not at first have admitted even so much to herself. Yet the fact was not thereby altered, and first the fact and later the feeling had given her much distress of mind. Who he was whose image would not down, for a long time she did not know. This, alone, was torture; not merely because it was mystery, but because it helped to force upon her consciousness that her affections, spite of her, were ready and waiting for him and he did not come after them. That he loved her, she knew; she had achieved at the ball an overwhelming victory, to her certain knowledge, or, depend upon it, she never would have unmasked — never.

But with this torture was mingled not only the ecstasy of loving, but the fear of her daughter. This is a world that allows nothing without its obverse and reverse. Strange differences are often seen between the two sides; and one of the strangest and most inharmonious in this world of human relations is that coinage which a mother sometimes finds herself offering to a daughter, and which reads on one side, Bridegroom, and on the other, Stepfather.

Then, all this torture to be hidden under smiles! Worse still, when by and by Messieurs Agoussou, Assonquer, Danny and others had been appealed to and a Providence boundless in tender compassion had answered in their stead, she and her lover had simultaneously discovered each other's identity only to find that he was a Montague to her Capulet. And the source of her agony must be hidden, and falsely attributed to the rent deficiency and their unprotected lives. Its true nature must be concealed even from Clotilde. What a secret — for what a spirit — to keep from what a companion! — a secret yielding honey to her, but, it might be, gall to Clotilde. She felt like one locked in the Garden of Eden all alone — alone with all the ravishing flowers, alone with all the lions and tigers. She wished she had told the secret when it was small and had let it increase by gradual accretions in Clotilde's knowledge day by day. At first it had been but a garland, then it had become a chain, now it was a ball and chain; and it was oh! and oh! if Clotilde would only fall in love herself! How that would simplify matters! More than twice or thrice she had tried to reveal her over-strained heart in broken sections; but on her approach to the very outer confines of the matter, Clotilde had always behaved so strangely, so nervously, in short, so beyond Aurora's comprehension, that she invariably failed to make any revelation.

And now, here in the very central darkness of this cloud of troubles, comes in Clotilde, throws herself upon the defiant little bosom so full of hidden suffering, and weeps tears of innocent confession that in a moment lay the dust of half of Aurora's perplexities. Strange world! The tears of the orphan making the widow weep for joy, if she only dared.

The pair sat down opposite each other at their little dinner-table. They had a fixed hour for dinner. It is well to have a fixed hour; it is in the direction of system. Even if you have not the dinner, there is the hour. Alphonsina was not in perfect harmony with this fixed-hour idea. It was Aurora's belief, often expressed in hungry moments with the laugh of a vexed Creole lady (a laugh worthy of study), that on the day when dinner should really be served at the appointed hour, the cook would drop dead of apoplexy and she of fright. She said it to-day, shutting her arms down to her side, closing her eyes with her eyebrows raised, and dropping into her chair at the

table like a dead bird from its perch. Not that
she felt particularly hungry; but there is a certain
desultoriness allowable at table more than elsewhere,
and which suited the hither-thither movement of
her conflicting feelings. This is why she had
wished for dinner.

Boiled shrimps, rice, claret-and-water, bread —
they were dining well the day before execution.
Dining is hardly correct, either, for Clotilde, at
least, did not eat; they only sat. Clotilde had,
too, if not her unknown, at least her unconfessed
emotions. Aurora's were tossed by the waves, hers
were sunken beneath them. Aurora had a faith
that the rent would be paid — a faith which was
only a vapor, but a vapor gilded by the sun — that
is, by Apollo, or, to be still more explicit, by
Honoré Grandissime. Clotilde, deprived of this
confidence, had tried to raise means wherewith to
meet the dread obligation, or, rather, had tried to
try and had failed. To-day was the ninth, to-
morrow, the street. Joseph Frowenfeld was hurt;
her dependence upon his good offices was gone.
When she thought of him suffering under public
contumely, it seemed to her as if she could feel the
big drops of blood dropping from her heart; and
when she recalled her own actions, speeches, and
demonstrations in his presence, exaggerated by the
groundless fear that he had guessed into the deepest springs of her feelings, then she felt those drops
of blood congeal. Even if the apothecary had been
duller of discernment than she supposed, here was

Aurora on the opposite side of the table, reading
every thought of her inmost soul. But worst of
all was 'Sieur Frowenfel's indifference. It is true
that, as he had directed upon her that gaze of
recognition, there was a look of mighty gladness,
if she dared believe her eyes. But no, she dared
not; there was nothing there for her, she thought,
— probably (when this anguish of public disgrace
should by any means be lifted) a benevolent smile
at her and her betrayal of interest. Clotilde felt as
though she had been laid entire upon a slide of
his microscope.

Aurora at length broke her reverie.

"Clotilde," — she spoke in French — "the matter with you is that you have no heart. You never
did have any. Really and truly, you do not care
whether 'Sieur Frowenfel' lives or dies. You do
not care how he is or where he is this minute. I
wish you had some of my too large heart. I not
only have the heart, as I tell you, to think kindly
of our enemies, those Grandissime, for example " —
she waved her hand with the air of selecting at ran-
dom — " but I am burning up to know what is the
condition of that poor, sick, noble 'Sieur Frowenfel',
and I am going to do it!"

The heart which Clotilde was accused of not
having gave a stir of deep gratitude. Dear, pretty
little mother! Not only knowing full well the
existence of this swelling heart and the significance,
to-day, of its every warm pulsation, but kindly
covering up the discovery with make-believe re-

proaches. The tears started in her eyes; that was her reply.

"Oh, now! it is the rent again, I suppose," cried Aurora, "always the rent. It is not the rent that worries *me*, it is 'Sieur Frowenfel', poor man. But very well, Mademoiselle Silence, I will match you for making me do all the talking." She was really beginning to sink under the labor of carrying all the sprightliness for both. "Come," she said, savagely, "propose something."

"Would you think well to go and inquire?"

"Ah, listen! Go and what? No, Mademoiselle, I think not."

"Well, send Alphonsina."

"What? And let him know that I am anxious about him? Let me tell you, my little girl, I shall not drag upon myself the responsibility of increasing the self-conceit of any of that sex."

"Well, then, send to buy a picayune's worth of something."

"Ah, ha, ha! An emetic, for instance. Tell him we are poisoned on mushrooms, ha, ha, ha!"

Clotilde laughed too.

"Ah, no," she said. "Send for something he does not sell."

Aurora was laughing while Clotilde spoke; but as she caught these words she stopped with open-mouthed astonishment, and, as Clotilde blushed, laughed again.

"Oh, Clotilde, Clotilde, Clotilde!" — she leaned forward over the table, her face beaming with love

and laughter — "you rowdy! you rascal! You
are just as bad as your mother, whom you think so
wicked! I accept your advice. Alphonsina!"

"Momselle!"

The answer came from the kitchen.

"Come go — or, rather, — *vini 'ci courri dans
boutique de l'apothecaire.* Clotilde," she continued,
in better French, holding up the coin to view,
"look!"

"What?"

"The last picayune we have in the world — ha,
ha, ha!"

CHAPTER XXXVII

HONORÉ MAKES SOME CONFESSIONS

"*Comment çà va, Raoul?*" said Honoré Grandissime; he had come to the shop according to the
proposal contained in his note. "Where is Mr.
Frowenfeld?"

He found the apothecary in the rear room,
dressed, but just rising from the bed at sound of
his voice. He closed the door after him; they
shook hands and took chairs.

"You have fever," said the merchant. "I have
been troubled that way myself, some, lately." He
rubbed his face all over, hard, with one hand, and
looked at the ceiling. "Loss of sleep, I suppose,
in both of us; in your case voluntary — in pursuit
of study, most likely; in my case — effect of

anxiety." He smiled a moment and then suddenly sobered as after a pause he said :

" But I hear you are in trouble ; may I ask ——— "

Frowenfeld had interrupted him with almost the same words :

" May I venture to ask, Mr. Grandissime, what ——— "

And both were silent for a moment.

" Oh," said Honoré, with a gesture. " My trouble — I did not mean to mention it ; 't is an old matter — in part. You know, Mr. Frowenfeld, there is a kind of tree not dreamed of in botany, that lets fall its fruit every day in the year — you know ? We call it — with reverence — ' our dead father's mistakes.' I have had to eat much of that fruit ; a man who has to do that must expect to have now and then a little fever."

" I have heard," replied Frowenfeld, " that some of the titles under which your relatives hold their lands are found to be of the kind which the State's authorities are pronouncing worthless. I hope this is not the case."

" I wish they had never been put into my custody," said M. Grandissime.

Some new thought moved him to draw his chair closer.

" Mr. Frowenfeld, those two ladies whom you went to see the other evening ——— "

His listener started a little :

" Yes."

" Did they ever tell you their history ? "

"No, sir; but I have heard it."

"And you think they have been deeply wronged, eh? Come, Mr. Frowenfeld, take right hold of the acacia-bush." M. Grandissime did not smile.

Frowenfeld winced. "I think they have."

"And you think restitution should be made them, no doubt, eh?"

"I do."

"At any cost?"

The questioner showed a faint, unpleasant smile, that stirred something like opposition in the breast of the apothecary.

"Yes," he answered.

The next question had a tincture even of fierceness:

"You think it right to sink fifty or a hundred people into poverty to lift one or two out?"

"Mr. Grandissime," said Frowenfeld, slowly, "you bade me study this community."

"I adv— yes; what is it you find?"

"I find — it may be the same with other communities, I suppose it is, more or less — that just upon the culmination of the moral issue it turns and asks the question which is behind it, instead of the question which is before it."

"And what is the question before me?"

"I know it only in the abstract."

"Well?"

The apothecary looked distressed.

"You should not make me say it," he objected.

"Nevertheless," said the Creole, "I take that liberty."

"Well, then," said Frowenfeld, "the question behind is Expediency and the question in front, Divine Justice. You are asking yourself——"

He checked himself.

"Which I ought to regard," said M. Grandissime, quickly. "Expediency, of course, and be like the rest of mankind." He put on a look of bitter humor. "It is all easy enough for you, Mr. Frowenfeld, my-de'-seh; you have the easy part—the theorizing."

He saw the ungenerousness of his speech as soon as it was uttered, yet he did not modify it.

"True, Mr. Grandissime," said Frowenfeld; and after a pause—"but you have the noble part—the doing."

"Ah, my-de'-seh!" exclaimed Honoré; "the noble part! There is the bitterness of the draught! The opportunity to act is pushed upon me, but the opportunity to act nobly has passed by."

He again drew his chair closer, glanced behind him and spoke low:

"Because for years I have had a kind of custody of all my kinsmen's property interests, Agricola's among them, it is supposed that he has always kept the plantation of Aurore Nancanou (or rather of Clotilde—who, you know, by our laws is the real heir). That is a mistake. Explain it as you please, call it remorse, pride, love—what you like—while I was in France and he was managing

my mother's business, unknown to me he gave
me that plantation. When I succeeded him I
found it and all its revenues kept distinct — as
was but proper — from all other accounts, and
belonging to me. 'T was a fine, extensive place,
had a good overseer on it and — I kept it. Why?
Because I was a coward. I did not want it or its
revenues; but, like my father, I would not offend
my people. Peace first and justice afterwards —
that was the principle on which I quietly made
myself the trustee of a plantation and income
which you would have given back to their owners,
eh?"

Frowenfeld was silent.

"My-de'-seh, recollect that to us the Grandissime
name is a treasure. And what has preserved it so
long? Cherishing the unity of our family; that
has done it; that is how my father did it. Just or
unjust, good or bad, needful or not, done elsewhere
or not, I do not say; but it is a Creole trait. See,
even now" (the speaker smiled on one side of his
mouth) "in a certain section of the territory certain
men, Creoles" (he whispered, gravely), "*some Grandissimes among them*, evading the United States
revenue laws and even beating and killing some
of the officials: well! Do the people at large
repudiate those men? My-de'-seh, in no wise,
seh! No; if they were *Américains* — but a Louisianian — is a Louisianian; touch him not; when
you touch him you touch all Louisiana! So with
us Grandissimes; we are legion, but we are one.

Now, my-de'-seh, the thing you ask me to do is to cast overboard that old traditional principle which is the secret of our existence."

" *I* ask you?"

" Ah, bah! you know you expect it. Ah! but you do not know the uproar such an action would make. And no ' noble part ' in it, my-de'-seh, either. A few months ago — when we met by those graves — if I had acted then, my action would have been one of pure — even violent — *self*-sacrifice. Do you remember — on the levee, by the Place d'Armes — me asking you to send Agricola to me? I tried then to speak of it. He would not let me. Then, my people felt safe in their land-titles and public offices; this restitution would have hurt nothing but pride. Now, titles in doubt, government appointments uncertain, no ready capital in reach for any purpose, except that which would have to be handed over with the plantation (for to tell you the fact, my-de'-seh, no other account on my books has prospered), with matters changed in this way, I become the destroyer of my own flesh and blood! Yes, seh! and lest I might still find some room to boast, another change moves me into a position where it suits me, my-de'-seh, to make the restitution so fatal to those of my name. When you and I first met, those ladies were as much strangers to me as to you — as far as I *knew*. Then, if I had done this thing —— but now — now, my-de'-seh, I find myself in love with one of them! "

M. Grandissime looked his friend straight in the eye with the frowning energy of one who asserts an ugly fact.

Frowenfeld, regarding the speaker with a gaze of respectful attention, did not falter; but his fevered blood, with an impulse that started him half from his seat, surged up into his head and face; and then ——

M. Grandissime blushed.

In the few silent seconds that followed, the glances of the two friends continued to pass into each other's eyes, while about Honoré's mouth hovered the smile of one who candidly surrenders his innermost secret, and the lips of the apothecary set themselves together as though he were whispering to himself behind them, "Steady."

"Mr. Frowenfeld," said the Creole, taking a sudden breath and waving a hand, "I came to ask about *your* trouble; but if you think you have any reason to withhold your confidence —— "

"No, sir; no! But can I be no help to you in this matter?"

The Creole leaned back smilingly in his chair and knit his fingers.

"No, I did not intend to say all this; I came to offer my help to you; but my mind is full — what do you expect? My-de'-seh, the foam must come first out of the bottle. You see "—he leaned forward again, laid two fingers in his palm and deepened his tone —" I will tell you: this tree — 'our dead father's mistakes' — is about to drop another rotten apple. I spoke just now of the uproar this restitution would make; why, my-de'-seh, just the mention of the lady's name at my house, when we lately held the *fête de grandpère*, has given rise to a quarrel which is likely to end in a duel."

"Raoul was telling me," said the apothecary.

M. Grandissime made an affirmative gesture.

"Mr. Frowenfeld, if you—if any one—could teach my people—I mean my family—the value of peace (I do not say the duty, my-de'-seh; a merchant talks of values); if you could teach them the value of peace, I would give you, if that was your price"—he ran the edge of his left hand knife-wise around the wrist of his right—"that. And if you would teach it to the whole community—well—I think I would not give my head; maybe you would." He laughed.

"There is a peace which is bad," said the contemplative apothecary.

"Yes," said the Creole, promptly, "the very kind that I have been keeping all this time—and my father before me!"

He spoke with much warmth.

"Yes," he said again, after a pause which was not a rest, "I often see that we Grandissimes are a good example of the Creoles at large; we have one element that makes for peace; that—pardon the self-consciousness—is myself; and another element that makes for strife—led by my uncle Agricola; but, my-de'-seh, the peace element is that which

ought to make the strife, and the strife element is
that which ought to be made to keep the peace!
Mr. Frowenfeld, I propose to become the strife-
maker; how then, can I be a peacemaker at the
same time? There is my diffycultie."

"Mr. Grandissime," exclaimed Frowenfeld, "if
you have any design in view founded on the high
principles which I know to be the foundations of
all your feelings, and can make use of the aid of a
disgraced man, use me."

"You are very generous," said the Creole, and
both were silent. Honoré dropped his eyes from
Frowenfeld's to the floor, rubbed his knee with his
palm, and suddenly looked up.

"You are innocent of wrong?"

"Before God."

"I feel sure of it. Tell me in a few words all
about it. I ought to be able to extricate you. Let
me hear it."

Frowenfeld again told as much as he thought he
could, consistently with his pledges to Palmyre,
touching with extreme lightness upon the part
taken by Clotilde.

"Turn around," said M. Grandissime at the
close; "let me see the back of your head. And it
is that that is giving you this fever, eh?"

"Partly," replied Frowenfeld; "but how shall
I vindicate my innocence? I think I ought to go
back openly to this woman's house and get my hat.
I was about to do that when I got your note; yet
it seems a feeble — even if possible — expedient."

" My friend," said Honoré, " leave it to me.   I
see your whole case, both what you tell and what
you conceal.   I guess it with ease.   Knowing Palmyre so well, and knowing (what you do not) that
all the voudous in town think you a sorcerer, I
know just what she would drop down and beg you
for—a *ouangan*, ha, ha! You see?   Leave it all
to me — and your hat with Palmyre, take a febri-
fuge and a nap, and await word from me."

" And may I offer you no help in your difficulty ? "
asked the apothecary, as the two rose and grasped
hands.

" Oh ! " said the Creole, with a little shrug, " you
may do anything you can—which will be nothing."

CHAPTER XXXVIII

TESTS OF FRIENDSHIP

FROWENFELD turned away from the closing door,
caught his head between his hands and tried to
comprehend the new wildness of the tumult within.
Honoré Grandissime avowedly in love with one
of them — *which one ?*   Doctor Keene visibly in
love with one of them — *which one ?* And he !
What meant this bounding joy that, like one gorgeous moth among innumerable bats, flashed to and
fro among the wild distresses and dismays swarming
in and out of his distempered imagination ?   He
did not answer the question ; he only knew the

confusion in his brain was dreadful. Both hands could not hold back the throbbing of his temples; the table did not steady the trembling of his hands; his thoughts went hither and thither, heedless of his call. Sit down as he might, rise up, pace the room, stand, lean his forehead against the wall — nothing could quiet the fearful disorder, until at length he recalled Honoré's neglected advice and resolutely lay down and sought sleep; and, long before he had hoped to secure it, it came.

In the distant Grandissime mansion, Agricola Fusilier was casting about for ways and means to rid himself of the heaviest heart that ever had throbbed in his bosom. He had risen at sunrise from slumber worse than sleeplessness, in which his dreams had anticipated the duel of to-morrow with Sylvestre. He was trying to get the unwonted quaking out of his hands and the memory of the night's heart-dissolving phantasms from before his inner vision. To do this he had resort to a very familiar, we may say time-honored, prescription — rum. He did not use it after the voudou fashion; the voudous pour it on the ground — Agricola was an anti-voudou. It finally had its effect. By eleven o'clock he seemed, outwardly at least, to be at peace with everything in Louisiana that he considered Louisianian, properly so-called; as to all else he was ready for war, as in peace one should be. While in this mood, and performing at a sideboard the solemn rite of *las onze*, news incidentally reached him, by the mouth of his busy second,

Hippolyte, of Frowenfeld's trouble, and despite 'Polyte's protestations against the principal in a pending "affair" appearing on the street, he ordered the carriage and hurried to the apothecary's.

When Frowenfeld awoke, the fingers of his clock were passing the meridan. His fever was gone, his brain was calm, his strength in good measure had returned. There had been dreams in his sleep, too ; he had seen Clotilde standing at the foot of his bed. He lay now, for a moment, lost in retrospection.

"There can be no doubt about it," said he, as he rose up, looking back mentally at something in the past.

The sound of carriage-wheels attracted his attention by ceasing before his street door. A moment later the voice of Agricola was heard in the shop greeting Raoul. As the old man lifted the head of his staff to tap on the inner door, Frowenfeld opened it.

"Fusilier to the rescue!" said the great Louisianian, with a grasp of the apothecary's hand and a gaze of brooding admiration.

Joseph gave him a chair, but with magnificent humility he insisted on not taking it until "Professor Frowenfeld" had himself sat down.

The apothecary was very solemn. It seemed to him as if in this little back room his dead good name was lying in state, and these visitors were coming in to take their last look. From time to time he longed for more light, wondering why the gravity of his misadventure should seem so great.

"H-m-h-y dear Professor!" began the old man. Pages of print could not comprise all the meanings of his smile and accent; benevolence, affection, assumed knowledge of the facts, disdain of results, remembrance of his own youth, charity for pranks, patronage — these were but a few. He spoke very slowly and deeply and with this smile of a hundred meanings. "Why did you not send for me, Joseph? Sir, whenever you have occasion to make a list of the friends who will stand by you, *right or wrong* — h-write the name of Citizen Agricola Fusilier at the top! Write it large and repeat it at the bottom! You understand me, Joseph? — and, mark me, — right or wrong!"

"Not wrong," said Frowenfeld, "at least not in defence of wrong; I could not do that; but, I assure you, in this matter I have done ——"

"No worse than any one else would have done under the circumstances, my dear boy! — Nay, nay, do not interrupt me; I understand you, I understand you. H-do you imagine there is anything strange to me in this — at my age?"

"But I am ——"

"—— all right, sir! that is *what* you are. And you are under the wing of Agricola Fusilier, the old eagle; that is *where* you are. And you are one of my brood; that is *who* you are. Professor, listen to your old father. *The — man — makes — the — crime!* The wisdom of mankind never brought forth a maxim of more gigantic beauty. If the different grades of race and society did not have corresponding moral and civil liberties, varying in degree as they vary — h-why! *this* community, at least, would go to pieces! See here! Professor Frowenfeld is charged with misdemeanor. Very well, who is he? Foreigner or native? Foreigner by sentiment and intention, or only by accident of birth? Of our mental fibre — our aspirations — our delights — our indignations? I answer for you, Joseph, yes! — yes! What then? H-why, then the decision! Reached how? By apologetic reasonings? By instinct, sir! h-h-that guide of the nobly proud! And what is the decision? Not guilty. Professor Frowenfeld, *absolvo te!*"

It was in vain that the apothecary repeatedly tried to interrupt this speech. "Citizen Fusilier, do you know me no better?" — "Citizen Fusilier, if you will but listen!" — such were the fragments of his efforts to explain. The old man was not so confident as he pretended to be that Frowenfeld was that complete proselyte which alone satisfies a Creole; but he saw him in a predicament and cast to him this life-buoy, which if a man should refuse, he would deserve to drown.

Frowenfeld tried again to begin.

"Mr. Fusilier —— "

"*Cit*izen Fusilier!"

"Citizen, candor demands that I undeceive —— "

"Candor demands — h-my dear Professor, let me tell you exactly what she demands. She demands that in here — within this apartment — we understand each other.   That demand is met."

" But —— " Frowenfeld frowned impatiently.

"That demand, Joseph, is fully met!   I understand the whole matter like an eye-witness!   Now there is another demand to be met, the demand of friendship!   In here, candor; outside, friendship; in here, one of our brethren has been adventurous and unfortunate; outside " — the old man smiled a smile of benevolent mendacity — " outside, nothing has happened."

Frowenfeld insisted savagely on speaking; but Agricola raised his voice, and gray hairs prevailed.

"At least, what *has* happened?   The most ordinary thing in the world; Professor Frowenfeld lost his footing on a slippery gunwale, fell, cut his head upon a protruding spike, and went into the house of Palmyre to bathe his wound; but finding it worse than he had at first supposed it, immediately hurried out again and came to his store.   He left his hat where it had fallen, too muddy to be worth recovery.   Hippolyte Brahmin-Mandarin and others, passing at the time, thought he had met with violence in the house of the hair-dresser, and drew some natural inferences, but have since been better informed; and the public will please understand that Professor Frowenfeld is a white man, a gentleman, and a Louisianian, ready to vindicate his honor, and that Citizen Agricola Fusilier is his friend!"

The old man looked around with the air of a bull on a hill-top.

Frowenfeld, vexed beyond degree, restrained himself only for the sake of an object in view, and contented himself with repeating for the fourth or fifth time, —

"I cannot accept any such deliverance."

"Professor Frowenfeld, friendship — society — demands it; our circle must be protected in all its members. You have nothing to do with it. You will leave it with me, Joseph."

"No, no," said Frowenfeld, "I thank you, but ——"

"Ah! my dear boy, thank me not; I cannot help these impulses; I belong to a warm-hearted race. But " — he drew back in his chair sidewise and made great pretence of frowning — "you decline the offices of that precious possession, a Creole friend?"

"I only decline to be shielded by a fiction."

"Ah-h!" said Agricola, further nettling his victim by a gaze of stagy admiration. "'*Sans peur et sans reproche*' — and yet you disappoint me. Is it for naught, that I have sallied forth from home, drawing the curtains of my carriage to shield me from the gazing crowd? It was to rescue my friend — my vicar — my coadjutor — my son — from the laughs and finger-points of the vulgar mass. H-I might as well have stayed at home — or better, for my peculiar position to-day rather requires me to keep in ——"

"No, citizen," said Frowenfeld, laying his hand upon Agricola's arm, "I trust it is not in vain that you have come out. There *is* a man in trouble whom only you can deliver."

The old man began to swell with complacency.

" H-why, really —— "

" *He*, Citizen, is truly of your kind —— "

" He must be delivered, Professor Frowenfeld —— "

" He is a native Louisianian, not only by accident of birth but by sentiment and intention," said Frowenfeld.

The old man smiled a benign delight, but the apothecary now had the upper hand, and would not hear him speak.

" His aspirations," continued the speaker, " his indignations — mount with his people's. His pulse beats with yours, sir. He is a part of your circle. He is one of your caste."

Agricola could not be silent.

" Ha-a-a-ah! Joseph, h-h-you make my blood tingle! Speak to the point; who —— "

" I believe him, moreover, Citizen Fusilier, innocent of the charge laid —— "

" H-innocent? H-of course he is innocent, sir! We will *make* him inno —— "

" Ah! Citizen, he is already under sentence of death!"

" *What?* A Creole under sentence!" Agricola swore a heathen oath, set his knees apart and grasped his staff by the middle. " Sir, we will liberate him if we have to overturn the government!"

Frowenfeld shook his head.

"You have got to overturn something stronger than government."

"And pray what ——"

"A conventionality," said Frowenfeld, holding the old man's eye.

"Ha, ha! my b-hoy, h-you are right. But we will overturn — eh?"

"I say I fear your engagements will prevent. I hear you take part to-morrow morning in ——"

Agricola suddenly stiffened.

"Professor Frowenfeld, it strikes me, sir, you are taking something of a liberty."

"For which I ask pardon," exclaimed Frowenfeld. "Then I may not expect ——"

The old man melted again.

"But who is this person in mortal peril?"

Frowenfeld hesitated.

"Citizen Fusilier," he said, looking first down at the floor and then up into the inquirer's face, "on my assurance that he is not only a native Creole, but a Grandissime ——"

"It is not possible!" exclaimed Agricola.

"—— a Grandissime of the purest blood, will you pledge me your aid to liberate him from his danger, 'right or wrong'?"

"*Will* I? H-why, certainly! Who is he?"

"Citizen —— it is Sylves ——"

Agricola sprang up with a thundering oath.

The apothecary put out a pacifying hand, but it was spurned.

"Let me go! How dare you, sir? How dare you, sir?" bellowed Agricola.

He started toward the door, cursing furiously and keeping his eye fixed on Frowenfeld with a look of rage not unmixed with terror.

"Citizen Fusilier," said the apothecary, following him with one palm uplifted, as if that would ward off his abuse, "don't go! I adjure you, don't go! Remember your pledge, Citizen Fusilier!"

Agricola did not pause a moment; but when he had swung the door violently open the way was still obstructed. The painter of "Louisiana refusing to enter the Union" stood before him, his head elevated loftily, one foot set forward and his arm extended like a tragedian's.

"Stan' bag-sah!"

"Let me pass! Let me pass, or I will kill you!"

Mr. Innerarity smote his bosom and tossed his hand aloft.

"Kill me-firse an' pass aftah!"

"Citizen Fusilier," said Frowenfeld, "I beg you to hear me."

"Go away! Go away!"

The old man drew back from the door and stood in the corner against the book-shelves as if all the horrors of the last night's dreams had taken bodily shape in the person of the apothecary. He trembled and stammered:

"Ke — keep off! Keep off! My God! Raoul, he has insulted me!" He made a miserable show of drawing a weapon. " No man may insult me and live ! If you are a man, Professor Frowenfeld, you will defend yourself ! "

Frowenfeld lost his temper, but his hasty reply was drowned by Raoul's vehement speech.

" 'T is not de trute ! " cried Raoul. " He try to save you from hell-'n'-damnation w'en 'e h-ought to give you a good cuss'n ! " — and in the ecstasy of his anger burst into tears.

Frowenfeld, in an agony of annoyance, waved him away and he disappeared, shutting the door.

Agricola, moved far more from within than from without, had sunk into a chair under the shelves. His head was bowed, a heavy grizzled lock fell down upon his dark, frowning brow, one hand clenched the top of his staff, the other his knee, and both trembled violently. As Frowenfeld, with every demonstration of beseeching kindness, began to speak, he lifted his eyes and said, piteously :

" Stop ! Stop ! "

" Citizen Fusilier, it is you who must stop. Stop before God Almighty stops you, I beg you. I do not presume to rebuke you. I *know* you want a clear record. I know it better to-day than I ever did before. Citizen Fusilier, I honor your intentions —— "

Agricola roused a little and looked up with a miserable attempt at his habitual patronizing smile.

" H-my dear boy, I overlook " — but he met in Frowenfeld's eyes a spirit so superior to his dissimulation that the smile quite broke down and gave

way to another of deprecatory and apologetic distress.
He reached up an arm.

" I could easily convince you, Professor, of your
error " — his eyes quailed and dropped to the floor
— " but I — your arm, my dear Joseph ; age is
creeping upon me." He rose to his feet. " I am
feeling really indisposed to-day — not at all bright ;
my solicitude for you, my dear b —— "

He took two or three steps forward, tottered,
clung to the apothecary, moved another step or
two, and grasping the edge of the table stumbled
into a chair which Frowenfeld thrust under him.
He folded his arms on the edge of the board and
rested his forehead on them, while Frowenfeld sat
down quickly on the opposite side, drew paper and
pen across the table and wrote.

" Are you writing something, Professor ? " asked
the old man, without stirring. His staff tumbled
to the floor. The apothecary's answer was a low,
preoccupied one. Two or three times over he
wrote and rejected what he had written.

Presently he pushed back his chair, came around
the table, laid the writing he had made before the
bowed head, sat down again and waited.

After a long time the old man looked up, trying
in vain to conceal his anguish under a smile.

" I have a sad headache."

He cast his eyes over the table and took mechanically the pen which Frowenfeld extended toward
him.

" What can I do for you, Professor ? Sign

something ?   There is nothing I would not do for Professor Frowenfeld. What have you written, eh ?"

He felt helplessly for his spectacles.

Frowenfeld read :

" *Mr. Sylvestre Grandissime : I spoke in haste.*"

He felt himself tremble as he read. Agricola fumbled with the pen, lifted his eyes with one more effort at the old look, said, " My dear boy, I do this purely to please you," and to Frowenfeld's delight and astonishment wrote :

" *Your affectionate uncle, Agricola Fusilier.*"

CHAPTER XXXIX

LOUISIANA STATES HER WANTS

" 'Sieur Frowenfel'," said Raoul as that person turned in the front door of the shop after watching Agricola's carriage roll away — he had intended to unburden his mind to the apothecary with all his natural impetuosity ; but Frowenfeld's gravity as he turned, with the paper in his hand, induced a different manner. Raoul had learned, despite all the impulses of his nature, to look upon Frowenfeld with a sort of enthusiastic awe. He dropped his voice and said — asking like a child a question he was perfectly able to answer —

" What de matta wid Agricole ? "

Frowenfeld, for the moment well-nigh oblivious of his own trouble, turned upon his assistant a look in which elation was oddly blended with solemnity, and replied as he walked by :

"Rush of truth to the heart."

Raoul followed a step.

"'Sieur Frowenfel'—— "

The apothecary turned once more. Raoul's face bore an expression of earnest practicability that invited confidence.

"'Sieur Frowenfel', Agricola writ'n' to Sylvestre to stop dat dool ? "

"Yes."

"You goin' take dat lett' to Sylvestre ? "

"Yes."

"'Sieur Frowenfel', dat de wrong g-way. You got to take it to 'Polyte Brahmin-Mandarin, an' 'e got to take it to Valentine Grandissime, an' 'e got to take it to Sylvestre. You see, you got to know de manner to make. Once 'pon a time I had a diffycultie wid —— "

"I see," said Frowenfeld; "where may I find Hippolyte Brahmin-Mandarin at this time of day ? "

Raoul shrugged.

"If the pre-parish-ions are not complitted, you will not find 'im ; but if they har complitted — you know 'im ? "

"By sight."

"Well, you may fine him at Maspero's, or helse in de front of de Veau-qui-tête, or helse at de Café Louis Quatorze — mos' likely in front of de Veau-qui-tête. You know, dat diffycultie I had, dat arise itseff from de discush'n of one of de mil-littery mov'ments of ca-valry; you know, I —— ”

“ Yes,” said the apothecary; “ here, Raoul, is some money; please go and buy me a good, plain hat.”

“ All right.” Raoul darted behind the counter and got his hat out of a drawer. “ W'ere at you buy your hats?”

“ Anywhere.”

“ I will go at *my* hatter.”

As the apothecary moved about his shop awaiting Raoul's return, his own disaster became once more the subject of his anxiety. He noticed that almost every person who passed looked in. “ This is the place,”— “ That is the man,”— how plainly the glances of passers sometimes speak! The people seemed, moreover, a little nervous. Could even so little a city be stirred about such a petty, private trouble as this of his? No; the city was having tribulations of its own.

New Orleans was in that state of suppressed excitement which, in later days, a frequent need of reassuring the outer world has caused to be described by the phrase “ never more peaceable.” Raoul perceived it before he had left the shop twenty paces behind. By the time he reached the first corner he was in the swirl of the popular current. He enjoyed it like a strong swimmer. He even drank of it. It was better than wine and music mingled.

"Twelve weeks next Thursday, and no sign of re-cession!" said one of two rapid walkers just in front of him. Their talk was in the French of the province.

"Oh, re-cession!" exclaimed the other angrily. "The cession is a reality. That, at least, we have got to swallow. Incredulity is dead."

The first speaker's feelings could find expression only in profanity.

"The cession — we wash our hands of it!" He turned partly around upon his companion, as they hurried along, and gave his hands a vehement dry washing. "If Incredulity is dead, Non-participation reigns in its stead, and Discontent is prime minister!" He brandished his fist as they turned a corner.

"If we must change, let us be subjects of the First Consul!" said one of another pair whom Raoul met on a crossing.

There was a gathering of boys and vagabonds at the door of a gun-shop. A man inside was buying a gun. That was all.

A group came out of a "coffee-house." The leader turned about upon the rest:

"*Ah, bah! cette* Amayrican libetty!"

"See! see! it is this way!" said another of the number, taking two others by their elbows, to secure an audience, "we shall do nothing ourselves; we are just watching that vile Congress. It is going to tear the country all to bits!"

"Ah, my friend, you have n't got the *inside*

news," said still another — Raoul lingered to hear him
— " Louisiana is going to state her wants ! We have
the liberty of free speech and are going to use it ! "

His information was correct ; Louisiana, no
longer incredulous of her Americanization, had laid
hold of her new liberties and was beginning to run
with them, like a boy dragging his kite over the
clods. She was about to state her wants, he said.

" And her don't-wants," volunteered one whose
hand Raoul shook heartily. " We warn the world.
If Congress does n't take heed, we will not be responsible for the consequences ! "

Raoul's hatter was full of the subject. As Mr.
Innerarity entered, he was saying good-day to a
customer in his native tongue, English, and so
continued :

" Yes, under Spain we had a solid, quiet government — Ah ! Mr. Innerarity, overjoyed to see you!
We were speaking of these political troubles. I
wish we might see the last of them. It's a terrible
bad mess ; corruption to-day — I tell you what —
it will be disruption to-morrow. Well, it is no
work of ours; we shall merely stand off and see it."

" Mi-frien'," said Raoul, with mingled pity and
superiority, " you have n't got doze *inside* nooz ;
Louisiana is goin' to state w'at she want."

On his way back toward the shop Mr. Innerarity
easily learned Louisiana's wants and don't-wants by
heart. She wanted a Creole governor ; she did not
want Casa Calvo invited to leave the country ; she
wanted the provisions of the Treaty of Cession hur-

ried up; "as soon as possible," that instrument said; she had waited long enough; she did not want "dat trile bi-ju'y"—execrable trash! she wanted an *unwatched import trade!* she did not want a single additional Américain appointed to office; she wanted the slave trade.

Just in sight of the bare-headed and anxious Frowenfeld, Raoul let himself be stopped by a friend.

The remark was exchanged that the times were exciting.

"And yet," said the friend, "the city was never more peaceable. It is exasperating to see that coward governor looking so diligently after his police and hurrying on the organization of the Américain volunteer militia!" He pointed savagely here and there. "M. Innerarity, I am lost in admiration at the all but craven patience with which our people endure their wrongs! Do my pistols show *too* much through my coat? Well, good-day; I must go home and clean my gun; my dear friend, one don't know how soon he may have to encounter the Recorder and Register of Land-titles."

Raoul finished his errand.

"'Sieur Frowenfel', excuse me—I take dat lett' to 'Polyte for you if you want." There are times when mere shopkeeping—any peaceful routine—is torture.

But the apothecary felt so himself; he declined his assistant's offer and went out toward the Veau-qui-tête.

CHAPTER XL

FROWENFELD FINDS SYLVESTRE

THE Veau-qui-tête restaurant occupied the whole
ground floor of a small, low, two-story, tile-roofed,
brick-and-stucco building which still stands on the
corner of Chartres and St. Peter streets, in company with the well-preserved old Cabildo and the
young Cathedral, reminding one of the shabby and
swarthy Creoles whom we sometimes see helping
better-kept kinsmen to murder time on the banquettes of the old French Quarter.   It was a favorite rendezvous of the higher classes, convenient to
the court-rooms and municipal bureaus.   There you
found the choicest legal and political gossips, with
the best the market afforded of meat and drink.

Frowenfeld found a considerable number of persons there.   He had to move about among them
to some extent, to make sure he was not overlooking the object of his search.

As he entered the door, a man sitting near it
stopped talking, gazed rudely as he passed, and
then leaned across the table and smiled and murmured to his companion.   The subject of his jest
felt their four eyes on his back.

There was a loud buzz of conversation throughout the room, but wherever he went a wake of
momentary silence followed him, and once or twice
he saw elbows nudged.   He perceived that there

was something in the state of mind of these good citizens that made the present sight of him particularly discordant.

Four men, leaning or standing at a small bar, were talking excitedly in the Creole patois. They made frequent anxious, yet amusedly defiant, mention of a certain *Pointe Canadienne*. It was a portion of the Mississippi River "coast" not far above New Orleans, where the merchants of the city met the smugglers who came up from the Gulf by way of Barrataria Bay and Bayou. These four men did not call it by the proper title just given; there were commercial gentlemen in the Creole city, Englishmen, Scotchmen, Yankees, as well as French and Spanish Creoles, who in public indignantly denied, and in private tittered over, their complicity with the pirates of Grand Isle, and who knew their trading rendezvous by the sly nickname of " Little Manchac." As Frowenfeld passed these four men they, too, ceased speaking and looked after him, three with offensive smiles and one with a stare of contempt.

Farther on, some Creoles were talking rapidly to an Américain, in English.

" And why ? " one was demanding. " Because money is scarce. Under other governments we had any quantity ! "

" Yes," said the venturesome Américain in retort, " such as it was ; *assignats, liberanzas, bons* — Claiborne will give us better money than that when he starts his bank."

"Hah! his bank, yes! John Law once had a bank, too; ask my old father. What do we want with a bank? Down with banks!" The speaker ceased; he had not finished, but he saw the apothecary. Frowenfeld heard a muttered curse, an inarticulate murmur, and then a loud burst of laughter.

A tall, slender young Creole whom he knew, and who had always been greatly pleased to exchange salutations, brushed against him without turning his eyes.

"You know," he was saying to a companion, "everybody in Louisiana is to be a citizen, except the negroes and mules; that is the kind of liberty they give us — all eat out of one trough."

"What we want," said a dark, ill-looking, but finely-dressed man, setting his claret down, "and what we have got to have, is" — he was speaking in French, but gave the want in English — "Representesh'n wizout Taxa——" There his eye fell upon Frowenfeld and followed him with a scowl.

"Mah frang," he said to his table companion, "wass you sink of a mane w'at hask-a one neegrow to 'ave-a one shair wiz 'im, eh? — in ze sem room?"

The apothecary found that his fame was far wider and more general than he had supposed. He turned to go out, bowing as he did so, to an Américain merchant with whom he had some acquaintance.

"Sir?" asked the merchant, with severe politeness, "wish to see me? I thought you —— As

I was saying, gentlemen, what, after all, does it sum up?"

A Creole interrupted him with an answer:

" Leetegash'n, Spoleeash'n, Pahtitsh'n, Disintegrhash'n ! "

The voice was like Honoré's. Frowenfeld looked; it was Agamemnon Grandissime.

" I must go to Maspero's," thought the apothecary, and he started up the rue Chartres. As he turned into the rue St. Louis, he suddenly found himself one of a crowd standing before a newly-posted placard, and at a glance saw it to be one of the inflammatory publications which were a feature of the times, appearing both daily and nightly on walls and fences.

" One Amerry-can pull' it down, an' Camille Brahmin 'e pas'e it back," said a boy at Frowenfeld's side.

Exchange Alley was once *Passage de la Bourse*, and led down (as it now does to the State House — late St. Louis Hotel) to an establishment which seems to have served for a long term of years as a sort of merchants' and auctioneers' coffee-house, with a minimum of china and a maximum of glass : Maspero's — certainly Maspero's as far back as 1810, and, we believe, Maspero's the day the apothecary entered it, March 9, 1804. It was a livelier spot than the Veau-qui-tête ; it was to that what commerce is to litigation, what standing and quaffing is to sitting and sipping. Whenever the public mind approached that sad state of public sentiment in which sanctity signs politicians' memorials and chivalry breaks into the gun-shops, a good place to feel the thump of the machinery was in Maspero's.

The first man Frowenfeld saw as he entered was M. Valentine Grandissime. There was a double semi-circle of gazers and listeners in front of him ; he was talking, with much show of unconcern, in Creole French.

" Policy ?   I care little about policy."   He waved his hand.   " I know my rights — and Louisiana's.   We have a right to our opinions.   We have " — with a quiet smile and an upward turn of his extended palm — " a right to protect them from the attack of interlopers, even if we have to use gunpowder.   I do not propose to abridge the liberties of even this army of fortune-hunters.   *Let* them think."   He half laughed.   " Who cares whether they share our opinions or not ?   Let them have their own.   I had rather they would. But let them hold their tongues.   Let them remember they are Yankees.   Let them remember they are unbidden guests."   All this without the least warmth.

But the answer came aglow with passion, from one of the semicircle, whom two or three seemed disposed to hold in check.   It also was in French, but the apothecary was astonished to hear his own name uttered.

" But this fellow Frowenfeld " — the speaker did not see Joseph — " has never held his tongue.   He has given us good reason half a dozen times, with his too free speech and his high moral whine, to hang him with the lamppost rope! And now, when we have borne and borne and borne and borne with him, and he shows up, all at once, in all his rottenness, you say let him alone! One would think you were defending Honoré Grandissime!" The back of one of the speaker's hands fluttered in the palm of the other.

Valentine smiled.

"Honoré Grandissime? Boy, you do not know what you are talking about. Not Honoré, ha, ha! A man who, upon his own avowal, is guilty of affiliating with the Yankees. A man whom we have good reason to suspect of meditating his family's dishonor and embarrassment!" Somebody saw the apothecary and laid a cautionary touch on Valentine's arm, but he brushed it off. "As for Professor Frowenfeld, he must defend himself."

"Ha-a-a-ah!"—a general cry of derision from the listeners.

"Defend himself!" exclaimed their spokesman; "shall I tell you again what he is?" In his vehemence, the speaker wagged his chin and held his clenched fists stiffly toward the floor. "He is—he is—he is——"

He paused, breathing like a fighting dog. Frowenfeld, large, white, and immovable, stood close before him.

"Dey 'ad no bizniz led 'im come oud to-day," said a bystander, edging toward a pillar.

The Creole, a small young man not unknown to us, glared upon the apothecary; but Frowenfeld was far above his blushing mood, and was not disconcerted. This exasperated the Creole beyond bound; he made a sudden, angry change of attitude, and demanded:

"Do you interrup' two gen'lemen in dey conve'sition, you Yankee clown? Do vou igno' dad you 'ave insult me, off-scow'ing?"

Frowenfeld's first response was a stern gaze. When he spoke, he said:

"Sir, I am not aware that I have ever offered you the slightest injury or affront; if you wish to finish your conversation with this gentleman, I will wait till you are through."

The Creole bowed, as a knight who takes up the gage. He turned to Valentine.

"Valentine, I was sayin' to you dad diz pusson is a cowa'd and a sneak; I repead thad! I repead id! I spurn you! Go f'om yeh!"

The apothecary stood like a cliff.

It was too much for Creole forbearance. His adversary, with a long snarl of oaths, sprang forward and with a great sweep of his arm slapped the apothecary on the cheek. And then —

What a silence!

Frowenfeld had advanced one step; his opponent stood half turned away, but with his face toward the face he had just struck and his eyes glaring up into the eyes of the apothecary. The semicircle was dissolved, and each man stood in neutral isolation, motionless and silent. For one instant objects lost all natural proportion, and to the expectant on-lookers the largest thing in the room was the big, upraised, white fist of Frowenfeld. But in the next — how was this? Could it be that that fist had not descended?

The imperturbable Valentine, with one preventing arm laid across the breast of the expected victim and an open hand held restrainingly up for truce, stood between the two men and said:

"Professor Frowenfeld — one moment ——"

Frowenfeld's face was ashen.

"Don't speak, sir!" he exclaimed. "If I attempt to parley I shall break every bone in his body. Don't speak! I can guess your explanation — he is drunk. But take him away."

Valentine, as sensible as cool, assisted by the kinsman who had laid a hand on his arm, shuffled his enraged companion out. Frowenfeld's still swelling anger was so near getting the better of him that he unconsciously followed a quick step or two; but as Valentine looked back and waved him to stop, he again stood still.

"*Proffesseur* — you know, — " said a stranger, " daz Sylvestre Grandissime."

Frowenfeld rather spoke to himself than answered:

"If I had not known that, I should have —— " He checked himself and left the place.

While the apothecary was gathering these experiences, the free spirit of Raoul Innerarity was chafing

in the shop like an eagle in a hen-coop. One
moment after another brought him straggling evidences, now of one sort, now of another, of the
" never more peaceable " state of affairs without.
If only some pretext could be conjured up, plausible
or flimsy, no matter ; if only some man would pass
with a gun on his shoulder, were it only a blow-
gun ; or if his employer were any one but his beloved Frowenfeld, he would clap up the shutters as
quickly as he had already done once to-day, and be
off to the wars.   He was just trying to hear imaginary pistol-shots down toward the Place d'Armes,
when the apothecary returned.

" D' you fin' him ? "

" I found Sylvestre."

"'E took de lett' ? "

" I did not offer it."   Frowenfeld, in a few compact sentences, told his adventure.

Raoul was ablaze with indignation.

"'Sieur Frowenfel', gimmy dat lett' ! "   He extended his pretty hand.

Frowenfeld pondered.

" Gimmy 'er ! " persisted the artist ; " befo' I lose
de sight from dat lett' she goin' to be hanswer by
Sylvestre Grandissime, an' 'e goin' to wrat you one
appo-logie ! Oh ! I goin' mek 'im crah fo' shem ! "

" If I could know you would do only as I ——— "

" I do it ! " cried Raoul, and sprang for his hat ;
and in the end Frowenfeld let him have his way.

" I had intended seeing him ——— " the apothecary said.

"Nevvamine to see; I goin' tell him!" cried
Raoul, as he crowded his hat fiercely down over his
curls and plunged out.

CHAPTER XLI

TO COME TO THE POINT

IT was equally a part of Honoré Grandissime's
nature and of his art as a merchant to wear a look
of serene leisure. With this look on his face he
reëntered his counting-room after his morning visit
to Frowenfeld's shop. He paused a moment outside the rail, gave the weak-eyed gentleman who
presided there a quiet glance equivalent to a beckon,
and, as that person came near, communicated two
or three items of intelligence or instruction concerning office details, by which that invaluable diviner
of business meanings understood that he wished to
be let alone for an hour. Then M. Grandissime
passed on into his private office, and, shutting the
door behind him, walked briskly to his desk and
sat down.

He dropped his elbows upon a broad paper containing some recently written, unfinished memoranda
that included figures in column, cast his eyes quite
around the apartment, and then covered his face
with his palms — a gesture common enough for a
tired man of business in a moment of seclusion; but
just as the face disappeared in the hands, the look

of serene leisure gave place to one of great mental distress. The paper under his elbows, to the consideration of which he seemed about to return, was in the handwriting of his manager, with additions by his own pen. Earlier in the day he had come to a pause in the making of these additions, and, after one or two vain efforts to proceed, had laid down his pen, taken his hat, and gone to see the unlucky apothecary. Now he took up the broken thread. To come to a decision; that was the task which forced from him his look of distress. He drew his face slowly through his palms, set his lips, cast up his eyes, knit his knuckles, and then opened and struck his palms together, as if to say: "Now, come; let me make up my mind."

There may be men who take every moral height at a dash; but to the most of us there must come moments when our wills can but just rise and walk in their sleep. Those who in such moments wait for clear views find, when the issue is past, that they were only yielding to the devil's chloroform.

Honoré Grandissime bent his eyes upon the paper. But he saw neither its figures nor its words. The interrogation, "Surrender Fausse Rivière?" appeared to hang between his eyes and the paper, and when his resolution tried to answer "Yes," he saw red flags; he heard the auctioneer's drum; he saw his kinsmen handing house-keys to strangers; he saw the old servants of the great family standing in the marketplace; he saw kinswomen pawning their plate; he saw his clerks (Brahmins, Mandarins, Grandissimes) standing idle and shabby in the arcade of the Cabildo and on the banquettes of Maspero's and the Veau-qui-tête; he saw red-eyed young men in the Exchange denouncing a man who, they said, had, ostensibly for conscience's sake, but really for love, forced upon the woman he had hoped to marry a fortune filched from his own kindred. He saw the junto of doctors in Frowenfeld's door charitably deciding him insane; he saw the more vengeful of his family seeking him with half-concealed weapons; he saw himself shot at in the rue Royale, in the rue Toulouse, and in the Place d'Armes: and, worst of all, missed.

But he wiped his forehead, and the writing on the paper became, in a measure, visible. He read:

Total mortgages on the lands of all the Grandissimes	\$—
Total present value of same, titles at buyers' risk	—
Cash, goods, and accounts	—
Fausse Rivière Plantation account	—

There were other items, but he took up the edge of the paper mechanically, pushed it slowly away from him, leaned back in his chair and again laid his hands upon his face.

"Suppose I retain Fausse Rivière," he said to himself, as if he had not said it many times before.

Then he saw memoranda that were not on any paper before him — such a mortgage to be met on such a date; so much from Fausse Rivière Plantation account retained to protect that mortgage from foreclosure; such another to be met on such a date

— so much more of same account to protect it. He saw Aurora and Clotilde Nancanou, with anguished faces, offering woman's pleadings to deaf constables. He saw the remainder of Aurora's plantation account thrown to the lawyers to keep the question of the Grandissime titles languishing in the courts. He saw the fortunes of his clan rallied meanwhile and coming to the rescue, himself and kindred growing independent of questionable titles, and even Fausse Rivière Plantation account restored, but Aurora and Clotilde nowhere to be found. And then he saw the grave, pale face of Joseph Frowenfeld.

He threw himself forward, drew the paper nervously toward him, and stared at the figures. He began at the first item and went over the whole paper, line by line, testing every extension, proving every addition, noting if possibly any transposition of figures had been made and overlooked, if something was added that should have been subtracted, or subtracted that should have been added. It was like a prisoner trying the bars of his cell.

Was there no way to make things happen differently? Had he not overlooked some expedient? Was not some financial manœuvre possible which might compass both desired ends? He left his chair and walked up and down, as Joseph at that very moment was doing in the room where he had left him, came back, looked at the paper, and again walked up and down. He murmured now and then to himself: "*Self*-denial —that is not the hard

work. Penniless myself — *that* is play," and so on.
He turned by and by and stood looking up at that
picture of the man in the cuirass which Aurora had
once noticed. He looked at it, but he did not see
it. He was thinking — "Her rent is due to-
morrow. She will never believe I am not her
landlord. She will never go to my half-brother."
He turned once more and mentally beat his breast
as he muttered : "Why do I not decide?"

Somebody touched the door-knob. Honoré
stepped forward and opened it. It was a mortgager.

"*Ah! entrez, Monsieur.*"

He retained the visitor's hand, leading him in
and talking pleasantly in French until both had
found chairs. The conversation continued in that
tongue through such pointless commercial gossip
as this :

"So the brig *Equinox* is aground at the head of
the Passes," said M. Grandissime.

" I have just heard she is off again."

" Aha ? "

" Yes ; the Fort Plaquemine canoe is just up
from below. I understand John McDonough has
bought the entire cargo of the schooner *Freedom*."

"No, not all; Blanque et Fils bought some
twenty boys and women out of the lot. Where is
she lying?"

" Right at the head of the Basin."

And much more like this ; but by and by the
mortgager came to the point with the casual
remark :

" The excitement concerning land titles seems to increase rather than subside."

" They must have *something* to be excited about, I suppose," said M. Grandissime, crossing his legs and smiling. It was tradesman's talk.

" Yes," replied the other; " there seems to be an idea current to-day that all holders under Spanish titles are to be immediately dispossessed, without even process of court. I believe a very slight indiscretion on the part of the Governor-General would precipitate a riot."

" He will not commit any," said M. Grandissime with a quiet gravity, changing his manner to that of one who draws upon a reserve of private information. " There will be no outbreak."

" I suppose not. We do not know, really, that the American Congress will throw any question upon titles; but still —— "

" What are some of the shrewdest Americans among us doing ? " asked M. Grandissime.

" Yes," replied the mortgager, " it is true they are buying these very titles; but they may be making a mistake ? "

Unfortunately for the speaker, he allowed his face an expression of argumentative shrewdness as he completed this sentence, and M. Grandissime, the merchant, caught an instantaneous full view of his motive; he wanted to buy. He was a man whose known speculative policy was to " go in " in moments of panic.

M. Grandissime was again face to face with the

question of the morning. To commence selling
must be to go on selling. This, as a plan, included
restitution to Aurora; but it meant also dissolution
to the Grandissimes, for should their *sold* titles be
pronounced bad, then the titles of other lands
would be bad; many an asset among M. Grandissime's memoranda would shrink into nothing,
and the meagre proceeds of the Grandissime estates,
left to meet the strain without the aid of Aurora's
accumulated fortune, would founder in a sea of
liabilities; while should these titles, after being
parted with, turn out good, his incensed kindred,
shutting their eyes to his memoranda and despising
his exhibits, would see in him only the family
traitor, and he would go about the streets of his
town the subject of their implacable denunciation,
the community's obloquy, and Aurora's cold eva-
sion. So much, should he sell. On the other
hand, to decline to sell was to enter upon that
disingenuous scheme of delays which would enable
him to avail himself and his people of that favorable wind and tide of fortune which the Cession
had brought. Thus the estates would be lost, if
lost at all, only when the family could afford to
lose them, and Honoré Grandissime would continue to be Honoré the Magnificent, the admiration of the city and the idol of his clan. But
Aurora — and Clotilde — would have to eat the
crust of poverty, while their fortunes, even in his
hands, must bear all the jeopardy of the scheme.
That was all. Retain Fausse Rivière and its wealth,

and save the Grandissimes; surrender Fausse Rivière, let the Grandissime estates go, and save the Nancanous. That was the whole dilemma.

"Let me see," said M. Grandissime. "You have a mortgage on one of our Golden Coast plantations. Well, to be frank with you, I was thinking of that when you came in. You know I am partial to prompt transactions — I thought of offering you either to take up that mortgage or to sell you the plantation, as you may prefer. I have ventured to guess that it would suit you to own it."

And the speaker felt within him a secret exultation in the idea that he had succeeded in throwing the issue off upon a Providence that could control this mortgager's choice.

"I would prefer to leave that choice with you," said the coy would-be purchaser; and then the two went coquetting again for another moment.

"I understand that Nicholas Girod is proposing to erect a four-story brick building on the corner of Royale and St. Pierre. Do you think it practicable? Do you think our soil will support such a structure?"

"Pitot thinks it will. Boré says it is perfectly feasible."

So they dallied.

"Well," said the mortgager, presently rising, "you will make up your mind and let me know, will you?"

The chance repetition of those words "make up

your mind" touched Honoré Grandissime like a
hot iron.   He rose with the visitor.

" Well, sir, what would you give us for our title
in case we should decide to part with it ?"

The two men moved slowly, side by side, toward
the door, and in the half-open doorway, after a little
further trifling, the title was sold.

" Well, good-day," said M. Grandissime.   " M.
de Brahmin will arrange the papers for us to-
morrow."

He turned back toward his private desk.

" And now," thought he, " I am acting without
resolving.   No merit;   no strength of will;   no
clearness of purpose ;   no emphatic decision ;   nothing but a yielding to temptation."

And M. Grandissime spoke truly ;   but it is only
whole men who so yield — yielding to the temptation to do right.

He passed into the counting-room, to M. De
Brahmin, and standing there talked in an inaudible
tone, leaning over the upturned spectacles of his
manager, for nearly an hour.   Then, saying he
would go to dinner, he went out.   He did not dine
at home nor at the Veau-qui-tête, nor at any of the
clubs ; so much is known; he merely disappeared
for two or three hours and was not seen again until
late in the afternoon, when two or three Brahmins
and Grandissimes, wandering about in search of
him, met him on the levee near the head of the rue
Bienville, and with an exclamation of wonder and
a look of surprise at his dusty shoes, demanded to

know where he had hid himself while they had been ransacking the town in search of him.

"We want you to tell us what you will do about our titles."

He smiled pleasantly, the picture of serenity, and replied:

"I have not fully made up my mind yet; as soon as I do so I will let you know."

There was a word or two more exchanged, and then, after a moment of silence, with a gentle "Eh, bien," and a gesture to which they were accustomed, he stepped away backward, they resumed their hurried walk and talk, and he turned into the rue Bienville.

CHAPTER XLII

AN INHERITANCE OF WRONG

"I TELL you," Doctor Keene used to say, "that old woman's a thinker." His allusion was to Clemence, the *marchande des calas*. Her mental activity was evinced not more in the cunning aptness of her songs than in the droll wisdom of her sayings. Not the melody only, but the often audacious, epigrammatic philosophy of her tongue as well, sold her *calas* and gingercakes.

But in one direction her wisdom proved scant. She presumed too much on her insignificance. She was a "study," the gossiping circle at Frowenfeld's used to say; and any observant hearer of her odd aphorisms could see that she herself had made a life-study of herself and her conditions; but she little thought that others — some with wits and some with none — young hare-brained Grandissimes, Mandarins and the like — were silently, and for her most unluckily, charging their memories with her knowing speeches; and that of every one of those speeches she would ultimately have to give account.

Doctor Keene, in the old days of his health, used to enjoy an occasional skirmish with her. Once, in the course of chaffering over the price of *calas*, he enounced an old current conviction which is not without holders even to this day; for we may still hear it said by those who will not be decoyed down from the mountain fastnesses of the old Southern doctrines, that their slaves were "the happiest people under the sun." Clemence had made bold to deny this with argumentative indignation, and was courteously informed in retort that she had promulgated a falsehood of magnitude.

"W'y, Mawse Chawlie," she replied, "does you s'pose one po' nigga kin tell a big lie? No, sah! But w'en de whole people tell w'at ain' so — if dey know it, aw if dey don' know it — den dat *is* a big lie!" And she laughed to contortion.

"What is that you say?" he demanded, with mock ferocity. "You charge white people with lying?"

"Oh, sakes, Mawse Chawlie, no! De people don't mek up dat ah; de debble pass it on 'em.

Don' you know de debble ah de grett cyount'-feiteh? Ev'y piece o' money he mek he tek an' put some debblemen' on de under side, an' one o' his pootiess lies on top; an' 'e gilt dat lie, and 'e rub dat lie on 'is elbow, an' 'e shine dat lie, an' 'e put 'is bess licks on dat lie; entel ev'ybody say: 'Oh, how pooty!' An' dey tek it fo' good money, yass — and pass it! Dey b'lieb it!"

"Oh," said some one at Doctor Keene's side, disposed to quiz, "you niggers don't know when you are happy."

"Dass so, Mawse — *c'est vrai, oui!*" she answered quickly: "we donno no mo'n white folks!"

The laugh was against him.

"Mawse Chawlie," she said again, "w'a's dis I yeh 'bout dat Eu'ope country? 's dat true de niggas is all free in Eu'ope!'"

Doctor Keene replied that something like that was true.

"Well, now, Mawse Chawlie, I gwan t' ass you a riddle. If dat is *so*, den fo' w'y I yeh folks bragg'n 'bout de 'stayt o' s'iety in Eu'ope'?"

The mincing drollery with which she used this fine phrase brought another peal of laughter. No-body tried to guess.

"I gwan tell you," said the *marchande*; "'t is becyaze dey got a 'fixed wuckin' class.'" She sputtered and giggled with the general ha, ha. "Oh, ole Clemence kin talk proctah, yass!"

She made a gesture for attention.

"D' y' ebber yeh w'at de cya'ge-hoss say w'en 'e

see de cyaht-hoss tu'n loose in de sem pawstu'e wid
he, an' knowed dat some'ow de cyaht gotteh be
haul'? W'y 'e jiz snawt an' kick up 'is heel'"—
she suited the action to the word—"an' tah' roun'
de fiel' an' prance up to de fence an' say: 'Whoopy!
shoo! shoo! dis yeh country gittin' *too* free!'"

"Oh," she resumed, as soon as she could be
heard, "white folks is werry kine. Dey wants us
to b'lieb we happy — dey *wants to b'lieb* we is. W'y,
you know, dey 'bleeged to b'lieb it — fo' dey own
cyumfut. 'T is de sem weh wid de preache's; dey
buil' we ow own sep'ate meet'n-houses; dey b'liebs
us lak it de bess, an' dey *knows* dey lak it de bess."

The laugh at this was mostly her own. It is
not a laughable sight to see the comfortable fractions of Christian communities everywhere striving,
with sincere, pious, well-meant, criminal benevolence, to make their poor brethren contented with
the ditch. Nor does it become so to see these
efforts meet, or seem to meet, some degree of
success. Happily man cannot so place his brother
that his misery will continue unmitigated. You
may dwarf a man to the mere stump of what he
ought to be, and yet he will put out green leaves.
"Free from care," we benignly observe of the
dwarfed classes of society; but we forget, or have
never thought, what a crime we commit when we
rob men and women of their cares.

To Clemence the order of society was nothing.
No upheaval could reach to the depth to which she
was sunk. It is true, she was one of the popula-

tion. She had certain affections toward people and places; but they were not of a consuming sort.

As for us, our feelings, our sentiments, affections, etc., are fine and keen, delicate and many; what we call refined. Why? Because we get them as we get our old swords and gems and laces — from our grandsires, mothers, and all. Refined they are — after centuries of refining. But the feelings handed down to Clemence had come through ages of African savagery; through fires that do not refine, but that blunt and blast and blacken and char; starvation, gluttony, drunkenness, thirst, drowning, nakedness, dirt, fetichism, debauchery, slaughter, pestilence and the rest — she was their heiress; they left her the cinders of human feelings. She remembered her mother. They had been separated in her childhood, in Virginia when it was a province. She remembered, with pride, the price her mother had brought at auction, and remarked, as an additional interesting item, that she had never seen or heard of her since. She had had children, assorted colors — had one with her now, the black boy that brought the basil to Joseph; the others were here and there, some in the Grandissime households or field-gangs, some elsewhere within occasional sight, some dead, some not accounted for. Husbands — like the Samaritan woman's. We know she was a constant singer and laugher.

And so on that day, when Honoré Grandissime had advised the Governor-General of Louisiana to be very careful to avoid demonstration of any sort if he wished to avert a street war in his little capital, Clemence went up one street and down another, singing her song and laughing her professional merry laugh. How could it be otherwise? Let events take any possible turn, how could it make any difference to Clemence? What could she hope to gain? What could she fear to lose? She sold some of her goods to Casa Calvo's Spanish guard and sang them a Spanish song; some to Claiborne's soldiers and sang them Yankee Doodle with unclean words of her own inspiration, which evoked true soldiers' laughter; some to a priest at his window, exchanging with him a pious comment or two upon the wickedness of the times generally and their Américain Protestant-poisoned community in particular; and (after going home to dinner and coming out newly furnished) she sold some more of her wares to the excited groups of Creoles to which we have had occasion to allude, and from whom, insensible as she was to ribaldry, she was glad to escape. The day now drawing to a close, she turned her steps toward her wonted crouching-place, the willow avenue on the levee, near the Place d'Armes. But she had hardly defined this decision clearly in her mind, and had but just turned out of the rue St. Louis, when her song attracted an ear in a second-story room under whose window she was passing. As usual, it was fitted to the passing event:

> " *Apportez moi mo' sabre,*
> *Ba boum, ba boum, boum, boum.*"

"Run, fetch that girl here," said Dr. Keene to the slave woman who had just entered his room with a pitcher of water.

"Well, old eavesdropper," he said, as Clemence came, "what is the scandal to-day?"

Clemence laughed.

"You know, Mawse Chawlie, I dunno noth'n' 'tall 'bout nobody. I 'se a nigga w'at mine my own business."

"Sit down there on that stool, and tell me what is going on outside."

"I d' no noth'n' 'bout no goin's on; got no time fo' sit down, me; got sell my cakes. I don't goin' git mix' in wid no white folks's doin's."

"Hush, you old hypocrite; I will buy all your cakes. Put them out there on the table."

The invalid, sitting up in bed, drew a purse from behind his pillow and tossed her a large price. She tittered, courtesied and received the money.

"Well, well, Mawse Chawlie, 'f you ain' de fun-ni'st gen'leman I knows, to be sho!"

"Have you seen Joseph Frowenfeld to-day?" he asked.

"He, he, he! W'at I got do wid Mawse Frowenfel'? I goes on de off side o' sich folks — folks w'at cann' 'have deyself no bette'n dat — he, he, he! At de same time I did happen, jis chancin' by accident, to see 'im."

"How is he?"

Dr. Keene made plain by his manner that any

sensational account would receive his instantaneous contempt, and she answered within bounds.

" Well, now, tellin' the simple trufe, he ain' much hurt."

The doctor turned slowly and cautiously in bed.

" Have you seen Honoré Grandissime ? "

" W'y — das funny you ass me dat. I jis now see 'im dis werry minnit."

" Where ? "

" Jis gwine into de house wah dat laydy live w'at 'e runned over dat ah time."

" Now, you old hag," cried the sick man, his weak, husky voice trembling with passion, " you know you 're telling me a lie."

" No, Mawse Chawlie," she protested with a coward's frown, " I swah I tellin' you de God's trufe ! "

" Hand me my clothes off that chair."

" Oh ! but, Mawse Chawlie —— "

The little doctor cursed her. She did as she was bid, and made as if to leave the room.

" Don't you go away."

" But Mawse Chawlie, you' undress' — he, he ! "

She was really abashed and half frightened.

" I know that ; and you have got to help me put my clothes on."

" You gwan kill yo'se'f, Mawse Chawlie," she said, handling a garment.

" Hold your black tongue."

She dressed him hastily, and he went down the stairs of his lodging-house and out into the street. Clemence went in search of her master.

CHAPTER XLIII

THE EAGLE VISITS THE DOVES IN THEIR NEST

ALPHONSINA — only living property of Aurora and Clotilde — was called upon to light a fire in the little parlor. Elsewhere, although the day was declining, few persons felt such a need; but in No. 19 rue Bienville there were two chilling influences combined requiring an artificial offset. One was the ground under the floor, which was only three inches distant, and permanently saturated with water; the other was despair.

Before this fire the two ladies sat down together like watchers, in that silence and vacuity of mind which come after an exhaustive struggle ending in the recognition of the inevitable; a torpor of thought, a stupefaction of feeling, a purely negative state of joylessness sequent to the positive state of anguish. They were now both hungry, but in want of some present friend acquainted with the motions of mental distress who could guess this fact and press them to eat. By their eyes it was plain they had been weeping much; by the subdued tone, too, of their short and infrequent speeches.

Alphonsina, having made the fire, went out with

a bundle. It was Aurora's last good dress. She was going to try to sell it.

"It ought not to be so hard," began Clotilde, in a quiet manner of contemplating some one else's difficulty, but paused with the saying uncompleted, and sighed under her breath.

"But it *is* so hard," responded Aurora.

"No, it ought not to be so hard——"

"How, not so hard?"

"It is not so hard to live," said Clotilde; "but it is hard to be ladies. You understand——" she knit her fingers, dropped them into her lap and turned her eyes toward Aurora, who responded with the same motions, adding the crossing of her silk-stockinged ankles before the fire.

"No," said Aurora, with a scintillation of irrepressible mischief in her eyes.

"After all," pursued Clotilde, "what troubles us is not how to make a living, but how to get a living without making it."

"Ah! that would be magnificent!" said Aurora, and then added, more soberly; "but we are compelled to make a living."

"No."

"No-o? Ah! what do you mean with your 'no'?"

"I mean it is just the contrary; we are compelled not to make a living. Look at me: I can cook, but I must not cook; I am skillful with the needle, but I must not take in sewing; I could keep accounts; I could nurse the sick; but I must not.

I could be a confectioner, a milliner, a dressmaker, a vest-maker, a cleaner of gloves and laces, a dyer, a bird-seller, a mattress-maker, an upholsterer, a dancing-teacher, a florist —— "

"Oh!" softly exclaimed Aurora, in English, "you could be — you know w'ad? — an egcellen' drug-cl' — ah, ha, ha!"

"Now —— "

But the threatened irruption was averted by a look of tender apology from Aurora, in reply to one of martyrdom from Clotilde.

"My angel daughter," said Aurora, "if society has decreed that ladies must be ladies, then that is our first duty; our second is to live. Do you not see why it is that this practical world does not permit ladies to make a living? Because if they could, none of them would ever consent to be married. Ha! women talk about marrying for love; but society is too sharp to trust them, yet! It makes it *necessary* to marry. I will tell you the honest truth; some days when I get very, very hungry, and we have nothing but rice — all because we are ladies without male protectors — I think society could drive even me to marriage! — for your sake, though, darling; of course, only for your sake!"

"Never!" replied Clotilde; "for my sake, never; for your own sake if you choose. I should not care. I should be glad to see you do so if it would make you happy; but never for my sake and never for hunger's sake; but for love's sake, yes; and God bless thee, pretty maman."

"Clotilde, dear," said the unconscionable widow, "let me assure you, once for all, — starvation is preferable. I mean for me, you understand, simply for me; that is my feeling on the subject."

Clotilde turned her saddened eyes with a steady scrutiny upon her deceiver, who gazed upward in apparently unconscious reverie, and sighed softly as she laid her head upon the high chair-back and stretched out her feet.

"I wish Alphonsina would come back," she said. "Ah!" she added, hearing a footfall on the step outside the street door, "there she is."

She arose and drew the bolt. Unseen to her, the person whose footsteps she had heard stood upon the doorstep with a hand lifted to knock, but pausing to "make up his mind." He heard the bolt shoot back, recognized the nature of the mistake, and, feeling that here again he was robbed of volition, rapped.

"That is not Alphonsina!"

The two ladies looked at each other and turned pale.

"But you must open it," whispered Clotilde, half rising.

Aurora opened the door, and changed from white to crimson. Clotilde rose up quickly. The gentleman lifted his hat.

"Madame Nancanou."

"M. Grandissime?"

"Oui, Madame."

For once, Aurora was in an uncontrollable

flutter. She stammered, lost her breath, and even
spoke worse French than she needed to have done.

"Be pl — pleased, sir — to enter. Clotilde, my
daughter — Monsieur Grandissime. P-please be
seated, sir. Monsieur Grandissime," — she dropped
into a chair with an air of vivacity pitiful to behold,
— "I suppose you have come for the rent." She
blushed even more violently than before, and her
hand stole upward upon her heart to stay its violent beating. "Clotilde, dear, I should be glad if
you would put the fire before the screen; it is so
much too warm." She pushed her chair back and
shaded her face with her hand. "I think the
warmer is growing weather outside, is it — is it
not?"

The struggles of a wounded bird could not have
been more piteous. Monsieur Grandissime sought
to speak. Clotilde, too, nerved by the sight of her
mother's embarrassment, came to her support, and
she and the visitor spoke in one breath.

"Maman, if Monsieur — pardon —— "

"Madame Nancanou, the — pardon, Mademoiselle —— "

"I have presumed to call upon you," resumed
M. Grandissime, addressing himself now to both
ladies at once, "to see if I may enlist you in a
purely benevolent undertaking in the interest of
one who has been unfortunate — a common acquaintance —— "

"Common acquaint — " interrupted Aurora, with
a hostile lighting of her eyes.

"I believe so — Professor Frowenfeld." M. Grandissime saw Clotilde start, and in her turn falsely accuse the fire by shading her face: but it was no time to stop. "Ladies," he continued, "please allow me, for the sake of the good it may effect, to speak plainly and to the point."

The ladies expressed acquiescence by settling themselves to hear.

"Professor Frowenfeld had the extraordinary misfortune this morning to incur the suspicion of having entered a house for the purpose of — at least, for a bad design ——"

"He is innocent!" came from Clotilde, against her intention; Aurora covertly put out a hand, and Clotilde clutched it nervously.

"As, for example, robbery," said the self-recovered Aurora, ignoring Clotilde's look of protestation.

"Call it so," responded M. Grandissime. "Have you heard at whose house this was?"

"No, sir."

"It was at the house of Palmyre Philosophe."

"Palmyre Philosophe!" exclaimed Aurora, in low astonishment. Clotilde let slip, in a tone of indignant incredulity, a soft "Ah!" Aurora turned, and with some hope that M. Grandissime would not understand, ventured to say in Spanish, quietly:

"Come, come, this will never do."

And Clotilde replied in the same tongue:

"I know it, but he is innocent."

" Let us understand each other," said their visitor.
" There is not the faintest idea in the mind of one
of us that Professor Frowenfeld is guilty of even an
intention of wrong; otherwise I should not be
here.   He is a man simply incapable of anything
ignoble."

Clotilde was silent.   Aurora answered promptly,
with the air of one not to be excelled in generosity:

" Certainly, he is very incapabl'."

" Still," resumed the visitor, turning especially to
Clotilde, " the known facts are these, according to
his own statement: he was in the house of Palmyre
on some legitimate business which, unhappily, he
considers himself on some account bound not to
disclose, and by some mistake of Palmyre's old
Congo woman, was set upon by her and wounded,
barely escaping with a whole skull into the street,
an object of public scandal.   Laying aside the consideration of his feelings, his reputation is at stake
and likely to be ruined unless the affair can be explained clearly and satisfactorily, and at once, by his
friends."

" And you undertake —— " began Aurora.

" Madame Nancanou," said Honoré Grandissime,
leaning toward her earnestly, " you know — I must
beg leave to appeal to your candor and confidence
— you know everything concerning Palmyre that I
know.   You know me, and who I am ; you know
it is not for me to undertake to confer with Palmyre.
I know, too, her old affection for you ; she lives
but a little way down this street upon which you

live; there is still daylight enough at your disposal; if you will, you can go to see her, and get from her a full and complete exoneration of this young man. She cannot come to you; she is not fit to leave her room."

"Cannot leave her room?"

"I am, possibly, violating confidence in this disclosure, but it is unavoidable — you have to know: she is not fully recovered from a pistol-shot wound received between two and three weeks ago."

"Pistol-shot wound!"

Both ladies started forward with open lips and exclamations of amazement.

"Received from a third person — not myself and not Professor Frowenfeld — in a desperate attempt made by her to avenge the wrongs which she has suffered, as you, Madam, as well as I, are aware, at the hands of —— "

Aurora rose up with a majestic motion for the speaker to desist.

"If it is to mention the person of whom your allusion reminds me, that you have honored us with a call this evening, Monsieur —— "

Her eyes were flashing as he had seen them flash in front of the Place d'Armes.

"I beg you not to suspect me of meanness," he answered, gently, and with a remonstrative smile. "I have been trying all day, in a way unnecessary to explain, to be generous."

"I suppose you are incapabl'," said Aurora,

following her double meaning with that combination of mischievous eyes and unsmiling face of which she was master. She resumed her seat, adding: " It is generous for you to admit that Palmyre has suffered wrongs."

" It *would* be," he replied, " to attempt to repair them, seeing that I am not responsible for them, but this I cannot claim yet to have done. I have asked of you, Madam, a generous act. I might ask another of you both jointly. It is to permit me to say without offence, that there is one man, at least, of the name of Grandissime who views with regret and mortification the yet deeper wrongs which you are even now suffering."

" Oh ! " exclaimed Aurora, inwardly ready for fierce tears, but with no outward betrayal save a trifle too much grace and an over-bright smile, " Monsieur is much mistaken; we are quite comfortable and happy, wanting nothing, eh, Clotilde ? — not even our rights, ha, ha ! "

She rose and let Alphonsina in. The bundle was still in the negress's arms. She passed through the room and disappeared in the direction of the kitchen.

" Oh ! no, sir, not at all," repeated Aurora, as she once more sat down.

" You ought to want your rights," said M. Grandissime. " You ought to have them."

" You think so ? "

Aurora was really finding it hard to conceal her

growing excitement, and turned, with a faint hope
of relief, toward Clotilde.

Clotilde, looking only at their visitor, but feeling her mother's glance, with a tremulous and half-
choked voice, said eagerly :

" Then why do you not give them to us ? "

" Ah ! " interposed Aurora, " we shall get them
to-morrow, when the sheriff comes."

And, thereupon what did Clotilde do but sit
bolt upright, with her hands in her lap, and let the
tears roll, tear after tear, down her cheeks.

" Yes, Monsieur," said Aurora, smiling still,
" those that you see are really tears.   Ha, ha, ha !
excuse me, I really have to laugh ; for I just
happened to remember our meeting at the masked
ball last September.   We had such a pleasant evening and were so much indebted to you for our
enjoyment,— particularly myself,— little thinking,
you know, that you were one of that great family
which believes we ought to have our rights, you
know.   There are many people who ought to have
their rights.   There was Bras-Coupé ; indeed, he
got them — found them in the swamp.   Maybe
Clotilde and I shall find ours in the street.   When
we unmasked in the theatre, you know, I did not
know you were my landlord, and you did not know
that I could not pay a few picayunes of rent.   But
you must excuse those tears ; Clotilde is generally a
brave little woman, and would not be so rude as to
weep before a stranger ; but she is weak to-day —
we are both weak to-day, from the fact that we

have eaten nothing since early morning, although we have abundance of food — for want of appetite, you understand. You must sometimes be affected the same way, having the care of so much wealth *of all sorts*."

Honoré Grandissime had risen to his feet and was standing with one hand on the edge of the lofty mantel, his hat in the other dropped at his side and his eye fixed upon Aurora's beautiful face, whence her small nervous hand kept dashing aside the tears through which she defiantly talked and smiled. Clotilde sat with clenched hands buried in her lap, looking at Aurora and still weeping.

And M. Grandissime was saying to himself:

"If I do this thing now — if I do it here — I do it on an impulse; I do it under constraint of woman's tears; I do it because I love this woman; I do it to get out of a corner; I do it in weakness, not in strength; I do it without having made up my mind whether or not it is the best thing to do."

And then, without intention, with scarcely more consciousness of movement than belongs to the undermined tree which settles, roots and all, into the swollen stream, he turned and moved toward the door.

Clotilde rose.

"Monsieur Grandissime."

He stopped and looked back.

"We will see Palmyre at once, according to your request."

He turned his eyes toward Aurora.

"Yes," said she, and she buried her face in her handkerchief and sobbed aloud.

She heard his footstep again; it reached the door; the door opened — closed; she heard his footstep again; was he gone?

He was gone.

The two women threw themselves into each other's arms and wept. Presently Clotilde left the room. She came back in a moment from the rear apartment, with a bonnet and veil in her hands.

"No," said Aurora, rising quickly, "I must do it."

"There is no time to lose," said Clotilde. "It will soon be dark."

It was hardly a minute before Aurora was ready to start. A kiss, a sorrowful look of love exchanged, the veil dropped over the swollen eyes, and Aurora was gone.

A minute passed, hardly more, and — what was this? — the soft patter of Aurora's knuckles on the door.

"Just here at the corner I saw Palmyre leaving her house and walking down the rue Royale. We must wait until morn——"

Again a footfall on the doorstep, and the door, which was standing ajar, was pushed slightly by the force of the masculine knock which followed.

"Allow me," said the voice of Honoré Grandissime, as Aurora bowed at the door. "I should have handed you this; good-day."

She received a missive. It was long, like an official document; it bore evidence of having been carried for some hours in a coat-pocket, and was folded in one of those old, troublesome ways in use before the days of envelopes. Aurora pulled it open.

" It is all figures ; light a candle."

The candle was lighted by Clotilde and held over Aurora's shoulder ; they saw a heading and footing more conspicuous than the rest of the writing.

The heading read :

" *Aurora and Clotilde Nancanou, owners of Fausse Rivière Plantation, in account with Honoré Grandissime.*"

The footing read :

" *Balance at credit, subject to order of Aurora and Clotilde Nancanou, $105.000.00.*"

The date followed :

" *March 9, 1804.*"

and the signature :

" *H. Grandissime.*"

A small piece of torn white paper slipped from the account to the floor. Clotilde's eye followed it, but Aurora, without acknowledgement of having seen it, covered it with her foot.

In the morning Aurora awoke first. She drew from under her pillow this slip of paper. She had not dared look at it until now. The writing

on it had been roughly scratched down with a
pencil. It read:

*"Not for love of woman, but in the name of justice and the
fear of God."*

"And I was so cruel," she whispered.

Ah! Honoré Grandissime, she was kind to that
little writing! She did not put it back under her
pillow; she *kept it warm*, Honoré Grandissime,
from that time forth.

CHAPTER XLIV

BAD FOR CHARLIE KEENE

O N the same evening of which we have been telling, about the time that Aurora and Clotilde were dropping their last tear of joy over the document of restitution, a noticeable figure stood alone at the corner of the rue du Canal and the rue Chartres. He had reached there and paused, just as the brighter glare of the set sun was growing dim above the tops of the cypresses. After walking with some rapidity of step, he had stopped aimlessly, and laid his hand with an air of weariness upon a rotting China-tree that leaned over the ditch at the edge of the unpaved walk.

"Setting in cypress," he murmured. We need not concern ourselves as to his meaning.

One could think aloud there with impunity. In 1804, Canal street was the upper boundary of New Orleans. Beyond it, to southward, the open plain was dotted with country-houses, brick-kilns, clumps of live-oak and groves of pecan. At the hour mentioned the outlines of these objects were already darkening. At one or two points the sky was reflected from marshy ponds. Out to westward rose conspicuously the old house and willow-copse of Jean Poquelin. Down the empty street or road, which stretched with arrow-like straightness toward the northwest, the draining-canal that gave it its name tapered away between occasional over-hanging willows and beside broken ranks of rotting palisades, its foul, crawling waters blushing, gilding and purpling under the swiftly waning light, and ending suddenly in the black shadow of the swamp. The observer of this dismal prospect leaned heavily on his arm, and cast his glance out along the beautified corruption of the canal. His eye seemed quickened to detect the smallest repellant details of the scene; every cypress stump that stood in, or overhung, the slimy water; every ruined indigo-vat or blasted tree, every broken thing, every bleached bone of ox or horse — and they were many — for roods around. As his eye passed them slowly over and swept back again around the dreary view, he sighed heavily and said: " Dissolution," and then again — " Dissolution ! order of the day —— "

A secret overhearer might have followed, by

these occasional exclamatory utterances, the course
of a devouring trouble prowling up and down
through his thoughts, as one's eye tracks the shark
by the occasional cutting of his fin above the water.

He spoke again :

" It is in such moods as this that fools drown
themselves."

His speech was French. He straightened up,
smote the tree softly with his palm, and breathed
a long, deep sigh — such a sigh, if the very truth
be told, as belongs by right to a lover. And yet
his mind did not dwell on love.

He turned and left the place; but the trouble
that was plowing hither and thither through the
deep of his meditations went with him. As he
turned into the rue Chartres it showed itself thus :

" Right; it is but right ; " he shook his head
slowly — " it is but right."

In the rue Douane he spoke again :

" Ah ! Frowenfeld " — and smiled unpleasantly,
with his head down.

And as he made yet another turn, and took his
meditative way down the city's front, along the
blacksmith's shops in the street afterward called Old
Levee, he resumed, in English, and with a distinctness that made a staggering sailor halt and look
after him :

" There are but two steps to civilization, the first
easy, the second difficult; to construct — to recon-
struct — ah ! there it is ! the tearing down ! The
tear' —— "

He was still, but repeated the thought by a gesture of distress turned into a slow stroke of the forehead.

"Monsieur Honoré Grandissime," said a voice just ahead.

"*Eh, bien?*"

At the mouth of an alley, in the dim light of the streep lamp, stood the dark figure of Honoré Grandissime, f. m. c., holding up the loosely hanging form of a small man, the whole front of whose clothing was saturated with blood.

"Why, Charlie Keene! Let him down again, quickly — quickly; do not hold him so!"

"Hands off," came in a ghastly whisper from the shape.

"Oh, Chahlie, my boy ———"

"Go and finish your courtship," whispered the doctor.

"Oh Charlie, I have just made it forever impossible!"

"Then help me back to my bed; I don't care to die in the street."

CHAPTER XLV

MORE REPARATION

"THAT is all," said the fairer Honoré, outside Doctor Keene's sick-room about ten o'clock at night. He was speaking to the black son of Clemence, who had been serving as errand-boy for

some hours. He spoke in a low tone just without
the half-open door, folding again a paper which the
lad had lately borne to the apothecary of the rue
Royale, and had now brought back with Joseph's
answer written under Honoré's inquiry.

"That is all," said the other Honoré, standing
partly behind the first, as the eyes of his little menial
turned upon him that deprecatory glance of inquiry
so common to slave children. The lad went a little
way down the corridor, curled up upon the floor
against the wall, and was soon asleep. The fairer
Honoré handed the darker the slip of paper; it
was received and returned in silence. The question
was:

" Can you state anything positive concerning the duel?"

And the reply:

*" Positively there will be none. Sylvestre my sworn friend for
life."*

The half-brothers sat down under a dim hanging
lamp in the corridor, and except that every now and
then one or the other stepped noiselessly to the
door to look in upon the sleeping sick man, or in
the opposite direction to moderate by a push with
the foot the snoring of Clemence's "boy," they
sat the whole night through in whispered counsel.

The one, at the request of the other, explained
how he had come to be with the little doctor in
such extremity.

It seems that Clemence, seeing and understanding the doctor's imprudence, had sallied out with

the resolve to set some person on his track. We have said that she went in search of her master. Him she met, and though she could not really count him one of the doctor's friends, yet, rightly believing in his humanity, she told him the matter. He set off in what was for him a quick pace in search of the rash invalid, was misdirected by a too confident child and had given up the hope of finding him, when a faint sound of distress just at hand drew him into an alley, where, close down against a wall, with his face to the earth, lay Doctor Keene. The f. m. c. had just raised him and borne him out of the alley when Honoré came up.

"And you say that, when you would have inquired for him at Frowenfeld's, you saw Palmyre there, standing and talking with Frowenfeld? Tell me more exactly."

And the other, with that grave and gentle economy of words which made his speech so unique, recounted what we amplify:

Palmyre had needed no pleading to induce her to exonerate Joseph. The doctors were present at Frowenfeld's in more than usual number. There was unusualness, too, in their manner and their talk. They were not entirely free from the excitement of the day, and as they talked — with an air of superiority, of Creole inflammability, and with some contempt — concerning Camille Brahmin's and Charlie Mandarin's efforts to precipitate a war, they were yet visibly in a state of expectation. Frowenfeld, they softly said, had in his odd way been indiscreet

among these inflammables at Maspero's just when
he could least afford to be so, and there was no telling what they might take the notion to do to him
before bedtime.   All that over and above the independent, unexplained scandal of the early morning.
So Joseph and his friends this evening, like Aurora
and Clotilde in the morning, were, as we nowadays
say of buyers and sellers, "apart," when suddenly
and unannounced, Palmyre presented herself among
them.   When the f. m. c. saw her, she had already
handed Joseph his hat and with much sober grace
was apologizing for her slave's mistake.   All evidence of her being wounded was concealed.   The
extraordinary excitement of the morning had not
hurt her, and she seemed in perfect health.   The
doctors sat or stood around and gave rapt attention
to her patois, one or two translating it for Joseph,
and he blushing to the hair, but standing erect and
receiving it at second hand with silent bows.   The
f. m. c. had gazed on her for a moment, and then
forced himself away.   He was among the few who
had not heard the morning scandal, and he did not
comprehend the evening scene.   He now asked
Honoré concerning it, and quietly showed great
relief when it was explained.

Then Honoré, breaking a silence, called the attention of the f. m. c. to the fact that the latter had
two tenants at Number 19 rue Bienville.   Honoré
became the narrator now and told all, finally stating
that the die was cast — restitution made.

And then the darker Honoré made a proposition

to the other, which, it is little to say, was startling. They discussed it for hours.

"So just a condition," said the merchant, raising his whisper so much that the rentier laid a hand in his elbow, — "such mere justice," he said, more softly, "ought to be an easy condition. God knows" — he lifted his glance reverently — "my very right to exist comes after yours. You are the elder."

The solemn man offered no disclaimer.

What could the proposition be which involved so grave an issue, and to which M. Grandissime's final answer was "I will do it"?

It was that Honoré f. m. c. should become a member of the mercantile house of H. Grandissime, enlisting in its capital all his wealth. And the one condition was that the new style should be *Grandissime Brothers*.

CHAPTER XLVI

THE PIQUE-EN-TERRE LOSES ONE OF HER CREW

Ask the average resident of New Orleans if his town is on an island, and he will tell you no. He will also wonder how any one could have got that notion, — so completely has Orleans Island, whose name at the beginning of the present century was in everybody's mouth, been forgotten. It was once a question of national policy, a point of difference between Republican and Federalist, whether the

United States ought to buy this little strip of semi-
submerged land, or whether it would not be more
righteous to steal it. The Kentuckians kept the
question at a red heat by threatening to become an
empire by themselves if one course or the other was
not taken; but when the First Consul offered to sell
all Louisiana, our commissioners were quite robbed
of breath. They had approached to ask a hair
from the elephant's tail, and were offered the elephant.

For Orleans Island — island it certainly was until
General Jackson closed Bayou Manchac — is a
narrow, irregular, flat tract of forest, swamp, city,
prairie and sea-marsh, lying east and west, with
the Mississippi, trending southeastward, for its
southern boundary, and for its northern, a parallel
and contiguous chain of alternate lakes and bayous,
opening into the river through Bayou Manchac,
and into the Gulf through the passes of the Mal-
heureuse Islands. On the narrowest part of it
stands New Orleans. Turning and looking back
over the rear of the town, one may easily see from
her steeples Lake Pontchartrain glistening away to
the northern horizon, and in his fancy extend the
picture to right and left till Pontchartrain is linked
in the west by Pass Manchac to Lake Maurepas,
and in the east by the Rigolets and Chef Menteur
to Lake Borgne.

An oddity of the Mississippi Delta is the habit
the little streams have of running away from the
big ones. The river makes its own bed and its

own banks, and continuing season after season, through ages of alternate overflow and subsidence, to elevate those banks, creates a ridge which thus becomes a natural elevated aqueduct. Other slightly elevated ridges mark the present or former courses of minor outlets, by which the waters of the Mississippi have found the sea. Between these ridges lie the cypress swamps, through whose profound shades the clear, dark, deep bayous creep noiselessly away into the tall grasses of the shaking prairies. The original New Orleans was built on the Mississippi ridge, with one of these forest-and-water-covered basins stretching back behind her to westward and northward, closed in by Metairie Ridge and Lake Pontchartrain. Local engineers preserve the tradition that the Bayou Sauvage once had its rise, so to speak, in Toulouse street. Though depleted by the city's present drainage system and most likely poisoned by it as well, its waters still move seaward in a course almost due easterly, and empty into Chef Menteur, one of the watery threads of a tangled skein of "passes" between the lakes and the open Gulf. Three-quarters of a century ago this Bayou Sauvage (or Gentilly — corruption of Chantilly) was a navigable stream of wild and sombre beauty.

On a certain morning in August, 1804, and consequently some five months after the events last mentioned, there emerged from the darkness of Bayou Sauvage into the prairie-bordered waters of Chef Menteur, while the morning star was still luminous in the sky above and in the water below, and only the practised eye could detect the first glimmer of day, a small, stanch, single-masted, broad and very light-draught boat, whose innocent character, primarily indicated in its coat of many colors, — the hull being yellow below the water line and white above, with tasteful stripings of blue and red, — was further accentuated by the peaceful name of *Pique-en-terre* (the Sandpiper).

She seemed, too, as she entered the Chef Menteur, as if she would have liked to turn southward; but the wind did not permit this, and in a moment more the water was rippling after her swift rudder, as she glided away in the direction of Pointe Aux Herbes. But when she had left behind her the mouth of the passage, she changed her course and, leaving the Pointe on her left, bore down toward Petites Coquilles, obviously bent upon passing through the Rigolets.

We know not how to describe the joyousness of the effect when at length one leaves behind him the shadow and gloom of the swamp, and there bursts upon his sight the widespread, flower-decked, bird-haunted prairies of Lake Catharine. The inside and outside of a prison scarcely furnish a greater contrast; and on this fair August morning the contrast was at its strongest. The day broke across a glad expanse of cool and fragrant green, silver-laced with a network of crisp salt pools and passes, lakes, bayous and lagoons, that gave a good smell, the inspiring odor of interclasped sea and shore,

and both beautified and perfumed the happy earth,
laid bare to the rising sun. Waving marshes of
wild oats, drooping like sated youth from too much
pleasure; watery acres hid under crisp-growing
greenth starred with pond-lilies and rippled by
water-fowl; broad stretches of high grass, with
thousands of ecstatic wings palpitating above them;
hundreds of thousands of white and pink mallows
clapping their hands in voiceless rapture, and that
amazon queen of the wild flowers, the morning-
glory, stretching her myriad lines, lifting up the
trumpet and waving her colors, white, azure and
pink, with lacings of spider's web, heavy with pearls
and diamonds — the gifts of the summer night.
The crew of the *Pique-en-terre* saw all these and
felt them; for, whatever they may have been or
failed to be, they were men whose heartstrings
responded to the touches of nature. One alone of
their company, and he the one who should have
felt them most, showed insensibility, sighed laughingly and then laughed sighingly, in the face of his
fellows and of all this beauty, and profanely confessed that his heart's desire was to get back to his
wife. He had been absent from her now for nine
hours!

But the sun is getting high; Petites Coquilles
has been passed and left astern, the eastern end
of Las Conchas is on the after-larboard-quarter,
the briny waters of Lake Borgne flash far and wide
their dazzling white and blue, and, as the little boat
issues from the deep channel of the Rigolets, the

white-armed waves catch her and toss her like a
merry babe.   A triumph for the helmsman — he it
is who sighs, at intervals of tiresome frequency, for
his wife.   He had, from the very starting-place in
the upper waters of Bayou Sauvage, declared in
favor of the Rigolets as — wind and tide considered
— the most practicable of all the passes.   Now that
they were out, he forgot for a moment the self-
amusing plaint of conjugal separation to flaunt his
triumph.   Would any one hereafter dispute with
him on the subject of Louisiana sea-coast-naviga-
tion?   He knew every pass and piece of water
like A, B, C, and could tell, faster, much faster
than he could repeat the multiplication table (upon
which he was a little slow and doubtful), the
amount of water in each at ebb tide — Pass Jean
or Petit Pass, Unknown Pass, Petit Rigolet,
Chef Menteur,——

Out on the far southern horizon, in the Gulf —
the Gulf of Mexico — there appears a speck of
white.   It is known to those on board the *Pique-
en-terre*, the moment it is descried, as the canvas
of a large schooner.   The opinion, first expressed
by the youthful husband, who still reclines with the
tiller held firmly under his arm, and then by
another member of the company who sits on the
centreboard-well, is unanimously adopted, that she
is making for the Rigolets, will pass Petites Coquilles by eleven o'clock, and will tie up at the little
port of St. Jean, on the bayou of the same name,
before sundown, if the wind holds anywise as it is.

On the other hand, the master of the distant schooner shuts his glass, and says to the single passenger whom he has aboard that the little sail just visible toward the Rigolets is a sloop with a half-deck, well filled with men, in all probability a pleasure party bound to the Chandeleurs on a fishing and gunning excursion, and passes into comments on the superior skill of landsmen over seamen in the handling of small sailing craft.

By and by the two vessels near each other. They approach within hailing distance, and are announcing each to each their identity, when the young man at the tiller jerks himself to a squatting posture, and, from under a broad-brimmed and slouched straw hat, cries to the schooner's one passenger :

" Hello, Challie Keene."

And the passenger more quietly answers back :

" Hello, Raoul, is that you? "

M. Innerarity replied, with a profane parenthesis, that it was he.

" You kin hask Sylvestre ! " he concluded.

The doctor's eye passed around a semicircle of some eight men, the most of whom were quite young, but one or two of whom were gray, sitting with their arms thrown out upon the wash-board, in the dark négligé of amateur fishermen and with that exultant look of expectant deviltry in their handsome faces which characterizes the Creole with his collar off.

The mettlesome little doctor felt the odds against him in the exchange of greetings.

"Ola, Dawctah!"

"*Hé*, Doctah, *que-ce qui t'après fé?*"

"*Ho, ho, compère Noyo!*"

"*Comment va*, Docta?"

A light peppering of profanity accompanied each salute.

The doctor put on defensively a smile of superiority to the juniors and of courtesy to the others, and responsively spoke their names:

"'Polyte — Sylvestre — Achille — Émile — ah! Agamemnon."

The Doctor and Agamemnon raised their hats.

As Agamemnon was about to speak, a general expostulatory outcry drowned his voice. The *Pique-en-terre* was going about close abreast of the schooner, and angry questions and orders were flying at Raoul's head like a volley of eggs.

"Messieurs," said Raoul, partially rising but still stooping over the tiller, and taking his hat off his bright curls with mock courtesy, "I am going back to New Orleans. I would not give *that* for all the fish in the sea; I want to see my wife. I am going back to New Orleans to see my wife — and to congratulate the city upon your absence." Incredulity, expostulation, reproach, taunt, malediction — he smiled unmoved upon them all.

"Messieurs, I *must* go and see my wife."

Amid redoubled outcries he gave the helm to Camille Brahmin, and fighting his way with his pretty feet against half-real efforts to throw him overboard, clambered forward to the mast, whence a moment later, with the help of the schooner-master's hand, he reached the deck of the larger vessel. The *Pique-en-terre* turned, and with a little flutter spread her smooth wing and skimmed away.

" Doctah Keene, look yeh ! " M. Innerarity held up a hand whose third finger wore the conventional ring of the Creole bridegroom. " W'at you got to say to dat ? "

The little doctor felt a faintness run through his veins, and a thrill of anger follow it. The poor man could not imagine a love affair that did not include Clotilde Nancanou.

" Whom have you married ? "

" De pritties' gal in de citty."

The questioner controlled himself.

" M-hum," he responded, with a contraction of the eyes.

Raoul waited an instant for some kindlier comment, and finding the hope vain, suddenly assumed a look of delighted admiration.

" Hi, yi, yi ! Doctah, 'ow you har lookingue fine."

The true look of the doctor was that he had not much longer to live. A smile of bitter humor passed over his face, and he looked for a near seat, saying :

" How 's Frowenfeld ? "

Raoul struck an ecstatic attitude and stretched forth his hand as if the doctor could not fail to grasp it. The invalid's heart sank like lead.

" Frowenfeld has got her," he thought.

" Well ? " said he with a frown of impatience and restraint ; and Raoul cried:

" I sole my pig-shoe ! "

The doctor could not help but laugh.

" Shades of the masters ! "

" No ; ' Louizyanna rif-using to hantre de h-Union.' "

The doctor stood corrected.

The two walked across the deck, following the shadow of the swinging sail.   The doctor lay down in a low-swung hammock, and Raoul sat upon the deck *à la Turque.*

" Come, come, Raoul, tell me, what is the news ? "

" News ?   Oh, I donno.   You 'eard concernin' the dool ? "

" You don't mean to say —— "

" Yesseh ! "

" Agricola and Sylvestre ? "

" W'at de dev' !   No !   Burr an' 'Ammiltong ; in Noo-Juzzy-las-June.   Collonnel Burr, 'e —— "

" Oh, fudge !   yes.   How is Frowenfeld ? "

" ' E 's well.   Guess 'ow much I sole my pig-shoe."

" Well, how much ? "

" Two 'ondred fifty."   He laid himself out at length, his elbow on the deck, his head in his hand.   " I believe I 'm sorry I sole 'er."

" I don't wonder.   How's Honoré ?   Tell me what has happened.   Remember, I 've been away five months."

" No ; I am verrie glad dat I sole 'er. What?
Ha! I should think so! If it have not had been
fo' dat I would not be married to-day. You think
I would get married on dat sal'rie w'at Proffis-or
Frowenfel' was payin' me? Twenty-five dolla' de
mont'? Docta Keene, no gen'leman h-ought to
git married if 'e 'ave not anny'ow fifty dolla' de
mont'! If I wasn' a h-artiz I wouldn' git married ;
I gie you my word ! "

" Yes," said the little doctor, " you are right.
Now tell me the news."

" Well, dat Cong-ress gone an' make ——"

" Raoul, stop. I know that Congress has
divided the province into two territories ; I know
you Creoles think all your liberties are lost ; I
know the people are in a great stew because they
are not allowed to elect their own officers and legis-
latures, and that in Opelousas and Attakapas they
are as wild as their cattle about it —— "

" We 'ad two big mitting' about it," interrupted
Raoul ; " my bro'r-in-law speak at both of them ! "

" Who ? "

" Chahlie Mandarin."

" Glad to hear it," said Doctor Keene,— which
was the truth. " Besides that, I know Laussat has
gone to Martinique ; that the Américains have a
newspaper, and that cotton is two-bits a pound.
Now what I want to know is, how are my friends ?
What has Honoré done? What has Frowenfeld
done? And Palmyre,— and Agricole? They
hustled me away from here as if I had been

caught trying to cut my throat. Tell me every-thing."

And Raoul sank the artist and bridegroom in the historian, and told him.

CHAPTER XLVII

THE NEWS

"My cousin Honoré,— well, you kin jus' say 'e bitray' 'is 'ole fam'ly."

"How so?" asked Doctor Keene, with a hand-kerchief over his face to shield his eyes from the sun.

"Well,— ce't'nly 'e did! Di'n' 'e gave dat money to Aurora De Grapion? — one 'undred five t'ousan' dolla'? Jis' as if to say, 'Yeh 's de money my h-uncle stole from you' 'usban'.' Hah! w'en I will swear on a stack of Bible' as 'igh as yo' head, dat Agricole win dat 'abitation fair! — If I see it? No, sir; I don't 'ave to see it! I 'll swear to it! Hah!"

"And have she and her daughter actually got the money?"

"She — an'— heh — daughtah — ac — shilly — got-'at-money-sir! W'at? Dey livin' in de rue Royale in mag-*niffy*cen' style on top de drug-sto' of Proffis-or Frowenfel'."

"But how, over Frowenfeld's, when Frowenfeld's is a one-story ——"

"My dear frien'! Proffis-or Frowenfel' is *moove!*

You rickleck dat big new t'ree-story buildin' w'at jus' finished in de rue Royale, a lill mo' farther up town from his old shop? Well, we open dare *a big sto'*! An' listen! You think Honoré di'n' bitrayed' 'is family? Madame Nancanou an' heh daughtah livin' upstair an' rissy-ving de finess soci'ty in de Province! — an' *me?* — downstair' meckin' pill! You call dat justice?"

But Doctor Keene, without waiting for this question, had asked one:

"Does Frowenfeld board with them?"

"Psh-sh-sh! Board! Dey woon board de Marquis of Casa Calvo! I don't b'lieve dey would board Honoré Grandissime! All de king' an' queen' in de worl' couldn' board dare! No, sir! — 'Owever, you know, I think dey are splendid ladies. Me an' my wife, we know them well. An' Honoré — I think my cousin Honoré's a splendid gen'leman, too." After a moment's pause he resumed, with a happy sigh, "Well, I don' care, I 'm married. A man w'at's married, 'e don' care.

"But I di'n' t'ink Honoré could ever do lak dat odder t'ing."

"Do he and Joe Frowenfeld visit there?"

"Doctah Keene," demanded Raoul, ignoring the question, "I hask you now, plain, don' you find dat mighty disgressful to do dat way, lak Honoré?"

"What way?"

"W'at? You dunno? You don' yeh 'ow 'e gone partner' wid a nigga?"

"What do you mean?"

Doctor Keene drew the handkerchief off his face and half lifted his feeble head.

"Yesseh! 'e gone partner' wid dat quadroon w'at call 'imself Honoré Grandissime, seh!"

The doctor dropped his head again and laid the handkerchief back on his face.

"What do the family say to that?"

"But w'at *can* dey say? It save dem from ruin! At de sem time, me, I think it is a disgress. Not dat he h-use de money, but it is dat name w'at 'e give de h-establishmen' — Grandissime Frères! H-only for 'is money we would 'ave catch' dat quadroon gen'leman an' put some tar and fedder. Grandissime Frères! Agricole don' spik to my cousin Honoré no mo'. But I t'ink dass wrong. W'at you t'ink, Doctah?"

That evening, at candle-light, Raoul got the right arm of his slender, laughing wife about his neck; but Doctor Keene tarried all night in suburb St. Jean. He hardly felt the moral courage to face the results of the last five months. Let us understand them better ourselves.

CHAPTER XLVIII

AN INDIGNANT FAMILY AND A SMASHED SHOP

IT was indeed a fierce storm that had passed over the head of Honoré Grandissime. Taken up and carried by it, as it seemed to him, without volition,

he had felt himself thrown here and there, wrenched,
torn, gasping for moral breath, speaking the right
word as if in delirium, doing the right deed as if by
helpless instinct, and seeing himself in every case,
at every turn, tricked by circumstance out of every
vestige of merit.   So it seemed to him.   The long
contemplated restitution was accomplished.   On
the morning when Aurora and Clotilde had expected
to be turned shelterless into the open air, they had
called upon him in his private office and presented
the account of which he had put them in possession
the evening before.   He had honored it on the
spot.   To the two ladies who felt their own hearts
stirred almost to tears of gratitude, he was — as he
sat before them calm, unmoved, handling keen-
edged facts with the easy rapidity of one accustomed
to use them, smiling courteously and collectedly,
parrying their expressions of appreciation — to
them, we say, at least to one of them, he was " the
prince of gentlemen."   But, at the same time,
there was within him, unseen, a surge of emotions,
leaping, lashing, whirling, yet ever hurrying onward
along the hidden, rugged bed of his honest intention.

The other restitution, which even twenty-four
hours earlier might have seemed a pure self-sacrifice,
became a self-rescue.   The f. m. c. was the elder
brother.   A remark of Honoré made the night
they watched in the corridor by Doctor Keene's
door, about the younger's " right to exist," was but
the echo of a conversation they had once had to-

gether in Europe. There they had practised a familiarity of intercourse which Louisiana would not have endured, and once, when speaking upon the subject of their common fatherhood, the f. m. c., prone to melancholy speech, had said :

"You are the lawful son of Numa Grandissime ; I had no right to be born."

But Honoré quickly answered :

"By the laws of men, it may be ; but by the law of God's justice, you are the lawful son, and it is I who should not have been born."

But, returned to Louisiana, accepting with the amiable, old-fashioned philosophy of conservatism the sins of the community, he had forgotten the unchampioned rights of his passive half-brother. Contact with Frowenfeld had robbed him of his pleasant mental drowsiness, and the oft-encountered apparition of the dark sharer of his name had become a slow-stepping, silent embodiment of reproach. The turn of events had brought him face to face with the problem of restitution, and he had solved it. But where had he come out ? He had come out the beneficiary of this restitution, extricated from bankruptcy by an agreement which gave the f. m. c. only a public recognition of kinship which had always been his due. Bitter cup of humiliation !

Such was the stress within. Then there was the storm without. The Grandissimes were in a high state of excitement. The news had reached them all that Honoré had met the question of titles by selling one of their largest estates. It was received with wincing frowns, indrawn breath, and lifted feet, but without protest, and presently with a smile of returning confidence.

"Honoré knew; Honoré was informed; they had all authorized Honoré; and Honoré, though he might have his odd ways and notions, picked up during that unfortunate stay abroad, might safely be trusted to stand by the interests of his people."

After the first shock some of them even raised a laugh:

"Ha, ha, ha! Honoré would show those Yankees!"

They went to his counting-room and elsewhere, in search of him, to smite their hands into the hands of their far-seeing young champion. But, as we have seen, they did not find him; none dreamed of looking for him in an enemy's camp (19 Bienville) or on the lonely suburban commons, talking to himself in the ghostly twilight; and the next morning, while Aurora and Clotilde were seated before him in his private office, looking first at the face and then at the back of two mighty drafts of equal amount on Philadelphia, the cry of treason flew forth to these astounded Grandissimes, followed by the word that the sacred fire was gone out in the Grandissime temple (counting-room), that Delilahs in duplicate were carrying off the holy treasures, and that the uncircumcised and unclean — even an f. m. c.— was about to be inducted into the Grandissime priesthood.

Aurora and Clotilde were still there, when the various members of the family began to arrive and display their outlines in impatient shadow-play upon the glass door of the private office ; now one, and now another, dallied with the doorknob and by and by obtruded their lifted hats and urgent, anxious faces half into the apartment ; but Honoré would only glance toward them, and with a smile equally courteous, authoritative and fleeting, say :

" Good-morning, Camille " (or Charlie — or Agamemnon, as the case might be); " I will see you later ; let me trouble you to close the door."

To add yet another strain, the two ladies, like frightened, rescued children, would cling to their deliverer. They wished him to become the custodian and investor of their wealth. Ah, woman ! who is a tempter like thee ? But Honoré said no, and showed them the danger of such a course.

" Suppose I should die suddenly. You might have trouble with my executors."

The two beauties assented pensively ; but in Aurora's bosom a great throb secretly responded that as for her, in that case, she should have no use for money — in a nunnery.

" Would not Monsieur at least consent to be their financial adviser ? "

He hemmed, commenced a sentence twice, and finally said :

" You will need an agent ; some one to take full charge of your affairs; some person on whose sagacity and integrity you can place the fullest dependence."

" Who, for instance ? " asked Aurora.

" I should say, without hesitation, Professor Frowenfeld, the apothecary. You know his trouble of yesterday is quite cleared up. You had not heard? Yes. He is not what we call an enterprising man, but — so much the better. Take him all in all, I would choose him above all others ; if you —— "

Aurora interrupted him. There was an ill-concealed wildness in her eye and a slight tremor in her voice, as she spoke, which she had not expected to betray. The quick, though quiet eye of Honoré Grandissime saw it, and it thrilled him through.

" 'Sieur Grandissime, I take the risk ; I wish you to take care of my money."

" But, Maman," said Clotilde, turning with a timid look to her mother, " If Monsieur Grandissime would rather not —— "

Aurora, feeling alarmed at what she had said, rose up. Clotilde and Honoré did the same, and he said :

" With Professor Frowenfeld in charge of your affairs, I shall feel them not entirely removed from my care also. We are very good friends."

Clotilde looked at her mother. The three exchanged glances. The ladies signified their assent and turned to go, but M. Grandissime stopped them.

" By your leave, I will send for him. If you will be seated again —— "

They thanked him and resumed their seats ; he

excused himself, passed into the counting-room, and sent a messenger for the apothecary.

M. Grandissime's meeting with his kinsmen was a stormy one.   Aurora and Clotilde heard the strife begin, increase, subside, rise again and decrease. They heard men stride heavily to and fro, they heard hands smite together, palms fall upon tables and fists upon desks, heard half-understood statement and unintelligible counter-statement and derisive laughter; and, in the midst of all, like the voice of a man who rules himself, the clear-noted, unimpassioned speech of Honoré, sounding so loftily beautiful in the ear of Aurora that when Clotilde looked at her, sitting motionless with her rapt eyes lifted up, those eyes came down to her own with a sparkle of enthusiasm, and she softly said:

"It sounds like St. Gabriel!" and then blushed.

Clotilde answered with a happy, meaning look, which intensified the blush, and then leaning affectionately forward and holding the maman's eyes with her own, she said:

"You have my consent."

"Saucy!" said Aurora.   "Wait till I get my own."

Some of his kinsmen Honoré pacified; some he silenced.   He invited all to withdraw their lands and moneys from his charge, and some accepted the invitation.   They spurned his parting advice to sell, and the policy they then adopted, and never afterward modified, was that "all or nothing" attitude

which, as years rolled by, bled them to penury in
those famous cupping-leeching-and-bleeding establishments, the courts of Louisiana. You may see
their grandchildren, to-day, anywhere within the
angle of the old rues Esplanade and Rampart,
holding up their heads in unspeakable poverty, their
nobility kept green by unflinching self-respect, and
their poetic and pathetic pride revelling in ancestral, perennial rebellion against common sense.

"That is Agricola," whispered Aurora, with lifted
head and eyes dilated and askance, as one deep-
chested voice roared above all others.

Agricola stormed.

"Uncle," Aurora by and by heard Honoré say,
"shall I leave my own counting-room?"

At that moment Joseph Frowenfeld entered,
pausing with one hand on the outer rail. No one
noticed him but Honoré, who was watching for
him, and who, by a silent motion, directed him into
the private office.

"H-whe shake its dust from our feet!" said Agricola, gathering some young retainers by a sweep
of his glance and going out down the stair in the
arched way, unmoved by the fragrance of warm bread.
On the banquette he harangued his followers.

He said that in such times as these every lover
of liberty should go armed; that the age of trickery
had come; that by trickery Louisianians had been
sold, like cattle, to a nation of parvenues, to be
dragged before juries for asserting the human right
of free trade or ridding the earth of sneaks in the

pay of the government; that laws, so-called, had been forged into thumbscrews, and a Congress which had bound itself to give them all the rights of American citizens — sorry boon! — was preparing to slip their birthright acres from under their feet, and leave them hanging, a bait to the vultures of the Américain immigration. Yes; the age of trickery! Its apostles, he said, were even then at work among their fellow-citizens, warping, distorting, blasting, corrupting, poisoning the noble, unsuspecting, confiding Creole mind. For months the devilish work had been allowed, by a patient, peace-loving people, to go on. But shall it go on forever? (Cries of " No!" " No!") The smell of white blood comes on the south breeze. Dessalines and Christophe had recommenced their hellish work. Virginia, too, trembles for the safety of her fair mothers and daughters. We know not what is being plotted in the canebrakes of Louisiana. But we know that in the face of these things the prelates of trickery are sitting in Washington allowing throats to go unthrottled that talked tenderly about the " negro slave;" we know worse: we know that mixed blood has asked for equal rights from a son of the Louisiana noblesse, and that those sacred rights have been treacherously, pusillanimously surrendered into its possession. Why did we not rise yesterday, when the public heart was stirred? The forbearance of this people would be absurd if it were not saintly. But the time has come when Louisiana must protect her-

self! If there is one here who will not strike
for his lands, his rights and the purity of his race,
let him speak! (Cries of "We will rise now!"
"Give us a leader!"   "Lead the way!")

"Kinsmen, friends," continued Agricola, "meet
me at nightfall before the house of this too-long-
spared mulatto. Come armed. Bring a few feet
of stout rope. By morning the gentlemen of color
will know their places better than they do to-day;
h-whe shall understand each other! H-whe shall
set the negrophiles to meditating."

He waved them away.

With a huzza the accumulated crowd moved off.
Chance carried them up the rue Royale; they sang
a song; they came to Frowenfeld's. It was an
Américain establishment; that was against it. It
was a gossiping place of Américain evening loungers;
that was against it. It was a sorcerer's den — (we
are on an ascending scale); its proprietor had refused employment to some there present, had
refused credit to others, was an impudent con-
demner of the most approved Creole sins, had been
beaten over the head only the day before; all these
were against it. But, worse still, the building was
owned by the f. m. c., and unluckiest of all, Raoul
stood in the door and some of his kinsmen in the
crowd stopped to have a word with him. The
crowd stopped. A nameless fellow in the throng
— he was still singing — said: "Here's the place,"
and dropped two bricks through the glass of the
show-window. Raoul, with a cry of retaliative

rage, drew and lifted a pistol; but a kinsman jerked it from him and three others quickly pinioned him and bore him off struggling, pleased to get him away unhurt. In ten minutes, Frowenfeld's was a broken-windowed, open-doored house, full of un-recognizable rubbish that had escaped the torch only through a chance rumor that the Governor's police were coming, and the consequent stampede of the mob.

Joseph was sitting in M. Grandissime's private office, in council with him and the ladies, and Aurora was just saying:

"Well, anny'ow, 'Sieur Frowenfel', ad laz you consen'!" and gathering her veil from her lap, when Raoul burst in, all sweat and rage.

"'Sieur Frowenfel', we ruin'! Ow pharmacie knock all in pieces! My pig-shoe is los'!"

He dropped into a chair and burst into tears.

Shall we never learn to withhold our tears until we are sure of our trouble? Raoul little knew the joy in store for him. 'Polyte, it transpired the next day, had rushed in after the first volley of missiles, and while others were gleefully making off with jars of asafœtida and decanters of distilled water, lifted in his arms and bore away unharmed "Louisiana" firmly refusing to the last to enter the Union. It may not be premature to add that about four weeks later Honoré Grandissime, upon Raoul's announce-ment that he was "betrothed," purchased this painting and presented it to a club of *natural con-noisseurs*.

CHAPTER XLIX

OVER THE NEW STORE

THE accident of the ladies Nancanou making
their new home over Frowenfeld's drug-store occurred in the following rather amusing way. It
chanced that the building was about completed at
the time that the apothecary's stock in trade was
destroyed ; Frowenfeld leased the lower floor.
Honoré Grandissime f. m. c. was the owner. He
being concealed from his enemies, Joseph treated
with that person's inadequately remunerated em-
ployé. In those days, as still in the old French
Quarter, it was not uncommon for persons, even of
wealth, to make their homes over stores, and build-
ings were constructed with a view to their partition
in this way. Hence, in Chartres and Decatur
streets, to-day — and in the cross-streets between —
so many store-buildings with balconies, dormer windows, and sometimes even belvideres. This new
building caught the eye and fancy of Aurora and
Clotilde. The apartments for the store were entirely
isolated. Through a large *porte-cochère*, opening
upon the banquette immediately beside and abreast
of the store-front, one entered a high, covered carriage-way with a tessellated pavement and green
plastered walls, and reached, — just where this way
(corridor, the Creoles always called it) opened into a
sunny court surrounded with narrow parterres, — a

broad stairway leading to a hall over the "corridor" and to the drawing-rooms over the store. They liked it! Aurora would find out at once what sort of an establishment was likely to be opened below, and if that proved unexceptionable she would lease the upper part without more ado.

Next day she said:

"Clotilde, thou beautiful, I have signed the lease!"

"Then the store below is to be occupied by a — what?"

"Guess!"

"Ah!"

"Guess a pharmacien!"

Clotilde's lips parted, she was going to smile, when her thought changed and she blushed offend-edly.

"Not——"

"'Sieur Frowenf——ah, ha, ha, ha!—*ha, ha, ha!*"

Clotilde burst into tears.

Still they moved in — it was written in the bond; and so did the apothecary; and probably two sensible young lovers never before nor since behaved with such abject fear of each other — for a time. Later, and after much oft-repeated good advice given to each separately and to both together, Honoré Grandissime persuaded them that Clotilde could make excellent use of a portion of her means by reenforcing Frowenfeld's very slender stock and well filling his rather empty-looking store, and so they signed regular articles of copartnership, blushing frightfully.

Frowenfeld became a visitor, Honoré not; once Honoré had seen the ladies' moneys satisfactorily invested, he kept aloof. It is pleasant here to remark that neither Aurora nor Clotilde made any waste of their sudden acquisitions; they furnished their rooms with much beauty at moderate cost, and their *salon* with artistic, not extravagant, elegance, and, for the sake of greater propriety, employed a decayed lady as housekeeper; but, being discreet in all other directions, they agreed upon one bold outlay — a volante.

Almost any afternoon you might have seen this vehicle on the Terre aux Bœuf, or Bayou, or Tchoupitoulas Road; and because of the brilliant beauty of its occupants it became known from all other volantes as the " meteor."

Frowenfeld's visits were not infrequent; he insisted on Clotilde's knowing just what was being done with her money. Without indulging ourselves in the pleasure of contemplating his continued mental unfolding, we may say that his growth became more rapid in this season of universal expansion; love had entered into his still compacted soul like a cupid into a rose, and was crowding it wide open. However, as yet, it had not made him brave. Aurora used to slip out of the drawing-room, and in some secluded nook of the hall throw up her clasped hands and go through all the motions of screaming merriment.

" The little fool ! "—it was of her own daughter
she whispered this complimentary remark — " the
little fool is afraid of the fish ! "

" You ! " she said to Clotilde, one evening after
Joseph had gone, " you call yourself a Creole
girl ! "

But she expected too much.   Nothing so terror-
izes a blushing girl as a blushing man.   And then
— though they did sometimes digress — Clotilde
and her partner met to talk " business " in a purely
literal sense.

Aurora, after a time, had taken her money into
her own keeping.

" You mighd gid robb' ag'in, you know, 'Sieur
Frowenfel'," she said.

But when he mentioned Clotilde's fortune as
subject to the same contingency, Aurora replied :

" Ah ! bud Clotilde mighd gid robb' ! "

But for all the exuberance of Aurora's spirits,
there was a cloud in her sky.   Indeed, we know it
is only when clouds are in the sky that we get the
rosiest tints ; and so it was with Aurora.   One
night, when she had heard the wicket in the *porte-
cochère* shut behind three evening callers, one of
whom she had rejected a week before, another of
whom she expected to dispose of similarly, and
the last of whom was Joseph Frowenfeld, she began
such a merry raillery at Clotilde and such a hilarious
ridicule of the " Professor " that Clotilde would
have wept again had not Aurora, all at once, in
the midst of a laugh, dropped her face in her

hands and run from the room in tears.   It is one of
the penalties we pay for being joyous, that nobody
thinks us capable of care or the victim of trouble
until, in some moment of extraordinary expansion,
our bubble of gayety bursts.   Aurora had been
crying of nights.   Even that same night, Clotilde
awoke, opened her eyes and beheld her mother
risen from the pillow and sitting upright in the bed
beside her ; the moon, shining brightly through
the mosquito-bar revealed with distinctness her
head slightly drooped, her face again in her hands
and the dark folds of her hair falling about her
shoulders, half-concealing the richly embroidered
bosom of her snowy gown, and coiling in continuous abundance about her waist and on the slight
summer covering of the bed.   Before her on
the sheet lay a white paper.   Clotilde did not try
to decipher the writing on it ; she knew, at sight,
the slip that had fallen from the statement of
account on the evening of the ninth of March.
Aurora withdrew her hands from her face — Clotilde
shut her eyes ; she heard Aurora put the paper in
her bosom.

    " Clotilde," she said, very softly.

    " Maman," the daughter replied, opening her
eyes, reached up her arms and drew the dear head
down.

    " Clotilde, once upon a time I woke this way,
and, while you were asleep, left the bed and made
a vow to Monsieur Danny. Oh ! it was a sin !
but I cannot do those things now ; I have been

frightened ever since. I shall never do so any
more. I shall never commit another sin as long
as I live!"

Their lips met fervently.

"My sweet sweet," whispered Clotilde, "you
looked so beautiful sitting up with the moonlight
all around you!"

"Clotilde, my beautiful daughter," said Aurora,
pushing her bedmate from her and pretending to
repress a smile, "I tell you now, because you don't
know, and it is my duty as your mother to tell
you — the meanest wickedness a woman can do in
all this bad, bad world is to look ugly in bed!"

Clotilde answered nothing, and Aurora dropped
her outstretched arms, turned away with an involuntary, tremulous sigh, and after two or three hours
of patient wakefulness, fell asleep.

But at daybreak next morning, he that wrote the
paper had not closed his eyes.

CHAPTER L

A PROPOSAL OF MARRIAGE

THERE was always some flutter among Frowenfeld's employés when he was asked for, and this
time it was the more pronounced because he was
sought by a housemaid from the upper floor. It
was hard for these two or three young Ariels to
keep their Creole feet to the ground when it was

presently revealed to their sharp ears that the "prof-fis-or" was requested to come upstairs.

The new store was an extremely neat, bright, and well-ordered establishment ; yet to ascend into the drawing-rooms seemed to the apothecary like going from the hold of one of those smart old packet-ships of his day into the cabin. Aurora came for-ward, with the slippers of a Cinderella twinkling at the edge of her robe. It seemed unfit that the floor under them should not be clouds.

" Proffis-or Frowenfel', good-day ! Teg a cha'." She laughed. It was the pure joy of existence. " You 's well ? You lookin' verrie well ! Halways bizzie ? You fine dad agriz wid you' healt', 'Sieur Frowenfel' ? Yes ? Ha, ha, ha ! " She suddenly leaned toward him across the arm of her chair, with an earnest face. " 'Sieur Frowenfel', Palmyre wand see you. You don' wan' come ad 'er 'ouse, eh ? — an' you don' wan' her to come ad yo' bureau. You know, 'Sieur Frowenfel', she drez the hair of Clo-tilde an' mieself. So w'en she tell me dad, I juz say, ' Palmyre, I will sen' for Proffis-or Frowenfel' to come yeh ; but I don' thing 'e comin'. ' You know, I din' wan' you to 'ave dad troub' ; but Clotilde — ha, ha, ha ! Clotilde is sudge a foolish — she nevva thing of dad troub' to you — she say she thing you was too kine-'arted to call dad troub' — ha, ha, ha ! So anny'ow we sen' for you, eh ! "

Frowenfeld said he was glad they had done so, whereupon Aurora rose lightly, saying :

" I go an' sen' her." She started away, but

turned back to add: "You know, 'Sieur Frowenfel', she say she cann' truz nobody bud y'u." She
ended with a low, melodious laugh, bending her
joyous eyes upon the apothecary with her head
dropped to one side in a way to move a heart of
flint.

She turned and passed through a door, and by
the same way Palmyre entered. The philosophe
came forward noiselessly and with a subdued expression, different from any Frowenfeld had ever before
seen. At the first sight of her a thrill of disrelish
ran through him of which he was instantly ashamed;
as she came nearer he met her with a deferential
bow and the silent tender of a chair. She sat
down, and, after a moment's pause, handed him a
sealed letter.

He turned it over twice, recognized the handwriting, felt the disrelish return, and said:

"This is addressed to yourself."

She bowed.

"Do you know who wrote it?" he asked.

She bowed again.

"*Oui, Miché.*"

"You wish me to open it? I cannot read
French."

She seemed to have some explanation to offer,
but could not command the necessary English;
however, with the aid of Frowenfeld's limited
guessing powers, she made him understand that
the bearer of the letter to her had brought word
from the writer that it was written in English pur-

posely that M. Frowenfeld — the only person he was willing should see it — might read it. Frowenfeld broke the seal and ran his eye over the writing, but remained silent.

The woman stirred, as if to say "Well?" But he hesitated.

"Palmyre," he suddenly said, with a slight, dissuasive smile, "it would be a profanation for me to read this."

She bowed to signify that she caught his meaning, then raised her elbows with an expression of dubiety, and said:

"'E hask you —— "

"Yes," murmured the apothecary. He shook his head as if to protest to himself, and read in a low but audible voice:

"Star of my soul, I approach to die. It is not for me possible to live without Palmyre. Long time have I so done, but now, cut off from to see thee, by imprisonment, as it may be called, love is starving to death. Oh, have pity on the faithful heart which, since ten years, change not, but forget heaven and earth for you. Now in the peril of the life, hidden away, that absence from the sight of you make his seclusion the more worse than death. Halas! I pine! Not other ten years of despair can I commence. Accept this love. If so I will live for you, but if to the contraire, I must die for you. Is there anything at all what I will not give or even do if Palmyre will be my wife? Ah, no, far otherwise, there is nothing!" . . .

Frowenfeld looked over the top of the letter. Palmyre sat with her eyes cast down, slowly shaking her head. He returned his glance to the page, coloring somewhat with annoyance at being made a proposing medium.

"The English is very faulty here," he said, without looking up. " He mentions Bras-Coupé." Palmyre started and turned toward him; but he went on without lifting his eyes. " He speaks of your old pride and affection toward him as one who with your aid might have been a leader and deliverer of his people." Frowenfeld looked up. "Do you under —— "

" *Allez, Miché,*" said she, leaning forward, her great eyes fixed on the apothecary and her face full of distress. "*Mo comprend bien.*"

" He asks you to let him be to you in the place of Bras-Coupé."

The eyes of the philosophe, probably for the first time since the death of the giant, lost their pride. They gazed upon Frowenfeld almost with piteousness; but she compressed her lips and again slowly shook her head.

"You see," said Frowenfeld, suddenly feeling a new interest, " he understands their wants. He knows their wrongs. He is acquainted with laws and men. He could speak for them. It would not be insurrection — it would be advocacy. He would give his time, his pen, his speech, his means, to get them justice — to get them their rights."

She hushed the over-zealous advocate with a sad and bitter smile and essayed to speak, studied as if for English words, and, suddenly abandoning that

attempt, said, with ill-concealed scorn and in the
Creole patois :

"What is all that? What I want is vengeance ! "

" I will finish reading," said Frowenfeld, quickly,
not caring to understand the passionate speech.

"Ah, Palmyre ! Palmyre ! What you love and hope to love
you because his heart keep itself free, he is loving another ! "

" *Qui ci ça, Miché ?* "

Frowenfeld was loth to repeat. She had understood, as her face showed; but she dared not believe.
He made it shorter :

"He means that Honoré Grandissime loves
another woman."

" 'T is a lie ! " she exclaimed, a better command
of English coming with the momentary loss of
restraint.

The apothecary thought a moment and then
decided to speak.

" I do not think so," he quietly said.

" 'Ow you know dat ? "

She, too, spoke quietly, but under a fearful strain.
She had thrown herself forward, but, as she spoke,
forced herself back into her seat.

" He told me so himself."

The tall figure of Palmyre rose slowly and silently
from her chair, her eyes lifted up and her lips moving noiselessly. She seemed to have lost all
knowledge of place or of human presence. She
walked down the drawing-room quite to its cur-

tained windows and there stopped, her face turned
away and her hand laid with a visible tension on
the back of a chair. She remained so long that
Frowenfeld had begun to think of leaving her so,
when she turned and came back. Her form was
erect, her step firm and nerved, her lips set together
and her hands dropped easily at her side; but when
she came close up before the apothecary she was
trembling. For a moment she seemed speechless,
and then, while her eyes gleamed with passion, she
said, in a cold, clear tone, and in her native patois:

"Very well: if I cannot love I can have my revenge." She took the letter from him and bowed
her thanks, still adding, in the same tongue, "There
is now no longer anything to prevent."

The apothecary understood the dark speech.
She meant that, with no hope of Honoré's love,
there was no restraining motive to withhold her
from wreaking what vengeance she could upon
Agricola. But he saw the folly of a debate.

"That is all I can do?" asked he.

"*Oui, merci, Miché,*" she said; then she added,
in perfect English, "but that is not all *I* can do,"
and then — laughed.

The apothecary had already turned to go, and
the laugh was a low one; but it chilled his blood.
He was glad to get back to his employments.

CHAPTER LI

BUSINESS CHANGES

WE have now recorded some of the events which characterized the five months during which Doctor Keene had been vainly seeking to recover his health in the West Indies.

"Is Mr. Frowenfeld in?" he asked, walking very slowly, and with a cane, into the new drug-store on the morning of his return to the city.

"If Professo' Frowenfel' 's in?" replied a young man in shirt-sleeves, speaking rapidly, slapping a paper package which he had just tied, and sliding it smartly down the counter. "No, seh."

A quick step behind the doctor caused him to turn; Raoul was just entering, with a bright look of business on his face, taking his coat off as he came.

"Docta Keene! *Teck* a chair. 'Ow you like de noo sto'? See? Fo' counters! T'ree clerk'! De whole interieure paint undre mie h-own direction! If dat is not a beautiful! eh? Look at dat sign."

He pointed to some lettering in harmonious colors near the ceiling at the farther end of the house. The doctor looked and read:

MANDARIN, AG'T, APOTHECARY.

"Why not Frowenfeld?" he asked.
Raoul shrugged.

" 'T is better dis way."

That was his explanation.

" Not the De Brahmin Mandarin who was Honoré's manager ? "

" Yes. Honoré was n' able to kip 'im no long-er. Honoré is n' so rich lak befo'."

" And Mandarin is really in charge here ? "

" Oh, yes. Profess-or Frowenfel' all de time at de ole corner, w'ere 'e *con*tinue to keep 'is private room and h-use de ole shop fo' ware'ouse. 'E h-only come yeh w'en Mandarin cann' git 'long widout 'im."

" What does he do there ? *He's* not rich."

Raoul bent down toward the doctor's chair and whispered the dark secret:

" Studyin' ! "

Doctor Keene went out.

Everything seemed changed to the returned wanderer. Poor man ! The changes were very slight save in their altered relation to him. To one broken in health, and still more to one with a broken heart, old scenes fall upon the sight in broken rays. A sort of vague alienation seemed to the little doctor to come like a film over the long-familiar vistas of the town where he had once walked in the vigor and complacency of strength and distinction. This was not the same New Orleans. The people he met on the street were more or less familiar to his memory, but many that should have recognized him failed to do so, and others were made to notice him rather by his cough than by his face. Some

did not know he had been away. It made him
cross.

He had walked slowly down beyond the old
Frowenfeld corner and had just crossed the street to
avoid the dust of a building which was being torn
down to make place for a new one, when he saw
coming toward him, unconscious of his proximity,
Joseph Frowenfeld.

"Doctor Keene!" said Frowenfeld, with almost
the enthusiasm of Raoul.

The doctor was very much quieter.

"Hello, Joe."

They went back to the new drug-store, sat down
in a pleasant little rear corner enclosed by a railing
and curtains, and talked.

"And did the trip prove of no advantage to
you?"

"You see. But never mind me; tell me about
Honoré; how does that row with his family progress?"

"It still continues; the most of his people hold
ideas of justice and prerogative that run parallel
with family and party lines, lines of caste, of custom
and the like; they have imparted their bad feeling
against him to the community at large; very easy
to do just now, for the election for President of the
States comes on in the fall, and though we in
Louisiana have little or nothing to do with it, the
people are feverish."

"The country's chill-day," said Doctor Keene;
"dumb chill, hot fever."

"The excitement is intense," said Frowenfeld. "It seems we are not to be granted suffrage yet; but the Creoles have a way of casting votes in their mind. For example, they have voted Honoré Grandissime a traitor; they have voted me an encumbrance; I hear one of them casting that vote now."

Some one near the front of the store was talking excitedly with Raoul:

"An'—an'—an' w'at are the consequence? The consequence are that we smash his shop for him an' 'e 'ave to make a noo-start with a Creole partner's money an' put 'is sto' in charge of Creole'! If I know he is yo' frien'? Yesseh! Valuable citizen? An' w'at we care for valuable citizen? Let him be valuable if he want; it keep' him from gettin' the neck broke; but—he mus'-tek-kyeh—'ow—he—talk'! He-mus'-tek-kyeh 'ow he stir the 'ot blood of Louisyanna!'"

"He is perfectly right," said the little doctor, in his husky undertone; "neither you nor Honoré is a bit sound, and I should n't wonder if they would hang you both, yet; and as for that darkey who has had the impudence to try to make a commercial white gentleman of himself—it may not be I that ought to say it, but—he will get his deserts—sure!"

"There are a great many Americans that think as you do," said Frowenfeld, quietly.

"But," said the little doctor, "what did that fellow mean by your Creole partner? Mandarin is in charge of your store, but he is not your partner, is he ? Have you one ? "

" A silent one," said the apothecary

" So silent as to be none of my business ? "

" No."

" Well, who is it, then ? "

" It is Mademoiselle Nancanou."

" Your partner in business ? "

" Yes."

" Well, Joseph Frowenfeld, —— "

The insinuation conveyed in the doctor's manner was very trying, but Joseph merely reddened.

" Purely business, I suppose," presently said the doctor, with a ghastly ironical smile. " Does the arrangem'—" his utterance failed him — " does it end there ? "

" It ends there."

" And you don't see that it ought either not to have begun, or else ought not to have ended there ? "

Frowenfeld blushed angrily. The doctor asked :

" And who takes care of Aurora's money ? "

" Herself."

" Exclusively ? "

They both smiled more good-naturedly.

" Exclusively."

" She's a coon ; " and the little doctor rose up and crawled away, ostensibly to see another friend, but really to drag himself into his bedchamber and lock himself in. The next day — the yellow fever was bad again — he resumed the practice of his profession.

"'T will be a sort of decent suicide without the element of pusillanimity," he thought to himself.

CHAPTER LII

LOVE LIES A-BLEEDING

WHEN Honoré Grandissime heard that Doctor Keene had returned to the city in a very feeble state of health, he rose at once from the desk where he was sitting and went to see him ; but it was on that morning when the doctor was sitting and talking with Joseph, and Honoré found his chamber door locked.   Doctor Keene called twice, within the following two days, upon Honoré at his counting-room ; but on both occasions Honoré's chair was empty.   So it was several days before they met. But one hot morning in the latter part of August, — the August days were hotter before the cypress forest was cut down between the city and the lake than they are now, — as Doctor Keene stood in the middle of his room breathing distressedly after a sad fit of coughing, and looking toward one of his windows whose closed sash he longed to see opened, Honoré knocked at the door.

"Well, come in !" said the fretful invalid. "Why, Honoré, — well, it serves you right for stopping to knock.   Sit down."

Each took a hasty, scrutinizing glance at the other ; and, after a pause, Doctor Keene said :

" Honoré, you are pretty badly stove."

M. Grandissime smiled.

" Do you think so, Doctor? I will be more complimentary to you; you might look more sick."

" Oh, I have resumed my trade," replied Doctor Keene.

" So I have heard; but, Charlie, that is all in favor of the people who want a skilful and advanced physician and do not mind killing him; I should advise you not to do it."

" You mean" (the incorrigible little doctor smiled cynically) " if I should ask your advice. I am going to get well, Honoré."

His visitor shrugged.

" So much the better. I do confess I am tempted to make use of you in your official capacity, right now. Do you feel strong enough to go with me in your gig a little way?"

" A professional call?"

" Yes, and a difficult case; also a confidential one."

" Ah! confidential!" said the little man, in his painful, husky irony. " You want to get me into the sort of scrape I got our ' professor ' into, eh?"

" Possibly a worse one," replied the amiable Creole.

" And I must be mum, eh?"

" I would prefer."

" Shall I need any instruments? No?" — with a shade of disappointment on his face.

He pulled a bell-rope and ordered his gig to the street door.

"How are affairs about town?" he asked, as he made some slight preparation for the street.

"Excitement continues. Just as I came along, a private difficulty between a Creole and an Américain drew instantly half the street together to take sides strictly according to belongings and without asking a question. My-de'-seh, we are having, as Frowenfeld says, a war of human acids and alkalies."

They descended and drove away. At the first corner the lad who drove turned, by Honoré's direction, toward the rue Dauphine, entered it, passed down it to the rue Dumaine, turned into this toward the river again and entered the rue Condé. The route was circuitous. They stopped at the carriage-door of a large brick house. The wicket was opened by Clemence. They alighted without driving in.

"Hey, old witch," said the doctor, with mock severity; "not hung yet?"

The houses of any pretension to comfortable spaciousness in the closely built parts of the town were all of the one, general, Spanish-American plan. Honoré led the doctor through the cool, high, tessellated carriage-hall, on one side of which were the drawing-rooms, closed and darkened. They turned at the bottom, ascended a broad, iron-railed staircase to the floor above, and halted before the open half of a glazed double door with a

28

clumsy iron latch.   It was the entrance to two
spacious chambers, which were thrown into one by
folded doors.

The doctor made a low, indrawn whistle and
raised his eyebrows — the rooms were so sump-
tuously furnished; immovable largeness and heavi-
ness, lofty sobriety, abundance of finely wrought
brass mounting, motionless richness of upholstery,
much silent twinkle of pendulous crystal, a soft
semi-obscurity — such were the characteristics.
The long windows of the farther apartment could
be seen to open over the street, and the air from
behind, coming in over a green mass of fig-trees that
stood in the paved court below, moved through the
rooms, making them cool and cavernous.

"You don't call this a hiding place, do you —
in his own bed-chamber?" the doctor whispered.

"It is necessary, now, only to keep out of sight,"
softly answered Honoré.   "Agricole and some
others ransacked this house one night last March
— the day I announced the new firm; but of
course, then, he was not here."

They entered, and the figure of Honoré Grandissime, f. m. c., came into view in the centre of the
farther room, reclining in an attitude of extreme
languor on a low couch, whither he had come from
the high bed near by, as the impression of his form
among its pillows showed.   He turned upon the
two visitors his slow, melancholy eyes, and, without
an attempt to rise or speak, indicated, by a feeble
motion of the hand, an invitation to be seated.

"Good morning," said Doctor Keene, selecting·a light chair and drawing it close to the side of the couch.

The patient before him was emaciated. The limp and bloodless hand, which had not responded to the doctor's friendly pressure but sank idly back upon the edge of the couch, was cool and moist, and its nails slightly blue.

"Lie still," said the doctor, reassuringly, as the rentier began to lift the one knee and slippered foot which was drawn up on the couch and the hand which hung out of sight across a large, linen-covered cushion.

By pleasant talk that seemed all chat, the physician soon acquainted himself with the case before him. It was a very plain one. By and by he rubbed his face and red curls and suddenly said :

"You will not take my prescription."

The f. m. c. did not say yes or no.

"Still," — the doctor turned sideways in his chair, as was his wont, and, as he spoke, allowed the corners of his mouth to take that little satirical downward pull which his friends disliked, "I 'll do my duty. I 'll give Honoré the details as to diet ; no physic ; but my prescription to you is, Get up and get out. Never mind the risk of rough handling ; they can but kill you, and you will die anyhow if you stay here." He rose. "I 'll send you a chalybeate tonic ; or — I will leave it at Frowenfeld's to-morrow morning, and you can call there and get it. It will give you an object for going out."

The two visitors presently said adieu and retired together. Reaching the bottom of the stairs in the carriage "corridor," they turned in a direction opposite to the entrance and took chairs in a cool nook of the paved court, at a small table where the hospitality of Clemence had placed glasses of lemonade.

"No," said the doctor, as they sat down, "there is, as yet, no incurable organic derangement; a little heart trouble easily removed; still your — your patient —— "

"My half-brother," said Honoré.

"Your patient," said Doctor Keene, "is an emphatic 'yes' to the question the girls sometimes ask us doctors — Does love ever kill?' It will kill him *soon*, if you do not get him to rouse up. There is absolutely nothing the matter with him but his unrequited love."

"Fortunately, the most of us," said Honoré, with something of the doctor's smile, "do not love hard enough to be killed by it."

"Very few." The doctor paused, and his blue eyes, distended in reverie, gazed upon the glass which he was slowly turning around with his attenuated fingers as it stood on the board, while he added: "However, one *may* love as hopelessly and harder than that man upstairs, and yet not die."

"There is comfort in that — to those who must live," said Honoré with gentle gravity.

"Yes," said the other, still toying with his glass.

He slowly lifted his glance, and the eyes of the two men met and remained steadfastly fixed each upon each.

"You 've got it bad," said Doctor Keene, mechanically.

"And you?" retorted the Creole.

"It is n't going to kill me."

"It has nct killed me. And," added M. Grandissime, as they passed through the carriage-way toward the street, "while I keep in mind the numberless other sorrows of life, the burials of wives and sons and daughters, the agonies and desolations, I shall never die of love, my-de'-seh, for very shame's sake."

This was much sentiment to risk within Doctor Keene's reach; but he took no advantage of it.

"Honoré," said he, as they joined hands on the banquette beside the doctor's gig, to say good-day, "if you think there 's a chance for you, why stickle upon such fine-drawn points as I reckon you are making? Why, sir, as I understand it, this is the only weak spot your action has shown; you have taken an inoculation of Quixotic conscience from our transcendental apothecary and perpetrated a lot of heroic behavior that would have done honor to four-and-twenty Brutuses; and now that you have a chance to do something easy and human, you shiver and shrink at the 'looks o' the thing.' Why, what do you care ——— "

"Hush!" said Honoré; "do you suppose I have not temptation enough already?"

He began to move away.

"Honoré," said the doctor, following him a step, "I could n't have made a mistake — It's the little Monk,— it's Aurora, is n't it?"

Honoré nodded, then faced his friend more directly, with a sudden new thought.

"But, Doctor, why not take your own advice? I know not how you are prevented; you have as good a right as Frowenfeld."

"It would n't be honest," said the doctor; "it would n't be the straight up and down manly thing."

"Why not?"

The doctor stepped into his gig——

"Not till I feel all right *here*." (In his chest.)

CHAPTER LIII

FROWENFELD AT THE GRANDISSIME MANSION

ONE afternoon — it seems to have been some time in June, and consequently earlier than Doctor Keene's return — the Grandissimes were set all a-tremble with vexation by the discovery that another of their number had, to use Agricola's expression, "gone over to the enemy," — a phrase first applied by him to Honoré.

"What do you intend to convey by that term?" Frowenfeld had asked on that earlier occasion.

"Gone over to the enemy means, my son, gone over to the enemy!" replied Agricola. "It implies affiliation with Américains in matters of business and of government! It implies the exchange of social amenities with a race of upstarts! It implies a craven consent to submit the sacredest prejudices of our fathers to the new-fangled measuring-rods of pert, imported theories upon moral and political progress! It implies a listening to, and reasoning with, the condemners of some of our most time-honored and respectable practices! Reasoning with? N-a-hay! but Honoré has positively sat down and eaten with them! What? — and h-walked out into the stre-heet with them, arm in arm! It implies in his case an act — two separate and distinct acts — so base that — that — I simply do not understand them! *H-you* know, Professor Frowenfeld, what he has done! You know how ignominiously he has surrendered the key of a moral position which for the honor of the Grandissime-Fusilier name we have felt it necessary to hold against our hereditary enemies! And — you — know —— " here Agricola actually dropped all artificiality and spoke from the depths of his feelings, without figure — "h-h-he has joined himself in business h-with a man of negro blood! What can we do? What can we say? It is Honoré Grandissime. We can only say, 'Farewell! He is gone over to the enemy.'"

The new cause of exasperation was the defection of Raoul Innerarity. Raoul had, somewhat from a distance, contemplated such part as he could understand of Joseph Frowenfeld's character with ever-broadening admiration. We know how devoted he became to the interests and fame of "Frowenfeld's." It was in April he had married. Not to divide his generous heart he took rooms opposite the drug-store, resolved that "Frowenfeld's" should be not only the latest closed but the earliest opened of all the pharmacies in New Orleans.

This, it is true, was allowable. Not many weeks afterward his bride fell suddenly and seriously ill. The overflowing souls of Aurora and Clotilde could not be so near to trouble and not know it, and before Raoul was nearly enough recovered from the shock of this peril to remember that he was a Grandissime, these last two of the De Grapions had hastened across the street to the small, white-walled sick-room and filled it as full of universal human love as the cup of a magnolia is full of perfume. Madame Innerarity recovered. A warm affection was all she and her husband could pay such ministration in, and this they paid bountifully; the four became friends. The little madame found herself drawn most toward Clotilde; to her she opened her heart — and her wardrobe, and showed her all her beautiful new underclothing. Raoul found Clotilde to be, for him, rather — what shall we say? — starry; starrily inaccessible; but Aurora was emphatically after his liking; he was delighted with Aurora. He told her in confidence that "Profess-or Frowenfel'" was the best man in the world;

but she boldly said, taking pains to speak with a
tear-and-a-half of genuine gratitude, — " Egcep'
Monsieur Honoré Grandissime," and he assented,
at first with hesitation and then with ardor. The
four formed a group of their own ; and it is not
certain that this was not the very first specimen
ever produced in the Crescent City of that social
variety of New Orleans life now distinguished as
Uptown Creoles.

Almost the first thing acquired by Raoul in the
camp of the enemy was a certain Aurorean audacity ; and on the afternoon to which we allude,
having told Frowenfeld a rousing fib to the effect
that the multitudinous inmates of the maternal
Grandissime mansion had insisted on his bringing
his esteemed employer to see them, he and his
bride had the hardihood to present him on the
front veranda.

The straightforward Frowenfeld was much pleased
with his reception. It was not possible for such as
he to guess the ire with which his presence was
secretly regarded. New Orleans, let us say once
more, was small, and the apothecary of the rue
Royale locally famed ; and what with curiosity and
that innate politeness which it is the Creole's boast
that he cannot mortify, the veranda, about the top
of the great front stair, was well crowded with
people of both sexes and all ages. It would be
most pleasant to tarry once more in description of
this gathering of nobility and beauty ; to recount
the points of Creole loveliness in midsummer dress ;

to tell in particular of one and another eye-kindling face, form, manner, wit; to define the subtle qualities of Creole air and sky and scene, or the yet more delicate graces that characterize the music of Creole voice and speech and the light of Creole eyes; to set forth the gracious, unaccentuated dignity of the matrons and the ravishing archness of their daughters. To Frowenfeld the experience seemed all unreal. Nor was this unreality removed by conversation on grave subjects; for few among either the maturer or the younger beauty could do aught but listen to his foreign tongue like unearthly strangers in the old fairy tales. They came, however, in the course of their talk to the subject of love and marriage. It is not certain that they entered deeper into the great question than a comparison of its attendant Anglo-American and Franco-American conventionalities; but sure it is that somehow — let those young souls divine the method who can — every unearthly stranger on that veranda contrived to understand Frowenfeld's English. Suddenly the conversation began to move over the ground of inter-marriage between hostile families. Then what eyes and ears! A certain suspicion had already found lodgement in the universal Grandissime breast, and every one knew in a moment that, to all intents and purposes, they were about to argue the case of Honoré and Aurora.

The conversation became discussion, Frowenfeld, Raoul and Raoul's little seraph against the whole host, chariots, horse and archery. Ah! such strokes

as the apothecary dealt! And if Raoul and
"Madame Raoul" played parts most closely re-
sembling the blowing of horns and breaking of
pitchers, still they bore themselves gallantly. The
engagement was short; we need not say that nobody surrendered; nobody ever gives up the ship
in parlor or veranda debate: and yet — as is generally the case in such affairs — truth and justice
made some unacknowledged headway. If anybody
on either side came out wounded — this to the
credit of the Creoles as a people — the sufferer had
the heroic good manners not to say so. But the
results were more marked than this; indeed, in
more than one or two candid young hearts and
impressible minds the wrongs and rights of sov-
ereign true love began there on the spot to be more
generously conceded and allowed. "My-de'-seh,"
Honoré had once on a time said to Frowenfeld,
meaning that to prevail in conversational debate
one should never follow up a faltering opponent,
"you mus' *crack* the egg, not smash it!" And
Joseph, on rising to take his leave, could the more
amiably overlook the feebleness of the invitation to
call again, since he rejoiced, for Honoré's sake, in
the conviction that the egg was cracked.

Agricola, the Grandissimes told the apothecary,
was ill in his room, and Madame de Grandissime,
his sister — Honoré's mother — begged to be excused that she might keep him company. The
Fusiliers were a very close order; or one might
say they garrisoned the citadel.

But Joseph's rising to go was not immediately upon the close of the discussion; those courtly people would not let even an unwelcome guest go with the faintest feeling of disrelish for them. They were casting about in their minds for some momentary diversion with which to add a finishing touch to their guest's entertainment, when Clemence appeared in the front garden walk and was quickly surrounded by bounding children, alternately begging and demanding a song. Many of even the younger adults remembered well when she had been "one of the hands on the place," and a passionate lover of the African dance. In the same instant half a dozen voices proposed that for Joseph's amusement Clemence should put her cakes off her head, come up on the veranda and show a few of her best steps.

"But who will sing?"

"Raoul!"

"Very well; and what shall it be?"

"'Madame Gaba.'"

No, Clemence objected.

"Well, well, stand back — something better than 'Madame Gaba.'"

Raoul began to sing and Clemence instantly to pace and turn, posture, bow, respond to the song, start, swing, straighten, stamp, wheel, lift her hand, stoop, twist, walk, whirl, tiptoe with crossed ankles, smite her palms, march, circle, leap, — an endless improvisation of rhythmic motion to this modulated responsive chant:

RAOUL.   " *Mo pas l'aimein ça.*"

CLEMENCE.   " *Miché Igenne, oap! oap! oap!*"

HE.   " *Yé donné vingt cinq sous pou' manzé poulé.*"

SHE.   " *Miché Igenne, dit — dit — dit ——*"

HE.   " *Mo pas l'aimein ça!*"

SHE.   " *Miché Igenne, oap! oap! oap!*"

HE.   " *Mo pas l'aimein ça!*"

SHE.   " *Miché Igenne, oap! oap! oap!*"

Frowenfeld was not so greatly amused as the ladies thought he should have been, and was told that this was not a fair indication of what he would see if there were ten dancers instead of one.

How much less was it an indication of what he would have seen in that mansion early the next morning, when there was found just outside of Agricola's bedroom door a fresh egg, not cracked, according to Honoré's maxim, but smashed, according to the lore of the voudous. Who could have got in in the night? And did the intruder get in by magic, by outside lock-picking, or by inside collusion? Later in the morning, the children playing in the basement found — it had evidently been accidentally dropped, since the true use of its contents required them to be scattered in some person's path — a small cloth bag, containing a quantity of dogs' and cats' hair, cut fine and mixed with salt and pepper.

" Clemence ? "

" Pooh! Clemence. No! But as sure as the sun turns around the world — Palmyre Philosophe!"

CHAPTER LIV

" CAULDRON BUBBLE "

THE excitement and alarm produced by the practical threat of voudou curses upon Agricola was
one thing, Creole lethargy was quite another; and
when, three mornings later, a full quartette of
voudou charms was found in the four corners of
Agricola's pillow, the great Grandissime family
were ignorant of how they could have come there.
Let us examine these terrible engines of mischief.
In one corner was an acorn drilled through with
two holes at right angles to each other, a small
feather run through each hole; in the second a
joint of cornstalk with a cavity scooped from the
middle, the pith left intact at the ends, and the
space filled with parings from that small callous
spot near the knee of the horse, called the " nail ; "
in the third corner a bunch of parti-colored feathers;
something equally meaningless in the fourth. No
thread was used in any of them. All fastening was
done with the gum of trees. It was no easy task
for his kindred to prevent Agricola, beside himself
with rage and fright, from going straight to Palmyre's house and shooting her down in open day.

" We shall have to watch our house by night,"
said a gentleman of the household, when they had
at length restored the Citizen to a condition of
mind which enabled them to hold him in a chair.

" Watch this house?" cried a chorus. "You don't suppose she comes near here, do you? She does it all from a distance. No, no; watch *her* house."

Did Agricola believe in the supernatural potency of these gimcracks? No, and yes. Not to be foolhardy, he quietly slipped down every day to the levee, had a slave-boy row him across the river in a skiff, landed, re-embarked, and in the middle of the stream surreptitiously cast a picayune over his shoulder into the river. Monsieur D'Embarras, the imp of death thus placated, must have been a sort of spiritual Cheap John.

Several more nights passed. The house of Palmyre, closely watched, revealed nothing. No one came out, no one went in, no light was seen. They should have watched in broad daylight. At last, one midnight, 'Polyte Grandissime stepped cautiously up to one of the batten doors with an auger, and succeeded, without arousing any one, in boring a hole. He discovered a lighted candle standing in a glass of water.

" Nothing but a bedroom light," said one.

" Ah, bah!" whispered the other; "it is to make the spell work strong."

" We will not tell Agricola first; we had better tell Honoré," said Sylvestre.

" You forget," said 'Polyte, "that I no longer have any acquaintance with Monsieur Honoré Grandissime."

They told Agamemnon; and it would have gone

hard with the "*milatraise*" but for the additional
fact that suspicion had fastened upon another
person; but now this person in turn had to be
identified. It was decided not to report progress to
old Agricola, but to wait and seek further developments. Agricola, having lost all ability to sleep in
the mansion, moved into a small cottage in a grove
near the house. But the very next morning, he
turned cold with horror to find on his doorstep
a small black-coffined doll, with pins run through
the heart, a burned-out candle at the head and
another at the feet.

"You know it is Palmyre, do you?" asked
Agamemnon, seizing the old man as he was going
at a headlong pace through the garden gate.
"What if I should tell you that by watching the
Congo dancing-ground at midnight to-night, you
will see the real author of this mischief — eh?"

"And why to-night?"

"Because the moon rises at midnight."

There was firing that night in the deserted Congo
dancing-grounds under the ruins of Fort St. Joseph,
or, as we would say now, in Congo Square, from
three pistols — Agricola's, 'Polyte's, and the weapon
of an ill-defined, retreating figure answering the
description of the person who had stabbed Agricola
the preceding February. "And yet," said 'Polyte,
"I would have sworn that it was Palmyre doing
this work."

Through Raoul these events came to the ear of
Frowenfield. It was about the time that Raoul's

fishing party, after a few days' mishaps, had returned home. Palmyre, on several later dates, had craved further audiences and shown other letters from the hidden f. m. c. She had heard them calmly, and steadfastly preserved the one attitude of refusal. But it could not escape Frowenfeld's notice that she encouraged the sending of additional letters. He easily guessed the courier to be Clemence; and now, as he came to ponder these revelations of Raoul, he found that within twenty-four hours after every visit of Clemence to the house of Palmyre, Agricola suffered a visitation.

CHAPTER LV

CAUGHT

The fig-tree, in Louisiana, sometimes sheds its leaves while it is yet summer. In the rear of the Grandissme mansion, about two hundred yards northwest of it and fifty northeast of the cottage in which Agricola had made his new abode, on the edge of the grove of which we have spoken, stood one of these trees, whose leaves were beginning to lie thickly upon the ground beneath it. An ancient and luxuriant hedge of Cherokee-rose started from this tree and stretched toward the northwest across the level country, until it merged into the green confusion of gardened homes in the vicinity of Bayou St. Jean, or, by night, into the common

obscurity of a starlit perspective. When an un-
clouded moon shone upon it, it cast a shadow as
black as velvet.

Under this fig-tree, some three hours later than
that at which Honoré bade Joseph good-night, a
man was stooping down and covering something with
the broad, fallen leaves.

"The moon will rise about three o'clock," thought
he. "That, the hour of universal slumber, will
be, by all odds, the time most likely to bring
developments."

He was the same person who had spent the most
of the day in a blacksmith's shop in St. Louis street,
superintending a piece of smithing. Now that he
seemed to have got the thing well hid, he turned to
the base of the tree and tried the security of some
attachment. Yes, it was firmly chained. He was
not a robber; he was not an assassin; he was not
an officer of police; and what is more notable,
seeing he was a Louisianian, he was not a soldier
nor even an ex-soldier; and this although, under his
clothing, he was encased from head to foot in a
complete suit of mail. Of steel? No. Of brass?
No. It was all one piece — *a white skin;* and on
his head he wore an invisible helmet — the name of
Grandissime. As he straightened up and withdrew
into the grove, you would have recognized at once
— by his thick-set, powerful frame, clothed seemingly in black, but really, as you might guess, in
blue cottonade, by his black beard and the general
look of a seafarer — a frequent visitor at the Gran-

dissime mansion, a country member of that great family, one whom we saw at the *fête de grandpère.*

Capitain Jean-Baptiste Grandissime was a man of few words, no sentiments, short methods; materialistic, we might say; quietly ferocious; indifferent as to means, positive as to ends, quick of perception, sure in matters of saltpetre, a stranger at the customhouse, and altogether — *take him right* — very much of a gentleman. He had been, for a whole day, beset with the idea that the way to catch a voudou was — to catch him; and as he had caught numbers of them on both sides of the tropical and semi-tropical Atlantic, he decided to try his skill privately on the one who — his experience told him — was likely to visit Agricola's doorstep to-night. All things being now prepared, he sat down at the root of a tree in the grove, where the shadow was very dark, and seemed quite comfortable. He did not strike at the mosquitoes; they appeared to understand that he did not wish to trifle. Neither did his thoughts or feelings trouble him; he sat and sharpened a small penknife on his boot.

His mind — his occasional transient meditation — was the more comfortable because he was one of those few who had coolly and unsentimentally allowed Honoré Grandissime to sell their lands. It continued to grow plainer every day that the grants with which theirs were classed — grants of old French or Spanish under-officials — were bad. Their sagacious cousin seemed to have struck the right standard, and while those titles which he still

held on to remained unimpeached, those that he had
parted with to purchasers — as, for instance, the
grant held by this Captain Jean-Baptiste Grandissime — could be bought back now for half what he
had got for it.   Certainly, as to that, the Capitan
might well have that quietude of mind which enabled
him to find occupation in perfecting the edge of his
penknife and trimming his nails in the dark.

By and by he put up the little tool and sat looking out upon the prospect.   The time of greatest
probability had not come, but the voudou might
choose not to wait for that; and so he kept watch.
There was a great stillness.   The cocks had finished
a round and were silent.   No dog barked.   A few
tiny crickets made the quiet land seem the more
deserted.   Its beauties were not entirely overlooked
— the innumerable host of stars above, the twinkle
of myriad fireflies on the dark earth below.   Between a quarter- and a half-mile away, almost in a
line with the Cherokee hedge, was a faint rise of
ground, and on it a wide-spreading live-oak.   There
the keen, seaman's eye of the Captain came to a
stop, fixed upon a spot which he had not noticed
before.   He kept his eye on it, and waited for the
stronger light of the moon.

Presently behind the grove at his back she rose;
and almost the first beam that passed over the tops
of the trees, and stretched across the plain, struck
the object of his scrutiny.   What was it?   The
ground, he knew; the tree, he knew; he knew
there ought to be a white paling enclosure about the

trunk of the tree: for there were buried — ah! — he
came as near laughing at himself as ever he did in
his life; the apothecary of the rue Royale had lately
erected some marble headstones there, and ——

"Oh! my God!"

While Captain Jean-Baptiste had been trying to
guess what the tombstones were, a woman had been
coming toward him in the shadow of the hedge. She
was not expecting to meet him; she did not know
that he was there; she knew she had risks to run,
but was ignorant of what they were; she did not
know there was anything under the fig-tree which
she so nearly and noiselessly approached. One
moment her foot was lifted above the spot where
the unknown object lay with wide-stretched jaws
under the leaves, and the next, she uttered that cry
of agony and consternation which interrupted the
watcher's meditation. She was caught in a huge
steel-trap.

Captain Jean-Baptiste Grandissime remained perfectly still. She fell, a snarling, struggling, groaning
heap, to the ground, wild with pain and fright, and
began the hopeless effort to draw the jaws of the
trap apart with her fingers.

"*Ah! bon Dieu, bon Dieu!* Quit a-*bi-i-i-i-tin'
me!* Oh! Lawd 'a' mussy! Ow-ow-ow! lemme
go! Dey go'n' to kyetch an' hang me! Oh! an'
I hain' done nutt'n' 'gainst *no*body! Ah! *bon Dieu!
ein pov' vié négresse!* Oh! Jemimy! I cyan' gid
dis yeh t'ing loose — oh! m-m-m-m! An' dey'll
tra to mek out 't I voudou' Mich-Agricole! An'

I did n' had nutt'n' do wid it! Oh Lawd, oh
Lawd, you'll be mighty good ef you lemme loose!
I'm a po' nigga! Oh! dey had n' ought to mek
it so *pow*'ful!'"

Hands, teeth, the free foot, the writhing body,
every combination of available forces failed to spread
the savage jaws, though she strove until hands and
mouth were bleeding.

Suddenly she became silent; a thought of pre-
caution came to her; she lifted from the earth a
burden she had dropped there, struggled to a half-
standing posture, and, with her foot still in the trap,
was endeavoring to approach the end of the hedge
near by, to thrust this burden under it, when she
opened her throat in a speechless ecstasy of fright
on feeling her arm grasped by her captor.

"O-o-o-h! Lawd! o-o-oh! Lawd!'" she cried,
in a frantic, husky whisper, going down upon her
knees, "*Oh, Miché! pou' l'amou' du bon Dieu!
Pou' l'amou' du bon Dieu ayez pitié d'ein pov' négresse!
Pov' négresse, Miché*, w'at nevva done nutt'n' to nobody on'y jis sell *calas!* I iss comin' 'long an'
step inteh dis-yeh bah-trap by acci*dent!* Ah! *Miché,
Miché*, ple-e-ease be good! *Ah! mon Dieu!* — an'
de Lawd'll reward you — 'deed 'E will, *Miché!*'"

"*Qui ci ça?*'" asked the Capitain, sternly, stooping and grasping her burden, which she had been
trying to conceal under herself.

"Oh, Miché, don' trouble dat! Please jes tek
dis yeh trap offen me — da's all! Oh, don't,
mawstah, ple-e-ease don' spill all my wash'n' t'ings!

'Tain't nutt'n' but my old dress roll' up into a ball. Oh, please — now, you see? nutt'n' but a po' nigga's dr — *oh! fo' de love o' God, Miché Jean-Baptiste, don' open dat ah box! Y'en a rien du tout ladans, Miché Jean-Baptiste; du tout, du tout!* Oh, my God! *Miché*, on'y jis teck dis-yeh t'ing off'n my laig, ef yo' *please*, it's bit'n' me lak a *dawg!* — if you *please, Miché!* Oh! you git kill' if you open dat ah box, Mawse Jean-Baptiste! *Mo' parole d'honneur le plus sacre* — I'll kiss de cross! Oh, *sweet Miché Jean, laisse moi aller!* Nutt'n' but some dutty close *la-dans*." She repeated this again and again, even after Capitain Jean-Baptiste had disengaged a small black coffin from the old dress in which it was wrapped. "*Rien du tout, Miché;* nutt'n' but some wash'n' fo' one o' de boys."

He removed the lid and saw within, resting on the cushioned bottom, the image, in myrtle-wax, moulded and painted with some rude skill, of a negro's bloody arm cut off near the shoulder — a *bras coupé* — with a dirk grasped in its hand.

The old woman lifted her eyes to heaven; her teeth chattered; she gasped twice before she could recover utterance. "*Oh, Miché* Jean-Baptiste, I di' n' mek dat ah! *Mo' té pas fé ça!* I swea' befo' God! Oh, no, no, no! 'Tain' nutt'n' nohow but a lill play-toy, *Miché*. Oh, sweet *Miché Jean*, you not gwan to kill me? I di' n' mek it! It was — ef you lemme go, I tell you who mek it! Sho's I live I tell you, *Miché Jean* — ef you lemme go! Sho's God's good to me — ef you lemme go! Oh,

God A'mighty, *Miché Jean*, sho 's God 's good to me."

She was becoming incoherent.

Then Captain Jean-Baptiste Grandissime for the first time spoke at length:

"Do you see this?" he spoke the French of the Atchafalaya. He put his long flintlock pistol close to her face. "I shall take the trap off; you will walk three feet in front of me; if you make it four I blow your brains out; we shall go to Agricole. But right here, just now, before I count ten, you will tell me who sent you here; at the word ten, if I reach it, I pull the trigger. One — two — three ———"

"Oh, *Miché*, she gwan to gib me to de devil wid *houdou* ef I tell you — Oh, good *Lawdy!*"

But he did not pause.

"Four — five — six — seven — eight———"

"Palmyre!" gasped the negress, and grovelled on the ground.

The trap was loosened from her bleeding leg, the burden placed in her arms, and they disappeared in the direction of the mansion.

A black shape, a boy, the lad who had carried the basil to Frowenfeld, rose up from where he had all this time lain, close against the hedge, and glided off down its black shadow to warn the philosophe.

When Clemence was searched, there was found on her person an old table-knife with its end ground to a point.

CHAPTER LVI

BLOOD FOR A BLOW

I⊤ seems to be one of the self-punitive characteristics of tyranny, whether the tyrant be a man, a
community, or a caste, to have a pusillanimous fear
of its victim. It was not when Clemence lay in
irons, it is barely now, that our South is casting off
a certain apprehensive tremor, generally latent, but
at the slightest provocation active, and now and
then violent, concerning her "blacks." This fear,
like others similar elsewhere in the world, has
always been met by the same one antidote — terrific cruelty to the tyrant's victim. So we shall
presently see the Grandissime ladies, deeming themselves compassionate, urging their kinsmen to
"give the poor wretch a sound whipping and let
her go." Ah! what atrocities are we unconsciously
perpetrating North and South now, in the name of
mercy or defence, which the advancing light of pro-
gressive thought will presently show out in their
enormity?

Agricola slept late. He had gone to his room
the evening before much incensed at the presump-
tion of some younger Grandissimes who had brought
up the subject, and spoken in defence, of their
cousin Honoré. He had retired, however, not to
rest, but to construct an engine of offensive warfare
which would revenge him a hundred-fold upon the

miserable school of imported thought which had
sent its revolting influences to the very Grandissime hearthstone ; he wrote a "*Phillipique Générale
contre la Conduite du Gouvernement de la Louisiane*,"
and a short but vigorous chapter in English on
" The Insanity of Educating the Masses." This accomplished, he had gone to bed in a condition of
peaceful elation, eager for the next day to come
that he might take these mighty productions to
Joseph Frowenfeld, and make him a present of
them for insertion in his book of tables.

Jean-Baptiste felt no need of his advice, that he
should rouse him ; and, for a long time before the
old man awoke, his younger kinsmen were stirring
about unwontedly, going and coming through the
hall of the mansion, along its verandas and up and
down its outer flight of stairs. Gates were opening
and shutting, errands were being carried by negro
boys on bareback horses, Charlie Mandarin of St.
Bernard parish and an Armand Fusilier from Faubourg Ste. Marie had on some account come — as
they told the ladies — " to take breakfast ; " and
the ladies, not yet informed, amusedly wondering
at all this trampling and stage whispering, were up
a trifle early. In those days Creole society was a
ship, in which the fair sex were all passengers and
the ruder sex the crew. The ladies of the Grandissime mansion this morning asked passengers'
questions, got sailors' answers, retorted wittily and
more or less satirically, and laughed often, feeling
their constrained insignificance. However, in a

house so full of bright-eyed children, with mothers and sisters of all ages as their confederates, the secret was soon out, and before Agricola had left his little cottage in the grove the topic of all tongues was the abysmal treachery and *ingratitude* of negro slaves. The whole tribe of Grandissime believed, this morning, in the doctrine of total depravity — of the negro.

And right in the face of this belief, the ladies put forth the generously intentioned prayer for mercy. They were answered that they little knew what frightful perils they were thus inviting upon themselves.

The male Grandissimes were not surprised at this exhibition of weak clemency in their lovely women; they were proud of it; it showed the magnanimity that was natural to the universal Grandissime heart, when not restrained and repressed by the stern necessities of the hour. But Agricola disappointed them. Why should he weaken and hesitate, and suggest delays and middle courses, and stammer over their proposed measures as "extreme"? In very truth, it seemed as though that drivelling, woman-beaten Deutsch apotheke — ha! ha! ha! — in the rue Royale had bewitched Agricola as well as Honoré. The fact was, Agricola had never got over the interview which had saved Sylvestre his life.

" Here, Agricole," his kinsmen at length said, " you see you are too old for this sort of thing; besides, it would be bad taste for you, who might be presumed to harbor feelings of revenge, to have a voice in this council." And then they added to one another: "We will wait until 'Polyte reports whether or not they have caught Palmyre; much will depend on that."

Agricola, thus ruled out, did a thing he did not fully understand; he rolled up the "*Philippique Générale*" and "The Insanity of Educating the Masses," and, with these in one hand and his staff in the other, set out for Frowenfeld's, not merely smarting but trembling under the humiliation of having been sent, for the first time in his life, to the rear as a non-combatant.

He found the apothecary among his clerks, preparing with his own hands the "chalybeate tonic" for which the f. m. c. was expected to call. Raoul Innerarity stood at his elbow, looking on with an amiable air of having been superseded for the moment by his master.

"Ha-ah! Professor Frowenfeld!"

The old man flourished his scroll.

Frowenfeld said good-morning, and they shook hands across the counter; but the old man's grasp was so tremulous that the apothecary looked at him again.

"Does my hand tremble, Joseph? It is not strange; I have had much to excite me this morning."

"W'at's de mattah?" demanded Raoul, quickly.

"My life — which I admit, Professor Frowenfeld, is of little value compared with such a one as

yours — has been — if not attempted, at least
threatened."

"How?" cried Raoul.

"H-really, Professor, we must agree that a trifle
like that ought not to make old Agricola Fusilier
nervous. But I find it painful, sir, very painful.
I can lift up this right hand, Joseph, and swear I
never gave a slave — man or woman — a blow in
my life but according to my notion of justice.
And now to find my life attempted by former slaves
of my own household, and taunted with the righteous hamstringing of a dangerous runaway! But
they have apprehended the miscreants; one is actually in hand, and justice will take its course; trust
the Grandissimes for that — though, really, Joseph,
I assure you, I counselled leniency."

"Do you say they have caught her?" Frowenfeld's question was sudden and excited; but the
next moment he had controlled himself.

"H-h-my son, I did not say it was a 'her'!"

"Was it not Clemence? Have they caught her?"

"H-yes ——"

The apothecary turned to Raoul.

"Go tell Honoré Grandissime."

"But, Professor Frowenfeld ——" began Agricola.

Frowenfeld turned to repeat his instruction, but
Raoul was already leaving the store.

Agricola straightened up angrily.

"Pro-hofessor Frowenfeld, by what right do you
interfere?"

"No matter," said the apothecary, turning half-way and pouring the tonic into a vial.

"Sir," thundered the old lion, "h-I demand of you to answer! How dare you insinuate that my kinsmen may deal otherwise than justly?"

"Will they treat her exactly as if she were white, and had threatened the life of a slave?" asked Frowenfeld from behind the desk at the end of the counter.

The old man concentrated all the indignation of his nature in the reply.

"No-ho, sir!"

As he spoke, a shadow approaching from the door caused him to turn. The tall, dark, finely clad form of the f. m. c., in its old soft-stepping dignity and its sad emaciation, came silently toward the spot where he stood.

Frowenfeld saw this, and hurried forward inside the counter with the preparation in his hand.

"Professor Frowenfeld," said Agricola, pointing with his ugly staff, "I demand of you, as a keeper of a white man's pharmacy, to turn that negro out."

"Citizen Fusilier!" exclaimed the apothecary; "Mister Grandis—— "

He felt as though no price would be too dear at that moment to pay for the presence of the other Honoré. He had to go clear to the end of the counter and come down the outside again to reach the two men. They did not wait for him. Agricola turned upon the f. m. c.

" Take off your hat ! "

A sudden activity seized every one connected with the establishment as the quadroon let his thin right hand slowly into his bosom, and answered in French, in his soft, low voice :

" I wear my hat on my head."

Frowenfeld was hurrying toward them ; others stepped forward, and from two or three there came half-uttered exclamations of protest ; but unfortunately nothing had been done or said to provoke any one to rush upon them, when Agricola suddenly advanced a step and struck the f. m. c. on the head with his staff. Then the general outcry and forward rush came too late ; the two crashed together and fell, Agricola above, the f. m. c. below, and a long knife lifted up from underneath sank to its hilt, once — twice — thrice, — in the old man's back.

The two men rose, one in the arms of his friends, the other upon his own feet. While every one's attention was directed toward the wounded man, his antagonist restored his dagger to its sheath, took up his hat and walked away unmolested. When Frowenfeld, with Agricola still in his arms, looked around for the quadroon, he was gone.

Doctor Keene, sent for instantly, was soon at Agricola's side.

" Take him upstairs ; he can't be moved any further."

Frowenfeld turned and began to instruct some

one to run upstairs and ask permission, but the little doctor stopped him.

"Joe, for shame! you don't know those women better than that? Take the old man right up!"

CHAPTER LVII

VOUDOU CURED

"Honoré," said Agricola, faintly, "where is Honoré!"

"He has been sent for," said Doctor Keene and the two ladies in a breath.

Raoul, bearing the word concerning Clemence, and the later messenger summoning him to Agricola's bedside, reached Honoré within a minute of each other. His instructions were quickly given, for Raoul to take his horse and ride down to the family mansion, to break gently to his mother the news of Agricola's disaster, and to say to his kinsmen with imperative emphasis, not to touch the *marchande des calas* till he should come. Then he hurried to the rue Royale.

But when Raoul arrived at the mansion he saw at a glance that the news had outrun him. The family carriage was already coming round the bottom of the front stairs for three Mesdames Grandissime and Madame Martinez. The children on all sides had dropped their play, and stood about, hushed and staring. The servants moved with quiet rapidity.   In the hall he was stopped by two beautiful girls.

" Raoul! Oh, Raoul, how is he now? Oh! Raoul, if you could only stop them! They have taken old Clemence down into the swamp — as soon as they heard about Agricole — Oh, Raoul, surely that would be cruel! She nursed me — and me — when we were babies!"

" Where is Agamemnon?"

" Gone to the city."

" What did he say about it?"

" He said they were doing wrong, that he did not approve their action, and that they would get themselves into trouble: that he washed his hands of it."

" Ah-h-h!" exclaimed Raoul, " wash his hands! Oh, yes, wash his hands? Suppose we all wash our hands? But where is Valentine? Where is Charlie Mandarin?"

" Ah! Valentine is gone with Agamemnon, saying the same thing, and Charlie Mandarin is down in the swamp, the worst of all of them!"

" But why did you let Agamemnon and Valentine go off that way, you?"

" Ah! listen to Raoul! What can a woman do?"

" What can a woman — Well, even if I was a woman, I would do something!"

He hurried from the house, leaped into the saddle and galloped across the fields toward the forest.

Some rods within the edge of the swamp, which, at this season, was quite dry in many places, on a spot where the fallen dead bodies of trees overlay one another and a dense growth of willows and vines and dwarf palmetto shut out the light of the open fields, the younger and some of the harsher senior members of the Grandissime family were sitting or standing about, in an irregular circle whose centre was a big and singularly misshapen water-willow. At the base of this tree sat Clemence, motionless and silent, a wan, sickly color in her face, and that vacant look in her large, white-balled, brown-veined eyes, with which hope-forsaken cowardice waits for death. Somewhat apart from the rest, on an old cypress stump, half-stood, half-sat, in whispered consultation, Jean-Baptiste Grandissime and Charlie Mandarin.

" *Eh bien*, old woman," said Mandarin, turning, without rising, and speaking sharply in the negro French, " have you any reason to give why you should not be hung to that limb over your head ? "

She lifted her eyes slowly to his, and made a feeble gesture of deprecation.

" *Mo té pas fé cette bras*, Mawse Challie — I di'n't mek dat ahm; no 'ndeed I di'n', Mawse Challie. I ain' wuth hangin', gen'lemen; you'd oughteh jis gimme fawty an' lemme go. I — I — I — I di'n' 'ten' no hawm to Mawse-Agricole; I wa'n't gwan to hu't nobody in God's worl' ; 'ndeed I wasn'. I done tote dat old case-knife fo' twenty year' — *mo po'te ça dipi vingt ans*. I 'm a po' ole

marchande des calas ; mo courri 'mongs' de sojer
boys to sell my cakes, you know, and da's de
onyest reason why I cyah dat ah ole fool knife."
She seemed to take some hope from the silence
with which they heard her. Her eye brightened
and her voice took a tone of excitement. " You'd
oughteh tek me and put me in calaboose, an' let
de law tek 'is co'se. You's all nice gen'lemen —
werry nice gen'lemen, an' you sorter owes it to
yo'sev's fo' to not do no sich nasty wuck as hangin'
a po' ole nigga wench ; 'deed you does. 'T ain' no
use to hang me ; you gwan to kyetch Palmyre yit ;
li courri dans marais ; she is in de swamp yeh,
sum'ers ; but as concernin' me, you'd oughteh jis
gimme fawty an lemme go. You mus'n't b'lieve
all dis-yeh nonsense 'bout insurrectionin' ; all fool-
nigga talk. W'at we want to be insurrectionin'
faw ? We de happies' people in de God's worl' ! "
She gave a start, and cast a furtive glance of alarm
behind her. "Yes, we is ; you jis' oughteh gimme
fawty an' lemme go ! Please, gen'lemen ! God 'll
be good to you, you nice, sweet gen'lemen ! "

Charlie Mandarin made a sign to one who stood
at her back, who responded by dropping a rawhide
noose over her head. She bounded up with a cry
of terror ; it may be that she had all along hoped
that all was make-believe. She caught the noose
wildly with both hands and tried to lift it over her
head.

"Ah ! no, mawsteh, you cyan' do dat ! It's
ag'in' de law ! I 's 'bleeged to have my trial, yit.

Oh, no, no! Oh, good God, no! Even if I is a
nigga! You cyan' jis' murdeh me hyeh in de
woods! *Mo dis la zize!* I tell de judge on you!
You ain' got no mo' biznis to do me so 'an if I
was a white 'oman! You dassent tek a white
'oman out 'n de Pa'sh Pris'n an' do 'er so! Oh,
sweet mawsteh, fo' de love o' God! Oh, Mawse
Challie, *pou' l'amou' du bon Dieu n'fè pas ça!* Oh,
Mawse 'Polyte, is you gwan to let 'em kill ole
Clemence? Oh, fo' de mussy o' Jesus Christ,
Mawse 'Polyte, leas' of all, *you!* You dassent help
to kill me, Mawse 'Polyte! You knows why! Oh
God, Mawse 'Polyte, you knows why! Leas' of
all you, Mawse 'Polyte! Oh, God 'a' mussy on
my wicked ole soul! I aint fitt'n to die! Oh,
gen'lemen, I kyan' look God in de face! *Oh,
Michés, ayez pitié de moin!* Oh, God A'mighty ha'
mussy on my soul! Oh, gen'lemen, dough yo' kinfolks kyvvah up yo' tricks now, dey 'll dwap f'um
undeh you some day! *Solé levé là, li couché là!*
Yo' tu'n will come! Oh, God A'mighty! de God
o' de po' nigga wench! Look down, oh God, look
down an' stop dis yeh foolishness! Oh, God, fo'
de love o' Jesus! *Oh, Michés, y'en a ein zizement!*
Oh, yes, deh's a judgmen' day! Den it wont be
a bit o' use to you to be white! Oh, oh, oh, oh,
oh, oh, fo', fo', fo', de, de, *love o' God! Oh!*"

They drew her up.

Raoul was not far off. He heard the woman's
last cry, and came threshing through the bushes on
foot. He saw Sylvestre, unconscious of any ap-

proach, spring forward, jerk away the hands that
had drawn the thong over the branch, let the
strangling woman down and loosen the noose.
Her eyes, starting out with horror, turned to him;
she fell on her knees and clasped her hands. The
tears were rolling down Sylvestre's face.

"My friends, we must not do this! You *shall*
not do it!"

He hurled away, with twice his natural strength,
one who put out a hand.

"No, sirs!" cried Raoul, "you shall not do it!
I come from Honoré! Touch her who dares!"

He drew a weapon.

"Monsieur Innerarity," said 'Polyte, "*who is*
Monsieur Honoré Grandissime? There are two
of the name, you know, — partners — brothers.
Which of — but it makes no difference; before
either of them sees this assassin she is going to be a
lump of nothing!"

The next word astonished every one. It was
Charlie Mandarin who spoke.

"Let her go!"

"Let her go!" said Jean-Baptiste Grandissime;
"give her a run for life. Old woman, rise up. We
propose to let you go. Can you run? Never
mind, we shall see. Achille, put her upon her feet.
Now, old woman, run!"

She walked rapidly, but with unsteady feet, toward
the fields.

"Run! If you don't run I will shoot you this
minute!"

She ran.

" Faster ! "

She ran faster.

" Run ! "

" Run ! "

" Run, Clemence ! Ha, ha, ha ! " It was so funny to see her scuttling and tripping and stumbling. *"Courri! courri, Clemence! c'est pou' to' vie!* ha, ha, ha —— "

A pistol-shot rang out close behind Raoul's ear; it was never told who fired it. The negress leaped into the air and fell at full length to the ground, stone dead.

CHAPTER LVIII

DYING WORDS

DRIVERS of vehicles in the rue Royale turned aside before two slight barriers spanning the way, one at the corner below, the other at that above, the house where the aged high-priest of a doomed civilization lay bleeding to death. The floor of the store below, the pavement of the corridor where stood the idle volante, were covered with straw, and servants came and went by the beckoning of the hand.

" This way," whispered a guide of the four ladies from the Grandissime mansion. As Honoré's mother turned the angle half-way up the muffled stair, she saw at the landing above, standing as if about to part, yet in grave council, a man and a woman, the fairest — she noted it even in this moment of extreme distress — she had ever looked upon. He had already set one foot down upon the stair, but at sight of the ascending group drew back and said :

" It is my mother ; " then turned to his mother and took her hand ; they had been for months estranged, but now they silently kissed.

" He is sleeping," said Honoré. " Maman, Madame Nancanou."

The ladies bowed — the one looking very large and splendid, the other very sweet and small. There was a single instant of silence, and Aurora burst into tears.

For a moment Madame Grandissime assumed a frown that was almost a reminder of her brother's, and then the very pride of the Fusiliers broke down. She uttered an inaudible exclamation, drew the weeper firmly into her bosom, and with streaming eyes and choking voice, but yet with majesty, whispered, laying her hand on Aurora's head :

" Never mind, my child ; never mind ; never mind."

And Honoré's sister, when she was presently introduced, kissed Aurora and murmured :

" The good God bless thee ! It is He who has brought us together."

" Who is with him just now ? " whispered the two other ladies, while Honoré and his mother stood a moment aside in hurried consultation.

" My daughter," said Aurora, " and ——— "

" Agamemnon," suggested Madame Martinez.

" I believe so," said Aurora.

Valentine appeared from the direction of the sick-room and beckoned to Honoré. Doctor Keene did the same and continued to advance.

" Awake ? " asked Honoré.

" Yes."

" Alas ! my brother ! " said Madame Grandissime, and started forward, followed by the other women.

" Wait," said Honoré, and they paused. " Charlie," he said, as the little doctor persistently pushed by him at the head of the stair.

" Oh, there 's no chance, Honoré, you 'd as well all go in there."

They gathered into the room and about the bed. Madame Grandissime bent over it.

" Ah ! sister," said the dying man, " is that you ? I had the sweetest dream just now — just for a minute." He sighed. " I feel very weak. Where is Charlie Keene ? "

He had spoken in French ; he repeated his question in English. He thought he saw the doctor.

" Charlie, if I must meet the worst I hope you will tell me so ; I am fully prepared. Ah ! excuse — I thought it was ———

" My eyes seem dim this evening. *Est-ce-vous*, Honoré ? Ah, Honoré, you went over to the enemy, did you ? — Well, — the Fusilier blood would al — ways — do as it pleased. Here 's your old uncle's hand, Honoré. I forgive you, Honoré — my noble-hearted, foolish — boy." He spoke feebly, and with great nervousness.

"Water."

It was given him by Aurora. He looked in her face; they could not be sure whether he recognized her or not. He sank back, closed his eyes, and said, more softly and dreamily, as if to himself, " I forgive everybody. A man must die — I forgive — even the enemies — of Louisiana."

He lay still a few moments, and then revived excitedly. " Honoré! tell Professor Frowenfeld to take care of that *Philippique Générale*. 'T is a grand thing, Honoré, on a grand theme! I wrote it myself in one evening. Your Yankee Government is a failure, Honoré, a drivelling failure. It may live a year or two, not longer. Truth will triumph. The old Louisiana will rise again. She will get back her trampled rights. When she does, remem'——" His voice failed, but he held up one finger firmly by way of accentuation.

There was a stir among the kindred. Surely this was a turn for the better. The doctor ought to be brought back. A little while ago he was not nearly so strong. " Ask Honoré if the doctor should not come." But Honoré shook his head. The old man began again.

" Honoré! Where is Honoré? Stand by me, here, Honoré; and sister? — on this other side. My eyes are very poor to-day. Why do I perspire so? Give me a drink. You see — I am better now; I have ceased — to throw up blood. Nay, let me talk." He sighed, closed his eyes, and opened them again suddenly. " Oh, Honoré, you and the Yankees — you and — all — going wrong — education — masses — weaken — caste — indiscr'— quarrels settl' — by affidav' — Oh! Honoré."

" If he would only forget," said one, in an agonized whisper, " that *philippique générale!* "

Aurora whispered earnestly and tearfully to Madame Grandissime. Surely they were not going to let him go thus ! A priest could at least do no harm. But when the proposition was made to him by his sister, he said :

" No; — no priest. You have my will, Honoré, — in your iron box. Professor Frowenfeld," — he changed his speech to English, — " I have written you an article on — "his words died on his lips.

" Joseph, son, I do not see you. Beware, my son, of the doctrine of equal rights — a bottomless iniquity. Master and man — arch and pier — arch above — pier below." He tried to suit the gesture to the words, but both hands and feet were growing uncontrollably restless.

" Society, Professor," — he addressed himself to a weeping girl, — " society has pyramids to build which make menials a necessity, and Nature furnishes the menials all in dark uniform. She — I cannot tell you — you will find — all in the *Philippique Générale*. Ah! Honoré, is it —— "

He suddenly ceased.

" I have lost my glasses."

Beads of sweat stood out upon his face.   He grew frightfully pale.   There was a general dismayed haste, and they gave him a stimulant.

"Brother," said the sister, tenderly.

He did not notice her.

"Agamemnon!   Go and tell Jean-Baptiste——" his eyes drooped and flashed again wildly.

"I am here, Agricole," said the voice of Jean-Baptiste, close beside the bed.

"I told you to let — that negress——"

"Yes, we have let her go.   We have let all of them go."

"All of them," echoed the dying man, feebly, with wandering eyes.   Suddenly he brightened again and tossed his arms.   "Why, there you were wrong, Jean-Baptiste; the community must be protected." His voice sank to a murmur.   "He would not take off — you must remem'—" He was silent.   "You must remem'—those people are — are not — white people."   He ceased a moment.   "Where am I going?"   He began evidently to look, or try to look, for some person; but they could not divine his wish until, with piteous feebleness, he called:

"Aurore De Grapion!"

So he had known her all the time.

Honoré's mother had dropped on her knees beside the bed, dragging Aurora down with her.

They rose together.

The old man groped distressfully with one hand. She laid her own in it.

"Honoré!

" What could he want? " wondered the tearful family. He was feeling about with the other hand.

" Hon'— Honoré " — his weak clutch could scarcely close upon his nephew's hand.

" Put them — put — put them —— "

What could it mean? The four hands clasped.

" Ah! " said one, with fresh tears, " he is trying to speak and cannot."

But he did.

" Aurora De Gra— I pledge'— pledge' —pledged — this union — to your fa'— father — twenty — years — ago."

The family looked at each other in dejected amazement. They had never known it.

" He is going," said Agamemnon; and indeed it seemed as though he was gone; but he rallied.

" Agamemnon! Valentine! Honoré! patriots! protect the race! Beware of the "— that sentence escaped him. He seemed to fancy himself haranguing a crowd; made another struggle for intelligence, tried once, twice, to speak, and the third time succeeded:

" Louis'— Louisian'— a — for — ever! " and lay still.

They put those two words on his tomb.

CHAPTER LIX

WHERE SOME CREOLE MONEY GOES

AND yet the family committee that ordered the inscription, the mason who cut it in the marble — himself a sort of half-Grandissime, half-nobody — and even the fair women who each eve of All-Saints came, attended by flower-laden slave girls, to lay coronals upon the old man's tomb, felt, feebly at first, and more and more distinctly as years went by, that Forever was a trifle long for one to confine one's patriotic affection to a small fraction of a great country.

"And you say your family decline to accept the assistance of the police in their endeavors to bring the killer of your uncle to justice?" asked some *Américain* or other of 'Polyte Grandissime.

"'Sir, mie fam'lie do not want to fetch him to justice! — neither Palmyre! We are goin' to fetch the justice to them! And sir, when we cannot do that, sir, by ourselves, sir,— no, sir! no police!'"

So Clemence was the only victim of the family wrath; for the other two were never taken; and it helps our good feeling for the Grandissimes to know that in later times, under the gentler influences of a higher civilization, their old Spanish-colonial ferocity was gradually absorbed by the growth of better traits. To-day almost all the savagery that can justly be charged against Louisiana must — strange to say — be laid at the door of the *Américain*. The Creole character has been diluted and sweetened.

One morning early in September, some two weeks after the death of Agricola, the same brig which something less than a year before had brought the Frowenfelds to New Orleans crossed, outward bound, the sharp line dividing the sometimes tawny waters of Mobile Bay from the deep blue Gulf, and bent her way toward Europe.

She had two passengers; a tall, dark, wasted yet handsome man of thirty-seven or thirty-eight years of age, and a woman seemingly some three years younger, of beautiful though severe countenance; "very elegant-looking people and evidently rich," so the brig-master described them,— "had much the look of some of the Mississippi River 'Lower Coast' aristocracy." Their appearance was the more interesting for a look of mental distress evident on the face of each. Brother and sister they called themselves; but, if so, she was the most severely reserved and distant sister the master of the vessel had ever seen.

They landed, if the account comes down to us right, at Bordeaux. The captain, a fellow of the peeping sort, found pastime in keeping them in sight after they had passed out of his care ashore. They went to different hotels !

The vessel was detained some weeks in this harbor, and her master continued to enjoy himself in the way in which he had begun. He saw his late passengers meet often, in a certain quiet path under the trees of the Quinconce. Their conversations were low; in the patois they used they could have afforded to speak louder; their faces were always grave and almost always troubled. The interviews seemed to give neither of them any pleasure. The monsieur grew thinner than ever, and sadly feeble.

"He wants to charter her," the seaman concluded, "but she does n't like his rates."

One day, the last that he saw them together, they seemed to be, each in a way different from the other, under a great strain. He was haggard, woebegone, nervous; she high-strung, resolute,— with "eyes that shone like lamps," as said the observer.

"She's a-sendin' him 'way to lew-ard," thought he. Finally the Monsieur handed her — or rather placed upon the seat near which she stood, what she would not receive — a folded and sealed document, seized her hand, kissed it and hurried away. She sank down upon the seat, weak and pale, and rose to go, leaving the document behind. The mariner picked it up; it was directed to *M. Honoré Grandissime, Nouvelle Orléans, États Unis, Amérique.* She turned suddenly, as if remembering, or possibly reconsidering, and received it from him.

"It looked like a last will and testament," the seaman used to say, in telling the story.

The next morning, being at the water's edge and seeing a number of persons gathering about something not far away, he sauntered down toward it to see how small a thing was required to draw a crowd of these Frenchmen. It was the drowned body of the f. m. c.

Did the brig-master never see the woman again? He always waited for this question to be asked him, in order to state the more impressively that he did. His brig became a regular Bordeaux packet, and he saw the Madame twice or thrice, apparently living at great ease, but solitary, in the rue ——. He was free to relate that he tried to scrape acquaintance with her, but failed ignominiously.

The rents of Number 19 rue Bienville and of numerous other places, including the new drugstore in the rue Royale, were collected regularly by H. Grandissime, successor to Grandissime Frères. Rumor said, and tradition repeats, that neither for the advancement of a friendless people, nor even for the repair of the properties' wear and tear, did one dollar of it ever remain in New Orleans; but that once a year Honoré, "as instructed," remitted to Madame — say Madame Inconnue — of Bordeaux, the equivalent, in francs, of fifty thousand dollars. It is averred he did this without interruption for twenty years. "Let us see: fifty times twenty — one million dollars. That is only a *part* of the *pecuniary* loss which this sort of thing costs Louisiana."

But we have wandered.

CHAPTER LX

" ALL RIGHT "

THE sun is once more setting upon the Place
d'Armes. Once more the shadows of cathedral
and town-hall lie athwart the pleasant grounds
where again the city's fashion and beauty sit about
in the sedate Spanish way, or stand or slowly move
in and out among the old willows and along the
white walks. Children are again playing on the
sward ; some, you may observe, are in black, for
Agricola. You see, too, a more peaceful river, a
nearer-seeming and greener opposite shore, and
many other evidences of the drowsy summer's unwillingness to leave the embrace of this seductive
land ; the dreamy quietude of birds ; the spreading,
folding, re-expanding and slow pulsating of the all-
prevailing fan (how like the unfolding of an angel's
wing is ofttimes the broadening of that little instrument !) ; the oft-drawn handkerchief ; the pale, cool
colors of summer costume ; the swallow, circling
and twittering overhead or darting across the sight ;
the languid movement of foot and hand ; the reeking flanks and foaming bits of horses ; the ear-
piercing note of the cicada ; the dancing butterfly ;
the dog, dropping upon the grass and looking up
to his master with roping jaw and lolling tongue ;
the air sweetened with the merchandise of the
flower *marchandes.*

On the levee road, bridles and saddles, whips, gigs, and carriages, — what a merry coming and going! We look, perforce, toward the old bench where, six months ago, sat Joseph Frowenfeld. There is somebody there — a small, thin, weary-looking man, who leans his bared head slightly back against the tree, his thin fingers knit together in his lap, and his *chapeau-bras* pressed under his arm. You note his extreme neatness of dress, the bright, unhealthy restlessness of his eye, and — as a beam from the sun strikes them — the fineness of his short red curls. It is Doctor Keene.

He lifts his head and looks forward. Honoré and Frowenfeld are walking arm-in-arm under the furthermost row of willows. Honoré is speaking. How gracefully, in correspondence with his words, his free arm or hand — sometimes his head or even his lithe form — moves in quiet gesture, while the grave, receptive apothecary takes into his meditative mind, as into 'a large, cool cistern, the valued rain-fall of his friend's communications. They are near enough for the little doctor easily to call them; but he is silent. The unhappy feel so far away from the happy. Yet — "Take care!" comes suddenly to his lips, and is almost spoken; for the two, about to cross toward the Place d'Armes at the very spot where Aurora had once made her narrow escape, draw suddenly back, while the black driver of a volante reins up the horse he bestrides, and the animal himself swerves and stops.

The two friends, though startled apart, hasten

with lifted hats to the side of the volante, profoundly convinced that one, at least, of its two
occupants is heartily sorry that they were not
rolled in the dust. Ah, ah! with what a wicked,
ill-stifled merriment those two ethereal women bend
forward in the faintly perfumed clouds of their ravishing summer-evening garb, to express their equiv-
ocal mortification and regret.

" Oh! I 'm so sawry, oh! Almoze runned o'——
ah, ha, ha, ha ! "

Aurora could keep the laugh back no longer.

" An' righd yeh befo' haivry *boddie !* Ah, ha, ha!
'Sieur Grandissime, 't is *me-e-e* w'ad know 'ow dad
is bad, ha, ha, ha ! Oh! I assu' you, gen'lemen, id
is hawful ! "

And so on.

By and by Honoré seemed urging them to do
something, the thought of which made them laugh,
yet was entertained as not entirely absurd. It may
have been that to which they presently seemed to
consent ; they alighted from the volante, dismissed it,
and walked each at a partner's side down the grassy
avenue of the levee. It was as Clotilde with one
hand swept her light robes into perfect adjustment
for the walk, and turned to take the first step
with Frowenfeld, that she raised her eyes for the
merest instant to his, and there passed between
them an exchange of glance which made the heart
of the little doctor suddenly burn like a ball of
fire.

" Now we 're all right," he murmured bitterly

to himself, as, without having seen him, she took
the arm of the apothecary, and they moved
away.

Yes, if his irony was meant for this pair, he
divined correctly. Their hearts had found utterance across the lips, and the future stood waiting
for them on the threshold of a new existence, to
usher them into a perpetual copartnership in all
its joys and sorrows, its disappointments, its im-
perishable hopes, its aims, its conflicts, its rewards ;
and the true — the great — the everlasting God of
love was with them. Yes, it had been "all
right," now, for nearly twenty-four hours — an
age of bliss. And now, as they walked beneath
the willows where so many lovers had walked before them, they had whole histories to tell of the
tremors, the dismays, the misconstructions and
longings through which their hearts had come to
this bliss ; how at such a time, thus and so ; and
after such and such a meeting, so and so ; no part
of which was heard by alien ears, except a frag-
ment of Clotilde's speech caught by a small boy in
unintentioned ambush.

"—— Evva sinze de firze nighd w'en I big-in to
nurze you wid de fivver."

She was telling him, with that new, sweet bold-
ness so wonderful to a lately accepted lover, how
long she had loved him.

Later on they parted at the *porte-cochère*. Honoré
and Aurora had got there before them, and were
passing on up the stairs. Clotilde, catching, a mo-

ment before, a glimpse of her face, had seen that
there was something wrong; weather-wise as to its
indications she perceived an impending shower of
tears. A faint shade of anxiety rested an instant
on her own face. Frowenfeld could not go in.
They paused a little within the obscurity of the
corridor, and just to reassure themselves that everything *was* "all right," they ——

God be praised for love's young dream!

The slippered feet of the happy girl, as she
slowly mounted the stair alone, overburdened with
the weight of her blissful reverie, made no sound.
As she turned its mid-angle she remembered Aurora.
She could guess pretty well the source of her
trouble; Honoré was trying to treat that hand-
clasping at the bedside of Agricola as a binding
compact; "which, of course, was not fair." She
supposed they would have gone into the front
drawing-room; she would go into the back. But
she miscalculated; as she silently entered the door
she saw Aurora standing a little way beyond her,
close before Honoré, her eyes cast down, and the
trembling fan hanging from her two hands like a
broken pinion. He seemed to be reiterating, in a
tender undertone, some question intended to bring
her to a decision. She lifted up her eyes toward
his with a mute, frightened glance.

The intruder, with an involuntary murmur of
apology, drew back; but, as she turned, she was
suddenly and unspeakably saddened to see Aurora
drop her glance, and, with a solemn slowness whose

momentous significance was not to be mistaken, silently shake her head.

"Alas!" cried the tender heart of Clotilde. "Alas! M. Grandissime!"

CHAPTER LXI

" NO ! "

IF M. Grandissime had believed that he was prepared for the supreme bitterness of that moment, he had sadly erred. He could not speak. He extended his hand in a dumb farewell, when, all unsanctioned by his will, the voice of despair escaped him in a low groan. At the same moment, a tinkling sound drew near, and the room, which had grown dark with the fall of night, began to brighten with the softly widening light of an evening lamp, as a servant approached to place it in the front drawing-room.

Aurora gave her hand and withdrew it. In the act the two somewhat changed position, and the rays of the lamp, as the maid passed the door, falling upon Aurora's face, betrayed the again upturned eyes.

"'Sieur Grandissime —— "

They fell.

The lover paused.

"You thing I'm crool."

She was the statue of meekness.

" Hope has been cruel to me," replied M. Grandissime, " not you; that I cannot say. Adieu."

He was turning.

" 'Sieur Grandissime —— "

She seemed to tremble.

He stood still.

" 'Sieur Grandissime," — her voice was very tender, — " wad you' horry ? "

There was a great silence.

" 'Sieur Grandissime, you know — teg a chair."

He hesitated a moment and then both sat down. The servant repassed the door; yet when Aurora broke the silence, she spoke in English — having such hazardous things to say. It would conceal possible stammerings.

" 'Sieur Grandissime — you know dad riz'n I —— "

She slightly opened her fan, looking down upon it, and was still.

" I have no right to ask the reason," said M. Grandissime. " It is yours — not mine."

Her head went lower.

" Well, you know," — she drooped it meditatively to one side, with her eyes on the floor, — " 't is bick-ause — 't is bick-ause I thing in a few days I 'm goin' to die."

M. Grandissime said never a word. He was not alarmed.

She looked up suddenly and took a quick breath, as if to resume, but her eyes fell before his, and she said, in a tone of half-soliloquy :

" I 'ave so mudge troub' wit dad hawt."

She lifted one little hand feebly to the cardiac region, and sighed softly, with a dying languor.

M. Grandissime gave no response. A vehicle rumbled by in the street below, and passed away. At the bottom of the room, where a gilded Mars was driving into battle, a soft note told the half-hour. The lady spoke again.

" Id mague " — she sighed once more — "so strange, — sometime' I thing I 'm git'n' crezzy."

Still he to whom these fearful disclosures were being made remained as silent and motionless as an Indian captive, and, after another pause, with its painful accompaniment of small sounds, the fair speaker resumed with more energy, as befitting the approach to an incredible climax :

" Some day', 'Sieur Grandissime, — id mague me fo'gid my hage ! I thing I 'm young !"

She lifted her eyes with the evident determination to meet his own squarely, but it was too much ; they fell as before ; yet she went on speaking :

" An' w'en someboddie git'n' ti'ed livin' wid 'imsev an' big'n' to fill ole, an' wan' someboddie to teg de care of 'im an' wan' me to gid marri'd wid 'im — I thing 'e 's in love to me." Her fingers kept up a little shuffling with the fan. " I thing I 'm crezzy. I thing I muz be go'n' to die torecklie." She looked up to the ceiling with large eyes, and then again at the fan in her lap, which continued its spreading and shutting. " An' daz de riz'n, 'Sieur

Grandissime." She waited until it was certain he was about to answer, and then interrupted him nervously: "You know, 'Sieur Grandissime, id woon be righd! Id woon be de juztiz to *you!* An' you de bez man I evva know in my life, 'Sieur Grandissime!" Her hands shook. "A man w'at nevva wan' to gid marri'd wid noboddie in 'is life, and now trine to gid marri'd juz only to rip-ose de soul of 'is oncl' —— "

M. Grandissime uttered an exclamation of protest, and she ceased.

"I asked you," continued he, with low-toned emphasis, "for the single and only reason that I want you for my wife."

"Yez," she quickly replied; "daz all. Daz wad I thing. An' I thing daz de rad weh to say, 'Sieur Grandissime. Bick-ause, you know, you an' me is too hole to talg aboud dad *lovin'*, you know. An' you godd dad grade *rizpeg* fo' me, an' me I godd dad 'ighez rispeg fo' you; bud —— " she clutched the fan and her face sank lower still — "bud —— " she swallowed — shook her head — "bud —— " She bit her lip; she could not go on.

"Aurora," said her lover, bending forward and taking one of her hands. "I *do* love you with all my soul."

She made a poor attempt to withdraw her hand, abandoned the effort, and looked up savagely through a pair of overflowing eyes, demanding:

"*Mais*, fo' w'y you di' n' wan' to sesso?"

M. Grandissime smiled argumentatively.

"I have said so a hundred times, in every way but in words."

She lifted her head proudly, and bowed like a queen.

"*Mais*, you see, 'Sieur Grandissime, you bin meg one mizteg."

"Bud 't is corrected in time," exclaimed he, with suppressed but eager joyousness.

"'Sieur Grandissime," she said, with a tremendous solemnity, "I'm verrie sawrie, *mais* — you spogue too lade."

"No, no!" he cried, "the correction comes in time. Say that, lady; say that!"

His ardent gaze beat hers once more down; but she shook her head. He ignored the motion.

"And you will correct your answer; ah! say that, too!" he insisted, covering the captive hand with both his own, and leaning forward from his seat.

"*Mais*, 'Sieur Grandissime, you know, dad is so verrie unegspeg'."

"Oh! unexpected!"

"*Mais*, I was thing all dad time id was Clotilde wad you ——"

She turned her face away and buried her mouth in her handkerchief.

"Ah!" he cried, "mock me no more, Aurore Nancanou!"

He rose erect and held the hand firmly which she strove to draw away:

"Say the word, sweet lady; say the word!"

She turned upon him suddenly, rose to her feet, was speechless an instant while her eyes flashed into his, and crying out:

"No!" burst into tears, laughed through them, and let him clasp her to his bosom.